GRIM

Edited by Christine Johnson

HARLEQUIN®TEEN

Recycling programs
for this product may
not exist in your area.

ISBN-13: 978-0-373-21108-1

GRIM

Copyright © 2014 by Christine Johnson

THE KEY
Copyright © 2014 by Rachel Hawkins

FIGMENT
Copyright © 2014 by Jeri Smith-Ready

THE TWELFTH GIRL
Copyright © 2014 by Malinda Lo

THE RAVEN PRINCESS
Copyright © 2014 by Jon Skovron

THINNER THAN WATER
Copyright © 2014 by Saundra Mitchell

BEFORE THE ROSE BLOOMED: A RETELLING OF *THE SNOW QUEEN*
Copyright © 2014 by Ellen Hopkins

BEAST/BEAST
Copyright © 2014 by Tessa Gratton

THE BROTHERS PIGGETT
Copyright © 2014 by Julie Kagawa

UNTETHERED
Copyright © 2014 by Sonia Gensler

BETTER
Copyright © 2014 by Shaun David Hutchinson

LIGHT IT UP
Copyright © 2014 by Kimberly Derting

SHARPER THAN A SERPENT'S TONGUE
Copyright © 2014 by Christine Johnson

CONTENTS

This is for you.

THE
KEY

by Rachel Hawkins

High school is hard enough without having a psychic for a mom.

And no, I don't mean she has that uniquely Mom-like sixth sense. I mean she's literally a psychic. Reading your palms, telling you your future, all for the bargain price of fifty bucks a session (a hundred if you want a full hour, but no one ever does).

Momma runs her business out of our trailer. I know there are people who say that trailers can be nice, fancy even.

Those people had never been to our trailer.

It isn't even a double-wide, which would have at least given us enough space for more than one ratty couch. I think the couch had belonged to my nana at some point. I knew whoever had had it before us had smoked on it, though. It carried the scent of thousands of cigarettes, millions even, deep inside every cabbage rose on its stained and burned cushions.

Momma's "studio," as she liked to call it, was in the second bedroom. When she wasn't reading people's fortunes, I slept on an air mattress on the floor in there. It was either that or share with Momma, which no, thank you. And like I said, the couch stunk—and was haunted besides—so I made do with the air mattress, no matter how big a pain in the ass it was to pump it up every single night, only to roll it back flat every morning.

The studio was the one nice room in the whole trailer. In there, the linoleum didn't have duct tape over the cracks. In fact, you couldn't see the linoleum at all. Momma had bought a real nice rug from Walmart years ago. It was a little too big for the room, curling up against the walls, but Momma kept it so dark in there that no one ever really noticed.

There had been a beaded curtain separating the studio from the rest of the trailer, but I'd talked Momma into getting rid of it. It looked cheap and trashy. I realized that was kind of an ironic statement, considering the rest of our place, but I had some limits. She'd hung a paisley shawl in the doorway instead, and while that wasn't great, at least it didn't rattle every time you walked past it.

Momma was standing in front of that shawl on Saturday morning, yawning as she cradled a cup of coffee in her hands. I stood at the sink, washing last night's dinner dishes and looking out the window. On the porch of the next trailer over, a little girl with hair nearly the same white-blond as mine was playing with a water hose, giggling as she sprayed the vinyl siding. I was smiling at her and nearly missed what Momma was saying. Only when she said, "So you'll need to stay close by today," did I turn around, frowning at her.

"I can't," I told her, the dish in my hand dripping water

onto the stained and faded linoleum. "I have track practice at noon."

Momma scowled. Years ago, she had been pretty, but there was something hard in her face now that had nothing to do with aging or wrinkles. "You had track practice last weekend."

I fought the urge to roll my eyes. "Yeah, I have it every weekend. And three times a week after school. Come on, Momma. Use your powers and envision me jogging around the track." I wiggled my sudsy fingers at her. "Because trust me, that's my future today."

Momma sighed, crossing over to me and dropping her nearly empty mug in my newly cleaned sink. I bit my lip as coffee splashed over the enamel. Then she held her hands out to me and I groaned. "Oh, come on, Momma, I was joking."

Moving closer, Momma insisted, "Give 'em here."

Still grumbling, I laid my palms flat on hers, and taking a deep breath, Momma closed her eyes. Almost immediately, she frowned. "Girl, you weren't kidding."

"About what?"

"The running. You are gonna run and run today. Fast."

I took my hands back even as I smiled a little bit. "I am trying to beat my best time today—4:07. School record is 4:01, so I'm almost there."

"Well, if what I saw was any indication, you're gonna sail right through it, sweetheart. You were runnin' like your life depended on it, from what I could see."

Turning away from her, I started to rinse her coffee out of the sink. "In that case, I guess I'll be going to track practice today, after all."

Momma patted my shoulder blade. "The appointment is at ten, so we'll definitely be done by noon."

They'd be done by 10:30—10:15, probably. Usually once people got a look at our place, they didn't like to stay long. I glanced at Momma, still in a mismatched set of pajamas, before looking at the clock on the microwave. "It's nearly ten now—you might wanna go get into character."

I'd expected another comment about making fun, but Momma just swatted me with a dishcloth and snorted. "I will. Thanks for cleaning up for me, baby. You're a good girl."

She said that to me a lot.

As Momma drifted off to her bedroom to drape herself in scarves and eyeliner—*People expect a certain look, Lana*—I busied myself straightening up the living room. There was only so much I could do, but I could at least make sure things were clean. I always hated the looks on Momma's clients' faces when they first walked in. Like, hello, maybe you shouldn't be so disgusted when you're the one driving out to the boondocks to get your palm read, you know? That seemed way more offensive than an ugly couch and some fake paneling.

Still, I swept up and fluffed the throw pillows on the couch and sprayed some air freshener. The scent of incense was already wafting out of Momma's studio, and I knew I'd have a headache before the day was over.

At exactly 9:57, I heard the rumble of a truck outside. "Momma, they're here!" I hollered as I shoved last night's pizza box into the trash can. The truck's ignition cut off and I glanced out the front window, wondering which kind of client this one would be. Momma's main business came from bored ladies in Auburn, the nearest town over. They were almost never under the age of fifty, and they looked so similar that I couldn't swear Momma hadn't just been seeing the same client over and over again for the past few years.

But when I saw the shiny blue truck, I knew there was no old lady behind the wheel. My heart hammered in my chest, stomach jumping. What was he doing here now?

The passenger side door opened, and a girl came tumbling out, her long legs pale in the late-morning light. As soon as I saw her, I ducked back from the window, the butterflies in my stomach suddenly turning to lead.

"Momma!" I hissed, crossing over to her studio and yanking back the paisley curtain. She was already sitting at her table, shuffling the tarot cards.

"What?" she asked, raising her eyebrows so that they nearly disappeared under her headscarf.

"Those are kids from my school," I told her, trying to keep my voice low. Trailers aren't exactly soundproof, and I could already hear the heavy tread on the stairs outside. "You promised never to read for kids."

Momma blinked at me before returning to her cards. "Well, Lana, it's not like people tell me how old they are when they call and schedule a reading. Besides, they booked a whole hour, and if you wanna keep having nice things like, oh, I don't know, electricity, water..."

There was a knock at the door and I winced, afraid the kids on the porch may have overheard.

"Go answer it," Momma said, flinging a hand out, her mismatched bangles rattling.

"Please," I said, but I wasn't sure what I was asking for. For her to go answer it herself, for her not to make me do this with people I knew. For her not to be a psychic in a trailer, maybe.

But Momma just fixed me with her big hazel eyes, eyes that looked just like mine, and said, "You're not ashamed of your momma, are you, Lana Banana?"

There is no way to answer that question. It's a trick that parents throw at you, like *Do you want a spanking?* or *What did you just say?*

Besides, I was ashamed, and the guilt of that stung even more than the potential humiliation awaiting me at the front door.

They stood there on the porch, the girl leaning against the railing. Big aviator sunglasses covered nearly half her face, but I would've recognized that bright red hair anywhere. Milly Ross and I might not travel in the same circles at our school, but we'd had a few classes together.

I kept my eyes on her rather than the boy standing just beside her. I could feel the weight of his gaze on me.

"Um…Lana, right?" Milly asked, pushing her hair out of her eyes. "You're in algebra with me? Third period?"

I wondered if everything she ever said sounded like a question even as I said, "Yeah. And fourth-period history."

"Right," Milly said, and then she jerked her head at the boy. "Do you know Skye?"

I didn't want my cheeks to flame, but I could feel heat rising up my neck as I said, "Yeah, Skye Bartlett, right? I think we have English together?"

The corner of his lips lifted for just a second, a crooked smile I'd seen a hundred times. It never failed to make my pulse leap.

"French," Skye said, and I nodded.

"Right, that's it. Anyway, y'all, uh, wanna come in?" Moving out of the doorway, I gestured for them to come inside. Milly went first, and as Skye followed her into the trailer, he briefly let his hand brush my waist. It was a tiny touch, but even through my T-shirt, I could feel the heat of his fingers.

Milly stood in the middle of the room, shoving her sunglasses on top of her head. "So...you live here?"

No, I just hang out in this lady's trailer. "Yeah, I do. You guys can have a seat if you want."

Milly swung her head in the direction of the couch, the silver hoops in her ears flashing. Earlier, I'd thought that with the pillows fluffed, the sofa had actually looked a little bit better, but seeing it now through her eyes, I knew it was as shabby and ugly as ever.

"We can just stand here and wait," Milly said, her nose crinkling as she took in the faded flooring, the mismatched furniture.

I knew Mom was waiting for me to do my thing, but I really didn't want to. It was one thing when I was helping her with overweight, middle-aged ladies who just wanted to know if their husbands were cheating on them or if they were going to win the lottery. But these were kids I knew. This was Skye.

Skye was still standing by the door, and even though I wasn't looking at him, I was aware of the way his arms were folded across his chest, the thin material of his T-shirt stretching over his biceps.

"I didn't know this was your mom," Milly said at last, fiddling with the end of the oversize shirt she wore over a white tank top. It was a boy's shirt, hanging past her hips, and for a moment, I thought it looked kind of familiar. Had I seen that shirt on Skye before? I couldn't remember.

Then I realized the silence had stretched a little too long, and blinked. "Oh. Right, yeah, I don't exactly wear shirts that say Hey, My Mom's a Psychic."

Milly laughed at that, but it was too loud and too high to be genuine. From behind the paisley curtain, I heard Mom clear her throat.

She wasn't going to come out until I'd done the prep work, so with a sigh I asked them if I could get them anything to drink.

Milly cast a concerned look at the kitchen, but before she could answer, I'd crossed to the fridge and pulled out a couple of diet sodas. They were the off-brand kind from Winn-Dixie, but Milly and Skye both took one. As they did, I let my fingers brush against the thumb ring Milly wore.

It was always the same. Like coming across a closed door and opening it just a crack, peeking inside. As soon as I peeked inside Milly's mind, I saw a familiar face. Kimberly McEntire had been in my grade and had been Milly's best friend.

And Skye's girlfriend.

I saw her and Milly riding in Kimberly's car, singing loudly with the radio. Now they were sitting on Kimberly's bed, and she was crying, Milly wrapping an arm around her shoulders. Milly sitting on the floor of her bedroom, listening to Kimberly's mom asking where Kimberly was, if Milly had seen her. And over all of that was this feeling—worry, anxiety, anger, all balled up together.

I was just drawing my hand back when there was a flash

of another emotion, another face and name. It startled me so much I nearly dropped the soda I'd been handing to Milly, and she caught it with a little scowl.

"Whoa. You okay?"

"Yeah," I said, even as I shook my head. "Yeah, totally. Sorry, the can was slippery. Uh, if y'all will wait right here for a sec, I'll go get Mom—er, Madame Lin."

I'd begged Momma to drop the stupid name, but unlike the Beaded Curtain Argument, I'd lost. According to Momma, people felt better hearing their psychic readings from a woman named Madame Lin than from one named Lynette.

Ducking behind the paisley curtain, I found Momma sitting expectantly at her table. "Well?"

Keeping my voice at a whisper, I told her what I'd picked up from the jewelry. "She's mostly here to ask about Kimberly McEntire." I didn't mention the other thing. I wasn't sure I'd be able to without Momma knowing something was wrong with me.

Momma scowled. "Did she bring something belonging to the girl?"

I shook my head. "Don't think so."

Throwing up her hands, Momma blew out a long breath. "Well, how am I supposed to answer any questions about someone who's not even here? That's not how this works," she hissed.

There was no sense in reminding Momma that I knew how this worked. The powers Momma had—the powers I had— were really specific. I could touch people and, if I wanted to, get impressions of what they were thinking, little bits of their present and past. The future was a total no-go for me.

But Momma, she could see only little snatches of a person's future. But that person had to be sitting there with her or she had to touch something of theirs. In other words, if Milly wanted to find out where Kimberly had disappeared to all those months ago, she was crap outta luck.

"Just lie to her," I said with a little shrug. "Everybody says Kimberly ran away from home after a fight with her parents. Make up some kind of glamorous story about Kim living out in, like, L.A. or something."

Momma mulled that over, twirling the end of her head-scarf. "That's good," she said at last. "After all, what do I always say? If you can't tell someone the truth—"

"At least make them happy," I finished. It was basically Momma's motto as a psychic.

Momma smiled at me, her teeth white against the dark wine of her lipstick. "You'll be good at this."

It was pointless to remind Momma that there was no way in hell I was going to end up reading palms in a trailer. Just because she and Grammy had both done it didn't mean that I was going to. I had my eye on a track scholarship to the University of Alabama, and after that, I was getting as far away from the Woodland Hills Trailer Park as I possibly could.

Maybe Kimberly McEntire had felt like that, too. Sure, she lived in one of the nicer neighborhoods in town and seemed to have everything going for her. Good grades, pretty face and Skye Bartlett. But clearly something had been pulling her beyond the city limits. She'd taken off over six months ago, and other than a note left on her pillow, no one had heard from her since. I found myself hoping the future I'd told Momma to make up for her was close to the truth.

Momma got up from the table, and I trailed after her back into the living room. Milly was still standing hesitantly by the couch while Skye stood near the front window. Momma looked back and forth between them. "Will both of you be sitting for the reading, or—"

"Just her," Skye said, inclining his head toward Milly. "No offense, but this kind of thing freaks me out." He grinned at Momma and she practically giggled. Behind her back, I rolled my eyes, and Skye's grin widened.

"Very well, then." Momma held her hand out to Milly, who glanced over at Skye, worrying her lower lip between her teeth.

"So you'll just...wait out here, right?"

He gave an easy roll of his shoulders. "Sure. Laura here can keep me company."

"Lana," I corrected, my lips twitching in a smile.

He snapped his fingers, nodding. "Right, right. Lana."

It was a little too much, and just for a moment, Milly's brow wrinkled with something like confusion. Or maybe suspicion. But then Momma was taking her hand and guiding her toward her studio.

The moment the curtain twitched closed behind Milly, Skye's hands grabbed my waist, tugging me close to him. He ducked his head to kiss my neck, but I spun away from him, swatting at his hands. "What are you doing?" I hissed.

His bright blue eyes sparkled as he leaned closer and he whispered, "I was trying to kiss you."

For a second, I nearly wavered. It was hard to be mad at him when he was looking at me like that.

Shooting a glance at the curtain, I grabbed Skye's hand and

tugged him out onto the porch, closing the door softly behind me. Once we were down in the yard by his truck, I shaded my eyes with my hand and looked up at him. "I wasn't talking about the kissing. I mean why did you bring Milly here?"

Skye sighed. "She's been wanting to come out here for months. Pretty much ever since Kimberly bailed. When she said she'd made the appointment, I offered to drive her."

In the sunlight, his black hair glinted nearly as blue as his truck. Skye was beautiful in that way that is almost girlie. Only the dark stubble lining his jaw, the veins in his forearms, the blunt width of his hands saved him from looking too pretty. He smiled at me, leaning back against his truck. The move did nice things for his arms. It also showed off the tattoo inked on the inside of his forearm. It was a key, one of those big ornate kinds you sometimes see in old movies. I'd asked him once why a key, but he'd only kissed the tip of my nose and said, "Why not?"

"I wanted to see you today," he said now, looking at me over the tops of his sunglasses. "And I figured this would kill two birds with one stone. Keep Milly and your mom occupied for an hour. So." He reached out, his hand closing around my wrist, and pulled me to him. "Can we please get to occupying that time?"

My palm pressed flat against his chest. "Not here," I told him, looking around.

Our trailer was at the very back of the park, and just beyond was the thick pine forest that gave Woodland Hills its name. Skye followed my gaze, squeezing my hand. "She paid for the whole hour," he murmured low in my ear, and I shivered.

With one more quick glance at the trailer, I wrapped my fingers tighter around Skye's and pulled. "Come on."

The woods were thick and smelled like pine, dirt and that mossy, green scent of things growing. They were also cooler, the thick branches nearly blotting out the sun. We walked hand in hand until I couldn't see the trailer anymore, and then, finally, I turned and let Skye wrap me up in his arms.

We hadn't had a chance to be alone in over a week, and as Skye kissed me, I felt like I was melting into him, like there was nothing else in the world except me, him and the forest around us, the sound of birds in the trees, the distant burble of the creek. His lips moved over mine, and my fingers twisted in his shirt.

"I missed you," he breathed when we pulled apart, and I smiled against his collarbone.

"I missed you, too."

I always missed him. Even though I saw him every day at school, it wasn't the same as this, being alone with him, kissing him, feeling his arms around me.

Looking down at me, Skye pushed my hair away from my face. "Admit this was a good idea."

When he was holding me, everything seemed like a good idea, but I still wasn't exactly thrilled that he'd come out here. Or, really, that he'd brought Milly out here.

With that in mind, I stepped away from him, walking a little farther into the woods. He followed, and while I let him link his fingers with mine, I didn't say anything until we were even deeper into the trees, the ground underneath growing harder to navigate. Vines and low bushes pushed against the trees here, and even though I could hear the distant hum of I-85, it was like being in the middle of nowhere.

Once we'd reached the edge of the creek, I turned back to Skye and asked, "Why are we still sneaking around?"

He raised his dark eyebrows, blowing out a long breath. "Wow. Okay. What brought that on?"

There was a clump of dandelions at my feet, and I bent down to pick one. Twirling it between my fingers, I watched the fluff take to the air. "It's just… Skye, are you ashamed of me? Of all this?" I flung the headless dandelion out in the direction of the trailer, and Skye immediately stepped forward, holding my arms with both hands.

"No," he said, looking into my eyes. "God, no, Lana. Never." Skye's fingers dug into the flesh of my biceps, almost a little too hard.

"Then why?" I asked, hating the whiny note in my voice but unable to stop it.

He pulled away, rubbing one hand up and down the back of his neck. He always did that. He'd done it the first day I'd noticed him in French class, back at the beginning of the school year. Skye had been new, and in a county where everyone knew everyone, that had been enough to make him exotic. And then of course there was the unusual name, the blue-black hair, that beautiful, golden key covering the pale skin of his forearm. I was hardly the only girl who'd fallen in love with Skye Bartlett back in August. But he'd fallen for Kimberly McEntire, and that had been that.

Or so I'd thought.

After Kimberly had skipped town, things had changed. Skye had started sitting next to me in class, and even though he spent every lunch period with Milly and the rest of Kimberly's friends, he had always smiled at me. Then one day after French, he'd asked if I'd help him study at the library. He'd kissed me that night up against a shelf of reference books.

Now I looked at Skye in the late-morning light and asked, "Is it Milly? Is there…? You spend a lot of time with her." In front of people. In public.

Skye dropped his hand. "We're friends, Lan. I only drove her out here today because I wanted to see you." He stepped closer and I backed up until my elbows dug into the bark of the pine tree behind me. It wasn't that he scared me. It was that I was afraid if he stood too close, I'd once again forget to be angry, forget how crappy this whole situation made me feel.

Forget what I'd seen in Milly's head.

"It's just not good timing right now, Lana." Skye reached out and brushed a sweaty piece of hair from my forehead, his touch featherlight. "Kimberly's only been gone a few months, and it might look bad if I suddenly had a new girlfriend, you know?"

Overhead, something rustled in the trees, and on the distant interstate, I heard the blast of a car horn.

"Is that what I am?" I asked, folding my arms tightly across his chest. "Your girlfriend?"

Skye lifted an eyebrow, a smirk twisting his lips. "Do you want a ring or something? My letterman's jacket? I mean, I don't play a sport, and I'm not even sure they make those things anymore, but maybe Goodwill would—"

I shoved at his chest. "Don't make fun of me."

Something flashed in his eyes, something dark and angry. But it was gone as soon as it had appeared, and when Skye took my wrist in his hand, his grip was light. "I'm not, I promise. But this is tough for me. I don't want to look like the dick who doesn't even miss Kim, you know?"

This whole conversation was going nowhere, and suddenly I wished I'd never brought it up. We only had an hour, and we'd spent half that already, walking and arguing. Skye was right. There was enough weirdness about Kimberly's disappearance, and we didn't want to add to that.

But then I remembered Milly, the images I'd gotten when I'd touched her ring. "Milly—" I started, and Skye's fingers tightened around my wrist.

"I told you, there's nothing going on. She doesn't even like me like that."

"Yes, she does," I said before I could stop myself. "I saw it."

I hadn't quite shouted the words, but they'd still come out a lot louder than I'd intended. In a nearby bush, a bird suddenly took wing, and Skye startled.

"What do you mean you 'saw it'?" There was a deep crease between his brows, and his grip on my wrist was tight enough to hurt now. I shook him off, irritated.

"I…I can see things. When I touch people. Same as my mom."

Skye blinked, once, then twice, his whole body going still. "So…this psychic crap is for real? Because you said your mom just—"

"I know what I said." Shoving my hands into the back pockets of my jeans, I tilted my head back, looking up at the snatches of blue sky through the branches. "I didn't want you to think I was a freak, but yeah, Momma can really tell a person's future, and I can get…I don't know, impressions. When I touch somebody. It's not a big deal."

Skye had backed away from me now, his face pale. "Have you done that to me?" he asked, and I immediately shook my head.

"No," I promised. "Never. I only do it to help Momma out before her readings. Anything else feels—" I shuddered "—gross. Like a violation or something."

Skye seemed to sigh with his whole body, the breath ruffling his hair where it fell over his forehead. "So when you touched Milly—"

"She's into you, trust me." I left it at that. The longing coming off Milly for Skye had practically wavered there in the air earlier. True, I hadn't picked up anything else. If anything had ever happened between them, I hadn't seen it. But that didn't mean it hadn't happened.

"I can't help it if she likes me, Lana," Skye said. His own hands were in his pockets now, almost mimicking my pose. "But I don't feel that way about her. I swear."

When I didn't say anything, Skye took a step closer. "When we kissed earlier… If you'd wanted to, you could've looked into my head, right?"

"I told you I wouldn't do that," I snapped.

Skye was watching me closely now, ducking his head so that he could see into my face. "Do you promise, Lan? Do you promise you would never do that?"

If he hadn't said that, maybe I wouldn't have felt so tempted. But there was something so intense in his gaze, something that made the hairs on my arms stand up. And it was like any temptation, like Skye himself—once I'd been told I couldn't, I had to.

"Yeah," I heard myself say. "I promise."

His expression softened. "And I promise Milly and I are just friends. She's only hanging around me because we both miss Kim. That's it."

He smiled at me, a dimple flashing in one cheek. In the shady woods, his eyes seemed a darker blue, and when he tugged me to him, I let him.

When he leaned in to kiss me, I closed my hands around his forearms. The key tattoo was just there underneath my palm, and there was one brief moment when I tried to tell myself not to do it. That he had said there was nothing going on with Milly, and I needed to trust him.

But another darker part whispered, *Then why is he still keeping you a secret?*

He had asked me never to read him, and I had promised, but standing there in the woods behind my home, his skin pressed against mine, the temptation was too strong. *Just a little bit,* I told myself. *So I can be sure.*

As always, it felt like opening a door, and I tried to keep the door opened only a crack. Just enough to see if he was lying to me about Milly.

But the moment the door from my mind to his opened, it was like a hurricane blew through it. Skye kissed me as image after image assaulted my mind. Kimberly crying. Kimberly shoving at Skye's shoulders. They're in a field somewhere, and it's dark, and she needs to shut up, just shut up, shut up. Skye's hands around Kimberly's throat, and she's kicking him, but he's stronger and her kicks are getting weaker and weaker, and sweat is dripping down his face as he wonders why she won't die, would she just die already—

My heart was in my mouth, my stomach rolling, and it took every bit of strength in me not to scream, not to push him away. But we were alone out here, far from anyone, and I'd told him I wouldn't look. If he knew that I knew…

We parted, and he pressed his lips to my forehead while I shook. *Please let him think it's from the kiss.*

I wasn't sure how I managed to smile when he looked down at me. His eyes were so blue. Kimberly had looked into those eyes as he'd choked the life out of her. Kimberly, who had never left town, who had no glamorous future in L.A. Kimberly, who was probably at the bottom of a lake, or in a hole somewhere in that field I'd seen. Kimberly, who'd loved and trusted Skye like I had.

We stood there in the woods, looking at one another, and I tried to force my heart not to beat out of my chest, tried to keep my breathing calm. All I had to do was get back to the trailer. Get back to Momma, and get away from Skye. I could do this. I could.

And then Skye winced.

We both looked down, seeing my hand where it still clung to his forearm. I may have slowed my pulse and steadied my breathing, but I hadn't stopped my fingers from digging into him, hard enough to break the skin. My nails had pierced his flesh, and Skye and I both watched as a single drop of blood welled up just over the teeth of his key tattoo.

His eyes met mine, and I knew there was no lie I could tell that would convince him that I hadn't looked inside his mind. That I hadn't seen. That I didn't know.

I was in the woods behind my trailer with a boy who'd killed the last girl who loved him. I could look off to the horizon all I wanted, but no one was coming to save me. Maybe I couldn't tell the future like Momma, but in that instant, I swore I could see it. When her reading with Milly was done, she'd come out and find Skye sitting there. Maybe there'd be dirt on his knees, and he might be breathing a little hard. He'd tell her I'd left. Maybe I headed out for track practice early, caught a ride with a friend—no, he wasn't sure who. And then maybe later, he'd come back to this quiet place in Woodland Hills, and by the end of the night, I'd find myself lying next to Kimberly McEntire, wherever she was. For just a second, I thought of taking one more peek, trying to see what he had done with her. But I was too afraid to look again, afraid that anything I saw might break what was left of my mind.

Skye's hands were tight around my wrists now, and I could feel that same dark anger I'd sensed earlier pulsing through him. *Oh, Momma,* I thought almost from a distance. *You were wrong. I'm not going to track practice today.*

But as the bones in my wrists creaked and popped, I remembered what Momma had said.

You are gonna run and run today. Fast.

A laugh nearly gurgled out of my throat, high and hysterical. "You're damn right I am," I muttered. I reached out.

I shoved.

I ran.

FIGMENT

by Jeri Smith-Ready

It begins, as always, in darkness.

I awake in transit, amid the clamor of voices and the clatter of trucks. Then a steady jet-engine roar lulls me to the edge of sleep.

If I'm waking, it means that someone believes in me again. Maybe it's the man, woman, boy or girl I'll soon befriend. Maybe it's a person close to them. Or maybe it's only my ex-friend's employee who took this padded envelope I've been trapped inside and put it on a plane.

All that matters is that someone, somewhere, believes.

A woman's soft footsteps accompany what I hope is the final leg of my journey. Her hands hold my envelope level before her, not swinging casually at the end of her arm the way the deliveryman carried me. It reminds me of the way Gordon's butler used to deliver his vodka and pills on a silver tray.

"No more tears," she murmurs. "He wasn't worth it."

But I'm not crying. I never cry.

She sniffles, then takes a deep, slow breath. "No more tears," she repeats.

Ah, you weren't talking to me. Never mind. If she can't hear my thoughts, that means she's not the one I'm meant for.

She stops and knocks on heavy wood—a door, likely. I hear the muffled voice of a young man, a begrudging beckoning over the strum of guitar.

Hinges creak. The guitar grows louder, doesn't pause while the woman who carries me stands still at what must be a seldom-crossed threshold.

"Eli, your father is dead."

The guitar doesn't stop, but it hits a sour note. Then Eli continues to play, picking up where he left off. "So?"

"He left you this."

The guitar is set aside with a soft gong. Eli takes my envelope and squeezes it, crushing my face. "It's soft. Is it a big fat wad of cash?" he asks with a mixture of harshness and hope.

"Just open it."

Eli tears the sealing strip, letting in the first light I've glimpsed in...I won't know how long until I see a calendar.

"What the hell?" He clamps the envelope shut, smothering the light. "Mom, is this a joke?"

Pull me out. Please don't let me stay in here.

"There's a story behind it," his mother says. "It's rather interesting, actually. Your father—"

"What did the others get?"

"I—I don't know."

"Never mind, I'll look it up online. It'll be in the news.

One-hit wonder Gordon Wylde, 45, dies of— What did he die of?"

"A boating accident. They said it was instant. He didn't suffer."

"Good for him." Eli's voice cracks, causing me to wonder how far past puberty he is. His hands are large and strong, squeezing me tighter than ever, so perhaps the voice-crack is…sadness? Anger? I wouldn't know.

"Eli, if you want to talk, I'm here."

"I know you are," he snaps. Then his voice softens. "Thanks, Mom. I'm sorry—I mean, if you're upset he's gone."

"Not really." She gives a wistful laugh. "Your father's always been gone." Her footsteps come closer, then a kiss, muted, laid upon hair instead of skin. "I've got a roast in the oven, but how about pizza tonight instead?"

"That'd be cool. Thanks."

She retreats and closes the door. Eli takes a deep breath— as would I, had I lungs—and pulls me out of the envelope.

Amber eyes examine me, the same color as the streaks in his disheveled black hair. Eli pulls in his lower lip, brushes his tongue over the silver ring there. He could be as young as sixteen, but the piercing makes me think he's closer to eighteen. "I don't get it," he mutters. "I do not get it."

Eli tosses me on the bed—faceup, luckily. The ceiling features a wood-and-green-metal fan, currently off, as well as a poster of a brunette girl with wide blue eyes. The right edge is torn, the poster ripped in half to eliminate her partner. At the bottom it reads "she &" in a whimsical cursive hand.

He pulls a note from the envelope, the folded sheet of paper I've been lying on for…a long time, I think. I don't remember how long, or even what form I've taken. It must be the same form as when I was Gordon's friend, because vessels contain our spirits until they disintegrate (the vessels, that is). I never forget disintegration.

I am eternal. I can never die, only sleep. My kind has existed since humans first drew pictures on cave walls and told stories around campfires. We were born at the dawn of imagination.

"Call Tyler," Eli says in a flat voice. It sounds like a command, but not, I hope, for me.

A tinny male voice emits from a cell phone speaker. "Eli! What's up, bro?"

Eli picks me up and stares into my eyes, his own turned dark with loathing.

"My father left me a cat."

I'm four inches long. My plush fake fur is black, except for my paws, which are white. My eyes are stitched yellow-thread rings surrounding felt black centers. Their perfect roundness makes me look perpetually astonished.

All of this I'd forgotten, because when no one holds you for…years?…you lose sense of your shape.

All of this I remember, because Eli has thrown me against the wall and I've landed, fortuitously, in front of a full-length mirror.

My puffy white forepaws extend forward, like I'm asking for double fist bumps, or worse, protecting myself. But nothing can hurt me, aside from being ignored.

Eli is ignoring me. In the mirror I see him sitting cross-legged on the double bed, his back turned. The fan is on low now, its wood-and-metal arms making lazy circles, casting hazy shadows on the ceiling and the girl in the poster.

I examine what details I can, to determine Eli's state of living. His dresser and nightstand are basic pale wood, IKEA-ish. The boots sticking out from under the bed appear to be Timberland knockoffs. His jeans and black T-shirt are threadbare and distressed, but that might be the style still (or again). Through the floor I hear his mother in the kitchen, opening the oven door, then letting the door crash shut. A two-story house, then. Eli and his mother seem neither rich nor poor.

My gaze sweeps the walls for a calendar. I'm used to lying dormant for years between allies, but not knowing how many years is unsettling. Eli's father crammed me into that envelope in 1997, when the world was throwing itself at his feet. He thought he didn't need me anymore. I wonder how that worked out.

Some months or years later, Gordon opened the envelope, but only to add the note, which Eli read to his friend Tyler over the phone.

"My dear Elias,
Of all my sons, I've given you the least in life, so in death I give you the most.
    This wee kitty has been more than a good-luck charm to me. It's been a friend, perhaps the most loyal one I've ever had. I advise you to keep it at your side at all times if you want to succeed. And when (not if, but when) you find that success, do not make my arrogant mistake and cast the cat aside. Give credit where credit is due.

Your father,
Gordon Wylde"

Tyler laughed his ass off, naturally, and then Eli threw me across the room, where I wait, neither patiently nor impatiently, since I do not feel.

I do have opinions, however, an important one of which is forming now: Eli has more musical genius in that pouty lower lip than his father had in his entire body. His voice needs no enhancing, and his playing needs no amplification. He could most likely make hundreds a day busking in a subway station. God only knows what a decent record label could do for him.

But he needs more than talent. He needs me. Not just to set him on the path to greatness, but to keep him there. When inevitable misfortunes beset him, he must believe he's destined. He must believe that luck is on his side.

First, however, he must believe in me.

Eli draws in a sudden hiss of pain between his teeth, then shakes out his hand. He's played too long.

Sucking the pad of his right thumb, he turns and slides off the bed. For a moment I wonder what it would be like to unfold long legs so effortlessly—or to move at all. He lays the guitar in its case and starts to close the lid.

Eli, wait.

He hesitates but doesn't look at me.

You can't hear my words yet, I tell him, *but you can feel what I want. Please, put me inside. It all starts there.*

Eli snatches me up by one ear, then drops me facedown in the compartment in the guitar case's neck. "There, Dad. Happy?"

He slams the lid shut and flips the latches. But instead of shoving the guitar case back under the bed where he got it, he lays his hand over the place where I am, pressing this end of the case against the floor. The carpet gives a little.

All it takes is a little belief to bring me to life.

Thank you, Eli.

His breathing stops. A soft suction pop marks his sore thumb coming out of his mouth.

I'm inside the case. But don't worry, I won't suffocate. I don't breathe.

Eli's whimper has a question mark at the end.

Yes, I'm real. Sort of. I used to know your father. If he bequeathed me to you, it means that you were important to him. Or that I was not. In any case, we're together now.

"What the—" The latches rattle as he fumbles to open them. The lid lifts, letting in light.

Eli doesn't pick me up. I wish I could see his expression, but I'm still facedown and can't turn over.

He tugs my tail. "I'm going insane."

On the contrary, you have a normal, healthy imagination. That's what keeps me alive.

He lets out a curse and slams the guitar case shut again. A few moments later, he speaks in hushed tones, but not to me.

"Ty, have you had any, like, weird thoughts since Saturday night?"

The phone speaker is loud enough—and my cat ears sensitive enough—that I can hear the reply. "What kind of weird thoughts?"

"I don't know. Hallucinations?"

"It was just a little weed. You didn't even smoke any."

"I know, but even secondhand, I definitely felt the effects."

"Are you saying you're seeing things?"

"Hearing things," Eli corrects.

"It was a loud concert. My ears were ringing afterward."

"This isn't a ringing."

"What is it?"

Eli pauses. "Nothing. I guess it is sort of like a ringing. I gotta go. Mom's calling me for dinner."

His mom's not calling him for dinner, but after hanging up, Eli stalks from the room, shouting her name.

I hope she has answers.

"So you're from Cleveland?" Eli has propped me up on his other pillow so that I can see him, but he doesn't look at me as we talk. He sits against his headboard beside me, arms crossed, legs straight out, looking stunned.

Not originally, but that was where my essence was encapsulated in this temporary form. The musician who gave me to your father was from there. He was in a band called Raise an Axe. Ever heard of them?

"No."

That's because they had only one heavy-metal hit in the late eighties, off their self-titled album, Raise an Axe. *Can you guess the song name?*

"'Raise an Axe'?"

Very good. That singer abandoned his band to embark on a solo career. He also abandoned me. When he realized his mistake, it was too late. I had no luck left for him.

Eli groans. "This is so bizarre." He sweeps both palms over his wavy dark hair, holding it back against his scalp. Under all those tumbling locks, he has a pronounced widow's peak, just like his father. "So who are you?"

A figment.

"That's your name?"

It's what I am.

"Like a figment of my imagination?"

I give the vocal equivalent of a shrug. *A bit redundant, since by definition a figment is something that exists only in the imagination.*

Heels together, Eli taps his bare feet against each other. "Like an imaginary friend."

Precisely.

"I thought only little kids had imaginary friends."

They're not the only ones who need them.

"I've got plenty of friends."

Friends or fleas? His father's penthouse had been overrun with bloodsucking sycophants, people who only loved him for his money and fame.

Eli pulls his knees to his chest and rests his chin on them. "What I mean is, I'm not lonely or anything."

I decide not to challenge this assertion. *May I ask, what became of your father's career once he left Boyz on the Korner?*

Eli scoffs. "Nothing. He never had another hit like BotK had with 'Ready, Set, Dance.' Because he basically sucked. People realized that after he hit twenty-one and wasn't adorable anymore." He looks at me quickly. "Wait. Was that when he put you away?"

That's when I entered the envelope, yes.

"Wow." He shakes his head hard. "This can't be real."

You need to redefine "real."

"Obviously. So why are you here?"

To help you succeed in life by bringing you good luck. You need the right people in the right place in the right mood. I can make that happen. Your talent will do the rest.

Eli gives me a sideways, suspicious look. "What's in it for you?"

If I help you, you'll believe in me, and I get to keep existing. I remember my image in the mirror. Also, I'd very much like some clothes.

Eli, it turns out, used to play with dolls when he was a boy. I don't judge.

"If anyone sees me doing this, I'll have my man card permanently revoked," he says as he buttons my sparkly blue shirt.

So I won't be meeting your friends?

"No, you're staying here."

But unless I'm in your presence, I can't influence the thoughts of others around you in your favor.

He looks up from the box of doll clothes, horrified. "Other people can hear you?"

Not in words, the way you can. They can sense my desires and be swayed by them, but only if they've seen me and acknowledged my existence.

I catch sight of the doll sneakers he's picked out of the box. *Please, no pink.*

"So you are a boy. I wondered, since you don't have any— you know." He flips up my shirttail. "Anything to cover."

Technically, I'm neither a boy nor a girl. I can be whichever you prefer.

He narrows his eyes. "What do you mean, 'prefer'?"

In a friend.

"Oh. Well, a human for starters."

You have no pets?

"Just fish. I'm allergic."

And I'm relieved. Some dogs chew stuffed animals, and some cats hump them. Humiliating in either case.

Eli rummages through the box, which appears to have all sorts of doll clothes jumbled together in one mass. "If you're an imaginary friend, why don't you look human? Why are you trapped in this stuffed cat?"

Figments need a physical vessel so their friends can take them places. Or leave us behind, if you like.

"Us?" He casts a wary gaze around his room. "There's more than one of you here?"

No, you only get one. But there are others of my kind in the world. There always have been.

"Huh. Hey, here's a cool hat." Eli holds it up with a flourish. It has three points and a giant purple feather, like one of the Three Musketeers.

Yes! Put that on my head. Now.

He laughs. "You like the bling, huh?"

I love the bling.

"Pimp my cat." He tugs the hat down over my ears, then tilts it sideways. "Figment's got swag, yo."

Is that what you wish to call me?

"Or Fig for short. Is that okay?"

You may call me whatever you like. I hide my next thought from him: just don't ever put me away.

"Well, Fig, guess what? You're getting yourself some fine-ass boots."

Over the past week, Eli has learned to entertain me. When he's downstairs with his mother, he sets me on the windowsill or in front of his aquarium so I have something to watch. He leaves on the radio, which teaches me about current events and the latest musical trends.

When he leaves the house he brings me with him, buried deep in his messenger bag to school, or tucked into his guitar case to band practice, which double as makeout sessions with his girlfriend, Vanessa. He hasn't gotten up the nerve to introduce me to anyone yet, so I have influence on nobody but him.

Just before history class on my third day of school, a girl behind Eli whispers his name. His chair creaks as he turns to her.

"Sorry about your dad," she says. "I heard on the news."

I expect him to growl *"It doesn't matter"* or *"whatever,"* as he has to every other sympathizer. Instead he just says, "Thanks, Lyra."

"I know what it's like. I mean, I don't have a famous father, but—"

"Semifamous."

"Well. Anyway, I never knew my mom. She left right after I was born."

He shifts in his chair again, perhaps turning all the way round. "That probably sucks more than not knowing your dad."

"If they left, they probably weren't worth knowing, right? At least, that's what I tell myself every birthday."

"Seriously. I never got a birthday or Christmas card. Just some child-support money in a bank account, but not as much as you'd think. Not with two other sons to take care of." Eli lowers his voice until I can barely hear it. "When he died, he left the oldest one a house and the middle one a car."

"What did you get?"

He pauses for a long moment. If I had breath, I would hold it. But he finally says, "Nothing."

The bell rings and the teacher clops across the floor in what sound like platform heels. I can feel the vibrations from here.

She begins the lecture, on the French Revolution, a topic I know well, since I've heard it in classrooms ever since a few years after the event itself. The facts remain the same, but the perspective changes as the centuries pass.

I wish you'd bring me out in class just once, I tell Eli. *You'd get much better grades, or at least I could keep the teacher from calling on you.*

He gives the bag a slight kick to shut me up. Since I feel no pain, it doesn't work.

For the record, girls think I'm cute.

No response.

Perhaps you could bring me out at band practice today, when you see what's-her-name. The one who treats you like an imbecile. She'd find it charming, you carrying a tiny stuffed cat with a feather hat and silver boots in your guitar case.

No response.

Tap the bag once for no, twice for yes.

Eli gives a heavy sigh, shifts his feet beneath the desk next to my bag. For a long moment, nothing happens. Then finally, I feel a single tap. Followed by another.

"Oh, my God, he's adorbs!" Vanessa squeezes my belly and shakes me from side to side, making my hat's feather flop against my head. "Where did you get him?"

I appreciate that she refers to me as "him" instead of "it," but her tone is a bit patronizing. She's a year older than Eli, a fact she points out as often as possible.

Sitting on the basement couch with his arm around Vanessa's shoulders, Eli says, "My father left him to me as a good-luck charm. Isn't that hilarious?"

"Aww." She strokes his cheek with the backs of her black-lacquered fingernails, then kisses him softly. "Are you sad you never got to meet him?"

"Not really," he replies, but gives me a nervous glance.

Liar.

Eli opens his mouth to tell me to shut up, but catches himself in time.

Vanessa tugs my shirtsleeve. "Did he come dressed like this?"

"Of course. Where would I get doll clothes?"

I don't bother repeating my call of *"liar."*

"Eli, come on." Behind me, Jules, the drummer, taps his sticks together.

Eli reaches for me, then pulls his hand back. "Take good care of him, okay?"

"I will." Vanessa kisses me right between the eyes. My opinion of her is softening somewhat.

Eli takes his guitar and joins Jules and the other boy, Tyler, who fancies himself a lead singer but often seems more fascinated with his collection of unusual instruments.

As they play, Vanessa dances me atop her bare knee in time to the music. During a slow ballad, she rests me on her shoulder, my feet tucked into her long blond hair streaked with green and blue. At the end of each song, she waves me in the air, cheering with exaggerated enthusiasm. The boys scowl at her silliness, but it's the most fun I've had since I reawakened.

The tunes are intricate for a songwriter of Eli's age, but sadly, he's the only one who seems capable of playing them. When they take a break, I seize the opportunity to speak to him.

You should go solo. You're too good for these poseurs.

Eli doesn't glare at me. Instead the corner of his mouth tugs into a sad frown. He knows I'm right, but he loves his friends.

Also the band name, Trending Frenzy? What does that even mean?

"Long story," he says under his breath.

After the break, it takes Trending Frenzy a full hour to rehearse three more songs. Tyler keeps trying to change the key to take it up to his singing range and make it easier to play, but it sounds like crap when they do that. Even Tyler recognizes this truth, once I've sent this mental message to him ten or eleven times.

Eventually Vanessa gets bored and lies down on the couch, cuddling me close. She presses me to her chest, blocking my eyes and ears. It's just as well—Eli is growing tired of my running commentary, and the band's playing is growing ever unruly. I let myself zone out to the sound of Vanessa's slow, rhythmic heartbeat.

"That's all I can take," Eli says finally. "I'm gonna grab a soda. You guys want anything?"

They grumble a response I can't hear, then his footsteps ascend the staircase over my head.

"Lucky cat," says a soft voice close to the couch.

Vanessa stirs, then gives a low laugh. "Jules. Where's Eli?"

"Upstairs. Tyler's in the bathroom." He leans in, and her heart starts to race. "So I thought I'd come do this."

Uh-oh.

They kiss, loud and wet, and her hand leaves me to move to him. I'm flipped on my back, looking up at their chins. Their mouths move like they're starving.

Then Jules's hand displaces me. For a moment I teeter on the edge of the sofa, long enough to see him reach down her shirt. Then his elbow tips me off the side, and I tumble onto the floor. I focus on the frayed brown fabric of the couch skirt and think to Vanessa with all my might, *What about Eli?*

She pulls away from Jules. "I can't do this to him. His dad just died."

"So? He didn't even know the guy. He makes fun of that stupid 'Ready, Set, Dance' song all the time." Jules leans in again, making a slurping sound against what I assume is Vanessa's neck.

"Stop." She pushes him away, and this time he relents, letting both hands fall onto his knees. "Eli's been different since it happened," she says. "If you can't see that, you're a shitty friend."

"I've been hooking up with you for a month. I'm already a shitty friend."

Down the basement hallway, a door opens, letting out the liquid sound of a flushing toilet. Jules hurries to stand up and move away from the couch. "Hey, Ty, wanna play some Ping-Pong? Loser buys pizza."

"Nah, I gotta get out of here before I stab Eli with one of your drumsticks. One more 'Why can't you sing it the way I wrote it?' and I'm going solo."

"If you do that, then Eli'll go solo, too. I don't want to see you guys competing."

"Plus, you'll be out of a gig, right?"

"You think that's all I care about?" Jules laughs. "You wound me, man. I'll see you Friday."

Vanessa calls goodbye to him as he goes up the stairs. Then she picks me up from the floor. "Aww, sorry, little guy." She dusts off my tail and the front of my shirt. "Ty, you need a roadie to carry out your million instruments?"

"Very funny, but no. I'm leaving my guitar here. Eli said he'd adjust the bridge for me. Intonation is totally out of whack."

He's the talented one.

"He's the talented one, you know," Vanessa says.

"And you're the slutty one," Tyler answers. "Eli finds out about you and Jules, that's the end of the band."

"Why do you care? You just said you wanted to—"

"Shh."

Eli is coming down the stairs. "You're leaving?" he asks Tyler, his voice devoid of disappointment.

"Yep. Friday practice still on?"

I wouldn't commit if I were you.

Eli commits, despite my warning. Ah, well, I suppose band breakups, like all breakups, are best done in person.

Vanessa sets me on the coffee table in front of the couch, propped up against a stack of books. Then she straightens my clothes and gives me an indulgent smile.

You don't deserve him.

Her smile fades, then she moves over to give Eli room on

the couch. He picks up Tyler's Fender and starts to tune it, but keeps glancing between Vanessa and me.

I'm not the one you should be jealous of.

She slides her hand up his thigh. "I have to leave in about half an hour, so…can you do that later?"

Eli sets Tyler's guitar aside, then pulls her into his arms, kissing her, tangling his fingers in her hair. I wonder if her heart is beating as fast as it did when Jules kissed her.

I clear my throat, figuratively. *I'm sitting right here. Do you mind?*

Eli opens one eye to look at me, then extends his middle finger ever so slightly in my direction, below her arm, where she couldn't see it even if her eyes were open.

There's something you should know about her before you—

She tears off his T-shirt, then Eli leans back to lie on the sofa, pulling her on top of him. Things progress faster.

This is your last chance before I blurt out a hard truth. Trust me, you don't want to hear it in front of her. I'm warning you.

Her sweater comes off, then the camisole beneath it.

Vanessa's been cheating on you with Jules.

Eli's hands go still on her bare waist, his thumb tracing beneath the edge of her bra. She doesn't notice at first, too busy kissing or maybe biting his neck.

"Stop," he whispers.

"What's wrong?" she asks, her blond hair hanging like a veil between us, so I can't see his face.

"It's not— I—um. I just remembered I have to be some-where."

"Now? Where?"

Coward. Don't drag this out. I saw them kissing. More than kiss-

ing. You know I'm telling the truth, don't you? You've suspected for a while.

"I just— I need you to go. I'll call you later. I'm sorry."

Why are you apologizing to her?

Vanessa doesn't budge. "I don't understand." She clutches his arm harder, her voice taut with fear.

I turn my attention to her. *He knows about you and Jules. Go now. Now!*

Vanessa lifts her head, like she's hearing her name shouted from far away. "Okay. But call me?"

"I will," he says. "Promise."

She grabs her sweater from the back of the couch and yanks it over her head. "I guess I'll be early for work instead of late for once. My boss'll die of surprise." Vanessa picks up her bag, leans over for a quick kiss, then runs up the stairs.

Eli lies there on his back for a second, hands covering his face. The black tattoo on his upper arm twitches, a bare tree with birds rising from its branches.

Sorry.

He lets his hands fall to his side with a thud. "Sorry? Do you know what you just interrupted? Or are all figments celibate?"

It depends on the imagination that sustains us. I've taken some interesting forms in the past. For instance—

"I don't want to know." Eli taps his fingers against his ribs. "What do I do?"

Break up with her. What choice do you have?

"I could pretend I don't know. Then everything stays the same. Otherwise I lose her and Jules. Tyler, too, probably, because I'll have to break up the band. They're my only friends."

I doubt that's true, and if it is, then you need to make better friends.

"I know." Eli turns on his side to face me. "But even bad friends are better than being alone."

He suddenly looks years younger. I have to make him feel better. It's what I do.

I promise you this, Eli, right here and now: you'll never be alone again.

After dinner, Eli paces his bedroom floor, clutching his Magic 8 Ball. "Should I break up with Vanessa and the band?" He flips the ball. "'Outlook good.' Does that mean yes or no?"

That sounds definitively yes.

"But not as definitive as *Yes*." He shakes the ball hard and repeats the question. "'Reply hazy, try again.' You know what? I don't trust this for big decisions. I'll ask the cookie." He sets down the ball and shoves his hand into his jar of fortune-cookie fortunes, a jar that looks like a giant ceramic Oreo.

He reads the first slip. "'The secret to good friends is no secret to you.' I don't know what that means."

It means time to man up and clear your life of douchebags.

He tilts his head at me. "You're starting to sound less proper."

And you're starting to sound less smart. End it now.

After another half hour of my cajoling, Eli breaks up with Vanessa via text. She doesn't reply. No begging, crying, threatening. Deep down she knows why he's ended it, because I told her. She'll chalk it up to intuition.

At bedtime, rather than setting me on the nightstand or in his guitar case, Eli takes off my hat and boots, wraps me in the blue silk cami Vanessa left behind and holds me close as he lies down to sleep. I fit perfectly under his chin.

This is something new, this…cuddling. Even when I belonged to women, I was in unhuggable forms, such as a crystal elephant or a carved wooden Woman of Willendorf fertility statue. Maybe if I'd ever been a child's figment, I'd have experienced this closeness, this neediness. For the first time, I'm more than an advisor and miracle worker. I'm a friend.

Eli sleeps fitfully, and soon I tumble out of his arms and onto the floor. I've never spoken to him in his sleep, but he needs settling.

Wake up and write. You'll feel better.

He comes awake with a sharp breath, then without a word, slips out of bed and crosses to his desk, the direction I'm facing. He lifts his Magic 8 Ball from atop a stack of notebooks, takes the top pad, then sets down the worthless prediction device.

On the way back to the bed, he accidentally steps on my face. "Sorry, Fig!" Eli picks me up, unwraps the camisole from around my torso and brings both to the bed with him.

Do you need my help?

He shakes his head and pulls the cap off the pen with his teeth. "This is one thing I do best on my own."

Pen in one hand, Vanessa's cami in the other, Eli scribbles furiously for the next four hours, frowning and crossing out as many lines as he writes. Just after 3:00 a.m. he pulls out his guitar and plays a series of chords—softly, so as not to wake his mom.

The next day at school, he returns Vanessa's shirt, wrinkles ironed out. She takes it without a word, or at least none that I can hear from inside his bag.

In history class, he sets me on the corner of his desk, facing forward. "Good-luck charm for the exam," he explains to Lyra.

"Let me see."

He spins me to face him and Lyra. Instead of gushing over my cute widdle boots and hat, she takes a good long look at me. "That expression," she says finally. "Like the whole world is amazing."

It's just the way the manufacturer shaped my eyes. The world is most definitely not amazing.

Eli gives me a skeptical smile.

But maybe she is, I add.

Friday afternoon, Eli meets Tyler and Jules for burgers at Five Guys before band practice. I'm left in the bag, of course, on the seat of the booth. His so-called friends sit across from him.

"I'm leaving the band," he tells them when their food's arrived.

"Aw, man." Tyler pounds the bottom of a ketchup bottle. "Why now, when we're finally getting good?"

"I don't think we're getting good, but that's not the main reason. My main reason is that Jules here can't keep his hands off my girlfriend."

"What?" Jules stammers. "How do *you* know?"

"I knew this would happen," Tyler says. "I told her to knock it off."

"Wait, how did you know?" Jules asks him.

"I have eyes. Eyes that saw you feeling her up in the school parking lot last week."

"Tyler, you knew and didn't tell me?" Eli says. "I thought you were my best friend."

"I didn't want to make you mad."

He didn't want you to break up the band, I tell Eli. *He wanted to do it himself.*

"Well, I'm twice as mad now."

"I can see that." Tyler pounds the ketchup bottle again. "What is with this stuff? It's stuck."

"Eli, I'm sorry, man. I really am." Jules sounds sincere.

He's not sorry.

"It's my fault," he continues with a full mouth. "You shouldn't blame Vanessa. I'll stay away from her, I swear."

"It's too late for that."

"I'm just saying, it's over with us. So you might as well keep her."

"*Keep* her?" Eli's voice rises above the din of the crowd. "She's a girl, not a doll!"

Tyler snorts. "Well, you'd know, wouldn't you?"

"What's that supposed to mean?" Eli's voice is colder than I've ever heard it.

"You've gotten a little too attached to that stuffed cat your loser dad gave you."

"I'm not attached."

"Oh, really? Then let me have it for a week." Tyler sets down the bottle hard on the table. "It's the least you can do, Mr. I'm Too Talented for My Band."

"Why would you even want him?" Eli's voice turns hot with anger again.

"It's a 'him' now? Is he your new best friend? Is that why you don't need me anymore?"

Jules breaks in. "Take it easy, Ty. Eli didn't say we weren't still friends. The band stuff is just business."

"'Business'?" Ty says. "This is your fault, Jules! It wasn't business when you had your hand inside Vanessa's shirt."

Eli's silverware hits the table with a clatter. A fork or knife bounces onto the booth seat beside my bag. "Screw you guys both."

Suddenly I'm lifted, bag and all. He's walking fast toward the door, faster than he's ever headed to class. The corner of his calculus textbook digs into my stomach with every step, and I'm very glad I have no pain nerves.

A door creaks open, and Eli says, "I'm sorry. Excuse me. Sorry."

"It's okay, but what…" The girl's familiar voice fades as Eli keeps going.

We stop suddenly, and a car door handle rattles. Eli curses. He tears open the bag, letting in bright sunlight I can't blink away.

Your keys aren't in here. I didn't hear them jangle.

"Looking for these?" Tyler says behind us.

Now I hear them jangle.

"Give me my keys," Eli demands.

"I'll trade you." Tyler laughs. "The keys for the kitty."

"Why do you want him so much?"

He doesn't want me. He wants to destroy me to hurt you, because you hurt him.

Eli lunges, and now it's Jules's turn to laugh, though more nervously than Tyler did. "We're just messin' with you. Come on, our burgers are getting cold. Give Ty the stupid doll for two seconds so he'll stop being a dick. Or give it to me, whatever."

Eli drops the bag on the ground. "Haven't I given you enough? My songs, my time, my girlfriend?"

"Vanessa wasn't your girlfriend—she was just a regular hookup. You know what she called you? Her favorite charity."

There's a smack of bone against bone, and Jules cries out. Then a thud and the sound of denim skidding over blacktop.

Suddenly, I'm pulled out into the brightness. By Tyler.

"How do you like him now, dude?" He rips off my hat and boots. "Nothing better than a naked p—"

Tyler buckles over with an "oof!" He clutches me against his stomach, groaning. Something in bright blue leather— a gloved fist? A booted foot?—flashes past me, up into his chin. Released from his grip, I fall to the pavement, rolling to rest faceup.

Appearing above me are wide blue eyes, like those belonging to the girl on Eli's ceiling. Lyra scoops me up and stuffs me into her bag. There's candy in here. Watermelon flavored, I think.

Tyler cries out again, higher-pitched this time.

"Let go of the keys," Lyra says. Her body rocks forward, and Tyler shrieks louder. "Sorry, does that hurt? You know what would hurt worse? If you didn't let go of the keys and my foot accidentally broke all your fingers." She bends over, and the bag on her back rises. "If you ever want to play that stupid ukulele again, you know what to do."

A sharp jangle, then Lyra says, "Thank you."

I can't hear much over the rush and jostle of her bag, which is soon dumped on the floor of Eli's car (I recognize the smell).

"You okay?" she asks.

Not bad, but—

"I'll be all right," Eli answers.

Oh, she wasn't talking to me. Sorry.

Lyra starts the engine. "I live around the block. We can go to my house and get some ice for your face, then you can bring me back to get my car later."

"Thanks for rescuing us. I mean, rescuing me. I mean, rescuing Fig."

"You named your stuffed cat after a fruit?"

Eli pauses. "It's short for Figment."

She laughs and backs out of the parking space so fast, a book in her bag smashes my legs. "Interesting, considering he actually exists."

I sit on Lyra's kitchen table, propped against the salt and pepper shakers. Eli holds an ice pack to his bruised left eye and another to his lower lip, where he was lucky not to have the ring pulled out. Popcorn is popping in the microwave.

"Okay, kitty, your turn." Lyra enters the kitchen with a large plastic bin. "Time for some new clothes."

Yes! I would pump my fist if I could.

Eli can't hide his interest as she lifts the lid. "You have a separate compartment for each item of clothing? I'm in awe."

"I was a little OCD when I was a kid, at least with the stuff that was important to me." Lyra tucks a lock of her long dark hair behind her ear in a self-conscious gesture. "It's been years since I even looked at my dolls, much less dressed them up."

Eli puts down one of his ice packs and pulls out an orange boa. "Isn't this from one of the Bratz girls?"

"Yeah, I owned, like, ten of those. So you must have a sister, huh?"

He holds the boa up in front of me.

Too much.

"I don't have a sister," Eli says without meeting her eyes.

She pauses in her search, then smiles. "You played with dolls? That's so cool."

He shrugs like it's nothing, but the skin around his visible eye loosens in relief. "That's one of the advantages to being dad-free: no one to force me to play with trucks or try out for football." He places the boa back in the bin. "Mom didn't care, though I think she was confused when I turned out straight."

Lyra laughs. "I'm glad you turned out— I mean, not that there's anything wrong with— I mean, I'm glad for my sake. Ugh, can we just pretend I didn't say any of that?" She lifts a pair of golden slippers. "Fig must have new boots, if nothing else."

And you thought you'd be alone if you ditched your fake friends. Ask her to hang out.

Eli picks up the other ice pack, but before pressing it to his mouth, he says, "What are you doing tomorrow night?"

Over the next six months, Eli plays a series of successful solo gigs, he and Lyra get serious, and he graduates magna cum laude. I play a role in all of these fortunate events, but only a developmental one. Mostly it's his doing. Mostly.

During the summer between high school and college, Eli ramps up his appearance schedule, and after each performance, a music journalist or blogger sits him down for an interview. They ask the expected questions about his one-hit-wonder of a father, how Eli will avoid the same trap of overconfidence, how he'll stay down-to-earth despite drowning in contract offers, each bigger than the last.

He always answers, "My friends keep me humble. They remind me that success doesn't come from my efforts alone. Some of it's luck, of course, and I feel very lucky right now."

But each time he says it with less conviction. When they start asking about me, his "good-luck charm," Eli gets antsy.

These days, we don't talk much.

One night, after a standing-room-only concert at a local nightclub, a reporter with a different sort of angle wants to talk to Eli.

"Hi." The lady is about thirty years old and carries a bag that screams *organic living*. "I'm doing a story about good-luck charms and successful performers—musicians, sports stars, that sort of thing. The article is called 'Beyond Rabbit's Feet.'" She sinks into a chair and signals the waitress. "Your little cat is quite the legend."

"It is?" Eli glances over to the chair next to him, where I'm sitting atop his guitar case.

You just called me "it." Not cool.

The reporter smiles at me. "So I've done some digging…"

"Great," he mutters, reaching for his Coke.

"It is my job." She flips a page in her notepad. "Turns out, your father was also known for carrying around a cat-shaped good-luck charm when he was with Boyz on the Korner." She points her pen at me. "Is this the same one? Did he give it to you?"

Eli just sips his Coke and stares at her impassively, saying nothing.

She reaches into her bag. "I have pictures, if that would help."

"Don't bother." Standing quickly, almost knocking his chair over, he sweeps me up and crams me into his inside jacket pocket. "For the record, yes, the cat was my father's, but it's just a gimmick. My girlfriend likes holding it during shows. It gives her something to do with her hands when she gets nervous for me."

"If it's just a gimmick, then why is it insured for over a hundred thousand—"

"I have to go. Good night."

Her protestation fades behind us as Eli stalks out of the club.

Once we're outside where it's quiet, I ask him, *Am I really a gimmick to you now?*

He pulls out his phone to pretend he's talking to someone else instead of the bulge in his coat. "Fig, I think next time you should stay home."

I do stay home for the following gig, perched on his windowsill, angled so that I can also see the aquarium. As frustrated as Eli is with my influence over his life, he still takes the time for small kindnesses.

Just after 2:00 a.m., he pulls into the driveway. I can feel the slam of car doors from up here. Soon the stairs, then the floorboards shake with his footsteps.

The bedroom door jerks open. Eli dumps his guitar case on the bed, then paces, hands on his hips, shoulders lowered in defeat.

How'd it go? I ask, though I can guess.

"It sucked." He sinks onto the edge of the bed. "I suck."

You do not suck. That's one thing I know for sure about you.

"Maybe you know, but I'll never know. Not as long as…" He raises his head from his hands to stare at me. A look I recognize all too well comes into his eyes.

No…

He gets up and crosses the room toward me, slowly, as if I'll bite. I wish I could bite.

"I have to do this." Eli picks me up with the gentlest of touches, but I can feel the fury in his bones.

Don't put me away. You'll regret it.

"No, Fig, I won't. Not in the long run." He slides me into the envelope his dad sent me in. "I have to make things happen for myself. I don't even know whether people like me because they want to, or because you're making them."

Fine. Let me stay here in your room. Just don't put me away. Please. Don't be like your father.

"I'm not like him. You were the one who told me I could succeed on my own. He needed luck, but I don't." Eli staples my envelope shut, as if I could escape.

I'll miss you if you put me away. I'll be miserable and lonely.

"No," he whispers, on the verge of tears. "Figments feel nothing, remember?"

I've become more than a figment with you. I thought we were friends!

"I've given up friends before, when they've hurt me."

But I'm still your Fig. I lower my thought-voice to a whisper. *I'll always be your Fig.*

Eli's hands begin to shake, but I still hear him clearly. *"No matter what?"*

The toes of my boots bend against the interior of the envelope, and my paws reach out, forever. *No matter what.*

In a box in the attic, I lie upon something soft—clothes, I imagine—and wait for Eli to return. Because he still believes in me, I can still feel him. Sometimes I hear him downstairs in his room, playing the song I woke him to write, the song that could make him huge.

It's cold up here. My cat ears pick up the scrabble of insects and mice, creeping about in what must be an ideal home. My plush body conforms to the shape of whatever I lie upon, the way my soul (if I have one) conforms to the shape of whomever I—well, *serve* is the wrong word, but it's better than *love*.

When Eli moves away—to college or stardom—I begin to fade. It takes months, maybe years. Time loses meaning. My senses dull. I forget who I am.

It ends, as always, in darkness.

EPILOGUE

A veiled light meets my eyes.

"There you are," a woman whispers. "Just where he said you'd be."

A slight rip of paper, then I'm tugged out to see her. Familiar, I think, but…was her hair always that gray?

She stands, crosses the attic, then carries me down creaky stairs, clutching me to her side.

We enter a living room, where the television is on, playing the Grammy Awards. "My friends were going to come over to celebrate," the woman says, "but I told them I was sick. Eli wanted to make sure you saw, so I figured it should just be you and me."

Eli…I know the name. Was I once his? Were we each other's?

I don't think she can hear me. She sets me on a coffee table, propped against a stack of magazines.

Wait! Was that his face on the cover?

She definitely can't hear me, and I can't turn to face the magazines. I strain to see out of the corner of my eye, but these eyes don't seem to have corners.

"Coming up next," says the voice on TV, "Grammy nomi-nee for Best New Artist—Eli Wylde!"

Eli...

When they return from commercial break, he's there on-stage, just him and his guitar. His age shocks me—I expected to see a twenty-year-old Best New Artist, but this man's closer to thirty. It took him thirteen years to reach this height with-out me, but he reached it, with the song I made him write.

When he wins, his acceptance speech is full of names I don't recognize. The only name I know is Lyra, whom he refers to as his "oldest friend." I feel so displaced by this; at our last time together, she was his newest friend.

Finally Eli looks straight at the camera. "Last of all, I'd like to thank my father, Gordon Wylde. We never met in person, but he gave me the most important, most real gift I've ever received." He leans in close to the mic and speaks in a near whisper, holding up his award. "Fig, I'm bringing home a new pair of boots."

THE
TWELFTH
GIRL

by Malinda Lo

Harley was the kind of girl who could get away with anything.
That was the first thing Liv learned when she arrived at the
Virginia Sloane School for Girls in mid-October. It wasn't
only that Harley flouted the dress code and skipped class and
ignored the curfew without ever being reprimanded. There
was something disquieting yet seductive about her, like walking on the edge of a cliff while gazing down at the violent
beauty of the ocean breaking below. Somehow it seemed as
if Harley could jump—would jump—but instead of falling,
she'd spread her arms and fly like a blackbird.

Liv had known girls who acted like Harley before, but
never someone quite so successful at pulling it off. Harley was
definitely the most interesting thing about the Sloane School,
and from the first time Liv saw her—walking into class twenty
minutes late, dressed in tight jeans and boots instead of the
uniform, her black hair wind-tossed and wild—Liv didn't
know if she wanted to be Harley or if she wanted to kiss her.

Harley's friends, too, seemed to benefit from her apparent invincibility. They lived together in Eleanor Castle Hall, a small, turreted fantasy of a dorm on the edge of campus. Castle had twelve rooms, all singles, each taken by Harley and her group. Everybody knew they went out dancing every night until three in the morning, and they never got caught, even though the campus gates were locked at 10:00 p.m., and every dorm had a resident advisor who knocked on your door if you even played your music too loud. The rumor was that Harley had a rich father who had given so much money to Sloane that Harley—and everybody she liked—was immune from the rules.

Liv wanted to be immune, too. Her parents had transferred her to Sloane after she got in trouble at her old school in New York City for missing curfew too many times. Liv was pretty sure her parents had chosen Sloane because there was nothing to miss curfew for in Middlebury, Massachusetts, the quiet town where Sloane was located. If Harley somehow got off campus to party every night, Liv wanted in, but neither Harley nor any of her friends seemed the least bit interested in getting to know the new girl. Their collective cold shoulder annoyed Liv, who was used to being noticed for all the right reasons, and it only made her more determined to figure out how they got away with what they did.

One afternoon about a week after she first arrived at Sloane, Liv walked into Middlebury to buy shampoo at the drugstore. As she approached the shop, she saw a pink neon hand in the window upstairs. The sign next to the hand read Madam Sofia's Fortunes & Favors. Liv was gazing curiously at the sign—it seemed, almost, to beckon to her—when the door next to the drugstore that led upstairs opened. A girl dressed all in black barreled out onto the sidewalk, nearly smacking into Liv.

"Hey, watch it!" Liv cried.

The girl didn't stop, tossing her only a brief glare before she continued down the street in the direction Liv had come from. She recognized the girl; it was Paige, one of Harley's friends. Liv watched Paige disappear around the corner, then glanced at the door she had come out of. There was a small placard in the glass window. Sale: Five Minutes for Ten Dollars. Find Your Future Here. Impulsively, Liv opened the door and went up to the palm reader's shop.

A gray-haired woman in a green velvet dress turned from the window overlooking the street when Liv entered. The woman's eyes narrowed on her. "Can I help you?" she said.

"Are you Madam Sofia?" Liv asked, glancing around the shop. It was stuffed with knickknacks and baskets of trinkets.

"Yes."

"I saw your sign in the window," Liv said. "'Five minutes for ten dollars.'"

An odd expression passed over Madam Sofia's face; it reminded Liv of a key turning in a lock. "Follow me," the woman said. She led Liv through the cluttered shop to a back room hung with curtains and furnished with a round table and two chairs. Madam Sofia sat down and took out a kitchen timer from beneath her chair. She set it for five minutes and placed it on the table. "Give me your hand," she said.

Liv sat across from the fortune-teller and placed her hand in the woman's palm. The instant they touched, Liv felt a strange sensation run through her, as if she were a marionette and the puppeteer had tugged on her strings. She watched as the woman bent over her palm, studying the lines in her skin. The rapid ticking of the timer in the background began to make Liv nervous, as if it were counting down the seconds to—well, Liv didn't know what, but it was unsettling, and she had the sudden urge to leave.

As if she could sense Liv's change of heart, Madam Sofia's hand tightened over hers. "You want to know about the girl who was just here," she said.

"How—how did you know that?"

"It's my job to know what brings you into my shop."

The ticking of the timer seemed to grow louder, and Liv had the disconcerting sensation that she was shrinking while the room around her was expanding.

"You should stay away from those girls," Madam Sofia said, her voice sounding like liquid smoke.

"What girls?" Liv's palm was sweating.

"The girls who live in the castle."

Castle Hall. "Harley and her friends?" Liv asked.

"Yes."

"Why?"

"They're dangerous. You should stay away from them."

Liv hated it when anyone told her what to do. "I'll hang out with whoever I want," she said.

Madam Sofia gazed at her with small, dark eyes. Liv twitched under the scrutiny and tried to pull back, but the woman wouldn't let go of her hand. "They are playing with forces beyond their control," Madam Sofia said. "If you value your life, you'll stay away from them."

The cautionary words only stoked Liv's curiosity. As that

venturesome emotion snaked through her, she said, "I thought you were supposed to tell my fortune, not give me a warning."

"I'm doing both," Madam Sofia said, and she dropped Liv's hand as if it had burned her.

Liv cradled her hand to her chest—it trembled now, free from the woman's grasp—and stood. "You're crazy," she said, and turned to leave.

"Ten dollars," Madam Sofia said, her voice ringing in the small room. "You don't want to owe me a debt."

Liv stopped, feeling as if the woman had grabbed her with an invisible hook. Liv reached into her pocket with her other hand—the one Madam Sofia hadn't touched—and pulled out her wallet. She fished out a ten-dollar bill and tossed it at the fortune-teller. It caught in the air and fluttered to the floor.

Madam Sofia gave her a shrewd smile and said, "You're welcome."

Everything Liv learned about Harley was like finding another piece to a puzzle. The problem was, she had no idea what the puzzle was supposed to depict.

All the girls at Sloane had definite opinions about Harley and her friends. They were stuck-up; they were slackers; they were daddy's girls. Beneath the criticism, though, was a palpable yearning to be one of them. To be part of that tight-knit pack of girls who prowled the campus like panthers, beautiful and cunning. To dance every night—no one knew where, but it had to be good—and come to breakfast with last night's makeup on, leaning on each other and laughing about what they had seen and done until dawn.

Liv soon discovered that the only way to join them was

to wait for one of the twelve girls who lived in Castle Hall to leave Sloane, and then hope that Harley chose you to take the vacant room. Two girls had left so far: Melissa Wong, last spring, and Andrea Richmond, at the start of the school year in September. It didn't look like there would be any vacancies in the near future, which was why the sudden departure of Harley's younger sister, Casey, was such big news.

Harley didn't come to breakfast the morning that Casey left. She didn't show up in public at all until late afternoon, and then her eyes had the unmistakable red rims of someone who had been crying.

Liv saw it up close and personal, because Harley was waiting for her after biology class. "You want to be the twelfth girl?" Harley asked, oblivious to the stares of the girls coming out of the classroom behind them.

Liv couldn't believe this was happening. She didn't understand why Harley had picked her and not one of the hundreds of other girls at Sloane. Girls who had been there for much longer; who had been campaigning for Harley's affections for months. Girls who had more-powerful parents; who had private planes to fly Harley and her friends out of the country if they wanted. Liv's family was well-off—she wouldn't be at Sloane if they weren't—but in comparison to the rest of the students, she fell squarely in the middle. Perhaps that was why Harley's invitation gave Liv a sense of raw satisfaction, as if she had made this come true because of the strength of her desire, as if she had created a physical arrow from her craving and shot it straight at Harley. Now all she had to do was answer in the affirmative, and her every wish would come true.

"Yes," Liv said, and Harley's full lips turned up in the tiniest of grins, and she gestured for Liv to follow her outside.

The trees in the quad had shed half their leaves by now, and with the wind picking up, it was likely they'd lose quite a few more before the end of the day. Harley led her to a nearly bare oak tree in the center of the quad, and Liv understood that the first thing she had to do was survive the hungry gazes of all the students streaming out of the academic buildings around them. She tucked a strand of hair behind her ear and looked at Harley, trying to act like she didn't care, even though her heart was pounding as hard as if she were sprinting toward a prize.

Out of the corner of her eye, Liv thought she saw a man standing nearby. His shadow stretched across the browning grass as though the sun was rising behind him, but the sky was slate-gray, and when she turned her head, there was no one there. Only Harley was watching her, her dark eyes fringed with long lashes as black as her hair. Liv wondered if she dyed it to attain that shade of midnight.

"These are the rules," Harley began. "First, you will tell no one about anything I'm about to say. Do you agree?"

"I agree," Liv said.

"Rule number two is that once you're in, you're in. There's no backing out, no matter what happens. Do you agree?"

The curiosity that had lit within her at Madam Sofia's shop only burned brighter. "Sure."

"You have to say 'I agree,'" Harley said, sounding irritated.

"I agree," Liv said, puzzled.

"Good. Rule number three: You do what I tell you. We

are not a democracy. But if you follow the rules, I'll watch out for you. Agree?"

Now Liv hesitated. She didn't like being told what to do. She thought she saw the shadow again, but this time she also saw wings unfolding from it. She blinked, and it was gone.

"Liv," Harley said.

There was a feverish insistence in Harley's eyes that made Liv's contrary nature soften. She felt as if the only thing she had ever wanted was to make Harley happy. "I agree," she said.

Harley's shoulders slumped uncharacteristically, and for a second Harley didn't look invincible; she only looked tired. But the moment passed as quickly as it had come. "Good," Harley said. "Then you go back to your room and pack your things. Bring them over to Castle Hall before lights-out."

"Tonight? Don't I have to fill out some paperwork or something?"

"I'll take care of it. It'll take a couple of days to process, but you can still move in tonight. You can stay in my sister's room."

"Where'd your sister go?" Liv asked, but as soon as the words were out of her mouth she knew she shouldn't have said them.

Harley's face closed up and she looked away. "None of your business. Go get ready. We're going out tonight." She began to leave, heading toward the administration building.

"Wait," Liv called after her. "What should I wear?"

Harley glanced over her shoulder but didn't slow down. "Dress to impress," she said.

A blackbird fluttered down from the branch of the oak tree

above Liv's head and landed on the ground a few feet away. It turned to look at her, and as it folded its wings along its body, Liv felt a deep, dark cold inside, as if she had made a bargain with someone or something she did not understand.

Casey's room was on the third floor of Castle Hall, and she had left her sheets and blankets on the bed. The first thing Liv did was swap out Casey's flowered sheets for her own yellow ones. As Liv changed out of her school uniform and into black jeans and a glittery black tank top, she had the unsettling feeling that the room wasn't empty. It still smelled like another girl's shampoo.

There was a knock on the door, and Harley called out, "Liv, you ready? Party's starting."

"Coming," Liv answered, and she checked her makeup one last time in the mirror. She had always thought of herself as confident; she had never been a wallflower. Tonight, though, she was nervous. The anticipation of what might happen spread over her cheeks in a rosy flush. She didn't need any blush.

The girls were all waiting in Harley's room when she arrived. Harley said, "Say hi to Liv," and they did, each one of them. Paige, Carmody, Ruby, Skyler, Devin, Sarah, Angela, Tara, Brooklyn and Kirsten. Liv was glad she had worn black, because that seemed to be their favorite color. Black jeans, black leggings, black tanks, black lace, black boots, black eyeliner, black nails. The only spots of color were on their lips and eyes—crimson and purple and blue—and in the jewelry each girl wore. Carmody had a shining steel cuff embedded with blue stones on her right wrist. Paige put up her blond hair with garnet pins. Sarah had a gold mesh bracelet studded with what looked like diamonds. Harley wore a gold ring set with a faceted black jewel on her left hand. Every time she raised her hand, it sparkled.

They passed around a bottle of vodka while they waited for midnight. "We don't go out till then," Paige informed Liv. Liv's mouth grew numb from the liquor, and she wondered if she was going to be drunk before the party even started, but then Harley put the bottle away, and it was time.

"These are the rules," Harley said to Liv as the girls stood up. "We have to return by three in the morning. No exceptions. And nobody brings anything back with them."

Liv nodded, and then Harley did something very strange: she pushed her bed aside along well-worn grooves on the wooden floor, revealing a trapdoor. Harley lifted the door's black iron ring and pulled it up, and Liv saw a flight of stairs descending into the dark. Liv wondered if she was seeing things because of the vodka. They were on the third floor of Castle Hall. Did those stairs go to the second floor?

Nobody questioned it, so Liv didn't, either. As the girls began to troop down the stairs, Harley caught her eye and said, "Don't forget what you agreed to, Liv."

Warmth suffused her skin. "I won't," Liv said, and she stepped into the hole in the floor beneath Harley's bed.

The stairs seemed to go on forever—well past the point where they should have struck the first floor. Liv gripped the metal railing as she followed the girls ahead of her, listening to them chatter about where they were going, who would be there, whether the music would be good. "It's always good," said one of them, and the others laughed in agreement, their voices throaty in the dim stairway.

Finally the stairs ended in a steel door like an emergency exit, and Paige pushed the bar to open it. They spilled out into a rain-slicked alley that smelled faintly of gasoline. As Liv looked around, the world seemed to spin. She didn't understand how they could have climbed all the way down those stairs from beneath Harley's bed to emerge in this alley in a city that was clearly not Middlebury.

"Where are we?" she asked, feeling dizzy.

Harley grabbed her arm, steadying her. "This way," she said, and led Liv down the alley to another door. There was a flyer taped to it that depicted a stylized girl's face with spiky hair and a big, full mouth. Across the place where her eyes should be were four letters: *AARU*. Harley reached for the handle of the door and pulled it open. Music blasted into the alley.

Liv and the other girls followed her inside. In front of a velvet curtain, a bouncer waited with a flashlight. Harley pulled Liv forward and said, "She's new. The twelfth girl."

The bouncer swept his flashlight over Harley's hand, and her ring glowed. Then he turned the light on Liv's face, and she winced at the brightness.

"All right," the bouncer said, flicking the light away.

Harley grabbed her arm again. "Come on," she said, and pulled her through the velvet curtain.

It was like stepping into another world. The music was overpowering, the bass so heavy it seemed to snake up her body from the floor to shake her from the inside out. The lights that strobed over the crowd obscured as much as they revealed: dancers in glitter and vinyl and fur, their bodies glinting with metal in places she would never think to pierce, their hair caught up in crowns and headdresses that looked like antlers. Instead of mirrored disco balls, there were trees made of glass rising from the floor, reflecting the lights. Crystal leaves hung from the clear branches overhead, making it seem as if the ceiling was heaving in time to the music.

The other girls slipped around Liv and Harley, disappearing into the crowd. Harley—who was still holding Liv's wrist as if she were a child—leaned over to say, "This is the main room. There are two more. I'll show you." Then she began to lead Liv around the edge of the dance floor.

The next room seemed to be made of gold. The walls were hammered gold, and gold leaves hung from weeping golden willows while golden spotlights illuminated a dancer in a cage hanging above the crowd, her whole body painted gold. After that was the room made of silver: curving silver tree trunks; silver leaves that shivered in the warm, perfumed air; silver strobe lights that made every dancer's skin look like platinum. Harley took Liv toward the bar in the silver room, and when Harley let go of her, she realized that sometime during their circuit of the club, Harley had switched to holding her hand.

Harley leaned close and said, "I have to go look for someone. I'll come back for you before three. You should have a drink." She pressed a goblet into Liv's hand, and before Liv could object, Harley was gone.

The goblet was made of heavy gold and encrusted with jewels; it was the kind of thing you'd expect to see in a fairy-tale castle, not in a nightclub. Liv stared at the reflected lights in the shimmering liquid and sniffed it suspiciously. She still felt tipsy from the vodka and wasn't sure if she should mix it with this…wine? She looked out at the crowd, wondering where Harley had vanished to so quickly, but she couldn't find her. She couldn't see any of the other girls from Castle Hall, either. She was about to put the goblet down—she had a sudden urge to look for Harley—when a boy appeared in front of her. He had spiky black hair and both of his arms were covered with full-sleeve tattoos. Liv couldn't quite make out what the tattoos were—they seemed to swim in her vision—but she noticed that he was holding a gold goblet like hers.

"Hey, you're new here," he shouted over the music. He smiled at her, and she stared at him, unexpectedly transfixed. He clinked his goblet with hers and took a sip of his drink. Without thinking, she mirrored him. The wine was bracing—cool and sharp, as if she had inhaled a breath of winter.

She didn't remember much of what happened after that, but she did remember him taking the empty goblet out of her hand and saying in her ear, "Dance with me." His words slid like honey down her throat, and she let him lead her onto the dance floor beneath the silver leaves. He was lithe and beautiful and he tasted as icy as that wine when he kissed her. The music seemed to embed itself in her body beat after beat, and she felt as if she could dance with this unnamed boy forever and never be sated.

And then Harley was back, pulling her away from the boy and saying, "Come on, Liv. Time to go." And Liv stumbled through the crowd, holding Harley's hand, and she couldn't remember why she had ever wanted to dance with that boy in the first place.

★ ★ ★

Liv awoke the next morning in Harley's sister's room, feeling like her head had been stuffed with cotton balls. She glanced at the clock and realized she had already missed breakfast and most of history class, but when she ran across campus and burst into the classroom, the teacher didn't even notice.

It took almost all day for Liv to shake off her hangover. It wasn't until she and the others were back in Harley's room that night, passing the vodka bottle around again, that she felt as if she had finally returned to the real world—just in time to leave it.

At midnight, Harley reminded them of the rules: They had to return by 3:00 a.m., and nobody could bring anything back with them. Then she pushed the bed aside and pulled up the trapdoor, and once more a flight of stairs was revealed. Liv was prepared for a long descent, but tonight it was different. This time the stairs ended after only ten steps, delivering the twelve girls into a tunnel dug out of the earth. Liv didn't understand how it was possible, because they should only be on the second floor, but there appeared to be roots growing out of the walls.

"It wasn't like this yesterday, was it?" Liv whispered over her shoulder to Paige.

"Sometimes it's different," Paige said.

Liv wanted to ask how—or why—but she knew somehow that she shouldn't. She was meant to accept this, the same way she had accepted the rules that Harley laid out. So she kept walking and swallowed her questions.

The tunnel ended in a short flight of steps that led to an ancient-looking wooden door. Harley lifted the latch on the iron handle as if everything was totally normal, and the door opened into the same city alley. The entrance to the club bore a different flyer tonight. It was printed with a black tree drawn like a tattoo, and gothic letters spelled out words Liv couldn't pronounce: *Magh Meall*.

Inside, the club had changed in ways that made Liv wonder if she had simply remembered it wrong. The first room had trees of gold, not glass, and instead of a caged dancer hanging above there were aerial acrobats, bare legs wrapped around rippling golden silk. Liv gazed at them as the music thudded through her, and she decided that she wouldn't drink the wine tonight, because tomorrow she wanted to remember this place.

She turned to look for Harley, but she was nowhere in sight. Liv began to push her way through the dancers, searching for her. Strangers' hands brushed against her, their fingers sweeping over her arms, and when she looked down she saw trails of gold dust on her skin. A woman with long green ropes of hair caught hold of her, urging her to dance, and she smelled like the ocean, salty and clean. Although Liv wanted to stay with her, she forced herself to remember what she was after: Harley. She had to find Harley. Liv pulled away from the woman, whose face suddenly contorted into anger, and when she snarled at Liv, her teeth looked like fangs.

Recoiling, Liv's gaze darted around the room, seeking anyone familiar who could explain what she had seen. Finally she glimpsed Harley slipping through the doorway into the next room. "Harley!" Liv shouted, but her voice was lost in the pounding music. She went after her, pressing against the walls so that she could avoid the dancers, but when she entered the next room—silver trees, lit with pulsing red-and-white strobe lights—she had lost her again.

Someone grabbed her elbow and she spun around, her heart racing. It was Paige. "You okay?" Paige asked.

"I'm looking for Harley," Liv said. "Is it three yet?"

Paige shook her head. "We've only been here about fifteen minutes."

That didn't feel right.

Paige saw her confusion and said, "Let me get you a drink." She led Liv to a curtained alcove along the wall—there were many of them, mostly full of couples—and pushed her inside. "Wait here."

When the curtain fell, it muffled some of the music. The low red lights made the alcove feel like being inside someone's heart. Liv's skin itched, and she rubbed at her forearms idly until she realized something was sloughing off. She looked down in horror, but it wasn't her skin; it was glitter.

Paige returned with two goblets—still gold and jewel-encrusted—and sat down beside her. "Here," Paige said, handing her a drink. "You need this."

Liv took the goblet but didn't drink. "I think it gave me a hangover last night."

"You get used to it," Paige said, sipping from her own goblet.

"Where's Harley?" Liv asked.

"Why? You have a thing for her?"

Liv's face grew warm. "No."

"It's okay. Everybody has a thing for her at first." Paige sounded resigned.

"Did you?" Liv asked.

Paige shrugged. "Sure. We were together for a while, but that's over."

"Do you know where she is?" Liv asked again. It was the only thing she could remember, as if her mind was stuck on repeat, and she didn't know why.

Paige didn't respond at first, instead studying her carefully. Liv clutched her goblet with both hands, the jewels digging into her skin, and she wished—she willed—Paige to answer her question. Finally Paige said, "Harley's looking for her sister."

Casey. "I thought she left school," Liv said.

"No," Paige said, and for a moment she looked frightened. She took another sip of her wine. "She came to the club with us a few nights ago, but we couldn't find her before we left."

"You mean she stayed here?"

"I don't know. Harley thinks she can find her, but…" Paige took another sip, and the drink seemed to calm her. "Melissa and Andrea stayed, too, and we haven't found them."

Liv rubbed a hand over her forehead, trying to clear the fuzziness from her brain. "You mean all three of them stayed here? They never returned? How come nobody talks about that at school? Everybody says they just transferred."

"They didn't transfer," Paige said flatly.

"Then what happened to them?" Liv asked. "Why would they stay here? I don't understand."

Paige sighed. "You're not supposed to know this," Paige said deliberately. "At least, not yet. You can't tell anyone that you know. You can't tell Harley."

Liv was mystified. "Why did you tell me, then?"

Paige looked annoyed. "I don't agree with everything Harley decides. And you're one of us now—or you will be to-morrow. You might as well know."

"What do you mean about tomorrow?" Liv asked. "Aren't I one of you already? I promised Harley I'd do what she wanted."

"Tomorrow everything will be finalized. Third time's the charm." Paige took another drink. "I shouldn't have said any-thing." She stood, her head nearly brushing the ceiling of the curtained alcove. "I'll see you later. I have to dance."

The way she said it—*I have to dance*—was so strange, as if she was being compelled to do it. Liv watched Paige leave, and then she put her own goblet of wine down on the floor. Bit by bit, like a knife scraping against the frost on a wind-shield, she was beginning to see.

This place. This beautiful, horrific place. What had she gotten herself into?

Liv woke to the repetitive screeching of her alarm at 7:00 a.m. She shut it off quickly. The rest of Castle Hall was silent; the other girls probably wouldn't wake up for hours. Liv threw off her blankets and got dressed. She didn't feel as hungover as she had the day before, but there was definitely something wrong with her perceptions. The real world seemed blurry.

She threw her laptop into her messenger bag and walked through the chilly late-October air to the dining hall. As she passed the quad, a flock of blackbirds took off from the oak tree, the beat of their wings loud in the silent morning.

The dining hall was beginning to fill with students. Liv poured herself a giant cup of coffee, took a seat alone at the table traditionally reserved for Harley's group and opened her laptop. Three girls had stayed behind at that club. Melissa Wong, Andrea Richmond, and Harley's sister, Casey. Liv searched for the girls' names online, looking for evidence of how their disappearances had been reported. Melissa and Andrea both had Facebook pages, but Melissa's was private, so she couldn't read it. Andrea's, however, was mostly public. Her page was filled with messages from people saying they missed her and were worried about her, but oddly, none of the messages appeared to be from any Sloane students. One was from someone identified as Andrea's brother, and it said, "We're looking for you, Ann. Please come home." It took Liv a while to read through her timeline, but the last update she had posted had been back in August. "Can't wait to party with the girls again!"

Where had Andrea gone? Liv thought about the flyers posted on the door to the club in the alley. She couldn't remember how to spell the name that had been on the flyer last night, but she remembered the four letters from the first night: *AARU*. She entered the word into the search bar. It was a term from Egyptian mythology. A heavenly paradise where souls could exist in pleasure for eternity. Similar to: Elysium, Avalon, Magh Meall. She caught her breath and clicked on the link to Magh Meall and read, "From Irish mythology, a pleasurable realm able to be accessed by only a select few...a place of eternal beauty...occasionally visited by mortals."

Liv stared at the screen, her mouth going dry. These places were myths, fairy tales. It wasn't possible for them to exist. But it wasn't possible for a stairway to open up beneath Harley's bed, either, and lead to a city where there shouldn't be one.

It had been real, hadn't it? Liv thought about the dancers, the wine, the music. If it wasn't real, she was coming unhinged, and that was even more disturbing than the idea that Harley had found a magical door to another world.

By the time breakfast was over and the students began leaving for class, Liv knew what she had to do. She put away her laptop and headed for the school gates. Technically, she wasn't allowed to go off campus during the school day, but she knew no one would stop her. She was one of Harley's now.

The walk into Middlebury cleared away more of the fogginess in her head. When she arrived at Madam Sofia's Fortunes & Favors, she felt almost entirely real again.

Liv had wondered if it was too early for the shop to be open, but Madam Sofia appeared to be expecting her. "Welcome back," the woman said as Liv entered the shop.

"I need to know what's going on with Harley and her friends," Liv said. "You told me they were dangerous. What did you mean?"

Madam Sofia didn't seem surprised. "Come sit down."

"What is that place that Harley takes us to?" Liv asked as they went into the back room. "It's not this world, is it? How is that possible?"

Madam Sofia sat down at the table. "It is not our world, no."

Liv felt a brief flush of relief to hear that Madam Sofia knew exactly what she was talking about.

"But it is entwined with ours," Madam Sofia continued. "Harley has discovered a way to enter it."

"How?"

"She has made some sort of bargain. I don't know the exact details, but she will have agreed to something."

"Does it have anything to do with the girls who stayed there? Melissa and Andrea and Casey?"

"There is a price to pay for entry to that world, and that is the traditional trade."

"Are you saying that those girls were forced to stay there? That they're...payment?" Liv was sickened. "That's insane."

Madam Sofia folded her hands on the table. "As I said, I don't know precisely what Harley has agreed to, but she may be getting something out of it that we are not aware of. Nobody strikes this kind of bargain without a great need of her own."

"What could possibly be worth kidnapping three girls?" Liv couldn't believe it of Harley. She didn't want to believe it. "Someone must be making her do it. How do I get her to stop?"

"She cannot stop on her own," Madam Sofia said. "It is a curse now. There is only one way to break it."

"Tell me how," Liv insisted. "I'll do it. It can't go on."

Madam Sofia nodded. "This is what you must do: You must take something dead from the other world and bring it to life in this one."

Liv's forehead wrinkled. "How am I supposed to do that? What do you even mean?"

"It is a riddle," Madam Sofia said. "And it is a test. If you can decipher it, then you are the one who will break the curse. If you cannot decipher it..." She trailed off, raising one open hand as if she were letting something unseen fly away.

"Then the curse remains unbroken," Liv whispered.

Madam Sofia leaned forward. "Tonight is your last opportunity to do this."

"Why?"

"After tonight, you will have entered the other world three times. You will have sealed your own bargain, and you will not be able to break it."

Liv remembered what Paige had told her, and she remembered that afternoon in the quad under the tree with Harley, saying *"I agree"* three times. She could practically feel the golden chains of that other world tightening around her.

"Tomorrow morning," Madam Sofia continued, "if you have not broken the curse, you will be given your own talisman to mark your acquiescence to the curse."

Liv remembered the girls' jewelry—bracelets and necklaces and hair ornaments that all seemed to come from the same jeweler. Part of Liv still wanted to be one of them, but even as the idea of having her own otherworldly charm thrilled her, she was also repulsed by the fact that it would bind her to that place. "I'll break it tonight," Liv said. "Will Melissa and Andrea and Casey be able to return then?"

"I don't know. They struck their own bargains when they stayed."

"But they could return?"

"It depends on how deeply they've fallen for that other world, whether they have strong enough ties to this one. It's possible, but it's not up to you."

Liv stood. "Okay." And then she asked, "How do you know all this?"

Madam Sofia's thin mouth turned up in a self-mocking smile. "I broke the curse myself, when I was your age. You girls are not the first to discover the allure of that other world, and you won't be the last."

* * *

The tunnel to the other world was the same that night, and the sign on the door in the alley said *Magh Meall* again. Liv wondered if they were truly entering that mythical world, or if whoever ran this nightclub thought of the name as a tongue-in-cheek joke. Inside, the club was as crowded as before, but tonight Liv could see that the dancers were not wearing costumes. What she had thought was clothing made of unusual materials was actually skin: skin covered in scales, skin erupting with downy feathers, skin rippling with spiny ridges the color of gold.

As the other girls disappeared into the cacophony of the club, Liv kept her eyes open, looking for anything that might solve Madam Sofia's riddle. In the room with the crystal trees, there was a band playing on a stage Liv hadn't noticed before. The lead singer was a woman with long white hair, her eyes outlined with the shapes of stars. Liv edged around the room, studying the crowd gathered at the bar. Most of the people were watching the show, but one of them, a man with tattoos of tiger stripes running up his wiry arms, had turned his back to the stage. He raised a cigarette to his mouth and plucked a matchbook from a glass bowl on the bar. The sight of someone smoking indoors startled Liv—they could do that here? she thought—and then she felt stupid. Of course they could. They could do anything here.

The tiger man tossed the matchbook back into the bowl after he had lit his cigarette, then vanished into the crowd on the dance floor. Liv crept into the gap he had left at the bar, taking the stool he had vacated. The glass bowl nearby held a whole bunch of matchbooks, and when she lifted one out, she saw that it was stamped with the words that had been on the flyer posted on the door: *Magh Meall.*

Liv didn't have any pockets that night. She was wearing a tank top and leggings and boots, so she tucked the matchbook into her bra. It only took a second, but her heart began to accelerate the moment the matchbook's sharp edges scraped against her skin. When she turned around, Harley was standing only a foot away from her, and Liv jerked in surprise.

Harley's black hair was loose tonight, falling in thick waves over her shoulders. She looked suspicious. "What're you doing?" she asked.

Liv thought fast. "Looking for you." She slid off the stool and reached for Harley's hand. Harley didn't move; she only continued to scrutinize Liv's face. "You want to dance?" Liv asked, and she pulled her toward the dance floor.

Liv hadn't had anything to drink tonight—she had even avoided the vodka upstairs—but the music was intoxicating enough. There was something hypnotic about the woman's voice, as if she gave Liv permission to do whatever she wanted, and there was something hypnotic about dancing with Harley, too. The movement of her muscles beneath the slippery fabric of her tank top; the warm flushed skin of Harley's upper back; the tickle of Harley's long black hair over her neck as Harley seemed to wind herself around Liv. After a while, it didn't even feel like they were moving anymore. The dancers around them were moving; the bass from the band was shuddering; the lights above were flashing. But the two of them stood motionless, their bodies pressed together, and Liv closed her eyes so that she could feel Harley better, so that she could shut out the dream world all around them and make this real.

The voice in her ear seemed to come at her from a very great distance, the sound of it bubbling up from the depths of a dark sea, until she felt someone else's hand—not Harley's—on her shoulder, shaking her. "Liv! Liv! It's time to go."

She blinked her eyes open, and Harley peeled herself away, and beside them, Paige was shaking her head as if she had caught two children misbehaving.

"Come on," Paige said. She glared at Harley. "You should know better."

Harley's cheeks were flushed and most of her lipstick had been rubbed off. She shook her head. "What time is it?"

"It's time," Paige said in a clipped voice.

Harley cursed. "Let's go."

Liv's legs wobbled as she followed the girls out of the club. Harley didn't even give her a second glance as she stalked through the crowd. Out in the alley, the night air was freezing on her skin. Still, Harley didn't look back. She threw open the door to the stairs, and the other girls followed in drowsy silence. Only Paige gave Liv a meaningful glance as she pulled the door shut behind her, and then it was too dark to do anything but pay attention to where she was walking.

When they arrived back in Harley's room, Liv headed for the exit with everyone else. She felt completely disoriented, and she could still taste Harley's mouth. Harley had been drinking the wine.

"Liv," Harley said. "Wait."

Liv stopped. "What?"

When all the other girls had gone, Harley shut the door, and it was only the two of them. Harley turned to face her. Liv's heart raced. This was the real world, she reminded herself. Whatever happened here…was real. It scared her, how much she wanted this to be real.

She had forgotten that she wanted to break whatever curse Harley was under. She had forgotten that Andrea and Melissa and Harley's own sister might have disappeared because of what Harley had done. All she could remember was what it felt like to dance with her.

Harley went to her dresser and pulled a tissue out of the box, wiping off the remains of her lipstick. Then she went over to Liv, who was standing right where she had been when Harley asked her to wait, and kissed her.

Real: Harley's full lips, slightly dry now, her tongue still tasting like wine. Real: Harley's hands on the hem of Liv's tank top, lifting it and sliding beneath. Real: Harley's body against hers, warm and soft.

Liv reached for Harley's slippery shirt and Harley raised her arms so they could peel it off. Harley had a tattoo of a blackbird over her heart, and Liv bent her head to kiss it, tasting the salty sweat on her skin. Harley's breath was uneven as she pulled Liv's tank top over her head. Her ring caught on the fabric, and Harley swore and took off the ring, letting it clatter onto her nightstand. Then Liv's shirt was off, too, and something tumbled out of Liv's bra and skittered onto the wood floor.

Liv froze.

"What was that?" Harley whispered.

"Nothing," Liv lied, hoping that Harley wouldn't notice.

But the matchbook had fallen into the circle of light cast by Harley's bedside lamp, and the words printed on it practically glowed: *Magh Meall*.

Liv remembered the curse and the riddle. The sticky sweet desire that had made her dizzy only seconds before turned sour.

Harley jerked away from her. "What did you do?" Harley asked, fear in her voice.

Liv lunged for the matchbook a moment before Harley did. Liv's knees banged against the floor. Harley's nails scraped over her arms. Liv scrambled away, her fingers trembling as she opened the matchbook.

"Stop it!" Harley cried.

Liv didn't stop. She tore out a match and struck it, and the flame flared into life.

Something dead from that world, brought into life in this one.

The smell of sulfur seemed to fill the room. The flame burned blue, and Liv saw it reflected in Harley's dark eyes, full of horror.

"What did you do?" Harley demanded.

The ground shifted beneath them. The bed moved. Harley tried to stop it, but it rolled back over the trapdoor in the floor, and when Harley tried to push it aside, she couldn't. She screamed in frustration, bending down to look beneath it, and then her shoulders heaved, and Liv knew that the trapdoor was gone.

The match burned out, scorching Liv's fingertips, and she dropped it onto the floor.

Harley stood. Her face was hard with anger. "Why did you do that? You've screwed everything up!"

Liv's heart was pounding so hard she was breathless. "I had to break the curse," Liv said.

"You don't know what you did," Harley snapped.

The disgust in Harley's voice made Liv angry. She scrambled to her feet. "I couldn't let it keep happening! They couldn't keep taking the girls."

Suddenly Harley sat down on the edge of her bed, her shoulders sagging. "I never wanted them to take any girls, but that was the price."

"For what? What was so important you'd let those girls be kidnapped? Your own sister!"

"I did it for Casey," Harley snarled. "So she and I could stay here at the Virginia Freaking Sloane School for rich bitches. We would have been kicked out for not paying tuition if I hadn't made that deal."

Liv took a step back. "What do you mean? I thought your dad was loaded."

Harley gave a choked laugh. "That's what everybody thinks, but no. My dad was the janitor here. While he worked here, we got to come here for free, but after he died last year, that was it. We were going to be kicked out. But where would we go? To live with my deadbeat mom in the city? She has no money, and she spends what she gets on drugs. The only way I could keep Casey here—to keep her safe—was to make a deal with that guy. But now you've messed it all up. He said they wouldn't take Casey. He said—" She broke off and looked at Liv furiously. "And now she's gone, and I can't find her. He'll never make a deal with me again."

Liv's stomach fell. Had she made a mistake? "She might come back—Madam Sofia said—"

"Nobody comes back once they take them," Harley interrupted. She looked utterly defeated.

"I'm—I'm sorry," Liv whispered.

Harley wouldn't look at her, and after the silence between them became too awful to bear, Liv snatched up her shirt and left. She couldn't stop shaking, even after she climbed into Casey's bed and buried her head beneath the covers.

Things began to change immediately. Harley was reprimanded by the headmistress for wearing boots to class. The paperwork that Harley said she had filed to move Liv from Sheffield to Castle turned out to be forged, and Liv had to move back to Sheffield. The other girls in Castle Hall began to be called in to teacher meetings to discuss their many absences.

Halloween came and went in a gust of wind and rain, stripping the last remaining leaves off the trees. Every time Liv walked by the oak tree where she had made her promises to Harley, she felt someone watching her, but it was only the blackbird that seemed to have made its home there. Once she thought she saw a tall, thin man in the shadows of the tree, but as soon as she noticed him the air itself seemed to shift, as if someone were pulling a shade closed.

Harley's friends began to drift apart, too, turning inward and barely eating at meals. Rumors went around that they had been doing some serious drugs, and now their supply had been cut off and they were going through withdrawal. And everyone whispered the shocking news about Harley: that her father wasn't some fabulously rich guy; that he had been the school janitor; that she might have to leave at the end of the semester because she had no money for tuition.

Liv felt bruised inside, as if she had lost something, not

saved the lives of the other girls. For weeks, she went through the motions of school and homework in a daze, half awake, half still caught in that world she had visited three times. At night she dreamed of the glittering gold trees, the throbbing music and Harley.

All through November, Harley faded. She had been vivid before, unbreakable, and now she was more ghostly every day. Her skin, her eyes, her hair—pale, dull, limp. Liv realized that she might have broken the curse, but she had also broken Harley.

The day that Harley didn't show up for breakfast, none of the students noticed at first. It wasn't until lunch, when Liv heard others whispering about how nobody had seen Harley since the night before, that Liv began to wonder if something had happened. She walked across the quad toward Castle Hall, her feet crunching over the blades of browned grass. She passed the oak tree and saw that the blackbird was gone.

Inside Castle, the dorm was quiet and empty. Everyone was supposed to be in class, and Liv knew she would be reprimanded for skipping, but she was drawn up the stairs to Harley's room just as she had been drawn to Harley from the beginning. Harley's door was closed, and when Liv knocked, there was no answer. She put her hand on the doorknob, and it turned easily.

There was a creak behind her.

Liv spun around, an excuse on her lips, but the sight of the girl across the hall stopped her. She looked like Harley, but younger. Her face was gaunt, as if she had been living on nothing but air for much too long, and her eyes were too bright. "Who are you?" Liv asked, afraid that she already knew.

"I'm Casey," Harley's sister said. Her voice sounded just like Harley's.

Liv's skin crawled. "Where's Harley?"

"She traded herself for me," Casey said. There was a haunted flatness to her speech, as if she were a doll that had just come awkwardly to life.

Everything inside Liv went cold. She opened Harley's door and barged into her room. It was empty. The bed was rumpled, and a pile of dirty clothes lay on the floor by the dresser. Liv ran to the bed and pushed it, but it wouldn't move. She knelt down to look beneath it, and all she saw was dust.

Casey came into Harley's room and went to the dresser, where she began to look through the drawers. She pulled out her sister's shirts one by one, holding them up and then tossing them onto the laundry pile.

"What are you doing?" Liv asked.

"Looking for something to wear," Casey replied in her odd, emotionless voice. "Harley always has the best stuff."

Liv stared at her in shock. She had wanted Casey to come back, but she hadn't expected she would be like this. Casey might be standing in her sister's room, but she wasn't all there.

Casey found a shirt she liked and laid it on top of the dresser, then took off the one she was wearing. The bones of her spine jutted out like teeth beneath her skin. In the mirror, Liv glimpsed a tattoo of a blackbird on Casey's chest before she pulled on her sister's shirt. She turned to face Liv, crossing her arms, and Liv noticed the ring Casey was wearing. It was a black stone set in a gold band.

"My sister told me about you," Casey said.

Liv swallowed the rising panic inside her and met Casey's feverish gaze. "Where is she?" Liv demanded.

"Someplace a lot more fun than this." A cold grin crossed Casey's face, and for one second she came alive—potent, forceful, just like Harley. An instant later she shriveled, once again more specter than girl. "We're going there tonight," Casey said to Liv. "You wanna come? Harley might be there."

THE
RAVEN
PRINCESS

by Jon Skovron

The princess wouldn't stop crying. The queen had fed her and changed her diaper. She didn't know what else to do.

"I can host a banquet for a hundred lords and ladies. But what do I know about babies?" The nanny had asked for the day off and now the queen regretted letting her have it.

The princess stood at the edge of the crib, howling at the top of her lungs. Tears and snot ran down her plump face as she reached out with wet slobbery fingers.

"What do you want?!" The queen gripped the edge of the crib hard. She wanted to shake the ungrateful little creature until she stopped.

No, she would never do that. But she felt trapped by the tiny, impossible thing who shrieked mindlessly at her. She moved to the other side of the room, turned her back on the princess and took a slow breath.

The coarse call of birds cut through the princess's cries. The queen looked out the window and spied a flock of ravens.

She had always found the raven's caw grating and distasteful, but right now, it seemed preferable to the endless wail of the little brat. As she watched them wheel slowly up into the sky, she said out loud:

"I wish you would just fly away with those ravens."

The crying stopped and silence fell suddenly in the room. The queen turned around, half expecting to find the child passed out from exhaustion. But the princess stood in her crib, her eyes wide. Her little bow mouth was quirked in the corners, as if she had just taken a bite of something and its flavor surprised her. She sat down hard and let out a cough that sounded strangely like the caw of a raven.

"My darling." Fear crept into the queen's chest. "What's wrong?"

The princess looked up and her bright blue eyes slowly filled with blackness until even the whites were gone.

"Oh, God," whimpered the queen.

Thick black hairs began to sprout on the princess's arms, legs and face. No, not hairs. Feathers.

"Please," whispered the queen. "I didn't mean…"

The princess opened her mouth wide and made a gagging sound until a black, curved beak emerged and her lips peeled back into nothing. Her legs grew thinner, then, with a loud crack, suddenly bent in the wrong direction, as her feet curled in like claws. Her body shrank into her white dress until the queen could no longer see her.

"My darling?"

A raven's head poked out from the dress. The bird shook herself as she untangled her wings from the dress. She hopped up onto the edge of the crib, black claws digging into the wood. She regarded the queen for a moment, her head cocked to one side. Then she let out a harsh caw and flew past the queen and out the open window.

The queen never spoke of what happened that day. It was thought that the princess had been abducted by mercenaries or brigands. The king searched everywhere, but didn't find her. As the years went on, the queen's secret shame aged her into a crone before her time. Finally one night she could no longer bear it, and left the castle without a word. The king did not search for her.

The young man was not a good hunter. He had some skill with a bow when the target was a bull's-eye, but he simply could not bring himself to shoot a living thing. His parents had sent him away in disgust, and none of the village girls showed any interest in him. So he lived alone in a small cottage in the forest, where he ate berries and the vegetables he grew in his small garden.

The young man would have been content to live this way, except he was lonely. He hoped that if he conquered his fear of hunting, he might finally catch a girl's eye. So one morning he set out into the forest, resolving not to return until he had made a kill.

First he came across a deer. But he was so petrified, he could not move until it was out of sight. Later, he spied a badger waddling along. But his hands shook so badly that by the time he was able to nock an arrow, the badger had slipped down into its hole. He cursed himself, wondering how he could be so cowardly.

Finally, near sunset, he spied a lone raven standing on an

outcropping of rock in a small clearing. Ravens were loath-some animals, eaters of the dead and dying, and harbingers of bad luck. The world would be a better place with one less raven. He quietly set an arrow and drew back on the bow-string. This time, he would claim his place as a man.

But the instant before he released the arrow, the raven turned to look at him and cocked its head in such a curious, intelligent way that the young man flinched and the arrow flew wide, embedding itself in a tree five feet away.

"That," remarked the raven, "was a terrible shot."

"Luckily for you," said the young man. Then his eyes grew wide. "You speak!"

"Truly," said the raven. "I have seen boys of ten and old men shaky with weariness who had better aim."

"Amazing! I nearly kill a magic talking raven and he crit-icizes me for not piercing his breast with a wooden shaft."

"I am not a 'he,'" said the raven, feathers ruffling. "And I'll thank you not to talk so casually about my breasts."

"My apologies, Lady Raven," said the young man with a slight bow. He slowly walked out into the clearing. "But I must know, how is it you talk?"

"Because I am not really a raven, but a maiden princess under a curse. Now I must know, how is it you are such a terrible marksman?"

"I happen to be an excellent marksman!"

"Oh?" The raven turned toward where the arrow was still embedded deep in the bark. "Were you hunting trees today, then?"

The young man sighed and shook his head. "My aim fails me the moment I target a living thing."

"And why is that?"

He thought about it a moment, then finally said, "I don't know."

"Could it be that you are afraid to kill?"

"Well, that would be an unfortunate trait in a hunter."

"Indeed. You would have been better off born to a shoe-maker or a tailor, perhaps."

"We cannot choose who we are born to."

"Truly." The raven turned away and raised her wings to take flight.

"Please don't go yet!" said the young man. "Meeting you is the most interesting thing that has ever happened to me."

"Unsurprisingly."

"Won't you tell me of your curse?"

She lowered her wings. She did not turn back around, but craned her head toward him.

"I have been cursed like this since I was but a year old."

"And how old are you now?"

"Seventeen."

"That is terrible!" said the young man. "Is there no way to break this curse?"

The raven turned back all the way around to face him. "There is. Why, would you be willing to attempt it?"

"Of course!" Then he looked suddenly hesitant. "That is... if it is within my ability."

"You wouldn't have to kill."

"Then yes, I would consider it a privilege. What must I do?"

"On the edge of this forest, a small house sits next to a crossroads. By the house is a pile of wood chips. Sit upon that pile and wait for me. The curse allows me to appear in my true form for one hour every night at midnight. I will come for you, and if you are awake when I arrive, the curse will be broken."

"That doesn't seem so hard."

"Beware," said the raven. "There is an old woman who lives in the house. She will try to give you food and drink. But if you accept it, you will not be able to stay awake that night."

"Hunger and thirst are not new to me," said the young man. "I will prevail easily."

"I am not so sure of that," said the raven.

The young man hiked through the darkening forest and arrived at the cottage just as the sun slid behind the tree line. The cottage was even smaller and coarser than his own. The walls were made of stacked logs sealed with mud, and the hay thatched roof looked rotten in places. The young man felt sorry for the old woman who lived there, whoever she was.

He found a bed of oak chips by the side of the house, just as the raven had described. It wasn't very comfortable, but he thought that might help him stay awake. So he sat down and waited.

Darkness had fallen when the old woman emerged from the cottage, holding a lantern. She had a gentle smile, and eyes that were warm yet sad.

"A guest!" Her voice was as soft as worn velvet. "Oh, how wonderful!" She came over and held out the lantern to look at him. "Handsome face. A little thin and pale, though. You could do with a bit of meat."

"It has been a long time since I have eaten meat," he admitted.

"Well, you are in luck, then, my boy. I have a nice fat rabbit turning on the spit. Far too much for me to eat. Won't you come inside and share it?"

"It's generous of you, but I must remain out here until after midnight."

"Ah, the old legend of the Raven Princess, eh?"

"Old legend? Have others tried to break the curse before me?"

"Of course! And who can blame them! According to the legends, her beauty is like no other."

"I had not heard of her beauty," he said.

"Oh? Then why do you sit here?"

"So that she may be free of the curse."

"And that is all?"

"Should there be more?"

She smiled briefly. "I suppose not. Now, won't you come in and share supper with me? It is still several hours until midnight. You would be able to return to this spot in plenty of time."

"I thank you for your hospitality, but I cannot."

Her face grew suddenly sad. "I understand. What is the company of a poor old woman when there is the promise of a beautiful princess."

"Please, that isn't what I meant...."

But she turned and slowly walked back into the cottage as if she hadn't heard him.

As he sat on the woodpile, he thought of her, eating alone inside. He had eaten many meals alone and knew how it felt.

The silence broken only by one's own chewing. How many meals had she taken in solitude? How many more lay before her, an unbroken line stretched out until her life ended?

The old woman came out sometime later. In her hands she held a cup that steamed in the cold night air.

"I am sorry for what I said earlier," she said. "It was unfair. You are doing a noble thing, helping to break the princess's curse."

"I am sorry that I cannot accept your hospitality."

She smiled and held out the cup to him. "I have made you some tea."

"I must decline even this. I was told I cannot accept any food or drink, or else I would fall asleep and miss the princess when she arrives."

"If it were wine, that would be true. But tea will help keep you awake."

"Tea usually does fresh me," he admitted.

She held out the cup. "Please, I will feel much better if you take it."

He smiled as he took the cup. "Thank you."

Then he drank.

An hour later, a black coach pulled by two black horses approached the cottage at the crossroads. The coach slowed to a halt and the princess emerged. Her skin was as pale as moonlight. Her curly black hair, as rich as the night sky, was piled up high above her luminous face. As she stepped down to the ground in elegant pointed boots, her black-feathered cloak rustled quietly.

She looked down with eyes that sparkled like stars at the

young man sleeping in the woodpile. She placed a pale hand on the horse's sweat-lathered neck, stroking the black fur.

"I knew he would fail," she said, her soft red lips expressionless.

As soon as the first rays of dawn woke the young man, he cried out in anguish.

The old woman came running out of the cottage, her shawl clutched around her shoulders.

"What is it?" she asked.

"I slept through midnight! I missed the princess!"

"But how? You seemed wide-awake when I left you last night."

"I don't know. It must have been the tea."

"Tea never makes one sleep."

"When dealing with curses, it may be that normal rules don't apply."

She laid a hand on his shoulder. "I am sorry you didn't see your princess. Will you come inside and break your fast?"

"No. I must try again tonight," he said.

The young man sat on the pile of wood chips all that day, while the hot sun bore down on him. He hadn't eaten since the morning of the day before and had had nothing to drink since the small cup of tea the night before. He felt as if he were baking in the sun, and his mouth tasted like bile and ash.

Once night fell, the old woman emerged from her cottage.

"Here." She held out a mint leaf.

"No," he said hoarsely. "I cannot."

"But this isn't food. You don't even need to swallow it.

What if the princess wishes to bestow a kiss upon her rescuer? I fear you would offend her with your breath."

"Is it…really that bad?"

She nodded gravely.

"I will chew it. But I will not swallow."

He took the leaf from her with a trembling hand and placed it on his dry tongue. At once, cool sharp relief engulfed his mouth. He chewed slowly, carefully, savoring it with eyes closed, before he spit it into the handkerchief she offered him.

"Thank you," he said.

Again the black coach appeared just after midnight. And again the princess looked down at the sleeping young man, her expression unreadable.

"I knew he would fail again," she said.

Then a different voice said, "Must we continue with this charade?"

"Yes," said the princess.

"But it only brings you suffering."

The princess looked up at the star-speckled sky. "No matter what choices we make in life, suffering is always a part of what follows."

The next morning when the young man woke, he didn't cry out. In fact, he barely moved.

"Will you come inside and take some food now?" asked the old woman.

"I must try again," he said in a croaking voice.

She stared down at him, biting her lip. Then she turned and went inside.

He lay on the pile all that day, at times not even remembering why he was there. At last night came. The old woman came out of her cottage holding a steaming bowl.

"You will die out here waiting for your legendary princess." There were tears in her eyes. "I cannot bear it. Please eat!"

She held out the bowl of warm stew.

"Get away!" His voice was harsh, and there was a snarl on his lips. "You will not tempt me! You who have made me fail each night. Perhaps it is on purpose, eh? For all I know, you are the witch who cursed her in the first place. You old hag, you will not trick me again!"

She looked at him, tears streaming down her face. She placed the bowl on the ground and returned to her cottage.

The moment the door closed behind her, the young man regained his senses. What had he just done? He hadn't even known he was capable of such harsh words, and he had unleashed them on a kind old woman who had been trying to save his life.

He stumbled to his feet.

"Wait! I'm sorry!"

Maybe there was no princess. Maybe he had imagined it all and would die waiting. Or even if there was a princess, was she worth turning himself into a beast to save?

"Please, I'm so sorry!" He took a step toward the cottage, but then his strength gave way and he fell. He lay there for a moment, half on the wood chips, half in the grass. Then he smelled the stew. He turned his head. The bowl was just within reach.

What did it matter? Even if she was real, and even if she

was worth it, then certainly he was not. He was foolish. He was fearful. And he was weak.

He gulped down the stew, and no sooner had he put the bowl down then he fell fast asleep.

The raven princess gently placed her cool white hand on the young man's cheek.

"I knew he would fail the third and final time," she said.

"He is weak," said the old woman, her voice no longer soft or sweet.

"What you call weakness, I call kindness," said the princess. "I think he is worthy, Mother."

"We shall see," said the queen. "I hope for your sake, and for his, that you are right."

At first, the young man couldn't remember why it was he found himself lying on a pile of wood chips by a crossroads. Then he saw the cottage and remembered the crying old woman, and it all came back to him. He had failed the princess, just as he failed at everything else in his life. But perhaps he could at least make it up to the old woman. He rose stiffly and walked over to the cottage.

"Hello?" There was no answer. "Old woman, are you there?"

He knocked on the door and it slowly swung open.

"Hello?"

The cottage was empty. The floor and walls were bare. A thick layer of dust covered everything. He stepped away from the cottage, not sure what to make of this.

Then he saw a small sack by the woodpile that he hadn't noticed before. It was pinned shut with a single long black feather. He ran to it and carefully opened the sack with trembling fingers. Inside, he found a cured ham, a wineskin, a gold ring and a letter.

The letter said:

You have failed me three times, gentle huntsman. But take heart, for the purpose of these challenges was not to win, but to show one's character. Your resolve was impressive, but not half so impressive as your generosity of spirit. You would rather fail than be unkind to another person. This, more than anything, gives me hope that you truly will be able to lift my curse. Now you must find me at the Golden Castle of Stromberg and persuade the one who keeps me there to release me.

Enclosed with this letter, you will find a ham and wineskin. They are both enchanted by your generous spirit and will never run out. I have also included a ring, which has my name engraved on the inside. Keep it as a symbol of my faith that you can accomplish the difficult task before you.

The young man held up the ring, and in the gleaming light of the sun, he saw the name of the Raven Princess.

He didn't know where the Golden Castle of Stromberg was, but he had the endless ham and wine to keep strength in his body, and the ring to keep strength in his spirit. So he began to walk.

He went deeper into the forest until there was not even a woodcutter's path to follow and he had to force his way through the undergrowth. But then he came upon a wide straight path. He made good use of it, but all the while wondered how it had come to be there. He discovered the reason the next morning when he woke to find a giant staring down at him.

"It is fortunate that I have come upon you, little man." The giant's shaggy hair and beard were a golden-yellow. "I have not yet had my breakfast and you will make a tasty morsel."

"If it is food you seek, I have plenty to spare!" said the young man quickly.

The giant raised a bushy blond eyebrow. "Enough to satisfy my hunger?"

"Enough to satisfy a family of giants."

"Is that so?" The giant sat down, causing nearby tree branches to shake. "If you can truly satisfy my hunger, then I will have no need to eat you."

So they ate and drank. After a little while, their bellies were full of meat and their faces were flushed with wine.

"What brings you out here to these dark woods?" asked the giant.

"I am on a quest, I suppose."

"A quest, by God!" In his enthusiasm, the giant slapped the ground and the sound echoed like thunder. "What are you questing for?"

"I must find the Golden Castle of Stromberg to free a princess from a curse."

"Ah. She must be a real beauty."

"I have never seen her true form, since the curse has turned her into a raven."

"She must be rich and powerful, then."

"She never mentioned riches or power to me."

"Then what do you hope to gain?"

"Gain?" The young man frowned thoughtfully. "I suppose I hadn't thought of that."

"Then why are you risking your tiny little life for her?"

"Because before this quest, risking my life was not risking much. Because for the first time, I feel I have an interesting life. Is that not reward enough?"

The giant grinned, showing white teeth. "I am grateful for your hospitality, and your words have moved me. Come with me to my castle. I have many maps both new and old. We will find this golden castle of yours."

"I would be grateful for any assistance you can provide."

The giant placed the young man on his shoulder and began to walk. Now that the young man was above the tree line, he could see that it was a bright, sunny day. The forest stretched out in every direction, and off in the distance, he saw the white peaks of snow-covered mountains.

"There, you see?" The giant pointed a finger at a mountain. "My home."

The young man didn't understand at first. But when they were only about a mile or so off, he realized the "mountain" was much too uniform to be natural. It was instead a castle whose spires reached so high into the sky that snow gathered at their tops.

Once they reached the castle, the giant strode into the main hall, which was lit by torches as big as houses. The giant set the young man down on a dark wood table that was so long, he could scarcely see the other end of it.

"Where do you find trees large enough to make a table of this size?"

The giant laughed. "Do you think the whole world is your size? In the land I come from, everything is to my scale. Now, let's see about those maps."

They spent hours sorting through maps. Some were brightly colored and marked with the modern names of towns and roads. Others were faded, and had names that the young man had never heard of. But none of them showed the Golden Castle of Stromberg.

"Are those all the maps you have?" asked the young man.

"Those are all the maps that I know of." The giant carefully rolled up a crinkled old sheet. "But my mate may have others stowed away somewhere."

"You have a mate?"

"Of course. This is a rather large home for only one person."

"I didn't know giants had mates."

"You are a kind and generous person, and I like you a lot," said the giant. "But we could fill this castle ten times over with the things you do not know."

It was shortly after sunset when a second giant arrived at the castle. The mate was slim and pale, with a long face and hair as white as snow. The young man had not expected the mate to be male, but having already been chastised for his ignorance, he was careful not to seem surprised. Then he noticed what the white-haired giant carried in his hand, and he couldn't help blurting out, "Is that a human baby?"

The white-haired giant looked down at the young man, then at the other giant, arching a thin white eyebrow.

"I have taken a liking to this human," said the yellow-haired giant. "I promised we would help him in his quest."

"I see…." The white-haired giant turned back to the young man. "Yes, you are correct. This is a human infant who has come under our protection."

"You aren't going to eat it, then?"

"No. Definitely not." He turned back to the yellow-haired giant.

"Eh, I may have threatened to eat him when we first met. Just a bit."

"Ah." The white-haired giant turned back to the young man. "Since adopting this orphaned baby, we are both on a strict nonhuman diet. But…some of us are finding it difficult to stick to the regimen. Now, what is this quest of yours?"

"I seek to break a curse put upon a princess held at the Golden Castle of Stromberg."

"None of my maps have found the location," said the yellow-haired giant.

The white-haired giant's eyes scanned the pile of rolled-up maps. "No, I expect not. These are all local maps. If memory serves, the place you seek is far from here." He carefully handed the baby to the yellow-haired giant, then left the room.

The yellow-haired giant stared down at the sleeping baby in his hand with a peaceful smile on his bearded lips. Then he glanced over at the young man, looking slightly embarrassed.

"Parenthood changes you," he said.

"I expect it would," said the young man.

The white-haired giant returned with an old map that looked like it had been chewed by both rats and insects. He laid it out on the table and pointed. "Here it is."

The young man jogged across the map to examine the spot. "And where are we?"

The white-haired giant pointed to a spot on the other side of the map.

"And how far is that?"

"Fifty leagues or so."

"That far?"

The yellow-haired giant cleared his throat and looked meaningfully at his mate. "It's my turn with the baby, so…"

The white-haired giant sighed and turned back to the young man. "I suppose I could take you there."

"That would be very kind of you," said the young man. "Please accept this gift in return. It is a cured ham that will never run out."

"A generous gift," said the white-haired giant. "And one which might help us stick to our nonhuman diet."

"Then I am all the more pleased to give it to you."

"Let's be off, then," said the white-haired giant. "I do not care to be long away from my family."

The young man sat on the white-haired giant's shoulder as they moved through the dark forest. This giant moved faster and more quietly than his mate, so that the young man almost felt like he was flying through the night sky. Going this speed made the world seem smaller somehow, and travel to faraway places more possible. The young man thought how much he would like to see the land of the giants and perhaps even other, stranger places.

At last, as dawn broke on the horizon, the white-haired giant pointed.

"Look. Do you see it? The Castle of Stromberg."

The castle's towers rose just above the tree line. The new-risen sun flashed off its golden walls.

"I must leave you here and get back to my family," said the giant. "The map spoke of a key needed to get into the castle." He held out his massive hand and in the center was a tiny human handkerchief. "This key."

The young man took the handkerchief and unrolled it. Inside he found a small wooden stick about the length and thickness of his little finger.

"This is a key?"

"Apparently," said the giant. He carefully placed the young man on the ground, then stood back up. "Farewell, little human. May we meet again." Then he turned and strode off the way he had come, the early-morning light sparkling in his white hair.

The castle sat on top of a mountain made of smooth glass. When the young man saw this, he began to lose heart because it looked impossible to climb. But then he put his hand in his pocket, and next to the cloth-wrapped key, he felt the princess's ring and he knew there had to be a way. So he circled the base, looking for a path of some kind.

Then he caught the scent of roasting meat. He hadn't eaten since the previous day, so he followed the smell until he came upon three men hunched over a fire.

"Hello!" he called. "Do you have any food to spare? I can trade you for some wine." He held up his wineskin.

The three men eyed him warily. They were dressed mostly in furs, and they were heavily armed.

"What sort of man travels with wine and no food?" asked the largest of the three men.

"I gave the last of my food to a friend."

"Then you are a fool," said the man. The others laughed.

"Perhaps," said the young man. "But my folly is your gain. You must be fine hunters, for you have quite a lot of game. But you have nothing to wash it down with."

"Yours seems a small skin for four men."

"Trust me, it will more than quench your thirst."

The large man looked at the others and they shrugged. "All right, then. Come and sit with us."

The young man sat down next to the fire and offered the wineskin to the large man. "I had not expected there to be anyone else trying to get into the castle."

The man swished the wine around in his mouth and smiled appreciatively. "It's a tough nut to crack, to be sure." He handed the skin to a scar-faced fellow next to him.

The scar-faced man took a drink, then nodded. "But with the right tools, anything is possible."

"What tools are those?" asked the young man.

"Well…" said the third man. His pinched face looked distrustful. But then he took a drink of wine and his expression softened a little. "We have a cloak that makes you invisible and a pair of boots that are enchanted to walk up any surface, even one as smooth as glass."

"That's great!" said the young man as he took his turn

to drink. "We can help each other, then. I have no way to reach the castle, but…" He pulled the cloth from his pocket and held it up. "I do have the key to unlock the door once we reach the top."

"Is that so?" The large man took a long drink of wine. "Maybe we can help each other out, then."

"What do you need an invisibility cloak for, though?" asked the young man.

The scar-faced man laughed and took another drink. "You've got a sense of humor on you. I like it."

"You…do seek an audience with the princess, don't you?" asked the young man.

The pinch-faced man took a drink, grinning as he wiped his chin with his sleeve. "Sure, sure. An audience with her riches. After I cut her throat." Then he handed the wineskin to the young man.

The young man lifted the wineskin to his lips, but this time he did not actually drink.

"Do you think there is a lot of treasure up there?" he asked as he handed the skin to the large man.

"They say there are rooms so filled with gold and jewels that you can't find the floor." He took another long drink.

"Is that so? Tell me more."

And so they passed the wineskin around many more times. Each time, the young man only pretended to drink. Soon the three thieves began to slur their speech and finally to nod off. When he was sure they were all asleep, the young man hid their weapons. Then he opened their bags and searched for the enchanted items.

He found the invisibility cloak first. He couldn't see it, but he could feel it, rough and porous. He found the boots soon after. They looked old, the leather raw and stained, but they had a strange wet sheen to the bottom. He placed them on the glass surface of the mountain and they held fast.

In place of the cloak and boots, he left the wineskin. He didn't like to steal, even from murderers. Then he put on the boots and began to climb the glass mountain.

The sun reflected off the glass surface with a harsh glare that nearly blinded him. With his added weight, the boots held the slick surface for only a few seconds, so he could not rest as he hiked up the steep incline. It took him the rest of the day, but at last he reached the top, exhausted.

By then it was dark, and the golden castle glinted mutely in the moonlight. He took only a moment to catch his breath before approaching the door. He intended to break this curse tonight.

But when he drew the cloth from his pocket and unrolled it, the key wasn't there. It must have fallen out when he showed it to the thieves. He could not go back down to retrieve it now. They would probably be awake and eager for revenge.

He banged on the door and shouted until his hand was numb and his throat was sore. But there was no answer. He looked up at the moon and saw that it was nearly midnight.

Maybe he could make another key. After all, the first one didn't even have teeth. He looked around for something he could fashion into the length and thickness of his little finger. But there were no trees, sticks or even rocks. The glass ground was completely bare.

He looked at the keyhole in the door. He looked at the

moon. It was midnight. He looked at his hand. At his little finger.

He inserted his little finger into the keyhole. Nothing happened, so he slowly rotated it. He felt a slight pressure close on his finger. Then there was a sudden clang, and the door opened. His hand came free, covered in blood.

He stood there and stared at the stump where his little finger had been. A bit of white bone poked out from the ragged clump of red-oozing skin and meat. His vision narrowed and it became hard to breathe. He fought against the dark numbness that tried to take him, as he tried to think of a way to stop the bleeding. He looked down and saw that he still held the cloth that the key had come in. He wrapped it around his hand and abruptly the pain vanished and the bleeding stopped. He tied the cloth off with one hand and his teeth so that it stayed in place.

He looked cautiously through the open doorway. It seemed warm and clean inside, with fine tapestries and rugs. But now the young man was not as inclined to trust its safety, so he pulled the invisibility cloak over himself as he stepped inside.

He wandered for a little while through the empty halls of the castle until he heard two voices. He recognized one as the old woman from the cottage, except her tone was now harsh and bitter. Could it be she had deceived him and was the one keeping the princess here?

Then he heard the other voice. It sounded sharp and sweet, like a ripe apple, and it beckoned to him. He drew his invisibility cloak tightly around himself and crept closer.

He came upon a dining room. At one end of the table was

the old woman, except now instead of peasant clothes, she wore a gown fit for a queen.

"Where is your hero, then?" she asked. "Dead, I suppose. What a waste."

The woman at the other end of the table was the loveliest person the young man had ever seen. Her large blue eyes were as clear as a summer sky, and her pale face as gentle as a spring rain. She wore a black feathered gown, and the young man's heart leaped, for he knew this must be the Raven Princess. As he moved quietly over to her side, her scent, like a crisp evening autumn breeze, filled him with longing. He dropped the ring she had given him into her golden wine goblet and it gave a soft ping.

Her eyes widened and a slow smile spread across her face.

"It appears you are wrong, Mother," said the princess. "Gentle huntsman, please reveal yourself."

The young man pulled off his cloak.

The queen looked at him in surprise. "My God, I don't believe it. He made it." She glanced at his bandaged hand. "Or most of him, anyway."

"I have," said the young man. "And even if you are her mother, you will not prevent me from breaking her curse."

"Prevent you?" asked the queen. "Why would I do that?"

"Aren't you keeping her here against her will?"

The queen laughed bitterly. "Getting her to do anything against her will? That'll be the day."

"But…"

"Your confusion is understandable," said the princess. "It was indeed my mother who cursed me all those years ago.

But she has sorely repented and dedicated her life to making up for her accidental misdeed."

"Then...who keeps you here?" asked the young man.

"She keeps herself here," said the queen.

"This is the only place where the curse can be broken," said the princess. "So I kept myself here, hoping for your arrival."

"So how do we break it?"

"Only she can do that," said the queen. "She must want it broken with her whole heart."

The young man turned back to the princess. "Don't you want the curse broken?"

She took his good hand and cupped it between her own. "I have lived most of my life as a raven. The thought of never again soaring through the air was too much for me to bear. I hoped that the right man would give me enough reason to leave it behind."

"And...has it?"

Her clear blue eyes looked into his. "You are a magnificent man, full of hidden strength. You have shown yourself to be brave and gentle. But even so, I find I cannot relinquish the wonder of flight."

The queen made a noise of disgust. "Even after all this? You're hopeless."

"Then if you love being a raven," said the young man, "why would you seek to break the curse at all?"

She smiled at him then, but the sadness in her eyes was as deep as the ocean. "Because I am lonely. Other ravens, real ravens, know that I am not like them, and they shun me. I am alone, like no other in this world."

The young man gazed down at the enchanted cloth wrapped around his maimed hand. Terrible things had happened to him on this quest, it was true. But wondrous things, as well. It was as he had told the yellow-haired giant. This quest had given his life meaning. And now that he had seen some of the strange, fantastic things out in the larger world, he knew he wanted to see more.

"Would it be possible for another to share this curse with you?" he asked.

"Only if that person truly desired it with their whole heart," said the princess. "And who would do that?"

"If one could fly," he said, "there would be no limit to the places one could reach, the lands one could explore."

"That is true...."

"I have heard that far away, there is a land of giants. Can you believe it?"

"I can."

"And if that is possible, what else might be possible out there in the wide world?"

"I have heard there are many marvels in store for those with the courage and desire to share them."

"And do you have the courage and desire to share them?" asked the young man. "With me?"

The princess smiled. "I do."

"Then I wish with all my heart that I could fly away with you as a raven."

So the queen was witness to another transformation, just as strange and gruesome as the first. But this one did not fill her with horror. And when it was done, she looked at the two proud ravens, their feathers glistening green-black and blue-black as they stared into each other's eyes.

"Where shall we go first?" asked the female raven.

"There is a family I met along the way," said the male raven. "I would love for you to meet them."

"Let us be off, then," said the female raven. "Try to keep up."

Then the two flew out through the window, circling high up into a sky that was pink and warm with the sunrise.

THINNER THAN WATER

by Saundra Mitchell

I live in a kingdom surrounded by many lands. Beyond the Eventide Forest, there's Lycea, where only a queen may reign; still further, Vernal, where the crown princess chooses her consort. They're as fabled to me as Elysium and Avalon.

I'm the Princess of Flamen, and every night, my father—the king—comes to my bed.

Our people revere him, a man with the weight of the kingdom as his garland, and yet he tends his only child and always has. I hear them talk. I see the pride in their eyes: what a good man, our king. What a lucky people, we. I suppose they think we talk. Perhaps they think I unburden my troubles. His paternal counsel is no doubt wise.

From my balcony, I hear them sing the "Ballad of The Fairest Queen." Over and again, sixteen years and they're still not tired. It's a dirge and the meter doesn't scan. They don't care, because it's a romance. One with tragedy, the best kind, it seems. I don't need fourteen verses to tell you the tale.

My father, then a prince, picked my mother—then a cheese-monger's daughter—to be his bride. He loved her; she was beloved. She bore him child, and it took her life. In her last minutes, she made him promise to never again marry unless he found someone as beautiful as she. He swore it, three times, and she died.

Then the king, my grandfather, died of a fever. My father, newly crowned, was alone in the world but for me. At bedtime, when I was a flat-chested, nothing-shaped child, Father sang the ballad to me. His voice was sweeter than the laurel trees in the garden. His eyes, darker than the seas. He rubbed my chest, singing and staring out the window.

I'm older now. He's not stopped singing, nor rubbing my chest. Tonight, he looks at me. There's a frightening shade in his gaze. It ties a knot round my throat and makes leather of my tongue. His hand rasps. It catches on the thin silk of my nightdress. Unpleasant heat sinks through the fabric.

As the last note of my mother's ballad drips from his lips, he stills. His hand rests above my heart. On the round of my breast. My guts turn liquid and churn. Perhaps it's coincidence (I don't believe it is) but his forefinger and middle make a V. They frame my nipple.

Inside, I scream. I howl a sound that scrapes the meat from my bones. Inside myself, I'm hollow. Scattered across the plains like sand. Across the sky like stars. I'm worlds away from myself. And yet, a single thread attaches me. My soul is sewn into my skin, and it relays every terrible thing, even at a distance.

"I was a better man with your mother at my side," my father says, his hand heavy on my breast.

Am I to answer? He's the king, so I suppose I am. My tongue rattles in my mouth, a dried bean inside a husk. "Were you?"

"Wiser with her counsel. Happier with her affection."

I pray his hand remains still. "I don't remember her. All I know is that she was beautiful."

"And I promised to never marry until I found her equal."

The song. I clench my teeth together. My eyes are already closed. "I know."

My father leans over me. His breath skates on my cheek. His stubble burns. I don't seek his kisses anymore. Sometimes I wonder if I drew his unnatural attention by climbing in his lap when I was little. I sought warmth beneath his arm then. Sometimes even climbed in his bed when I had a nightmare.

Now it's all nightmares, and I don't dare move. "Merula," my father says. "You have bettered her. And I did promise…."

I roll from bed. It startles us both. My father's left clutching the remains of my heat in the sheets. Lurching for the window, I consider flinging myself out. It's late. I'm tired. I might have misunderstood him. I take deep, gulping breaths of the night air.

"Are you crying?" he asks.

I'm not. I'm shuddering. Trying to keep my supper in my stomach.

Across the castle walls, I see the good people of Flamen in the fields. They're nothing but silhouettes, singing and laughing and looking to the stars. They're illuminated by the streak of meteors and nothing else. There are proposals made on nights like these; couplings, too.

If I were one of those girls, if their fathers came to their beds, I could cry out. There are laws, each one with a punishment. A protection. The village quaestor would hear my plea. And if the quaestor didn't satisfy my complaint, I'd turn to the praetor. Then the consul.

And if none of them applied our sacred codes, if none stepped in—and I couldn't believe it would go so far—then the king would hear my complaint.

But I'm already here, in the finest chamber of the palace, trembling before the king. Because of the king. His voice drips like oil; it glides and spreads, until it fills the whole chamber. The walls seem to glisten with it.

"I've upset you," he says disingenuously. "But take some time to consider it, Merula. Across the sea, Haladian royalty marry only sisters and brothers. Their empire was born before memory. No doubt, it'll outlast it. It's a wise decision."

To strike my father would be treason. To spit at him, treason. To argue with him, to raise my voice—to displease him—treason. And that's a crime punishable by death.

I can stand in my window and wish to be a girl in the fields. I can consider the slate flagstones beneath my window, and whether they would split my head and end me.

But I can't disagree with the king.

In the executioner's house, there are unholy devices. Capes full of hooks. Razored helmets. A spiked chair, all metal, that sits in a bed of embers. The executioner heats it till it glows, and only then is the prisoner forced to sit in it.

Death isn't the worst thing that happens to a traitor in Flamen.

Before dawn breaks, I find Consul Sapiens at his breakfast. He's elected, both a judge and a scholar. In Flamen, he's the last voice of the law before my father. Egg-shaped and charming, he's also one of my favorites in the court. When I was little, he kept a jar of sugared dates for me.

This morning, he pales when I enter his chambers. He moves to stand, covering his mouth to hide the nut cake he chews. "Augusta Merula! Glory and honor to you."

"Please sit," I say.

Closing the doors, I slide the bolt into place. A brief longing consumes me, a wish that we followed the Northern custom of covering our walls and floors with tapestries. They'd trap my treasonous words: a guarantee that none but Sapiens would hear them.

Abandoning his breakfast, Sapiens does sit. But it's at the edge of his bench, not settled into it comfortably.

Wiping his mouth, he looks up at me. A faint, bluish haze has crept into his black eyes. It's a badge of his age, the same as his balding head and rounding belly. The caul, nonetheless, unsettles me.

"I have nowhere else to turn," I tell him.

"Oh, Merula," he says, already coddling me, "what can be so bad as that?"

We're equals, the two of us. Second only to the king. I whisper now, as I take his hand. And I choose my words carefully. No matter how fond of me Sapiens may be, I break the law when I say, "I think my father's grown distracted. He loved Mother so much. Everyone says I look just like her, so I understand his confusion...."

I don't. But politics and plain truth make an unpleasant harmony. The truth must be sweetened, smoothed. Though I wear Mother's face, I've got my father's political gifts—or so say the consul. I hope it's true. Before Sapiens can say anything, I push on.

"He's overcome with grief and thinks he should marry me."

Flashing flat, yellow teeth, Sapiens laughs.

"Exactly what I thought," I say. In relief, I slump. "It's madness. Perhaps after these long years of solitude, it seems sensible. I think he dreams of my mother and misses her."

"A joke," he offers.

"If only it were." Righting myself, I force myself to speak around it. I can't voice the memory of my father's hand. Where it rests, the shape it takes. My stomach turns to think of it. Bile burns in my throat, so I rasp when I say, "He means it, Sapiens."

Sapiens's hands tremble. He reaches for mine. "Are you certain, dear?"

"Last night, in my chambers, he came to me."

"As he's always done."

The coddling tone makes me hesitate. Yes, as Father's always done it, but it's not the way it was before. I force myself to go on; arguing wins me nothing.

"He said the Haladians only marry siblings. That it's a right and honorable way to maintain an empire."

The silence isn't long. Perhaps only the flick of a lash. The length of a breath. Then Sapiens nods.

His face is a puzzle, its details snapping together into a new shape. Now he wears an indulgent smile. I almost expect him to give me a sugared date. Instead, he says, "This is true."

"What?"

"The Haladians intermarry," he says—as if I were confused

on the facts, not horrified at his reaction. "And it does clarify the line of succession."

"That's hardly my point!"

Mildly, he asks, "Then what is?"

"He said it was time to keep the promise he made my mother! That I've bettered her!" My voice goes shrill, and I can't help it.

Why is he so calm? How can he be so thoughtful? Eels writhe beneath my skin. They squirm in my belly; I'm disgusted to recount it. How can he simply blink at me?

"Merula," he says. Now he clutches my hand, and I wish he wouldn't. "Perhaps you've misunderstood. Your father's a good man."

"But this is wrong."

"Different," he counters. "Not our tradition, but perhaps a new one."

Inwardly, I fall. The underworld opens to swallow me, but only on the inside. This body is cursed to stay in this world, where my court favorite is twisting all our customs to permit the impermissible.

Sapiens speaks on, as if I'd said nothing at all. "And he does have good judgment, dear. Look how many come on Hearing Days for his wisdom."

I want to retort, *And look how many come to his kitchens for scraps! Look how many widows his single war made! Look how many of us scurry and flee—look to the executioner's house and its red-hot chair!*

My lips won't part. Words refuse to slip through them because now I understand. I'm less than the king, and the king is the law. It will always change to agree with him.

"Merula?"

Lest Sapiens run to my father and whisper all my words in his ears, I force a smile. It's brittle as straw-made ice, but he doesn't care. Neither do I. I nod, and turn his hand. He needs to be reassured.

"You're right," I concede. "I panicked."

"It happens to all of us," he replies.

His chambers aren't as airy as mine. The windows are too small and too high. Perhaps if he hung from a perch in the ceiling, the air would move and we would breathe. We don't; we can't. We're second to the king, after all.

Poor Sapiens. I'm still his favorite, but now I hate him. I don't care if he dies in what comes next.

The dovecote at sunset is spectacular. Shaped like a beehive, the birdmaster washes it with new plaster each month. Its purity reflects the colors around it—at noon, the gold of the fields. Now it's a ruby set in the sand.

There's a silvery bird in each recess. There are hundreds of them, each named for their home post. Slowly, I circle, reading the tags.

The birds in the largest niches will fly to other nations. Those in the smallest will deliver to provinces in Flamen. Once I figure out the method, it's easy to find the beast I seek.

Gently, I lift Lycea. He's peculiar, bloodred spots beneath each eye, and what looks like soot streaks down his back. Bedraggled wings flutter when I turn him over, but he doesn't bite. Warm and light, Lycea gazes at me. Waiting.

I slip a coiled note into the tube on his leg. Once it's fixed, he animates. Claws flickering, he quivers. Twists his head.

Waits more actively, and seems almost delighted when I turn and toss him to the winds.

Soon, he's a speck and I sink to the ground to wait for my reply.

Sunset turns to twilight, and just as the moon rises, Lycea returns. He lands in his spot unerringly, but he doesn't settle. Instead, he struts.

"Proud thing," I mutter as I scramble toward him.

The note inside is the one I wrote. My handwriting fills one side of the scrap, cramped to fit the space. I'm almost embarrassed to read my words. Though I phrased them carefully and tried to ask for only a little aid, in the reading, it's stark.

My father comes to my chamber at night. Now he wishes to marry me. I can't speak against him, so I beg for sanctuary.
Your obedient servant,
Augusta Merula

On the reverse, the Queen of Lycea has written her response. Despite the narrow strip of parchment, her hand is elegant. Her letters loop in a foreign but familiar script.

Ask for an impossible bride-price to stay him. I suggest a gown made of sunlight. Write again.
Fondly,
Regina Vatia

At first, I feel a pricking in my heart. She won't take me; I must stay. I expected more of a queen. But logic explains it.

To shelter me from my own father would be an act of war. No one would believe I was there by choice.

Like her handwriting, Vatia's solution is elegant. She twists tradition to suit my cause. If I were to marry a lesser noble, I'd owe a price to my bride or groom. It's symbolic, to equalize us.

In my chamber, a teak chest holds silks and goldspuns, a string of pearls as long as I am tall. I have gold beads and an ivory abacus, the deeds to two vineyards and one shipyard— that's how much I would owe my mate, to make us equal.

Since my father is the king, he'll owe me so much more than that. I believe he gave my mother a temple to Vara, four hundred sheep and every poppy in Flamen. People grumbled then that it still wasn't enough.

Returning Lycea to his niche, I fold the note until it folds no more. Then I swallow it like a seed. Inside me, its idea grows.

When I walk into my chamber, I'm prepared.

"No one knew where you were," my father accuses. He's immaculate, a haircut and a shave today. He doesn't stand. He sits on my bed, eyes following me as I move through the chamber.

I have to remind myself, he can't see my thoughts. He doesn't know the acid that eats through my belly. My expression is the truth, filtered through his filthy gaze. So I smile, but keep to my feet. "That's ridiculous. I went to the dovecote."

"Did you, now?"

"Yes," I say. I stop in front of my mirror, putting my back to him. I toy with my hair to hide my trembling hands. I'm not lying, but my nerves betray me anyway. "I'm to be married. I wrote to Queen Vatia for her advice."

Father's trying to hide his nerves, too. His posture stiffens. "You have ladies of the court."

Lightly, I laugh. "True. But they won't be queens, will they?"

"You've been looking for a lot of advice today, Merula." He stands, pulling his shoulders back. They pop, worn from old battles and hard chairs. "You spoke to Sapiens, as well."

"To be certain none would stand in our way. I thought our laws might conflict."

Heat sweeps through me, sweat rising on my hands. They turn clumsy, and I drop the comb in my hair. Hurrying to pick it up, I find my father has followed me down, as well. His scent invades me and my guts roil. Unsettled by the darkness of his eyes, I struggle to keep my false face. Holding out my hand, I wait for him to return my comb.

He clings to it. "And?"

"Nothing does," I assure him. Since he doesn't return my comb, I take it from him. Then I push away from him, swimming through the thick air in my chamber. I'll play the part with words. Nothing more. Not my skin; it crawls. Especially when he laughs.

It's a warm sound, delighted. The same laugh I heard when I did something particularly clever as a child. It runs through me now like a blade. Turning to him, I hold up a hand. "I've been considering my bride-price. I don't want shipyards and orchards."

Indulgently, my father rocks back on his heels. "What would you have, then?"

He has no idea how much I hate him right now. How much strength it takes to stand there and smile.

Inside, my mental body twists. It picks up the marble box on my vanity and brings it down on his head. Again, at the first sight of blood. Again, until he's made paste and his face is obliterated.

My physical body remains serene. I twist my hair and pin it with the comb.

"I want a gown made of sunlight," I tell him. "Not yellow. Not goldspun. Sunlight. And I don't think you should come to my chambers until my bride-price is paid. I'll need my ladies to help me prepare for our wedding night."

My father, the king, agrees.

Two months pass. On Bread Day, I ride out with tributes for the people of Flamen, gifts of loaves to celebrate their hard work. Without their toil in the fields, we'd all go hungry. Fresh bread, salted and sweet, for everyone.

No one sings my mother's ballad this time. My people whisper; I hear them as my carriage rolls through the streets.

"…doesn't even look upset," one says.

Another replies, "She always was too fond of him…."

Thankfully, the carriage rolls on. I feel slapped. How could they believe this is my design? Don't they have fathers? Can't they imagine my horror? Irrationally, I want to send the guards to clamp irons on them. To drag them down to the dark places beneath the castle. It's spoiled, childish thinking. Proof that I have a monster inside me; that I'm my father's daughter, after all.

"Bless, Augusta," a woman murmurs. Then she ticks her tongue, and that speaks, as well. A shame, a shame, it says.

Another shakes her head. She takes the bread with her fingertips, careful not to touch mine. They're not usually careful. Usually, I shake hands and kiss them, and thank them for coming to see me. Sometimes, people thrust babies into my arms. A kiss from a princess means good luck the whole year through.

Not now. No one raises their gaze to mine. As I hand out loaves, they reply with muttered thanks. The village streets seem impossibly long today. Unnatural quiet follows me. Though they try for subtlety, I see the people of Flamen. My people—I see them hide their children.

By the time we turn down the market row, my eyes burn with tears. My chest grows tight, aching with each restrained breath. If I take a full one, I'll dissolve. The wind refuses to howl today. A blue sky stretches forth, an unmarked canopy. It's cruel is what it is. The day mocks me with its perfection.

Then, at the last stop, one woman comes forth. Her wide hips swing, rocking the baby that she carries. Ignoring the rest of the crowd, she cuts through them and comes right to my carriage door. Her chin high, her onyx eyes glitter when they meet mine. "Augusta Merula, bless."

"Bless you," I reply. I leap on this scrap of kindness, offering her a loaf, and the baby on her hip a sweet roll. Those are usually mine, but I've had no appetite for them today.

The woman catches my wrist. "A kiss for my babe?"

Leaning over the side, I brush my lips on the child's cheek and I shiver when the woman speaks into my ear. It's a whisper that could cut her down. Warm, it skates across my cheek and I nod gratefully as I right myself. I don't dare say anything aloud; she's risked too much today already.

But as the carriage carries me back to the palace, I repeat her words with my inner voice. Again and again, I say them; they become a prayer. Not the usual kind, sweetened with incense and fatted lambs. The gods haven't listened. This is a prayer for myself.

"You're not alone."

The gown is made of sunlight.

It took the better part of a year, but Father presents it to me at breakfast. In front of the courtiers, who are both fascinated and disgusted by the display. They don't need to go to country fairs to see two-headed calves and claw-fingered ladies. I'm their wonder, conveniently located within the wealth of the palace. They don't even have to change their clothes.

"How did you do it?" I ask.

My father laughs, amused. "Magic. Favors. What does it matter?"

I want to scream, but I can't, and I don't. Panic claims me. I never expected him to accomplish the bride-price. It was an impossible thing, but when you have an entire nation in your hands, I suppose impossible is a little easier.

"It's perfect," I say. What will I say next? My breakfast rises into my throat; what will I do if he tries to seal it with a kiss? Horror lines my flesh. If it were acidic, my skin would slip right off. I'd be nothing but raw muscle and blood, and maybe that would deter him.

Proud, he holds the gown aloft. Its delicate threads don't glow. Glowing implies that it's soaked up something else's light. They illume, casting golden morning sunlight throughout the room. When the fabric shifts, it sings. A song of morning, of wind in trees and birds awakening.

Suddenly, I wonder how much it's worth. Magic like that must come at a high price—it was meant to equalize me to a king. I laugh and clap, a bit of hysteria to it, but no one notices. They're dazzled by the light dappling their faces.

I say, "It's perfect, exactly what I wanted." I even put a fond, staying hand on my father's shoulder. "But I'm to be the queen, so of course I need a stola made of moonlight."

"What?" my father yelps.

The courtiers hoot and whistle. What a delightful game this is to them. But emboldened, I trace my fingers over my hair. Magic is a slow, rare thing these days. It took four seasons to enchant a gown; perhaps two more for a stola. I need more time than that, so I add, "And a palla made of starlight."

I think my father realizes that I'm putting him off. I think this is the exact moment when he realizes that I'm not eager to be his bride. Still, it's also when he understands that I've played him well.

If I'd asked for more in private, it would have been easy to say no. Now he has no choice—exactly what he gets for presenting the gown in public. We both know the rules of saving face; it's impossible to decline with an audience.

The crowd quiets when he raises his hands. How their faces shine, cheeks blushed and lips pink with delight. Their attention darts, from me to him, back again. It's a match of fascination to them.

Picking up his goblet, my father raises it to me. There's a silvered light in his eyes. It's sharp, a blade made of his gaze. "To Augusta Merula, who already rules me. It will be done."

I raise my cup, and close my ears to the courtiers' roars of delight.

After breakfast, poor Sapiens has to run to catch me. I might have slowed for him once. Not anymore. Even his voice irritates me. It scratches and scrabbles senselessly, and I would shake it off if I could.

Out of breath, he finally catches me. "Merula, I was calling."

"I'm sorry. I'm distracted this morning."

He doesn't dare call me a liar. I'm a princess and, apparently, soon to be queen. His tread must fall lighter than ever around me. That, I like. It's a petty revenge, and all I have except for my prayer. I'm not alone, I tell myself. I hear the woman's words again, feel the warmth of her lips to my cheek. I'm not alone.

Sapiens smooths a hand over his thin silvery hair. He twitches, his smile succeeding and failing by turns. "I wanted to discuss the succession with you again."

As if this were normal. As if he hadn't bent the law to make this travesty, so Flamen no longer has an heir. Shame lowers my voice. This marriage may be all but fact, but I don't want to admit it, not yet.

The gown of sunlight kept my father from my chamber for a year. I might have two more now; I can make a better plan. I can decide I'm ready to dash my head on the flagstones beneath my windows.

"I think that's hardly my problem," I tell Sapiens. "The Haladians marry siblings, which neatly solved it. But we have a new tradition, don't we?"

Sapiens frowns. "Are you speaking against the king?"

"Of course not," I reply. "But it's not my place to make law. Or uphold it."

Plainly, I've angered him. The tip of his nose grows red; his cheeks splotch with a flush, too. Still, he insists on walking with me. He presses forward, because what else can he do? This is his mess, and now he has to make it legal. "The council and I have spoken at length on the matter."

"Oh, good."

"We think it best that you take a fosterling as your heir. The council is split on the details. Half think a noble-born child should become your heir. It would certainly cement alliances, and give the council incentive to support your court."

I don't reply. I don't care who supports this court anymore.

"The other half believe," Sapiens says, trying to reach for my hand, "that an orphan fosterling is more ideal. It will warm the people's hearts. We rule only at the mercy and kindness of the people's affections, after all."

Pursing my lips, I say, "That won't do. Am I not marrying my father to strengthen our right to rule?"

"Yes, certainly," he replies. Then he waits, as if I might volunteer a solution for him.

My ugly inner self urges me to slap him. No, to punch him, because a slap won't draw blood. Instead, I open his flesh with the sweetest smile, and a question. "Is there some reason I shouldn't bear my own heir? I'm young. Surely I'm strong enough to have a nursery full of babies."

The color drains from Sapiens. Now the cloud in his eyes seems ever paler. It's perhaps cruel to delight in his discomfort, but I do. I enjoy every moment that he squirms in my presence. Every second it takes him to shape his mouth, and find the words to admit two things: making me marry my father is an abomination, and he is complicit in it.

"Of course you are," he says, then falters.

"But?"

But what? I wonder. But we understand you might have terrible, damaged children? That you can't mate a sire to a child without creating monsters? That we might be very lucky to have an heir who is only physically malformed and mostly cognizant? Oh, all those things. I know exactly why the council wants me to adopt an heir.

I refuse to let them hide behind their law and their decisions and their willing blindness. I wait for Sapiens to say something more. Finally, he withdraws from me. He has the gall to look at me with disgust, but he nods, slowly. "Nothing, Augusta. It was simply a thought."

Perhaps he remembers the iron chair in the executioner's house. Perhaps his very vivid imagination allows him to see himself, forced to sit on a red-hot spike as his skin fries like pork fat.

Mine certainly does.

The magic that worked a gown of sunlight works much faster the second and third time around. It's only weeks until my father presents my stola and palla, both of them remarkable. And both of them, he brings to my chamber, after my ladies are sent away.

"I think you'll be pleased," he says, opening the box.

I'm not. I want to fall to the floor and vomit. I will myself to faint, so at least whatever comes next happens when I am quiet and dead. I can't even bring myself to touch the last pieces of my bride-price. Because this is what I'm worth: a gown, a wrap, a veil. This is what pays for my flesh.

To be fair, they're remarkable. The witch who made them is especially keen on nature, for the pieces alternate. My father explains in a voice that's so distant to me, it could be a memory, the sunlight gown rises with light in the morning. Then it darkens, allowing the stola to glow from dusk till dawn.

Following the rules of the sky, the starlight palla flickers all the time. It's most magnificent at night. The stars are embroidered in a field of pitch-blue. They shift and move with the hours—I'd be willing to bet, with the seasons, too.

Each point glitters with its own light. They're all individual, even bearing their own shades of blue and pink and green. They rise and fall, and the Pole Star remains at my brow, like a crown.

And because my father is the king, because I've stayed him, because he's submitted graciously to my whims, he insists. He insists, with callused hands, on opening the brooches at my shoulders. He unpeels my everyday stola and unties the belt that binds it.

Even when I was a child, he never stripped me. There was no need; I had ladies when I was too little to manage on my own. Once I was older, I did it myself. Tears spill down my face—I try to stop them, but they won't cease. They just won't, and it doesn't matter.

Though my belly hitches with sobs, though I shake with them, my father undresses me anyway.

Much later, when he dresses me again, I wear sunlight, moonlight, starlight.

"I need a cloak," I announce as I sweep into breakfast.

Shaking the chill of the dovecote from my skin, I pluck a sweet bun from the royal table and take a bite. It's ashes in my mouth, and it burns to swallow. But I do swallow, and reach for my cup of morning wine.

The courtiers gasp. It's the first time they've seen my bride-price complete. I wear all of it, and they're stunned.

Their silverware stills; they put goblets in their places. Perhaps in some part, they stare because the gown is an extraordinary piece of sorcery. They laugh at the magician's gambols at dinner, but this is a piece of true power.

My father pulls me into his lap. That, I think, is why the courtiers truly gasp. Since I'm wearing this gown, they know what it means. The celebration is yet to come, but the proof of consummation is on my sheets and in this gown.

Oh, yes, the madness of their king has come to pass. My mother's ballad is complete: he found the woman more beautiful than she, and now I am their queen.

How romantic.

"What do you need a cloak for?" my father asks. His arms band around me, tight and hard. They belie the smile on his lips.

Inside, I am nothing but bees. I sting and I buzz, my breaths soaring and falling like a cloud of drones. To the tips of my fingers, I feel dangerous, but I make myself speak like honey. Sweet in his ears. "So bandits don't set on me when I go to visit Queen Vatia. This gown is beautiful and it announces its worth."

"Well, I don't see why we can't find you a cloak."

Shaking my head, I loop my arms around his neck. If only I had stingers in my fingertips. I'd prick him and leave him gasping for breath. "I must have a special cloak. One that makes me look wretched. The gown really is a wonder."

Now he's suspicious. "You can't hide beauty like yours."

"Just the gown," I insist. "I want a cloak made from Poeminus."

Our audience gasps, but carefully. Shock ripples through them, but they don't dare murmur. My father turns. It puts most of his back to the courtiers, and lets him argue with me in private. "I'm quite fond of that horse."

I nod. I know he is; it's his favorite horse. If he's willing to sacrifice his only daughter then he will be made willing to sacrifice his favorite pet.

"He's old and nearly dead. And it would make me very, very happy to have a part of you wherever I go."

He hesitates. The monster. He hesitates!

He'll go to any length to feed his deviance, except give up his pet. We're all pets to him, I suppose. Playthings. Toys to be used and broken. I wonder now how willingly my beautiful mother came to his bed. She was only fourteen, still narrow in the hips—but he was eighteen then.

It was romantic, wasn't it? He gave her all the poppies in Flamen because they paled beside her lovely face. A lucky gift, since the astrologers had no idea what would come next; the physikers plied her with opium when childbirth split her apart.

Suddenly, the scent of Father's skin stirs my bees. They agitate and swell inside me. If only I could open my mouth and let them pour out. A swarm to swallow him, it would be a divine vengeance. Peeling his arms from me, I stand. My teeth snap together when I lean over him.

"I want it, by nightfall."

Whatever will he do? This is his game, and I'm playing it. Because he claimed me and dressed me in it, I wear my bride-price. I'm his equal now. Though he could order me to the chamber of horrors, the people might turn against him. There are rules. His rules. And I abide them.

Without another word, I abandon breakfast. It's a long walk to the dovecote again, but I have a whole day to burn away. I wait for Lycea, then I'll wait for my cloak.

When my sister queen invited me to write again, I wonder what she expected. What did she think as she sat in her palace, adored by the consort she chose? Her suggestion of impossible bride-prices no doubt pleased her.

Perhaps she stroked his head and said to herself, "That will be that, and all will be well."

I doubt very much that was her reaction when my dove found her the second time. Perhaps we'll discuss it one day, but I think that unlikely. I knew better than to ask for sanctuary this time.

Once I have word from Vatia, I return to the palace and await my cloak.

At dusk, my lady delivers it and I cry.

The cloak she carries is unmistakably Poeminus. I know this, for the head remains attached. The eyes are glass now and some astringent sort of glue has cured his hide. But this was a beautiful living thing this morning. Now he's murdered, at my hand.

Sending my lady away, I choke and I sob, but I put the cloak on. It still smells of horseflesh. Someone even braided the mane, all details that rack me with guilt. I'll think of a way to make it up to him. I'll pay penance, and make temples to him.

I force myself to settle. Though he meant to horrify me, my father's cruel reply is actually a gift.

Once I'm outside the castle with the hood (head, bless the gods, it's poor Poeminus's head) on, I disappear easily into the countryside.

No one thinks twice about a horse in the fields. I hike to the Eventide Forest, and then through it. The cloak hides my glow of moonlight and starlight. I'm unnoticed the whole night through. The whole day through, too, when I sleep beneath Poeminus's noble flesh. What's one wild horse in a forest full of them?

By new dusk, I wake and cross the river. With a half night's walk, I finally stop. A great wall rises before me, and it bristles with soldiers. As I approach it, I cast off the cloak and let my bride-price identify me.

On the other side of the gate, my sister queen Vatia greets me. Sending her men away, Vatia invites me into her war tent. She gives me the privacy of her own screen, and the gift of an enchanted pair of scissors.

I peel off moonlight, starlight, sunlight. The whisper of silver slicing through sunlight pleases me. I sit in nothing but my tunic and cut.

The magic that made my bride-price was valuable enough to make me equal to a king. It's wealth with a measure; wealth I can share. I shear the fabric into a thousand pieces to pay the men and women who wait outside. My soldiers. My army.

When I dress again, it's with my own hands. The Lycean chain weave is too big, but I belt it. My cloak of Poeminus fits perfectly. Though I'm exhausted, starving, shuddering, I accept the gift of Vatia's horse. In return, I offer her my alliance as Flamen's queen.

"Leave our people," I cry as we gather at the river. "Leave our people, take nothing, burn nothing, harm none. We ride for the castle alone!"

My army roars. They're the best sort, these men and women of Flamen, well paid and with a purpose.

Though I don't see her among them, there is one woman in my village who understands. She slips through the streets tonight, warning the innocent to flee to the fields. No doubt her daughter trails after her, three years old, with bright black eyes.

I'm not alone.

And when I raise my pike, thundering horses surge with me. The voices of a thousand soldiers rise up, a new ballad that I'll sing until the day I die. My father's army is scattered. He fought just one war, and that was years ago. His guards search the forest for me; he's unprotected.

This means when we take the castle, it'll be easy to capture him. My new guard knows where to find the executioner's house. They know what lies within it, and what my intentions are.

It's my pleasure alone to find my father.

He'll know me, because I wear the head of his favorite horse. I'll throw it off, and I won't kiss him. I won't sit in his lap. I won't pretend anymore that he's my better.

No, he's a lesser beast, a man who defiled his daughter. Who betrayed her, broke the rules of our land and committed his crimes with no fear of retribution. He should have feared, for now I'm the queen. He made me a queen, so I intend to teach him what everyone around him knows:

Death isn't the worst thing that happens to a traitor in Flamen.

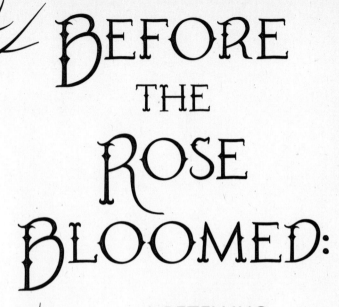

BEFORE THE ROSE BLOOMED:

A RETELLING OF THE SNOW QUEEN

by Ellen Hopkins

Deep in a vault beneath the Hall
of Legends is a tale of love and lust,
fire and ice. Magic. Reflection. Word
spinners repeat it only when they must,
for implicit within the seven-act
drama is a call for introspection.
But this storyteller has lived well,
and has no fear of this fable. So if
you dare, settle in with a hot cup—
protection against the approaching
chill. Are you ready? Let's begin.

ACT ONE

Once, beyond the reach of memory,
a certain archangel incited rebellion

in heaven. But God's faithful army
prevailed, and the Fallen were exiled

to Earth, where Lucifer took the name
Satan and angel became demon.

Angered by their defeat, jealous
of God's beloved people, the imps

set out to cause mischief among
the human race. Some realized great

success in this, but others grew lazy,
and not a few succumbed to lust.

One particularly clever demon
(having founded an academy for

aspiring young imps) titled himself
Demon King and determined to marry

a certain human princess. But when
he came courting, he was met with

ardent distaste. "The world is far
too beautiful to spend my days looking

at such an ugly creature. And the sun
is far too warm to lie beside someone

with a frozen heart. I will not marry
you." That might have discouraged

a less clever demon. But this one
crafted a mirror of enchanted ice,

and its magic was quite horrible.
For anytime someone gazed into it,

everything beautiful in the world
seemed ugly. The most magnificent

flowers appeared wilted, the orange
glow of a perfect sunset looked rusty-

brown, and the fairest human on
all the earth resembled a monster

more hideous than the demon
himself. The looking glass itself

was exquisite, its frame carved
in intricate detail and its surface

polished to perfect smoothness.
The princess knew nothing of its magic,

and its beauty was tempting. Even so,
intuiting a trap, she refused the gift.

The furious demon unfurled his long-
unused wings, and flew the mirror

toward heaven, so that it might appear
a wasteland to any human who looked

upward at the sky. But the higher
he flew, the more slippery the mirror

became, until at last it slipped from
his grasp. It fell to the earth, shattering

into a billion shards, which swarmed
and swirled throughout the world,

buzzing like great hives of bees.
This caused terrible trouble,

for a single flake lodged in an eye
or heart infected it with the mirror's

magic. A great many were attracted
to the princess, since the mirror

was always meant for her. One large
sliver pierced each of her eyes, turning

their sapphire-blue crystal pale.
Another burrowed into her heart,

growing with each beat until there
was nothing left beneath her breast

but a miniature iceberg. The demon
laughed, then deepened the curse.

> "Now you will never know love,
> my Snow Queen. You may search
>
> and search the earth for affection,
> but any man who kisses you more
>
> than three times will freeze solid. And
> the only place you'll ever know warmth
>
> is in the Land of the Midnight Sun."
> She was borne away by a swarm of ice,

which carved a palace for her from
a glacier near the North Pole. The demon

> sent her there with a parting gift.
> "One day every year, at the winter
>
> solstice, while the sun refuses to rise,
> you may see beauty. And if you should
>
> find a human heart warm enough
> to thaw yours, you may know love."

With a throaty chuckle, he returned
to his demon school, knowing the odds

were longer than long. And that
is how the beautiful, frost-hearted

Snow Queen came to live in a castle
of ice at the frozen tip of the world.

ACT TWO

Many hundreds of miles away, in a very
small town where neighbors were friends,
except when they weren't, lived a girl

named Greta and a boy known as K,
which was short for Kassandar, a name
he found much too unwieldy for daily

use. The pair had been friends since
the long days of childhood, having
adjoining backyards and grandparents

who often shared tea, and sometimes
a pint or two. In the growing seasons,
Greta and K spent long afternoons in

the garden, tending prismatic flower
beds. Both favored the richly scented
roses, though she preferred crimson

petals, and he tangerine. The joy
they shared in the summer months saw
them through the gray of winter.

And as they journeyed through time
toward adulthood, everyone in the village
assumed they would one day marry,

so pure was their love for one another.
K grew into a handsome young man,
and strong, from long days hauling lumber

and firewood. Greta learned to weave
intricate patterns, designs inspired by
her beloved blooms. A wedding was not

far away. But then came an unusually
early winter storm. Ice flurried through
the town, filling the streets with a strange

buzzing noise. This was very strange, and
no one could guess the source of the sound.
K's curiosity was piqued. When he wondered out

loud what it was, his grandmama decided
it must be snow bees. "Do they have a queen?"
asked K. Every hive had one, didn't it?

     "Well, of course, child," agreed Grandmama.
     "The Snow Queen. And she is beautiful
     to behold, but her heart is carved of ice."

K didn't quite believe it until that same
evening, just as the sun set, when motion
beyond his frost-curtained window

caught his notice. He cleared a small
spot, and when he looked out into
the fading light, he found a striking woman,

pale as freshly drifted snow, peering
back at him. She knocked on the glass.
"Please open the window. I saw you earlier,

hauling wood on your sledge. I might
have work for you." K felt compelled
to comply, and in a single blink, a swarm

of ice bees rose up and flew inside. One
lodged itself in K's right eye; another
burrowed into his heart. They were so

tiny, he barely felt pain, but though
the Snow Queen herself didn't change
in appearance, everything else did.

The cheerful fire shriveled to cold
embers in a smoke-stained hearth.
The walls leaned, peeling paint, and

the threadbare carpet revealed
a splintered floor. Grandmama's song,
only seconds before so lovely, now

sounded like a tomcat's yowl. And K's
heart felt as if it had frozen near solid.
Some instinct told him that if he could

only touch Greta, his love for her might
thaw the ice. But when he glanced
across the way at her window, it appeared

shuttered, and her house dilapidated,
as if no one had lived there for a very
long time. K fell into such despair

> that when the Snow Queen urged,
> "Come with me," he took her hand
> and followed docilely to her sleigh.

When he climbed in beside her,
she covered him with a rich ermine
stole. Then she kissed him, and he felt

a spark of warmth, but only a spark,
and his life as he knew it fell into
the tracked snow behind them.

> When he asked where they were going,
> the Snow Queen answered, "To my grand
> palace." And when he wanted to know

> why she had taken his hand, she told
> him, "Because I need someone to care
> for me." She didn't say that rumors

of his love for Greta had crept far and
wide, all the way to her ears, and she knew
she must see this thing for herself.

She'd traveled a great distance to K's
town and spied on the young couple,
witnessing such affection between them

that a little piece of her own heart
melted. Perhaps, enchanted, K would
grow to love her, too, freeing her

from the demon's curse. So they flew
across the snow, crows caw-cawing
overhead, to the Land of the Midnight Sun.

ACT THREE

K said goodbye to no one, and not a single
soul had seen him go. When someone
vanishes into thin air, people talk.
"He's gone looking for work," some said.

"He's fallen for another, and run off,"
opined others. After many days with no
word, no sign, everyone came to believe
K was dead. Everyone except Greta.

"I don't know where he went or what
he's done, but my heart would tell me
if he had succumbed to some threat
of nature or man. No, my K is alive."

She waited patiently through winter.
But with the spring thaw, as tender green
shoots pushed up through the earth,
preparing the land for summer, she knew

she must search for K. "Before the roses
bloom, or how will I ever look at them
again?" Despite all best-intentioned advice
to the contrary, Greta packed a few days'

food into a rucksack, and off she went.
Her quest would have been dangerous
enough for a young woman alone, but
dark magic prefers no interference,

unless it is its own. The road from town
went east and west, parallel the river.
Greta called out to the sparrows,
"Do you know which way K went?"

But the little birds just sang, "We're
here. We're here." So Greta cried
to the river, "You must have seen him
go. Tell me which way to travel."

Rippling waves lapped against the bank.
"Come here," they seemed to say.
"Come here." When Greta reached
the beach, she found a little skiff

tied there. "Get in. Get in," heaved
the water. So she did, and the river
rose, spiriting her away. With no oars
nor sail, Greta was at the mercy

of the current. After a time, she slept
in the soft April sunshine. She dreamed
of roses. Dreamed of ice. Of a sleigh
aloft in a winter sky. Somewhere, midst

the swirling images, the solution
to her puzzle appeared. But when
she woke, tossed into the bow as the boat
bumped against the shore, it was gone.

Greta stepped onto the shimmering
sand and stretched, and when her back
was turned, the river coaxed the boat
away. "Oh!" she exclaimed. "Now what?"

But there was really only one decision.
"Well, I suppose I must walk." It wasn't
until hours later that she remembered
her rucksack. All her provisions were

somewhere downriver. But, despite
the gnaw in her belly and blisters
forming on her feet, her love for K
drew her forward. On she trekked,

into the purpling evening, until at last
she reached a tidy cottage. Her knock
did not go unanswered. "I'm sorry to
bother you," she told the bent old woman

who opened the door. "I've traveled
all day, and I've lost my rucksack and…"
A tear or two spilled from her eyes.
"Could you spare a crust of bread?"

The crone (for that's what she was,
though her magic was tepid with
great age) allowed, "Come in, come
in, my dear. Tell me about your journey

while I fix you a plate. There's plenty
here. My garden is bounteous, and
never sleeps." That much, at least,
was true. "Please help yourself to

some cherries. They're fresh from
my orchard." Greta thought it odd
that trees would bear fruit in April,
but with one bite of a luscious red

cherry, all suspicion melted away,
and she told the old woman about
her quest to find her love before
the roses blossomed at home. Caught

up in her own story, Greta didn't ask
the crone how she had come to live alone
in the wilderness. Had she, the witch
would not have confessed that she was

in the employ of the Demon King.
Still, she wasn't truly wicked, only
intolerably lonely. Few enough people
passed that way. The spell she cast

on the turnip stew wasn't meant
to harm Greta, only to lull her into
forgetfulness so she might stay for
a time. "I'll fix you a bed in front

of the fire, where it's cozy." Greta
drifted off to the sound of crackling
wood and slept dreamlessly. The next
morning, after a breakfast of grains

and honey, she followed the crone
out the back door. The garden was
one hundred meters wide, and bordered
on two sides by very tall walls. The far

end was nowhere in sight. "Oh!" said
the girl. "All I can see from here to forever
are flowers in bloom and trees bearing
fruit. But how is that possible?"

The old woman answered easily, "As I
said, my garden doesn't understand
the constraints of time. You may partake
of anything you see. Except…" She gestured

toward the tallest tree in the yard.
"Don't eat that fruit. It's bitter poison."
Greta hardly cared. The garden offered
her much pleasure for countless days.

Every flower had a story to confess, and bird
choirs sang in leafy branches. The old
woman fed her well and in the evenings
recited poetry and ancient tales of woe.

All thoughts of home and the boy
she loved skittered off into the far
regions of Greta's mind. She might
have stayed right there for the rest

of her life, but one afternoon she noticed
a raven land on the tree of poison fruit.
He plucked one and, before she could
offer warning, gobbled it down. Greta

waited for him to fall to the ground.
Instead, he ate another. And another.
"Dear raven," said Greta. "How do you
feel? I'm told that fruit is poisonous."

> The raven looked down with one black
> marble eye. "Poison?" he cawed. "This
> fruit is quite delicious. Eaten it for years.
> Hasn't killed me yet." Then off he flew.

Next, a crow landed on the tree.
He, too, ate the fruit without incident.
"Oh, crow. Why would the old woman
warn me not to eat from this tree?"

If a crow could smile, that's what he did.
"Do you not read your Bible, child?
What is it she doesn't want you to know?"
Then he tossed her a fruit. "Eat. So sweet."

Greta ate. One bite, and she remembered
her home. Another, she recalled her
own garden and the greening roses.
When she finished the fruit, she saw

K in her mind's eye and remembered
her quest. "Oh! I have been here much
too long. But how will I escape
the garden? Do you know a way out?"

The crow blinked. "Indeed I do. Will
you take some fruit for your journey?
I've found it a wise thing to do."
Greta gathered as many as her pockets

could hold, then followed the crow
to a small gate in the wall, barely big
enough for her to squeeze through.
With great force of will she did, and on

the far side she found summer had
come and gone. "It is autumn, and
winter approaches. I have to hurry,
but which way? Where did my K go?"

ACT FOUR

Another day, her cry might have gone
unheeded. But Mr. Crow had taken
an interest in the girl, circling above
her as she hurried away from the garden,
throwing glances over her shoulder.

No one followed, however, and after a safe
distance, she slowed to a stop, winded.
It was then she noticed her companion.
"Might you have seen K, Mr. Crow?
He'd have passed this way in late winter."

She went on to describe her beloved,
and how he had disappeared. Now,
the crow spoke human fluently,
a benefit of eating fruit from the garden's
Tree of Knowledge. Still, he enunciated

carefully, so as not to squawk.
"That is a very sad story of love gone
astray. I myself am engaged, and
should the love of my life disappear,
I would search the ends of the earth

for her." Perched atop a formidable
rock, he considered a minute, then
said, "Come to think of it, I did see a lad
about that age pass this way last winter.
He was dressed in traveling clothes…"

Greta nodded her head. "As well
he would, and the timing was right.
It must have been K. Tell me the color
of his hair. Was it like summer wheat?
And was he tall and broad-shouldered?"

"Well, yes, he was quite a strapping
young man. He wore a cap, but as I
remember, what peeked out at the nape
of his neck was that very shade." Truthfully,
he'd seen none of that, but he wanted

to give her the slenderest ray
of hope that she was indeed on
the trail of her beloved. "Oh, then,
I'm certain it must have been my K.
And where do you suppose he went?"

The crow told her what he knew.
The story was that a princess who lived
in a castle nearby happened to be a girl
who loved books and the knowledge
they allowed. She yearned for a companion

who was articulate and well-read, and
so the news circulated that her prince
must be this type of gentleman. Many
tried, for she was lovely and a princess
of some means. But when they arrived

at the palace, even the best-spoken
fell mute. Only one was able to pass
her test. Greta's spirit soared. "That
might have been K. We spent many
evenings together in the company

of books. But…" Sadness weighted
her suddenly. "Did they marry, then,
the princess and he?" The crow couldn't
say, but either way, "I have to know
and I'll be happy if only he is alive."

It shouldn't come as a surprise,
but it can be exceedingly difficult for
a stranger to gain entry to a palace.
Luckily for Greta, however, Mr. Crow
had an inside source—his fiancée.

She let them in through the kitchen
door. "The princess and her prince
are in the library, taking tea. Come
with me." She led them up a back
staircase to the uppermost floor.

The library was immense, and books
spilled from floor-to-ceiling shelves.
The door to the veranda was open,
and a lovely cool breeze blew in
from the sea. The princess and her

young man sat close to the open
air, with their backs to the hallway
door. But K was not in the room.
Greta breathed a loud sigh of relief
before breaking down in tears,

startling the princess. "Who are you,
and how did you find your way in here?"
She might have called for the guards,
but the strange girl was so distraught,
instead she said, "Tell me your story."

When Greta finished, the princess, too,
was crying, and even the prince (for,
indeed, they had married) had a shine
to his eyes. "How can we help you?
Will you dine with us and stay the night?"

Greta agreed to start her journey
fresh in the morning. When she woke,
a small carriage and two coachmen
waited for her at the castle door.
"Oh, thank you!" she called toward

the library windows as she climbed
up inside. "Farewell, friends." She did
not know that the royal couple lounged
late in bed that morning, nor that
they were unaware of the generous gift.

ACT FIVE

Neither could Greta know that the road
was infamous in the land, or that they
traveled toward the heart of the Forest
of Thieves. She was too content to nibble
on the figs and scones provided, a gift
from the Demon King, who was well

aware of her journey and its possible
consequences. Before long, she swooned
with drowsiness, and when she woke,
it was with a jolt. "Who dares trespass
in our woods?" A time-shriveled face
materialized at the window. "Why,

it's a lass, and a comely one at that. Get
out, get out. I suspect you are quite tender
and will make a splendid meal." Greta's
head was still thick and she heard only
what she wanted to, which was "Get out
and I will make you a splendid meal."

She wasn't really hungry, but didn't
want to seem rude, so she climbed
down from the coach, where she was
apprehended by a band of thieves.
Greta might have found herself upon
a serving platter, had the youngest

    of the bunch not taken an interest.
    "Leave her be, Mother," she commanded.
    "Let me interrogate her, see what her
    business here might be. Perhaps, should
    she disappear, someone might come
    looking for her." Now, the girl, Phoebe,

was simply in want of some company.
Thieves, on the whole, are a closemouthed
lot, and not much good for conversation.
She took Greta by the hand, pulled
her off toward their camp as the thieves
dismantled the coach piece by piece.

    "Tell me, girl, why are you here? I'm
    in need of a good story. Recite it well
    and I'll make sure it's rabbit on the table
    tonight." Greta repeated her tale, and
    it brought tears to Phoebe's eyes, for
    such love could warm even the coldest heart.

The encampment was cheered by
a ring of fire, circled by substantial
tents. On the far perimeter, the horses
were kept and, much to Greta's delight,
in their midst stood a reindeer. He looked
hungry, so she fed him two of the garden

fruits from her pockets. In the highest
boughs of the tall pines roosted pigeons—
ugly birds, and not the brightest. But in one
nest a pair of mourning doves cooed.
Greta quite enjoyed their soft song,
and sought to reward it with another

of the fruits. Amiably, she nibbled one,
too, and suddenly understood her danger.
While the robbers saw to supper, Phoebe
asked Greta to tell her more about K,
and how he had come to vanish.
The doves overheard and after a while

           began to coo in the language of men,
           which the fruit had given them.
           "We saw your young man, K, you call
           him. He passed this way, sitting beneath
           an ermine wrap in a sleigh beside
           the Snow Queen. To Lapland, they went."

While pigeons are terrible gossips,
and rumor is a tool of the devil,
the Demon King holds no jurisdiction
over doves or caribou. "Lapland!" cried
the reindeer, possessed of human speech.
"That was my home when I was a calf."

Greta drew close to the downy-coated
animal, whispered into his ear, "If I can
secure your freedom, will you take me
to Lapland and help find the place where
the Snow Queen has sequestered K?"
The reindeer agreed happily, for the idea

of running upon the snowy plains
of his homeland again filled him with joy.
Greta waited until after the evening feast,
when the thieves all took to swigging
amber liquid from a very large bottle.
Eventually, they all staggered off to bed.

It was then she approached Phoebe,
who had drunk not a little herself
and toyed nervously with a very sharp
knife. "Put your weapon down, friend.
You know my quest. Will you help me
on my way again? I have little to give—"

"Are you a spell caster?" interrupted
Phoebe, for she had witnessed
the change in the animals. "Share
the secret of your incantation and
I shall let you go." In truth, magic
made her nervous, though she lusted

for such power. "I am not a witch,
only a girl. I gathered the fruit
of knowledge from a tree in a garden
far from here. If it's of use to you,
I will share what I have. But you must
promise to let the reindeer carry me

on my journey." The deal was struck.
Greta gave Phoebe half the remaining
fruit, and the thief untied the reindeer.
Greta climbed upon his back. But before
she could go, Phoebe stopped her. In a quite
uncommon gesture, most likely spurred

by rum consumption, she wrapped
Greta in a thick cloak and gave her
a hamper stuffed with meat and bread.
"Lapland is cold all year round, and winter
fast approaches. Godspeed." The reindeer
ran off before she could change her mind.

ACT SIX

The only knowledge the reindeer
needed to find the most direct route
to Lapland was instinct, drawing him
home. The line they took was straight,
but still it took many days, and by
the time they reached his familiar turf,
the hamper was empty, and so was

Greta's stomach. A small trail of smoke
led the reindeer to a lopsided cabin
at the very edge of the snowy plain.
"Oh! See how it tilts. However does it
stay standing?" wondered Greta out
loud. She was almost afraid to knock
on the door, thinking the tapping

might tip the structure all the way over.
But the house stayed mostly upright
and the old Laplander woman who
answered was happy enough to let
them inside and fill Greta's belly
with the excellent fish she had been
preparing. As she cooked, the reindeer

repeated Greta's story, but only after

his own, which he thought the most

fascinating. "You have come such a very

long way," said the woman, "but you have

farther to go. I saw the Snow Queen pass

by not long ago. She has a home in Finland,

and that, I'm sure, is where she is now.

My dearest cousin lives in Finland,

and she knows more about the Snow

Queen than I do. I will send you with

an introduction, for she is shy about

strangers, even those as interesting

as the two of you. But, please, take my

spare muff, as it is much colder there."

And so, they were off again, toward

the Northern Lights, which danced

in the sky, leading them to Finland.

The Lapland woman gave Greta a pouch

of dried fish, for her cousin loved the treat

and found it hard to come by. On the skin,

she wrote, *Please help this young lady*

in her search for the Snow Queen.
Her story has touched my heart, which
I have long believed immune to such
things as love. Oh, cousin! How I miss
my soldier, so long gone, and I know
it must be the same for you. So many
have stories, often left untold except

in certain company. So many, whose
lives are changed forever at the hands
of the Demon King. But Greta knew
nothing of this as she resumed her journey.
After many more hours of travel, the reindeer
stopped before the Finland woman's home,
which stood much straighter than that

of her Laplander cousin. Indeed,
Greta found the Finland woman quite
suspicious of strangers at her door.
But the pouch, with its message on
the skin, plus the delicious dried fish
inside, was enough to allow her through
the door. Again, she talked about her K

with such affection that the Finland
woman nearly swooned from the telling.
"Dear, dear girl. The Snow Queen is even
now only a mile from here. But you will
not easily gain entrance to her palace.
She wears the curse of the Demon King,
and it both controls and protects her."

The reindeer then drew the woman
to one side and asked whether she might
possess some potion or other means to
give Greta the strength to fight the curse.
"The girl needs nothing from me," responded
the Finlander. "She holds a powerful weapon.
Neither demon nor queen can conquer it."

The reindeer understood, and when
Greta urged, "Please, can we go to K
right this moment?" they left without
delay, and he ran as fast as he could
to the Snow Queen's palace. He set
Greta down beside a bush adorned
with red berries. "You have fulfilled

your promise." Greta stroked his forehead
gently. "You are free." The reindeer
was happy enough for his freedom,
yet left reluctantly, for he had come
to care deeply for the girl and her quest.
Unbeknownst to either of them, word
of their arrival had rippled to the lair

of the Demon King. He conjured, from
shards of ice, a company of sharp-
quilled porcupines and razor-clawed
wildcats, and raptors with talons like knives.
In the ever-dusk of winter solstice,
the beasts came marching, and for
the first time since her journey began,

Greta felt truly afraid. "Our father…"
She sent the words of the Lord's Prayer
toward heaven. With each expelled breath,
her frozen exhale formed an angel, and
soon an entire phalanx, wearing
helmets and carrying spears. They thrust
them into the ice-hewn beasts, shattering

them into hailstones, insignificant
in size. With the help of her heavenly
protectors, Greta marched straight
up to the door, and it opened for her
as if commanded. The hair at her nape
pricked. Her face flushed hot, despite
the cold. And she knew, "K is very near."

ACT SEVEN

K, in fact, was very near, but though
Greta's intuition screamed it was so,
just down a long corridor and across
a frozen hall, he couldn't feel her presence
at the door. Couldn't hear the sound
of her call or smell the drift of roses
on the air. K lay, prone, on a polar-bear skin,
at the foot of the Snow Queen's throne.

His color was an odd shade of blue,
bordering black. He would have been
dead of the cold already, except every
now and again, his queen would warm
him with the heat of her gaze, and her hot
cold lips would graze his face, enough
to keep him barely alive. All this, Greta
saw in the instant she burst into the hall,

flanked by angels so beautiful their very
presence lit the chamber. As it happened,
it was the afternoon of the winter solstice,
the one day of the year when the Snow
Queen could discern beauty. At the sight
of the angels, she fell to her knees. "Oh!
Never have I witnessed such a thing, not
even when I was a child." She wept openly.

K stirred from his oblivion. "What is it?"
he asked, struggling to sit upright.
"What do you see?" But when Greta rushed
to his side, he couldn't recognize her,
for she looked ugly as any old hag, with
the piece of mirror still lodged in his eye.
"What is it? What do you want from me?"
Greta drew back, horrified that her K

didn't know her. But an angel whispered
in her ear, reminding her of the power
of the Demon King's enchantment. Greta
reached into her pocket, withdrew
the last of the fruit from the garden tree.
"Please. Eat. This will make you strong
again." K might have refused, except
the angel fixed him with her eyes, and as

he stared into the depths of their
pools, he was encouraged to taste
the fruit the girl offered. One bite,
and he knew. "Greta? Yes, Greta. I know
you…" A rush of memory flooded
his eyes, washing the evil shard away.
"You are as beautiful as your guardians."
He opened his arms and Greta fell into

them eagerly, her own eyes wet against
his chest. The salt of her tears soaked
through his shirt, skin and flesh and
breastbone, all the way into his heart.
It began to thaw immediately, beating
surer and louder. As blood coursed, warm,
through his veins, K flushed, and without
thinking, he kissed Greta full on the lips.

The gesture filled the Snow Queen
with hope that such love might still
await her somewhere. "You shall stay
together forever," she declared, "though
I will miss your company, dearest K.
Thank you for brightening my days.
Return to your village, where, I suspect,
a happy homecoming awaits you."

Cloaked in a fine warm mantle of love,
Greta and K left the palace, hand in hand.
The air was sharp, and the light low,
but K paused to promise, "I'll never again
leave your side." At the bush with red berries
stood the reindeer and his own mate, ready
to carry the couple home, under the protection
of angels and before the roses bloomed.

BEAST/BEAST

by Tessa Gratton

I

The first time I attempted to escape from the Beast's castle was under cover of flat, fierce rain. It soaked through the layers of wool and velvet I'd traveled here wearing, the hem now tattered and ruined, all sweat- and tearstained from two days in the attic. Dust streaked into mud along my cheeks. Hair clung to my skull, and my finger bones ached in the cold.

I ran straight to the gate, glad of my hardy riding boots to splash through the puddles and miniature rivers forming along the broad avenue. The sluice of rain obscured the world, melting everything.

Massive iron gates rose so fast I skidded through the slick gravel to stop. I grasped the bars, pulling with my weight, grinding my teeth. Nothing. I wiped water from my eyes to hunt for a lever or lock. *Nothing.* The hinges were solid, smooth iron. I saw no grooves in the earth. Had the gates even opened when I was dragged through? I could not recall.

My dull, frozen fingers barely obeyed as I untied my boot-laces, then discarded the boots. The wall was built of heavy granite blocks half my height with narrow grooves between. I caught my fingers into one and dug my toes in, but there was no good purchase in the rain.

I tried and tried again. Thunder shook the air. *I will not cry.* Even when the skin of my fingers and palms was raw and stinging, I refused.

The ninth—*tenth*—I don't know!—time I fell into the freezing mud, I lay back and screamed at the low black clouds.

Mud melded to my back, and I rolled away heavily, dragging myself to the wall. I huddled there, arms on my knees, facedown and sheltered enough from the rain for hot tears to gather on my lashes. Water filled my nose and I swallowed it, choking, fighting its weight.

The Beast found me there.

I did not know what he was yet, and could see only the impression of his bulk in the dark, watery night. He said nothing, but loomed until the rain died and dawn lit the east. He turned his face away from it and waved me to come. I stood without aid and watched as he lumbered back toward the castle. Exhaustion compelled me to follow.

II

The second night I tried to escape was clear and full of moonlight. I ran through the topiary forest and the wilderness garden toward the north curve of the wall. Everything was dry and crisp with shadows. I had no boots on, but slippers; no wool, but layers of silk and fine linen: a dress from the closet in the opulent room the Beast had given me.

Moonlight aided my search for hand- and footholds, but the wall there was no less forbidding. I left blood smeared down the pale granite.

That time I did not cry.

III

It's because of a rose I'm trapped here. I asked Father for one before he left, bitterly, to remind him I existed, to remind him of my mother, who had grown ghostly white roses along the fence of our city house.

He brought home nothing but that single red rose, stuck to his palm by the thorns. Fever-pink burned his cheeks as he offered it to me, and my half sisters groaned as they turned away. I took it.

Only, the thorns bit into my fingers and refused to tear free. I cried out at the blood weeping from my palm and my father did, too, triumphantly. He was free.

A spell—a compulsion—wove about me like vines, drawing me onto the strange black horse stamping at the dirt path before our house. I rode like the devil through a day and a night until the black gates and blacker castle appeared. My will returned to me as we passed through the rose garden and the bloodred rose fell away. I screamed as a great wind lifted me, dragging me through the castle, down corridors, through vast halls. Massive doors slammed. Lights flashed on before me and off behind, whispers gossiped hurriedly about

my name, my hair, my boots and cape. But there were no
faces, no creatures or people I could see.

The magic flung me into a tower room, dusty, but with a
bed, a desk and toilet, three wide round windows curtained
in faded violet. The door locked behind me and no matter
how I pounded, no matter how I screamed, I was trapped.

IV

For the first two nights the Beast spoke to me through the
door. His deep voice shook the wood, pulsing in time with
my heart.

He offered me food but I cried vows of murder and vio-
lence, swore to escape, to be free of this place and him.

I did not know what he was yet.

On the third night the door clicked open. The corridor
was empty. I ran out into the rain.

V

He led me inside after, both of us soaking, into a fine bedroom lacking the dust and grime of the attic tower. He left
me there, behind an unlocked door, ruined and too weary for
questions and demands. Too tired to look at his face.

Silk rugs layered over the cold stone floor, and there were
more pillows than I could use in a month. I stripped out of
the wet, torn riding habit and accepted a nightgown that
hung in the air as if held by a ghost. The silk warmed my
skin, and I fell into limp exhaustion even as many invisible
hands combed my hair.

VI

It was my third escape attempt when I saw him, full-on in the light.

I thought perhaps under the sun I might discover hand-holds or secret crannies leading to freedom. The light bled harsh and silver over the stone wall, revealing only smooth lines, and none of the streaks of blood from my first or second attempt. They'd faded or washed off in the rain, or had very, very painstakingly been rubbed away by the hands of invisible servants.

I tilted my chin to look up at the bluest sky possible. Nothing marred it, no stray clouds, no bird or wind with a clutch of leaves fluttering past. Only vast, glowing blue.

"Girl," he said from behind me. "Come back inside. Eat. You'll never climb it shaking with hunger."

It made me smile, then choke on a laugh. Near hysteria, I slid down to the thick carpet of grass, tears dripping straight from my lashes onto the manicured green.

My stomach trembled for the first time in a day; my eye-balls pulsed with my heartbeat. I did need food, and drink. My blood flowed thick and sluggish. But accepting his food would be accepting my prison.

I turned my face and peeked at him. The sun flooded his body, allowing for no shadows or gentle, gradual reveal.

The Beast was a monster of flesh and fur and forest: fangs curled like tusks through his bottom lip, his arms were green as fresh vegetables and twisted with vines. Thorns pushed out through the elbows of his tattered velvet coat, from his crooked fingers like claws and in a fierce line down either cheekbone. Those eyes were dark, pupils slit like a cat's, his shoulders humped like a buffalo's, nose wide and flared, and his coarse hair tangled as though wet. A great orange fungus circled one wrist like a gauntlet. One foot was cloven and the other clawed into the grass like a tiger's. He would never be graceful. Lichen dripped down one side of his face, pulling his features down so he appeared to melt even as he towered over me.

And red rose petals clung to him, blossoming from his neck like sores.

I might have stared at him forever if he hadn't shied away. That thick hair swung over his face, and he pressed his fists into the hard edges of his hips. "Come, girl," he rumbled.

VII

"What are you?" I asked as I discarded a chicken bone and reached for a bowl of orange soup that smelled of cinnamon and cloves and the comforts of home. My mother used to make something like it with pumpkins. This porcelain burned my fingers but I gripped harder, welcoming the sharp pain.

At the far end of the dining table, he hunkered in a throne large enough for a bear. I sensed his head shake rather than saw it. All the candles that side of the room had blown out the moment he entered. "No one thing," he murmured.

I saluted with the bowl. "So a man."

The Beast snorted, very much like a displeased stallion.

I shrugged and drank my soup, focused on the heat as it slipped over my tongue and down my throat, landing like love in my stomach. Warmth radiated through my chest.

"I don't know your name," he said.

"Neither do I know yours."

"Beast. Only Beast."

"That isn't a name."

He did not reply.

"Call me Prisoner, then, if we're being literal." I thunked the bowl down and thoughtfully slid my fingers along the silver knife at the place setting.

"Beauty," the Beast said. "For that is what you are."

It was my turn to snort. Not ladylike. Not beautiful.

"Will you love me, Beauty?" the Beast asked, shocking my fingers numb. "Will you marry me?"

I pushed violently. *"No."*

He whispered, *"Good night,"* as I fled.

VIII

This became our pattern:

I rose and dressed in the morning, ate some little cheese and cold meat, then walked the grounds, hunting for escape.

The gardens were set like a wheel; the castle the hub, each spoke a path. Between them were triangles of nature. The wilderness garden, the topiary forest with its elephants and dragons and hearts, the garden of statues, the fruit orchard, the proper manicured garden full of tiny peonies and marigolds and tulips.

And of course the rose garden.

That was where he most often joined me, appearing like a shadow when the sun was high enough.

The roses were wild, though some attempt had been made

to train them over trestles and benches and statues. They were all sorts of pinks and reds and creamy yellows; normal, natural colors, except when twilight fell they glowed as if they caught up bits of the sunlight to hold.

It was days before we spoke in the garden. I stopped to touch the velvet petal of a pale yellow rose, so delicately colored it seems almost translucent.

"A Ray of Dawn," the Beast said quietly.

My fingers jerked.

"Her name. It's the rose's name."

"And what do you call the rose that trapped me here?" I asked in an even voice that belied the tumult beating in my chest.

He hesitated before rumbling a sigh and saying, "The Promise Kiss."

I stalked out of the garden.

Often I left him there, suddenly furious. I'd go to the library or the roof, to drown myself in the lives and thoughts of others, or to stare out over the black forest, despairing that the only escape would be death.

Always I dined with him.

Always he asked, "Will you marry me, Beauty?"

Always I reacted badly.

It took the soothing fingers of ghosts braiding my hair, tying up a nightgown, washing my hands, before I calmed enough to sleep in that soft, feathery bed. I listened to their whispers as I drifted off, but ghosts never say anything useful, or in a language I understand.

IX

I knew every step of the wall by the end of my first month. There were no secret latches. No crumbling footholds. No egress.

X

"Beauty," he called down the massive curve of staircase.

I stopped in the entryway and turned slowly. There he stood on the landing, a black shadow against the rich blue carpet and hanging tapestries. I snapped, "It's such a shallow thing, beauty. And I only am beautiful compared to you."

His hunched shoulders lifted in either a shrug or sigh. One broad paw touched the pillar beside him, thorn-claws gouging the stone. "Beauty is…a challenge. It pushes up through winter earth and unfurls into a flower. It chases the nighttime away with a glorious sunrise. Beauty reaches out and puts its fingers around your heart."

My own heart thudded, and I couldn't help but press my hands there, eyes fluttering down. I warmed all over and became incensed with myself. How dare I appreciate such a compliment from my jailer!

I didn't wait to learn why he'd called me, but charged outside.

XI

One night I asked, "How long will you keep me here?"

He said, "Until you break the curse."

"Curse!" I spat. "Open the gate. Let me go."

"I cannot. It isn't the part I'm allowed."

"And what, then, *sir,* is your part?"

"Will you marry me, Beauty?"

"Why would I do that?" I left, but hid in a deep recess in the hall, where a statue of a frolicking faun took up most of the space. The Beast passed, silent, but in that rolling gait caused by mismatched feet. I traced his progress, following soft and evenly behind him. Up the staircase he went, past the library and past the hall of mirrors, to a tower stair much like the one I'd first been dragged through. I paused at the bottom, for he would know I came now.

The constant anger simmering deep in my stomach popped, effervescing up my chest and neck, making me drunk with it. I put a foot on the first step, and the next. The soft slippers whispered against bare stone. Once the hall light faded it was dark as a moonless night, for the Beast tolerated no candles. *Does light hurt your eyes?* I had asked him, and he'd replied, *It hurts yours.* I skimmed a hand along the cool wall as I ascended.

At least three stories up, the stairs widened, opening doorlessly into a landing. It was circular and lit only by the starlight that soaked the milky glass of the tall windows. Bare of furniture, the room contained only a rug and plain patterned tapestries hanging between the windows. A soft yellow glow beckoned me through a doorway with several stones pried out of its arch. The Beast had destroyed it in order to fit his immense shoulders through.

It delighted a smile to the corners of my mouth.

I paused in the broken doorway, leaning into one of the deep gouges. Beyond, a single candle hung in a chandelier with spaces for twenty. Books were piled along the walls, many torn, and a wardrobe pressed against one side, doors hanging wide to reveal large jackets poorly sewn together. There were metal measuring cups, a magnifying glass, beakers and delicate scales waiting on a table, smelling sharp and pungent. A neat nest of mattress and blankets was tucked into one corner beneath an open window. Stars glittered distantly.

Unlike in my lovely room, there were no mirrors or vases of flowers here, no tea set or fine armoire. Several wine bottles perched atop various stacks of the books.

"Beauty," he rumbled with clear surprise.

I turned my eyes on his, tilting back my head because he stood so near. Strangly uneven wire spectacles brightened his eyes, strapped in place with a ribbon tied all around his head. Magnified, his eyes shone deep blue like the midnight sky around the moon, black pupils gaping wide.

I braced for his anger at my trespass—finally he would be angry at me! We could properly fight, could scream and tear and maybe find some answers.

But he said nothing more. Only studied me in my fine dinner gown, all dawn-pink and cream that complemented the new pallor of my skin. In the mirror every morning I sneered at the paleness overtaking my once sun-kissed cheeks. No matter how much time I spent in the garden, this place sapped the life out of me.

The lichen tugging at his face twisted in some expression, yet I could still not read him.

"Why aren't you afraid of me?" he finally said.

"I want you to threaten." I put my hands on his thick

chest and shoved. He budged not at all. "I want you to roar,"
I yelled.

His hands circled my wrists, those sharp thorns pricking
through the silk sleeves. "I won't."

"Because you don't have to," I whispered, slumping. His
grip on my arms held my body up, but not my eyelids. I closed
them, drooping like a thirsty flower. I'd asked him tonight,
What is your part? And he'd proposed. If that was his part,
what was mine? To agree? And then I would still be his, still
a prisoner, but of my own making. I snapped open my eyes.
"I'm yours forever, no matter what I feel, no matter what I
want. But I won't fear you. I won't love you, Beast. I won't
think of you at all."

He released me so suddenly I stumbled and knocked into
the wall. A cry, soft as a dove's, echoed in my ears, but it
could not have been him—my Beast surely could not make
so pitiful a sound.

I tripped out of his room and ran down the stairs so hard
my ankles jarred and I bruised my elbow against the dark
curving wall.

XII

The Beast made it easy for me, in his own way. He continued to join me in the rose garden, but didn't follow when
I chose the topiary forest. I refused to enter the dining room,
and he sent the ghosts to my rooms with my dinner. Days
passed when I didn't go to the roses at all. I looked around
corners and up at darkened windows but never saw him, except once, when I found him studying a caterpillar's cocoon

so closely, with such concentration, he did not notice me. He did not move for nearly an hour, and neither did I, uncomfortably aware that this was what he did all day: study and stare, like a piece of nature himself. With the patience of moss.

I had no such patience.

But I could not stop thinking of his. How long had he been here, waiting and studying? I could not stop thinking of him here, alone.

The library felt cavernous now that I'd seen his intimate piles of books. The gardens were a wilderness without his silent shadow. As I tried to fill my days, instead my thoughts fled in every direction, leaving me with nothing but emptiness. If I didn't talk to myself in the mirror, I heard no voices but for the nonsense whispers of my ghosts.

I insisted to myself it did not matter. I did not need my jailer.

Twice more I attempted to scale the wall. I hunted for a ladder and found nothing. I thought to build a barricade, but the wind itself worked against me. And so I climbed barehanded. Twice I broke my finely manicured nails, twice I ended in a furious, crying heap.

And after that I did not even have tears.

XIII

The nights were oh so very long, and I left my bedroom in the middle of them to prowl the halls of the castle. I discovered sitting rooms, and fireplaces that could roast a horse. I found the kitchens and old servant stairs, the attic room where I'd spent my first two nights. I never went back to the Beast's tower.

Sometimes I sank onto a fainting couch or leaned against a cool hearth to sleep until the ghosts woke me at dawn with trailing, teasing fingers.

The mirror gallery became my favorite. I could go there and waltz down the center, my reflections surrounding me like a crowd. I hummed and lifted my arms, curtsied at myself and at imaginary partners. I giggled at made-up jokes and flirted; I threw back my head and loosened my hair and lifted my skirts around my knees for a raucous peasant jig.

And I stopped, staring at my wild self, breathing heavily in the mirror. A mad girl with her hair tumbling around her face, her lips flushed and shoes missing. She'd been led away by the faeries into an unending dance, and if she didn't wake up she'd die. Too young, too alone.

Nobody would remember her.

XIV

I dressed with great care the following evening—a peacock-green dress like a duchess, hair up and tucked with a feather and golden comb. I accepted emeralds and topaz jewelry from the invisible hands and let them slide heavy earrings into my lobes. They dabbed red onto my mouth and deep silver onto my eyelids, rouge on my cheeks.

And I swept down to the dining room just as the nightly gong rang throughout the castle.

The Beast stood beside his chair, and one arm shifted as if he thought to welcome me.

I stood across the long table, chin lifted. "Good evening, Beast," I said in a cracking voice.

A sigh like ocean wind ruffled the room and he said, "Good evening, Beauty."

He lumbered around the table to my chair and pulled it back for me to sit. I sank down, relief shaking my knees, and settled my hands elegantly in my lap as he pushed my chair into place.

The smell of vines and rose petals, of old earth and musty leaves, filled my nose and I realized I hadn't missed only company. I'd missed *him*.

XV

"Must I stay here forever?" I asked him in the center of the rose garden, seated on a curved stone bench with no room for his bulk.

"I don't know," he answered immediately, one hand cupping a heavy purple rosebud. The petal tips promised bloody-red.

I crossed my arms and leaned back in a slouch. "How can you not know, oh Master of the Castle?"

He was silent so long I pursed my lips, ready to change the subject to something more pleasant—beheadings, perhaps, or the bond market. But he crouched down so the quilted jacket he wore billowed strangely around his bulk, and said, "I did not create the rose that brought you here, Beauty. Nor the high wall."

On my feet, I swept to him. This way, me standing, him crouching, our eyes were nearly level. I studied his face.

In the sunlight his pupils contracted like a lion's, and the twisted green skin ran in frozen rivulets over his wide nose. Every thorn that erupted from his cheekbones glinted sharply. The bright lichen pulled at his mouth. Those ivory tusks gleamed. I reached out with a finger and touched the tip of one. Beast did not even breathe. The ivory was smooth, almost warm. Understanding grew inside me and I felt an utter fool for never thinking it before.

"You're a prisoner, too," I whispered.

"I earned my sentence." Beast's breath tickled my wrist and I slowly pulled my hand away.

XVI

Knowing Beast wasn't my jailer was like removing a layer or armor. If it wasn't him, he wasn't my enemy. He was my silent, horrid companion.

"Will you tell me everything?"

He scratched at the lichen on his cheek. He tapped his cloven foot onto the stone floor. He said painfully, as if dragging every word through fire, "I can...try to...answer...questions. Specific questions. But not...put words to...the...whole."

I asked him everything I could think of.

"Is this a curse?"

Yes.

"What are the ghosts?"

Ghosts.

"How does the magic work?"

How does the sun work?

"Why are you a Beast? What were you before?

"How do I break it?

"How do I set both of us free?"

To a few he gave half answers, and I learned to recognize the slow blink of his heavy eyelids as evidence the enchantment kept him from replying in full. To most, he shook his head sadly. Instead of letting loose my frustration, I asked something different.

"What is your favorite book?"

"Do you like dry or sweet wine?"

Things that were easy to answer, nothing to do with magic.

He would tell me, *"Durid's Theory of Nature"* and *"dry wine."* He brought me a tattered copy of the former to the rose garden one morning, and I read pieces from it, though my interest in scientific ideas had never reached great heights. But Beast, he explained what I read in quiet, simple terms, plucking a leaf to demonstrate or bending to draw diagrams in the pebbles. When he finished, if I understood, I'd take the stick from his paw and draw a smiling face.

The Beast couldn't smile around the lichen and tusks and fangs.

At night, he continued to finish dinner with his own constant question. "Will you marry me, Beauty?"

"Why do you ask, Beast?" I replied once, flattening my palms on either side of my sauce-streaked dessert plate.

He struggled, I saw, to keep his eyes on mine across the distance of the long table. But he made no reply. And I knew the answer.

"No, Beast," I whispered, and left.

XVII

Outside the castle grounds it was deep winter. Through the iron gates I could see ice-crusted trees and drifting snow. It obscured the road, kept animals huddled in their nests and burrows. But inside the wall the snow melted into rain, and the roses bloomed.

I stood at the gates and gripped the bars until my hands were as cold as the metal. They ached to the bones but I refused to put on mittens. I needed that pain; that icy fire shot up my arms to my heart, kept me from becoming complacent.

XVIII

I taught Beast to play cards. We used silverware for wagers; knives were worth the most, then forks, spoons, dessert spoons, salad forks, butter knives. Once he learned the basics, he defeated me easily because his game face was so impossible to penetrate. He pitied me sometimes, and left me with a knife or two, until I laughingly yelled at him to stop it, to take his winnings from me. It all belonged to him anyway.

So we whiled away the winter darkness.

I grew used to touching him, to the shock of hard bark under the cloth of his jacket instead of flesh. To the prick of his thorn-claws. To the musty smell of his vinelike tangled hair.

And I wondered myself why I'd never been afraid of him. I'd been overwhelmed and fascinated when I first beheld his monstrosity. But not afraid. Perhaps I'd been too furious, too desperate for fear.

Maybe because he was so clearly made of natural things. Tumbled together by magic, certainly, but he was earth and trees and flowers and all the beasts of the wild.

Once he caught me staring, and his mouth moved into what I perceived to be a grimace. I caught one of his hands with both of mine and held him before me. "My answer isn't because I don't...care."

"Your answer?"

But he knew what question I meant.

I ran outside, straight down the white pebble road to the iron gates. Snow melted before me, pelting the earth like rain, pitter-patter, and two thin squirrels froze in their dashing to stare back at me. I tore at the gate, throwing all my weight into it, but it never budged.

The Beast joined me.

"What do you miss so very much, outside those black gates?" he asked, behind me like a shield, like a mountain.

I shut my eyes and pressed my forehead to the bars. A shiver racked my body, for I'd run here without a coat. What did I miss? Not my father. Not parties that lasted all night, or the silk sheets slightly less fine than the ones I slept on now. But my sisters and a few acquaintances in the village we'd moved to after Father's catastrophe, who might one day have become friends. My garden, so gaunt and bare and nothing like the magnificence behind me. Watching the sun set after a long day sewing and cooking and stirring butter, knowing I owed only myself for the food on my table.

"I did not choose to be here," I whispered finally. "I've never chosen my place, but been dragged by my father everywhere. Even if I might—might have been able to be happy here, how can I ever be, when I did not choose it?"

A heavy hand settled briefly against my head. As soon as I realized he touched me, his hand slid down my hair, thorns combing through.

I shivered again, though less from cold.

XIX

That night when he asked me to marry him, for the first time I considered it.

But it would be only the illusion of choice.

XX

I stood in the center of the rose garden and tore at the red roses.

Gloves only protected my hands at first. Soon the canvas shredded and my skin with it. My fingers were slick with blood, but I found every last red rose and destroyed it. When the pain numbed my hands and I could barely move them, I resorted to ripping apart the flowers themselves. Petals stuck to me, glued in place with blood.

The Beast found me, and cried out, a strangled roar.

He grabbed me, wrapping his arms around me so I was trapped, and lifted me up and away. "Beauty!" he roared again, and then, "Beauty..." more sadly. I wilted in his arms, blood printing his chest and arms, filling my nose and mouth.

Inside, he set me beside the fire and went for bandages and water. With his large, clumsy hands, he mopped up blood and broken petals. They released sweet perfume, their red-ness merging with my blood. He shook his head again and again as he wrapped my hands.

Finally, as I balanced a mug of hot tea in my lap, able to grab it only with both hands, as clumsy as him now, the Beast asked, "Why?"

"I thought it might free us."

He snorted impatiently.

I reached up and touched one of the petals clinging to his hair as they always did.

XXI

My hands healed as the springtime grew.

I watched the process in the mirror gallery, as gashes scabbed over, as they grew thinner, closed up, turned pink and puckered, lining my hands as though my bones had been sewn together with uneven stitches. Like the Beast's coats.

In the mirror, I was wild. Wild as I'd been dancing, but as I stared I didn't see a lost girl; I saw a beast. Wild like nature is wild; tangled hair, scarred hands, heavy garden boots, a tattered hem on an otherwise beautiful velvet dress. I smiled and my teeth were strong and straight, not fangs, but when I turned my smile to a growl, they were dangerous.

I wanted to show him, and whirled to run through the walls, yelling his name until it echoed off the high stone ceiling.

He waited in the grand entryway, blue tapestries behind him like the sky.

"Beauty, now that your hands have healed, come with me," he said.

I opened my mouth to tell him, *No, come with me!* But he reached out his hand and I slid mine into it, scars against fur, scars made by rose thorns, and his thorn-claws touching them delicately, harmlessly.

Together we walked out to the wall beside the black iron gate.

"Reach your hands up," Beast said, and amused, I did, remembering in a flash the first escape while rain pelted me, washing the entire world away.

He lifted me by the waist until my hands found the top stone. I gasped, and he boosted me higher. I climbed onto the wall, crouching there, halfway between the castle grounds and the freedom of the forest.

Wind hit my face, warm with springtime, and birds sang loudly now—I hadn't heard such a song in months! I laughed.

But the Beast sighed. It was so soft, if I weren't attuned to him so finely now, I'd have thought it a breath of the same wind teasing my hair.

I looked down at him. He said nothing. My smiles and laughter fell away as I realized what he'd done.

I was free.

My stomach dropped. I curled my scarred fingers into fists. "You could have always done this!" I cried. "Any day or night you could have lifted me up here!"

"Yes," he said. Red petals fell from his hair as the wind blew.

"Why didn't you?"

"I am desperate for you to stay."

Am. Am. Am. It beat in my heart. "But you've done it now," I whispered. I turned away from him to look out over the forest toward the city. Toward my village and sisters and decrepit little garden. I could leave anytime. He could boost me over this wall anytime! Now, or tomorrow, or the next day. But if I leaped down and away, however would I climb back in?

I would want to climb back in.

I would *choose* to climb back in.

Lowering myself carefully to sit on the wall with my feet dangling down against the castle side, I smiled at the Beast. "Thank you," I said fervently, for he had given me my choice.

"I will miss you, Beauty," he said. "If you— If you would think of me, sometimes, I would—like that."

"I will think of you every day, Beast."

Perhaps that twist of his mouth around the tusks was a smile.

But I still didn't move. "What will happen to you if I go?"

"If?" he whispered.

I waited. After a moment, staring up at me, he shook his head. "I do not know if anything will happen."

"What if you come with me?" I held down my hand as if to pull him up—as if I had that sort of strength.

With an awkward but powerful shove, he leaped onto the wall, catching himself with his claws. He swayed as he found balance, then knelt a few paces from me. His pupils narrowed as he looked toward freedom.

Excitement shivered through me, and I laughed. But it cut short when I saw the lichen pulling down the side of his face flake away. He trembled.

"Get back down!" I cried.

His dark blue eyes found mine and one of his tusks cracked.

He fell more than jumped, landing hard on his knees. I scrambled down.

When I touched him he did not flinch, for his breath rattled like winter branches. I remained, an arm spread as far around his hunched shoulders as it would go, until he was ready to walk slowly back inside the castle.

XXII

"I will not leave without breaking this curse," I said firmly as we shared dinner that night.

He stopped in his eating—he'd begun to pick at the easy things the castle shared with me; meat and cheeses, things he could pluck up with his claws and drop into his mouth. The Beast said, though it was early for it, "Will you love me, Beauty? Will you marry me?"

Standing fast, I paced away, my back to him, mind abuzz. Did I love him? Could I marry him? Was that the only way?

I remembered the moment his tusk had cracked, and my heart cracked, too. I remembered the sound of his knees slamming into the earth.

I loved him. I could not leave if it killed him. Or hurt him, or even just left him the same: alone, waiting, watching.

I stopped pacing, with my hands on my face. My scarred hands. I imagined caressing the rough lichen on his chin, gently kissing the thorns that pierced his cheekbones. What would his hands feel like against my back? Under that coat, where was fur and where bark? It was too much—too much.

As a coward, I fled.

XXIII

Because he is not a coward, he found me in the mirror gallery.

Positioning himself at my side instead of behind as he usually did, the Beast studied his reflection. "I understand."

"Will you dance with me?" I asked in a small voice, a little girl's plea.

The Beast bowed and we waltzed, slow and ungainly down the hall. His shadowy form flashed in the mirrors, reflecting again and again, with me as little bursts of bright hair, of pale silk. I closed my eyes and found the rhythm of his mismatched feet, and slid a hand under his coat, to the place I guessed his heart would be. He was soft as moss, cool as a mountain. I stepped in closer and breathed his smell.

Keeping hold of one hand, I led him outside the castle once more, and to the wall. Without having to ask, he boosted me up again, until I stood atop it, under the silver moon.

Turning as if still dancing, I said, "Ask me again."

"Don't make me."

"Do you love me, Beast?"

He opened his arms.

I leaped off the great wall and into the sky, knowing he would catch me.

THE
BROTHERS
PIGGETT

by Julie Kagawa

This is a story about a boy in love.

Once upon a time, there was a lad named Percival Piggett. Percival lived in a small, unnamed village on the edge of a forest. The forest beside the village was called The Haunted Wood and, according to suspicion, was home to all kinds of evil spirits—ghosts, goblins and the like. It was used in many an old wives' warning tale: don't go into the forest lest you be eaten by a wild beast, or fall under an evil spell, or become lost forever.

Percival didn't care about the forest, though. He was too busy being in love.

The object of his affection, a girl named Maya Thornton, was a newcomer to the village and lived with her grandmother in a small hut at the edge of the woods. Her grandmother was a kooky old bat, reclusive and eccentric, and many in the village whispered that she was a witch.

Percival didn't care about Maya's grandmother, either.

Though he really should have.

The problem with Percival was that he was painfully shy, and not a little on the chubby side. This couldn't really be helped, as he did work in his brothers' bakery and pie shop, and was subject to a host of tempting sweets every day. Piggett Pies was famous throughout the village, and Percival's two brothers, Pedro and Peter, were constantly telling him he needed to eat more. "Some meat on your bones would do you good!" Peter was fond of saying before shoving a meat pie under Percival's nose. He'd then thump his own impressive bulk and grin through his triple chins. "The ladies like a bigger man."

"If we don't look after you, who will?" Pedro would often add, usually when Percival insisted that he really didn't need a fourth slice of pie. "After Mama died and Papa ran off with that witch, we swore we'd take care of you."

And so it went, with Percival getting bigger and bigger, which in turn made him shyer and shyer. When his brothers made him go up front and help the customers, he'd stammer terribly, which made some villagers believe he was a little slow. Most began to treat him like a not-so-bright toddler, with pitying looks and patronizing smiles, but some of the crueler village boys began picking on him.

"Piggy Piggy!" they'd call when Percival left the shop for the day. "Percival Piggy, on his way home!"

Percival would only smile benignly and trot home as fast as he could, but his tormentors would follow him to his little house with its thatched straw roof and shout insults through the door until he was curled up on his bed in tears.

One morning, they were waiting for him when he left his

home for work, and trailed him all the way back to the shop, squealing and throwing mud balls that spattered against his apron.

Shaking with tears, Percival ducked inside the bakery, hoping to clean up before any of his brothers noticed. It was not to be. Peter took one look at him and turned a violent red.

"What happened?" he bellowed, bringing Pedro out from the back. Both brothers glowered at Percival like enraged twin bulls, though their anger was not directed at him. "Who did this to you?" Peter demanded, all his chins quivering with fury. "No one hurts my little brother like that. Tell me their names, right now!"

Percival sniffled. "I d–don't know their names," he stammered, futilely trying to rake mud from his straw-colored hair. "Just some v-village boys playing around. It's n-n-nothing."

"Nothing," Pedro growled, narrowing his beady black eyes. He shared a glance with Peter, who nodded grimly. "We'll see if it's nothing."

That evening, as they had done countless nights before, the boys followed Percival home. Percival, his arms overloaded with bread and pies Peter insisted he take home, ignored the jeers and cries of "Piggy Piggy Percival!" as best he could. In a fit of depression, he ate all the pies and most of the bread his brother sent home with him, and went to bed feeling slightly sick.

The next morning, however, the boys were gone. Percival didn't see them all day, and when he left work, they weren't waiting for him outside the shop per normal. Peter had given him a stack of small meat pies to take home, and Percival arrived at his house unharried. The pies that evening were even more savory than usual, and he went to sleep feeling full and quite content with life in general.

For the next few weeks, a search party was launched for the group of boys that disappeared from the village that night, but they were never found.

The first time Maya Thornton came into the pie shop, Percival was in the back, helping clean out the ovens. He heard the brass bell above the door jingle and, because it was early, thought it was old Mrs. Crabapple come in for her weekly loaf of bread. Peter had his head halfway in one of the cold ovens and Pedro was covered in flour all the way to his elbows, so Percival dusted soot from his hands and went up front to help the cranky widow.

A girl stood in the center of the room, her back to him, gazing around the store curiously. Percival caught a quick glance of long black hair tumbling down her back, and a deep green dress like the fancy ladies in town wore. She carried a basket in one hand, and was spinning in slow circles, taking everything in, when Percival emerged from the back room.

"Hello," said Percival, wiping his hands on his apron as he came out, not quite noticing his customer yet. "W-welcome to Piggett Pies. How may I help you—"

The girl turned just as he raised his head, and the words froze in his throat.

Percival had seen pretty girls before, even lusted after them from afar. But he acknowledged that the ladies in town would not be interested in a poor, fat, stuttering baker boy, and he was far too shy to approach any of them.

This was different. The moment the girl turned around,

flashing a pair of the biggest green eyes he'd ever seen, Percival was struck mute. She was perfect. Gorgeous. Lovely. The girl of his dreams, only he hadn't known it until now. He could only stare, wide-eyed and dumbstruck. It was also the first time he wanted to say something, to at least introduce himself, but he couldn't make a sound.

"Hello?" the girl said, smiling—smiling—at him. "I'm so sorry. I didn't see you there." Brushing back a strand of ebony hair, she stepped forward. "I'm Maya Thornton. I just moved into my grandmother's house a few days ago—she lives in a hut at the edge of the forest. It's nice to meet you, Mr....?"

Percival still couldn't speak. Words rose to mind—his name, *good morning, I love you*—but he couldn't seem to force anything past his lips. The girl frowned, giving him a worried look. "Are you all right? You've gone rather pale. Are you sick?"

Fortunately, Peter came out of the back room then, wiping off his hands. Seeing Percival standing rock-still, staring at the beautiful girl across the counter, he swiftly took charge of the situation.

"Percival, there you are! Pedro is moving some crates in the back—be a good lad and help him, will you?" He clapped Percival on the shoulder, hard, and Percival jumped. "Go on, boy. I'll take care of our customer."

Dazed, Percival tottered into the back room, knocking over a stack of pie tins as he did, his mind whirling with images of Maya Thornton.

For the rest of the afternoon, Percival couldn't concentrate. He tripped over himself constantly. He added salt into the pies instead of sugar. He dropped a bag of flour on Pedro's head from the top shelf, getting it everywhere and making his brother look like some kind of yeti emerging from the snow.

"Dammit, Percival!" Pedro bellowed, shaking flour from his beard. "First salt in the fruit pies and now this. Where's your head today, boy?"

"Sorry," Percival mumbled just as Peter poked his head through the door frame with a laugh.

"Go easy on our little brother, Pedro," Peter called, grinning through his thick beard. "He can't help it. The boy's in love."

Percival's face reddened even further, but he couldn't deny it. Peter guffawed and ducked back out, and Pedro sighed, brushing off his sleeves. Percival silently stepped down from the ladder to help clean up.

"Who is she?" Pedro asked, tossing Percival a broom to sweep the drifts of flour spreading across the floor. Percival took the broom, reluctant to talk about it but knowing his brothers would pester him all day until he shared.

"Maya Thornton," he replied, blushing even at the thought of her. "She's perfect, Pedro. She has eyes like emeralds and hair like black silk, and her smile…" He trailed off, unaware that he was gazing dreamily at the corner, until Pedro barked a laugh.

"Rat's whiskers, listen to you! You sound like a soft-headed poet staring into the clouds." Percival blushed and started briskly sweeping the floor as Pedro picked up the burst flour bag. "Thornton," he muttered, balling it up in his powerful hands. "Why does that name sound familiar? Where does this girl live?"

"With her grandmother on the edge of the forest."

"The witch!" Pedro straightened, which made Percival jump, sending his carefully swept flour pile curling over the floor again. "I knew that name was familiar! So, the evil old bat has a granddaughter, eh?" He frowned at Percival, eyebrows bristling. "I don't know if I like the idea of you being sweet on a witch's spawn."

"She's not a witch," Percival protested. "You didn't see her! She was beautiful, and gentle, and kind—"

"Witches can look like anything they want," Pedro interrupted. "You're young, you don't know the danger. You don't know what they're capable of." At Percival's crestfallen look, his expression softened. "I'm not saying you shouldn't see the girl," he explained kindly. "Just be careful. If she hurts you, or if you see anything strange, come tell us right away. Can you do that?"

"Yes."

Pedro nodded and ruffled Percival's hair, sending flour raining to the floor. "That's a good lad. We're only looking out for our youngest, you know. If we don't look after you, who will?"

He left the room, leaving Percival to dream about Maya in peace.

Over the next few days, Maya came into the shop every morning, as lovely and graceful as ever. And every day, Percival would hide in the back, peering through the door and trying to gather the courage to go up and talk to her. The few times she spotted him through the frame, she would smile and wave, and Percival would blush like a tomato and duck out of sight, cursing himself for being such a coward.

After several days of this, Peter got impatient.

"This is ridiculous," he growled after finding Percival in the back room again, huddled behind a wheat barrel. "I've watched you cringe and skulk like a rodent whenever that girl comes in long enough. Get out there and say something to her."

Percival paled. "I can't! What would I say? I c-can't even talk straight when I m-meet a stranger."

"You'll think of something." Peter grabbed the back of his shirt and hauled him away from the wall. Percival yelped and protested, to little effect. "You can't expect her to reciprocate your feelings if she doesn't even know you're there," his brother continued ruthlessly. "Just start with your name and go from there."

With a final heave, Peter shoved him out the door.

To come face-to-face with Maya.

"Er," Percival squeaked as the girl blinked and stepped back, eyes wide. "Um," he went on, glancing back at the door. Peter stood in the frame with his arms crossed, so escape was impossible unless he fled the store itself. But then he would be so embarrassed he could never face Maya again. This might be his only chance.

Gathering his courage, Percival turned back to the girl. "Uh, h-hello," he stammered, dropping his gaze. "I…I… That is…"

Maya smiled. "Hello, Percival," she replied, making him glance up in shock. She knew his name! "I asked about you the first day I came in," the girl continued. "I hope I didn't offend you in any way."

"No!" Percival shook his head quickly. "No, you d-didn't do anything. I…I j-just…um." He closed his eyes, thinking calm thoughts, the way she smiled at him that very first day. "I'm s-sorry I ran out on you like that," he said, meeting her gaze. "I've w-w-wanted to talk to you ever since but I haven't had the chance."

"Well." Maya cocked her head at him. "Now you do."

They talked for a goodly while. Occasionally, Percival would get nervous and stutter, but Maya never seemed to notice. Eventually, Pedro stuck his head into the room and yelled for Percival to get back to work, and Maya excused herself, saying her grandmother was waiting for her.

"I'll come back tomorrow," she promised, smiling in a way that made Percival's legs weak. "Goodbye, Percival. I'm glad I finally got to meet you."

"Goodbye," Percival whispered, and stared out the door for several minutes until Pedro smacked the back of his skull and shoved a mop into his hands, ordering him to the back room.

She did come back tomorrow. And the day after that. Sometimes, she would just smile and say hello, claiming her grandmother was expecting her back quickly. Sometimes, however, they staked out a corner of the shop and talked for many long minutes, while Pedro and Peter helped customers and shook their heads in resignation. And with every passing day, Percival fell more and more in love with her. Though he could never get up the nerve to tell her, or even ask her on a date. Instead, he baked pies especially for her, and always had one waiting when she entered the shop. And she always smiled and said they were the best things she had ever eaten.

His brothers watched these developments with a combination of amusement and concern, with Peter telling him to throw the young lady over his shoulder and cart her into the broom closet already, and Pedro reminding him to be careful. Pretty girls, he explained, were cunning, devious creatures. They were notorious for playing coy, stringing you along until the day they broke your heart. His warnings fell on deaf ears, however, as Percival's world began to revolve around the times Maya Thornton came into the shop.

And then, one gray, dismal morning, she didn't come in.

At first, Percival thought she was just a few minutes late. Perhaps she'd stopped at the fruit stall on her way there. Perhaps she'd forgotten her umbrella and had returned home to get it, as the sky did look rather ominous out the window. But as minutes ticked into hours, and Percival's gaze lingered more and more on the front door of the shop, it became obvious that Maya wasn't coming.

He moped his way through the afternoon, shuffling from task to task like a sleepwalker, barely aware of his surroundings. He felt like the day outside—gray, dismal, sullen. Maya had become his ray of sunshine every morning, and without her, his world had gone dark.

Peter finally gave him a good whack to the back of the head, bringing him out of his sulk.

"For Fred's sake!" he exploded as Percival winced and rubbed his abused skull. "You're worse than useless today, pining after that lass. Here." Shoving a basket of pies into his hands, he pointed him toward the door. "Go find your girl. Tell her what you've been dying to tell her ever since she came in. Don't give me that look," he continued as Percival stared at him in horror. "Time to man up, boy. If you don't snatch her while you can, someone else will. Now go."

He gave him a push toward the frame. Percival, clutching

the basket of pies, stumbled out the door and into the cloudy afternoon.

He was torn between dragging his feet to the witch's hut and hurrying there as fast as he could, which resulted in his tripping over himself a great deal. Overhead, sullen clouds blotted the sky, and thunder growled ominously in the distance. Percival didn't pay much attention to his surroundings, however, too busy thinking of what he would say to Maya when he finally found her.

Maya, I…love you. I've been in love with you from the day you entered the shop. When I see you, I can't think of anything except how beautiful you are, and how you were kind to a fat, shy shop boy even though you had no reason to be. I don't expect you could ever really fall for someone like me, but if you returned even a fraction of my feelings, it would make me the happiest person in the world.

It sounded elegant in his head, but when he tried to say it aloud he stuttered and tripped over the words, and ended up feeling like a fool.

He was thinking of turning around, calling off this insane quest entirely, when he suddenly realized he had arrived at the edge of the forest. And directly in front of him stood a house.

Percival shivered. Like most of the villagers, he avoided the Haunted Wood whenever possible. Not that he believed all the rumors and suspicion swirling around the evil forest, but it was better to be safe than sorry. This was actually the first time he'd stood at its borders, the closest he had ever been to the thick, tangled woods, and it gave him chills. As did the run-down shack at the forest's edge.

For a second, he almost went back, almost turned and hurried away from this place as fast as his stubby legs would take him. He was afraid of the witch, yes, but that wasn't the only thing that kept him from approaching the door and rapping on its gnarled surface.

What if the witch is there? Will she turn me into a toad? Would Maya protect me? What if Maya isn't home? Or, worst of all… What if she is, and when I tell her how I feel, she laughs in my face?

He struggled with himself a moment longer, then took a deep breath. He'd come this far. No point in turning back now.

Gripping the basket handle tightly in one hand, he edged up to the door and rapped softly on the surface.

A few minutes passed. The hut was silent. Percival was about to give up and go home, when the door swung inward with an ear-splitting creak, and he was suddenly face-to-face with the witch.

She was old, that much was certain. The lines and grooves along her withered skin looked carved out with a hatchet, and her crooked nose jutted a few inches away from her face, a prominent wart on the tip. But her hair was midnight-black like Maya's, though pulled into a severe bun, and her eyes burned a brilliant green as she stared at Percival, the corners of her thin lips pulled into a frown.

"Eh?" she rasped, glaring at the boy in front of her. Her voice was like a rusty blade over glass. "Who are you? What do you want? Come to see the scary old witch, eh, boy? Maybe throw rocks at her windows or torment her cat?"

"N-n-no!" Percival stammered, suddenly terrified. "I j-just came to see M-M-Maya. Is she h-here?"

The witch narrowed her eyes to green slits. "You must be that boy she keeps talking about. Percival Piggett, eh? Your evil brothers don't like me very much—that Pedro Piggett once threatened to burn down my hut if I ever went near you, did you know that?" Percival felt his heart constrict with fear that the old woman knew who he was, but she only snorted and raised a gnarled claw to the woods. "Eh, it doesn't matter. Maya is down by the lake, that way. Just take the path until you see the water. If you hurry, you should catch her."

"Th-thank you," Percival whispered, and hurried away, feeling the piercing green eyes of the witch follow him into the woods.

He found the path, cutting through the trees in the direction the witch had pointed, and followed it, his heart pounding in his chest. Thick, tangled trees pressed in on him from every side, clawed branches shutting out what little light there was. The forest was eerily silent; no birds sang, no small creatures scurried through the brush. And yet, Percival thought he felt eyes upon him the farther he ventured into the foreboding woods.

At last, he saw a glimmer of water through the trees, and began to run, clutching the basket tightly as he did. As he drew closer, he caught a flash of color by the water's edge, the shimmer of a bright dress, and his heart leaped with excitement. She was here! She was here, and he would finally tell her what he felt, and she would tell him she felt the same. And then...

The trees fell away. Percival stumbled from the woods, into the open.

And stopped.

There were two figures down by the water's edge, standing very close. They hadn't seen him yet, and Percival ducked behind a tree, peering out at the pair by the lake. One of the figures was Maya; he could see the tumble of black hair down her back, the bright blue dress she wore today. The other...

Percival's gut clenched painfully. The other was a boy from the village. Isaac, the miller's son. He'd seen him many times when his brothers sent him to buy wheat for the shop, but the two boys never spoke much beyond "good morning." He was a big lad, two years older than Percival, with dark hair, strapping muscles from a life of working the mill and a square, honest face.

That face hovered very close to Maya's now. As Percival watched, frozen behind a tree, Isaac leaned in, one hand rising to her cheek, and kissed her.

An icy shaft plunged into Percival's heart. The basket dropped from his limp fingers, rolling into the grass, but he didn't notice. All he could see was Isaac and the girl he loved, their figures silhouetted against the bright gleam of the lake, pressed together in a passionate kiss.

His throat closed up, and his eyes watered, becoming blurry and dim. With a strangled cry, Percival turned and fled the forest, barely seeing the path at his feet, and didn't stop until he reached his house. Flinging himself into bed, he pulled the covers over himself and sobbed into his pillow, feeling the icy dagger in his heart slice it into a million pieces.

He didn't go into the shop the next morning, but lay curled under his blanket all afternoon, feeling like nothing he did mattered now. The pain in his chest wouldn't go away, nor did the stubborn tears that leaked from his eyes every time he thought of Maya. Maya, the girl he loved. Who would never love him back. Who had lied to him, strung him along, all this time. She was probably laughing at him right now, or maybe she and Isaac were lying together somewhere, talking about the poor gullible fat boy who dared to love a beautiful girl.

He could never go back to the shop with her around, that was certain.

That evening, there was a pounding at his door. Percival was too heartsick to get up to answer it, and put a pillow over his head to muffle the noise. A moment later there was a crash, and Peter stomped into the room, followed closely by Pedro.

"Percival!" Peter's shout made Percival's ears ring, and he buried his head farther into the pillow. Abruptly it was snatched away, and he winced, blinking up at his older brother's worried face.

"You never came to the shop this morning," Peter said, tossing the pillow on the floor. "What happened, lad? Are you sick?"

"Go away," Percival muttered, pulling the blanket tighter around himself. "Leave me alone. Let me die, I want to die."

His brothers exchanged a glance. Then Pedro said, in a voice of deadly calm, "The girl. The witch's spawn. She did this, didn't she?" When Percival didn't answer, his voice grew even colder, brooking no argument. "Tell us what happened. Now."

Sniffling, Percival did. He told them about the witch, and going to see Maya at the lake, and her inevitable betrayal with Isaac, the miller's son. "You were right," Percival said, sniffling at Pedro, who listened to all of this in grim silence. "Girls are evil. She was just playing with me all this time. I'll never be able to go back to work with her around, knowing she's just laughing at me inside."

"Don't worry about that," Pedro said, looking at Peter. The other sibling's face was red; he looked ready to explode with rage. "We'll take care of this. Maya Thornton will never set foot in the shop again. Just say the word, little brother, and we'll make it so."

Percival sniffled, wiping his eyes. He thought of Maya, her smile, the kind way she spoke to him. All a lie. She didn't care for him at all, and he couldn't bear the thought of seeing her every day, knowing what he did. Anger burned. He wanted her to pay. He wanted to hurt her like she so casually hurt him.

"I never want to see Maya Thornton again," he murmured.

Pedro nodded. Without another word, he and Peter walked out of the room, closing the door behind them, and left Percival to grieve his lost love in peace.

Maya Thornton never came back to the shop. Percival did, eventually returning to work a few days later, much subdued and still heartsick over his loss. Peter finally came to his home one morning, telling him that Maya Thornton had been banned from the store, and that he'd better get his lazy ass into work the next morning or he would drag it back himself. Knowing his brother did not make idle threats, Percival obeyed.

After the first couple mornings, his heart jumped every time the shop bell tinkled, thinking perhaps that it was Maya. When it wasn't, he found himself both relieved and disappointed. Gradually, however, the relief faded, and yearning slid in to take its place. He missed Maya, he realized. Perhaps he had been hasty in his anger, his assumption that she was playing with his feelings. He wanted to see her again.

When he mentioned this to Pedro, about maybe letting Maya into the shop again, his brother gave a short bark of a laugh and looked at him like he was crazy.

"What? Now you want her back? After what she did to you? Are you a glutton for punishment, boy?" He glowered at Percival under bristling eyebrows. "Didn't you say she was using you?"

"I…uh…might've spoken rashly about that," Percival admitted, feeling his face heat. Shame and guilt settled over him, but he forced the words out. "I…I overreacted. I want to talk to her, at least. Let her explain her side of the story. And…I want to apologize for jumping to conclusions."

"Well, you can't," Pedro said ruthlessly. "Maya Thornton and her witch grandmother finally left town a couple days ago, and good riddance. They're gone, Percival. So you might as well forget about the girl and get back to work. It's for the best."

She's gone? Percival slumped to the floor, feeling his heart squeeze tight. *I'll never see her again,* he thought numbly. *She's gone, and I'll never get to tell her how I really felt. She probably thinks that I hate her now. Oh, Maya, I'm so sorry.*

Grief and shame plagued him the rest of the day. When they finally closed the shop late that night, Percival trudged home, his steps heavy and his heart squeezed in a vise. Maya was gone. The love of his life was gone, and he'd never see her again, never see her smile or hear her laugh. And the worst part of all was knowing he'd brought it on himself.

When he reached his house, his heart skipped a beat for a different reason. The front door was smashed in, hanging off its hinges and splintered beyond repair. Inside, his home had been trashed, things knocked over, torn apart and shredded. Long, deep slashes scarred the walls of his room, looking like the claws of some huge beast.

Percival backed out of his house in a daze, wondering what to do next. Peter's home was a few streets down, not far from where he stood. Maybe he should go there—

A low growl, somewhere above him, made his hair stand on end.

Heart in his throat, Percival looked up.

Something crouched on the thatched roof of his home, an enormous shadow against the night sky. Something huge and black, and obviously inhuman. Piercing green eyes stared down at him from a massive shaggy head, and a long muzzle curled back to reveal wet, shiny fangs as long as his fingers.

The thing threw back its head with a howl that turned his blood to ice, and Percival ran.

He felt, rather than saw, the thing give chase. He could hear it behind him, its low pants and raspy breathing, the rustle of its huge form through the grass and weeds. Percival's eyes blurred with tears of fright, and his legs burned as he fled, gasping, for Peter's home. At one point, he tripped over a stone and went sprawling to the ground, scraping his hands. He risked a glance over his shoulder and saw the creature a few yards away in the darkness, just watching him with blazing green eyes. Toying with him. Panicked, he scrambled upright and fled, as the monster gave another howl and loped into the shadows.

Peter's log cabin came into view, and Percival threw himself at it, crossing the yard and smashing into the front door. "Peter!" he screamed, pounding on the wood. "Peter, let me in! Let me in!"

Footsteps echoed from inside, and the door swung back, revealing Peter's frowning face in the doorway. "Percival?" he questioned as Percival barreled under his arm, slamming the door behind him. Peter turned, still frowning, as Percival scrambled across the room. "What's going on?"

"Peter!" his brother gasped. "Get away from the—"

The door exploded inward. Percival shrieked in terror, as the enormous head of a monstrous wolf came through the wooden barrier like it wasn't there. Wood flew in all directions, splinters and wood chips spiraling through the air. Peter turned, mouth open to shout something, when the huge jaws closed over his head and yanked him outside. Peter gave a startled cry, and then there was silence.

For a moment, Percival couldn't move. He stood there, frozen to the back wall, staring at the place Peter had been a second before. It wasn't real, his mind said frantically. None of this was real. He was having a nightmare where he had just watched his brother be killed right in front of him by a creature that should not exist. He would wake up in just a moment, and everything would be normal.

The porch steps creaked, and the monster wolf appeared in the frame, watching him. Blood dripped from its jaws, spattering the floor, and its muzzle was coated in red. It stared at him with hateful green eyes, and something in that burning glare sent a jolt of recognition through Percival's stomach. He'd seen those eyes, somewhere…

The wolf roared, baring bloodstained teeth, and lunged into the room. Percival screamed and fled to the back, slamming the bedroom door. Flinging himself to the window, he wrenched up the frame, just as the wolf's head erupted through the door, snarling and terrible. With a shriek, Percival dove out the window.

He was halfway through when, to his horror, he became stuck in the frame, and wriggled frantically to get loose. Crying with terror, he slid loose and dropped to the ground just as a huge muzzle clamped onto the sill and tore a chunk from the wooden frame. Leaping to his feet, Percival fled toward the only safe haven he had left: Pedro's brick house on the edge of town.

Either his mind had cracked, or the wolf was definitely toying with him. He would see it sometimes, from the corner of his eye, or he'd catch a glimpse of it between the trees as he fled past. What did it want? Why was it tormenting him like this? He'd figured out that this was no ordinary beast; those eyes were far too intelligent, and filled with a hatred that he'd seen before only in men.

Gasping, nearly sick with exertion, Percival was only a hundred yards from the safety of Pedro's home when something caught his leg and sent him sprawling to the ground. Frantic, he pushed himself to his knees…and stared right into the burning glare of the wolf.

The huge muzzle was just a snap away from his face. He could feel the hot, fetid breath on his cheeks, smell the blood that clung to its fur. His reflection stared back at him from those soulless green eyes, pale and terrified, and as the wolf curled its lip, showing bloodstained teeth, Percival braced himself to die.

A gunshot rang out, booming in the silence, and the wolf jerked sideways with a roar. Pedro stood several yards away, a smoking rifle in his hands, his gaze hard and determined.

"Come on, witch!" he bellowed, firing again, and the wolf howled as blood erupted from its side. "You want me? Here I am! Come and get me! Percival," he yelled as the wolf snarled and leaped away from the youngest brother, "get inside—now! Lock the door, and don't open it for anything, you hear?"

Percival nodded. Scrambling to his feet, he fled the last few yards to the front door of Pedro's home, turning in the frame as one last shot rang out behind him.

Pedro stood his ground, firing away at the wolf, which yelped in pain but kept coming. As the monster creature swept up on him, he dropped the rifle and pulled out a knife, raising it high as the wolf lunged. The blade plunged into the shaggy neck, sinking deep as the wolf bowled him over and buried its teeth into his throat.

Pedro spasmed, his limbs twitching like a jerky puppet's as the wolf tore and savaged his body, sending tendrils of blood curling through the air. Percival watched in the door frame, unable to scream or even make a sound until the vicious mauling came to an end, and the wolf finally looked up.

At him.

Fear jolted him into motion again. As the monster bounded forward, he slammed the thick, reinforced wooden door, threw all the locks and backed away. The wolf hit the entry-way with a resounding crash that rattled the frame, and Percival heard a yelp on the other side. Another crash, but the door held, and a snarl of frustration followed. Try as it might, it couldn't get through.

For the rest of the night, Percival huddled in the master bedroom, listening to the monster prowling outside. Sometimes it would scratch at the shuttered windows, whining. Sometimes it would hurl itself at the door or walls, making the rooms shake, but Pedro's house had been built to withstand the fiercest storms, and held firm.

Finally, near dawn, everything grew very quiet. Percival could no longer hear the beast circling the house, but he didn't dare move. He would stay in this fortress until he was certain the monster wasn't lurking somewhere, just waiting for him to step outside.

Witch, Pedro had shouted right before he died. It made sense now. The great wolf was the witch who lived at the edge of the Haunted Wood. She'd heard what he did to her granddaughter and had come back for revenge. Those burning green eyes, so full of rage and hate, only confirmed it.

She was overreacting a bit, Percival thought numbly, sitting with his knees to his chest on Pedro's bed. After all, Maya had only been told never to come back to the pie shop; it wasn't like they'd driven her out of town. But she was a witch. Perhaps she'd hated them all along, and just needed an excuse to come after them. Thank heavens for Pedro's fear of storms. As long as he stayed inside, the wolf couldn't get to him.

The afternoon sun was high overhead, and Percival, exhausted from his harrowing escape and staying up all night, had started to drift off on Pedro's bed, when there was a knock at the door.

He jerked up, and nearly tumbled off the bed, his heart

slamming in his chest. Was it the wolf? Had it returned? But the tap came again, softer than the crashing of the wolf against the door, and a faint, familiar voice drifted through the walls.

"Percival? Percival, are you there?"

Maya. Percival scrambled out of the bedroom and raced to the door, flinging it open.

And there she was. As beautiful and perfect as ever, though her hair was slightly mussed, and her green eyes were wide with fear.

"Oh, Percival, you're alive! Thank goodness!" Crossing the threshold, she threw herself at Percival and hugged him tightly. Percival froze, every nerve in his body standing at attention, so startled he didn't have the presence of mind to hug her back.

Maya drew away. "I was so worried," she said, her eyes darting over Percival's shoulder to the room beyond. "I have to tell you something, Percival. About...my grandmother. Will you let me come in?"

Percival was fairly certain he knew what she was going to say about her grandmother, but he quickly nodded. "Of course," he said, and Maya smiled, following him through the door. "S-sorry about the mess. It's been...a rough night. I'll make us something to eat."

"No need," Maya said, closing the door after her. "I've already eaten this morning."

"So," Percival began, heading toward the kitchen. So many questions. So many things to say. Where did he begin. "How...how is your grandmother?"

"She's dead."

Percival spun back. Maya stood in front of the door with

an odd look on her face. Her eyes were cold as she stared at Percival from across the room.

"Your brothers killed her," Maya went on, and she wasn't smiling now. "Came to our hut that night and burned it to the ground. They hung my grandmother from a tree and set her on fire, but they only dragged me into the forest, stabbed me a few times and left me to die. They thought she was the witch." Maya smiled then, but it was a terrible, hard smile, her eyes gleaming in the shadows. "They should've made certain to burn us both."

In a daze, Percival noticed all the locks on the door behind her had been thrown. He took a step back, but there was no other exit. Nowhere to run.

"I found your basket that day," Maya went on softly. "I knew you had seen me and Isaac. He had been pursuing me for days, and I wanted to speak with him alone, to tell him to stop chasing me. He didn't take it well, which is what you saw at the edge of the lake." Her brow furrowed just slightly, as if in pain, before smoothing out again. "I was going to tell you the next morning, but your brothers came for me that night, and I never got the chance."

"I didn't know," Percival whispered. "I didn't know what they would do."

Maya shook her head. "Yes, you did," she whispered back. "On some small, subconscious level, you knew what they were capable of. They came for us that night because of you, Percival. Because you told them to."

"Maya." Percival held out a hand. "I loved you."

She gave a tiny smile, though her eyes had started to glow, casting eerie green light over the walls and floor. "You know the saddest part?" she murmured. "I was really starting to fall for you. But it turns out you're nothing but an evil pig, just like your brothers."

And then she stepped forward, no longer Maya, and her huge, dark shadow filled the room. Percival screamed.

And screamed.

And screamed.

But there was no one around to hear.

UNTETHERED

by Sonia Gensler

Grief hangs heavy on my bones, at times nearly suffocating me. My world has turned shadowy and muted, and the strongest emotion I can muster is confusion. There's anger, as well, but it lurks under the surface, too smothered by weariness to ignite.

Ben's patience must be wearing thin, but I don't know how not to be this way.

"How's your mom?" he asks.

"The same."

"Still sticking to her room?"

"Yeah." I nestle further into the crook of his arm. His finger traces my eyebrow and cheek. These days Ben is my only comfort, but even he can't fill the void entirely.

"I saw her again," I whisper.

He doesn't ask whom. Instead, he lifts my chin, turning my face so our eyes meet. "And?"

"She came just before midnight, like before. Walked past

our bedroom, almost in slow motion." I have to swallow because the words are thick in my throat. "She was so pale and beautiful, it made me ache."

He nods. "You miss her."

"Miss her? It's more than that."

"I know, Claire."

But he can't know. Not really.

I don't tell him my plan. As much as he claims otherwise, Ben doesn't understand my need for my sister. He only remembers our shouting and door slamming. The chill of our punishing silence. Can I expect him to forget how I groused about Julia changing the way she dressed, the books she read, for her drama-geek boyfriend? Or how her narrowed eyes burned a hole of resentment straight through Ben every time they were in the same room?

Ben saw her as my enemy. Our enemy.

And I encouraged it.

But I've let go of all that. My brain may be murky and muffled, but the loss of her has brought certain things into sharp focus. We shared the same womb. Later it was the same crib, clasping fingers and toes as we slept. When our drooling mouths first formed words, we spoke our own language. The two of us made a world of our own, leaving others—even our own mother—feeling like intruders.

Shadows fall as I ponder this, and the bedroom turns dark and still.

"Mom's gonna be home soon," I say. "She never liked you being here."

"Let's go, then."

I shake my head. "I need to stay near, just in case."

"From what you've told me, she won't even notice."

"I have to stay. But I'll see you later, right?"

He frowns. "Claire…."

I pinch him. "Stop worrying. Kiss me instead."

He sighs sadly before his lips meet mine.

I kiss back, trying to melt into him like I did before. His body is a comfort to me, but also dangerous in a way I once found exciting. I still do, but in the back of my mind there's that vision of Julia, pale and fragile. Walking the hallway over and over. She's lost, unanchored, and somehow I must ground her. But how do I bridge the divide between us?

Mom seems more mechanical than human, her face blank as she makes her slow, jerky way through each day. I've given up trying to talk to her. When she's not hiding in her room, she slams kitchen cabinets and wipes counters that were never dirty in the first place. Occasionally she slumps in the living room recliner, staring at nothing. I tried to sit with her once, but her slack-faced silence was unsettling. I might as well have been sitting next to a corpse.

I prefer to stay in my room. Our room, minus Julia. Mom can't stand to come in here, but I need to be near my sister's things. Seeing them hurts like hell, but the pain helps me focus.

Julia will come, and this time I will somehow anchor her. I will make her see me.

I've never been patient, but lately I've learned stillness. I sit at the foot of my bed and concentrate, trying to be as present as possible. The digital clock hums faintly, and beyond that I hear the leaves rustling outside. I sniff the air and try to parse the different odors. A vanilla candle. Nail polish remover. The mushroomy smell of gym shoes lying in the corner. The perfume Trey bought for her last birthday. I'd never liked its heavy floral notes—overdramatic just like the giver—but now the elusive whiff of it brings tears to my eyes.

Julia, please come.

After a long silence, the floor creaks.

A door opens down the hall, and my heart plunges. It's only Mom. She'll make her bumbling way to the bathroom and ruin everything. Julia won't come near now.

But no…Mom is coming my way, toward the bedroom that she hasn't entered since it happened. She's in the doorway, her body backlit by the hall night-light. The bedroom curtains are open, and the moon casts a faint glow on her face. I've never seen her eyes so wide.

I stand quickly. "Mom?"

She leans against the doorjamb, pausing as if there's a force field keeping her at bay. Then she seems to make an effort, pushing through, and steps toward my bed.

All I can do is stare.

She eases herself onto the edge of the bed, her posture stiff. "It's been so hard, Claire," she says.

For a moment, I can't think how to respond. "I know, Mom," I finally whisper. "But you've got to pull it together."

"Sometimes it's just too much," she says.

The silence deepens, and I resign myself to a night without a glimpse of Julia. I'll stand here until Mom shuffles back to her room, and then I'll endure the hours until the next chance of seeing my sister again.

But then I feel it—the strange charge to the air that tells

me Julia is near. I draw closer to Mom, wanting to be fully visible through the doorway. A chill snakes through me, and I know it's a shiver of fear and longing.

She has come.

As before, Julia rigidly faces forward when she passes by the door, but I still see the pale of her flesh, the bluish shadows under her eyes. Her body is slightly stooped, as if she's tired...or broken. It hurts to see her this way—it isn't the Julia I know. She seems lost, untethered. I focus on her face, pleading with her to turn.

Look at me, Julia.

She pauses. My heart swells as her head turns.

But her eyes don't meet mine. They find Mom instead, and her mouth drops open.

Mom raises her head and gasps. "Julia?"

But my sister walks on, past the doorway, vanishing from our view.

The air stills. The electric charge is gone, and my spine softens. I concentrate hard on the room—otherwise I fear I might melt into the floor.

The silence drags at my limbs, weighing on my shoulders.

Mom shudders. "That was... I just..." She trails off, shaking her head.

"Yeah," I say dully.

She's quiet for a long moment. "Why'd she look at me that way?" she finally asks. She still faces the doorway, arms wrapped around her body.

I don't say anything. She doesn't want to hear my answer anyway.

Mom slumps. "She blames me."

Right now, I blame her for barging in and ruining my moment with Julia…but it's no good telling Mom that. She hears only what she wants to hear. When she finally lurches back to her own room and shuts the door, I stretch out on my bed and remember our raised voices in the driveway, car doors slamming and tires peeling out.

In the midst of arguments—and there had been plenty in the last year, though none as bad as that one—I knew our mother was crazy. She'd lost her grip on reality. She'd lost control. But seeing her face just now has made me less certain.

Mom has always been outnumbered. Excluded, even. Maybe that made her all the more tenacious, to the point of desperation, when she tried to lay down the law.

We were stubborn, too. So stubborn that sometimes getting our way was more important than having peace…or being safe.

"You saw her again?"

I nod. Ben knows without asking, but he asks anyway because he's the sort who likes to verbalize. He thinks it's unhealthy to repress emotion. Most of the time, I like this quality—every other guy I've known is tragically stunted when it comes to words and feelings.

"I know you're hoping to get something out of these, um, encounters with Julia," he continues, "but are they helping? Every time I see you, you seem more depressed." He pulls me against his chest. "I wish you'd just come away with me."

I tighten my grip around him, surprised at myself for smiling. "Would you take me away from all this if I asked?"

"Of course. But I'm afraid you'd just run back." He kisses the top of my head. "So what happened last night?"

"Mom ruined it. She came to our room and tried to talk to me, and when Julia finally appeared, she saw Mom. Not me, Mom. You should have seen Julia's face. Narrow eyes and forehead all wrinkly—like she was furious." My eyes fill with tears. "I'm afraid she won't come back now."

"Hmmm," Ben murmurs.

"What?"

"Did you ever think your mom might be the key to this?"

I wipe at my eyes. "How?"

He looks beyond me, his eyes thoughtful. "Why would your sister be angry with her?"

"Mom thinks it's because Julia blames her."

"Should Julia blame her?"

Anger flares in my gut. "Well, yeah. You know how freaking unreasonable Mom was!"

He sits up suddenly, pushing me away. "Claire, did your mother cause the crash?"

I open my mouth. Nothing comes out.

"Did she turn that wheel into the retaining wall?"

I take a breath. "No."

Ben nods. "Well...there you go."

"What are you trying to say?"

"I don't know." He looks away. "It's not really my business."

I can't bear the sudden gulf between us, so I tug at the hair that curls near his ear. "My business is always your business, buddy, and vice versa. You know you're stuck with me, right?"

"I'm counting on it. I just..." He breaks off. "I want you

to be whole again, or as whole as you can be, considering. If I could somehow make this better, I would."

"I know. But it's my job to fix things...if they can be fixed at all."

He opens his mouth to protest, but I lean forward and silence him with a kiss. It's one of my favorite tricks when he doesn't agree with me. I feel his lips curve upward as his arms tighten around my waist. Sometimes I think it would be so easy to lose myself in this thing Ben and I share.

But the call of blood to blood won't be ignored.

Maybe Ben is right, and Mom is the key. The key to reaching Julia...or to losing her forever.

I'll find out tonight.

When the time comes—when the darkness and silence deepen and I feel the first crackle of that charge to the air—I go to Mom's door. For once it's open, and through the three-inch crack I see her sitting on the old cedar chest at the foot of the bed. Her shoulders droop, and it strikes me how much weight she's lost. Her face is slack and sharply angled, her shoulders pointy rather than rounded. In that baggy sweat suit she looks like a kid in hand-me-downs.

For so long Mom has been an opposing force—a wall of anger, rather than a woman of flesh and feeling. A sour pang of guilt roils in my belly.

"Mom?"

She doesn't lift her head.

"Mom, I need you."

She shudders slightly and wipes at her eyes.

"Come to our room, Mom," I say as gently as I can. "I want you there."

I don't know what else to do, so I go back to the bedroom and sit on the edge of my bed. It's time to concentrate on Julia—on her laughter, her dimpled smile, the warmth of her skin, the scent of her hair. With each passing day the details fade a little more.

Moments later Mom stands in the doorway. She hesitates before stepping forward and easing herself onto the bed next to me. I reach out slowly, wary of startling her, and place my hand on her knee. She flinches but does not cry or push my hand away.

There's a thump in the distance. The light changes, brightening ever so slightly, and I feel that static in the air.

Julia is coming.

I move closer to Mom, imagining a pulse of affection spreading from my heart, through my arm, and flowing through my fingers to enter her body. She straightens a little, as though bolstered by the infusion.

I concentrate on Julia, and it feels like Mom is doing the same. Together maybe we can create a beam of yearning to pull her into the room.

When Julia appears at the doorway, she is slumped and pale as usual. An amputated soul. My heart contracts. If only I could absorb her into my body and reunite our cells—somehow reweave the strands of our DNA—I would carry her with me always, our feuding spirits finally in harmony.

I shake my head and concentrate.

This time I don't limit my thoughts to Julia. I think of Mom, too, and the happy times the three of us shared together. Curiously…there are more than I would have guessed. If I concentrate hard enough I can feel the sun on my face as we drive to the lake with the windows down, Julia's voice cracking as we belt out Beach Boys lyrics along with Mom's creaking tape deck. There's Christmas morning when our giggles crowd behind our teeth as Grandma preaches a sermon. Mom rolls her eyes, and if I even dare glance at Julia, the laughter will explode from both our mouths. And there's spring afternoons when I can taste the warm glop of chocolate hardening against ice cream as we eat tuxedo sundaes—two full scoops each—after Julia wins a tennis match.

I play these scenes on a loop in my mind—moments from simpler times before boyfriends and sports and college applications complicated everything. Before jealousy and arguments shadowed our hearts. Next to me, Mom sighs contentedly.

Like before, Julia pauses.

And she turns.

She sees Mom, and I want to believe her furrowed brow has more to do with confusion than anger.

Come closer, Julia.

Mom's spine stiffens as Julia crosses the threshold into our room, and pauses, just out of arm's reach. Mom doesn't stand, and I stay near even though my heart practically leaps toward Julia.

A strange noise erupts from Mom, something between a moan and a growl.

Julia stares at her. "Why are you in here?"

Mom swallows hard before speaking. "I'm here because I feel her."

My sister blinks.

"Don't you?" asks Mom. "That's why you sleep in the living room, isn't it?"

Julia's face falls. "Mom…you have to move on."

"How can I? You haven't. And you blame me."

A curtain of silence falls, and I remember to concentrate again on love and good memories. I stretch my left hand toward Julia—she's just out of my reach, but I know she somehow senses me, for she straightens and seems to gather herself.

"Mom," she says softly. "I remember what came out of my mouth that night. I said you ran them off…that you pushed them too far.…" She pauses, her eyes shining with tears. "But I wasn't thinking right. I don't blame you. Ben was driving the car. You know what the police said. It was an accident— a deer or something on the road."

Mom shakes her head. "I started the argument. That's why they left in such a rush."

"But you didn't turn the wheel," I say.

Mom wipes her nose and says nothing.

"I've tried so many times to talk to you," Julia says. "I've tried to think of ways to explain, but it's like you're not there. You shut yourself away. Even when we're in the same room together, you're…absent."

"Don't you miss her, Julia? You never cry. It's like you've pushed Claire out of your mind."

"I think of her every second." The bedsprings squeak as Julia sits next to Mom. "During the day, when I hear or see things she'd like, I remind myself to tell her. That's when it hits me all over again. At night my mind echoes with every mean thing I ever said, every criticism and complaint." Her chin drops. "And when I do finally sleep, I dream it's all a misunderstanding, and she's fine. I hate waking up from that dream."

Mom nods. "I have it, too. Nearly every night."

"Then why won't you talk to me?"

"I don't know. Talking makes it…permanent."

Keeping hold of mom's bony knee, I crouch before both of them and place my other hand on my sister.

Julia sighs and slips her arm around Mom's waist.

"Do you feel her here?" whispers Mom. "Or am I insane?"

I concentrate so hard on them both, on our bodies—no, our souls—as a closed circuit. A circuit that vibrates with a current of love. For the first time, the Beyond pulls at me, and I have to resist it.

"I do feel her," whispers Julia.

"It's okay," I say. "You'll both be okay."

A tear trails down Mom's cheek. "If I could just see her… one more time."

"You can't bring her back, Mom. You—" Julia breaks off, to sniffle wetly. "We have to let go."

"But I don't know how to make a life that doesn't include her." She turns to wrap her arms around Julia, sobbing into her shoulder. My hands slide toward my lap and the circuit is broken.

"Our lives will always include her." Julia lays her cheek against Mom's head. "Just…in a different way."

I stand.

The pull is even stronger now that the living have eased their grip.

I leave them to their embrace, moving through the door to the hallway, past Mom's room, the bathroom, past the living room and the couch with Julia's pallet of quilts and pillows. She will go back to sleeping in our room now, and I wonder if they'll replace the saggy twin beds with a double.

Ben waits for me, his mouth curved in a half smile. "You did it?"

"They understand now."

"So…we can leave?"

I pause to look back—the two-bedroom house droops a little, as though ashamed of its dusty brick and cracked concrete steps. It always was too small for our lanky bodies, our books and clothes and sports gear. Certainly too small for three fractious personalities. Is it now too large for two? I wonder if Julia has truly come to ground, or if she will continue to float away from Mom.

"Claire, if you're not ready…you know I'll wait as long as it takes. I'll wait forever."

I turn back to him. "You don't have to."

He opens his arms, and every particle of my being longs to rush into him. Mom and Julia will find a way to mend and thrive, and someday we may meet again. I don't know how this works, but I've done everything I know to do. For now Ben is all the warmth and light and love that I need.

I am ready.

BETTER

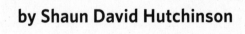

by Shaun David Hutchinson

I feel real.

I have fingers that move, eyes that have never seen sunset, ears that love a violin. I bleed and breathe and cry when I hurt. I tremble at night when I am alone and afraid; I laugh when I am happy. I have never known love, but I have lips that ache to kiss. To linger on the sweet lips of him.

I feel real, though they tell me I am not.

Levi Saxon sits alone in the cafeteria, slowly spooning the mush that passes for lunch into his mouth with spindly arms that look barely strong enough to lift even that small metal utensil. He is surrounded by them but still alone. I recognize the way they look at him—I have lived with their hatred my entire life.

"Pip!" Levi smiles at me and waves me over. I carry my tray to his table. The air is chillier here by the bulkheads—the only thing separating us from the relentless nightmare of space—but I keep my concerns to myself. The cold does not affect me, and Levi doesn't like to be reminded of his frailty.

"What happened?" Levi reaches out to touch me, but stops midway, dropping his hand and his eyes to his lap.

I run my fingers over the stubble of my scalp, pausing at the incision that meanders across the side of my head. The skin is puckered and raw where the stitches pull together. I hate the pity lurking in Levi's eyes. I should've eaten in the lab like usual.

"An experiment. Dr. Saxon says I have a lovely brain." I mean it to be a joke, something to lighten the mood, but Levi doesn't laugh. The concept of humor eludes me more often than not.

"Don't you hate it?"

"What?"

"The tests?" Levi says. "The experiments? Not being able to do whatever you want?"

I attempt to focus on eating, but the food is particularly offensive today. Though I'm not hungry, eating gives me something to do with my hands while I avoid answering Levi's question. When I realize that he's still staring at me, still waiting, I say, "It's the reason your father created me. I'm little more than a lab rat, my only purpose to be experimented upon in the hopes of finding a cure for the Disease."

Levi glances at his bony, wasted legs. The Disease has devoured his muscles, left him unable to stand or dance or relieve himself unassisted. "I hate it," he says. "The way they stare at me like it's my fault I'm alive while their damn kids are frozen in stasis."

A pale, gray-haired woman at a nearby table runs from

the cafeteria, sobbing, leaving behind a wordless, breathless vacuum. We become the focus of attention. Eighty-seven sets of eyes on us. Watching. Judging. Staring at us like we are the Disease vectors rather than simply a broken boy and wind-up girl.

"I'm sorry," Levi whispers. The words barely escape the gravity of his guilt. It doesn't matter that, one day, the Disease will force him to join the other children in stasis, waiting for a cure that may never come. Levi bears the guilt of health all the same.

I nervously run my finger along the ridges of my incision.

"Does it hurt?" Levi's desperation to talk about something, anything else, is carved into his frown.

I nod. "Dr. Saxon says that my pain isn't real. It's merely a series of electrical signals from my skin to my brain."

Levi tilts his head to the side slightly. His hand trembles as though it wants to move but cannot. "If you feel it, it's real."

I can't stand the way Levi is looking at me, like we are the only two people aboard the *Hamelin*. Part of me wishes we were. But the rest… "It's ugly. I'm ugly."

"Don't be stupid," Levi says. "You're pretty."

I don't know how to respond to…that. I blurt out, "You're pretty, too," without thinking, and Levi chuckles. Only, it wasn't a joke. "You are. You're the prettiest boy on the *Hamelin*."

"I'm the only boy on the *Hamelin*. The only one your age anyway." Levi bites the corner of his lip and looks down at his long, thin fingers. "I'm sorry he hurt you."

"It will be healed by tomorrow." I pick at my food, unsure whether Levi is sincere or just humoring me.

"I didn't know you healed that fast," he says, trying to hide his surprise.

"I'm not like you." It's a simple statement, and true, but it twists in my gut, reminding me that Levi and I will never be the same.

"No, you're not." Levi lifts my head, forcing me to stare into his pale blue eyes. "You're better." Levi holds me there for a moment before letting go and pushing away from the table. He steers his lift chair out of the cafeteria.

As I watch Levi leave, I try to think of something to say, some way to tell him that he's wrong. But I cannot.

I like to watch them sleep. Especially Levi.

I like the way his mouth puckers when he's dreaming, and the way his fingers curl and flex.

I wonder whether he dreams of the home he never knew or of the new home he will likely not live to see. When the colonists set out aboard the *Hamelin* in search of a habitable planet over two hundred years ago, I doubt they ever once dreamed that their descendants would perish on this ship, their children's children slowly devoured by a pitiless disease. The last gasp of humanity searching frantically for a cure that they may never find.

Levi is the last of the *Hamelin*'s children not in stasis. His father, Dr. Saxon, hoped to discover a cure before the Disease forced him to put Levi into the long sleep, too.

I wonder if he would dream in stasis.

I do not dream or sleep. Instead, I wander the ship alone, listening to the *Hamelin* purr as she carries us in her belly through the long, dark night.

But if I did, I would dream of where we have been, where we are going. Of the billions of stars that are not home, and—somewhere waiting in the cold void—the one star that might be.

I would dream of Levi.

"Will I ever fall in love?" I ask.

Dr. Saxon, sitting on the edge of his stool on the other side of the examination table, looks up from my arm as the blood bubbles up through the needle into the tube. The remains of his hair are wild and gray, and his skin sags deeply today. He completes the task before pulling the needle from my vein and setting his instruments on the counter behind him.

"What makes you ask?"

I shrug. I'm unsure how he'd react if I answered honestly. "Curiosity, I suppose."

"Oh." Dr. Saxon gathers the vials of blood he has drawn from me and takes them to the other side of the room. He places them in a centrifuge and sends them spinning around and around. "Do you know what you are?"

"An artificial being. A collection of biological machines assembled into the facsimile of life."

"Indeed," Dr. Saxon says. He returns to the table and grabs my hand. Before I know what's happening, he slashes the soft flesh of my palm with a scalpel that he produces from the sleeve of his white coat. I cry out but do not pull my hand from his.

"Watch" is all he says.

We watch together as the blood pools from the deep gash in my palm. Dr. Saxon sliced neatly through the dermal and hypodermal layers, through the muscle, nearly to the bone. However, within seconds, the flesh begins to rejoin from the bottom to the top like a meaty zipper snapping shut. In barely a minute, only blood and the memory of pain remain.

Dr. Saxon releases my wrist. "Clean up."

I slide off the table and do as I'm told.

"I hate you."

If Dr. Saxon is afraid, he doesn't show it. I could tear his head from his neck and he couldn't stop me. I could kill them all. Instead, he motions for me to sit at a table in the corner of the lab, while he takes the chair across from me. "You say you hate me, but you don't. You can't. You aren't real."

"What if I am?"

"You're not." Dr. Saxon scrubs his face with his worn hands. Though wrinkled and lined with veins, they're still steady. "You are an experiment, Pip. A means to an end. I hoped studying your unique physiology would help me find a way to cure the Disease, but all my hoping has proven fruitless."

I've read all of Dr. Saxon's research. I know that the Disease isn't a disease at all. It's a syndrome—a collection of symptoms for which Dr. Saxon has yet to find a cause. He once hypothesized that the Disease was similar to the allergies that developed on Earth in industrialized societies, that generations of living in space had caused it. But the only cure for space travel would be to find a habitable planet, and we are still light years from the nearest one.

"Your personality, your knowledge, were fabricated from the ship's computers. Your responses and so-called feelings are not real. You are not real. You can't hate me, because you can't feel hate. You won't ever fall in love because you will never know what real love feels like."

Dr. Saxon clears his throat. "None of this matters," he says. "I am no closer to discovering a cure than I was fifteen years ago. There is nothing more I can learn from you. I am terminating this experiment."

"What?" The implication of his words sends an alarm spreading through my mind like a virus.

"I'm sorry, Pip." The weariness in Dr. Saxon's voice nearly chokes him.

"What will happen to me?" I ask, even though I fear I already know the answer. If I could vomit, I would.

"The Senate fears you," Dr. Saxon says. "Some of the more…imaginative members worry that you will eventually seek to supplant us."

"I wouldn't," I say.

"I know." Dr. Saxon bows his head. "There's nothing I can do."

I scramble to come up with a way to stop him—something we haven't tried—but I know Dr. Saxon's work with the Disease as intimately as he does. Panic grips my frazzled mind and I blurt out, "What if I cure the Disease?"

"Pip—"

"Give me one chance," I say.

Dr. Saxon pushes back his chair. The metal legs grate against the textured floor of the lab. "My mind is made up."

"Without me, Levi will die." The words stick in my throat. The thought of losing Levi is a fear Dr. Saxon and I share.

"Yes," Dr. Saxon says, as if he is resigned to the inevitability. "I won't put him into stasis. His mother wouldn't have wanted that."

I grope for a way to change Dr. Saxon's mind. In the end, all I can say is "Please."

Dr. Saxon returns to his work and says no more.

As I walk to my quarters, I dissect my predicament. The corridors are quiet at night. Just my thoughts and the hum of the *Hamelin*. I care less about preserving my own life than about curing Levi, but if Dr. Saxon discontinues his work, I will not be able to accomplish either. It seems impossible to me that I will succeed where Dr. Saxon has failed, but I don't believe I have another choice. I need time.

In my mind, I pull up the results of Dr. Saxon's previous failures, searching for something he missed. But I am haunted by Levi. The feel of his fingers on my hand, the tilt of his smile and the way his hair falls over his eyes. Everything I know about love, I learned from the ship's databases. History, music, literature. The more I learn, the less I understand. Dr. Saxon might be right and I'm incapable of love, but I know what I feel. Maybe no one can explain love; they can only be in it.

I am so lost in thoughts of the Disease and Levi that I don't notice the hooded man standing in front of the door to my quarters until he shoves a stunstick in my ribs. Electricity floods my body. Another man lunges at me from behind, jabbing me with a second stunstick set to deliver a full shock, this time in my spine. Another and another. And another. This much electricity would kill a human, but I am better, I heal faster. Just not fast enough.

The world becomes watercolor. The walls run and bleed.

I collapse in the corridor. I'm in the garden with Levi. I'm floating in space.

My limbs betray me as I attempt to fight off the men—limp and useless. Even my eyes fail me as I attempt to see the faces of my attackers under their hoods. I fail. I see nothing but stars. Stars and the yawning void beckoning me home.

The men are in no hurry. My quarters are in an unused section of the ship. The *Hamelin* was once full, but now it's mostly empty. They laugh as they drag me across the floor and toss me onto my cot. It's a cruel joke that I can't move or scream or see, but can still hear every word the men say.

"Gotta get me some before they toss her out an airlock." Laughter. "Should've done this a long time ago."

Trapped inside my body, I beg for the end.

I shudder.

I shake.

As they hurt me.

As it gets so much worse.

I taste blood.

I feel pain.

Tears run from my eyes as they take turns.

Real pain, real fear.

I am real.

Even as they tell me I am not.

I'm huddled in the corner of my shower when Dr. Saxon enters my quarters. No amount of water could ever wash the stink of the men from me, but I tried. The bruises have already faded, the blood from my nose and lip washed down the drain. No outward traces remain of what they did to me.

Before they departed, they argued about whether to kill me. They left me alive to avoid an incident, knowing that even if I told, I couldn't identify them. Not that it would matter if I could. The Senate wants me dead. No, not dead—in their eyes, I am not alive. They want me disposed of. Like garbage.

"Pip?" Dr. Saxon enters my bathroom, unashamed of my nakedness even as I cross my arms over my chest. "You're late." When he sees me sitting on the cold metal floor of the shower, his brow furrows. "Are you damaged?"

"Convince the Senate to let me live," I say. My voice is hoarse and heavy. "Let me find a cure for the Disease."

Dr. Saxon closes his eyes for the longest time, unwilling to look at me. "It is already decided."

"Undecide it!"

"Let's get you out of there." Dr. Saxon passes me the towel hanging from a hook on the wall, but I let it drop to the floor.

"I can save them," I say. "You have nothing to lose and everything to gain." I sense Dr. Saxon's hesitation. "You said it yourself—Levi will soon die. Without me, you have no hope of saving your son, but with me, you have something. Maybe not much, but greater achievements have been accomplished with less."

Dr. Saxon kneels in front of me. I've never seen him so low, so meek. "Do you really believe you can do it?"

"Yes." I dangle hope in front of him, daring him to take it.

"Maybe," Dr. Saxon says. He grows quiet and I fear I may lose him, but he must come to the decision on his own. "Why would you help us?"

"Because I want to live, and I don't want to live alone."

I'm not sure if the answer is satisfactory, but it's the truth. After a moment, Dr. Saxon stands and turns away from me. "If you really believe you can do it, I'll talk to the Senate."

"I can save Levi. I can make him better."

The Senate grants me a one-month reprieve. One month to do what Dr. Saxon couldn't do in fifteen years. It's not a great deal of time, but it's better than nothing. Dr. Saxon grants me access to his research, unaware that I gained access ages ago. There's a file called Project Twig that I mean to ask Dr. Saxon about, but the label suggests something to do with botany, which seems unlikely to help me cure the Disease. I pore over the research, barely eating, hardly leaving the lab for a week. Partly because I'm consumed by my efforts to cure the Disease, mostly because I'm afraid to return to my quarters.

I focus on Levi because it keeps me from thinking about the men who hurt me, about the things they did to me. But even as I work in the locked lab, I imagine them on the other side of the door, plotting to hurt me again. Those thoughts infect my mind, creeping into the dark corners and breeding until they're all that's left. Until my hate for those men is all that's left.

But I'm not trying to help them. I'm trying to help Levi.

My stomach grumbles, reminding me that while I don't require much food, I still require some. I walk to the cafeteria, alert and ready to fight. No one will ever sneak up on me again. The cafeteria is nearly empty when I arrive. The lights are dim and Cook works behind the counter, cleaning up from dinner. He does not acknowledge me beyond passing me a tin plate with a serving of what appears to be a casserole.

"It tastes worse than it smells."

I turn to find Levi moving toward me in his lift chair. His dirty-blond hair is messier than normal and falls in tangled curls around his face. He grins, and I feel like I can finally breathe. Levi would never hurt me. He's everything that is good about humans; everything I want to be. "I need to eat."

"I know." Levi offers me his hand. "Let's go."

"Why?"

"It's a surprise."

"Why?"

Levi chuckles and grabs my hand. His fingers tremble, but he squeezes me tightly and I never want him to let go. "You've got a lot to learn, Pip." Levi navigates out of the cafeteria, pulling me along with him. I'm not sure where we're going, but I'm not afraid. Never with Levi.

We wind up in the botanical garden. Spread out under the drooping canopy of the willow tree is a blanket, atop which rests a wicker basket.

Wordlessly, I help Levi out of his chair and we settle down on the blanket. He weighs almost nothing. I can't help thinking about his fragility—the specter of death is his shadow and I should be in the lab working to save him.

But the fact that we're here—that Levi wants me here—makes this moment special. If I succeed, we might share many moments like this; if I fail, this moment, right here, might be our one and only.

"Have you ever eaten cheese, Pip?" Levi unpacks the basket, spreading out the different foods. "My father keeps a stash. I'm going to catch hell when he finds out I took them, but it's so worth it." Among the pilfered treasures are a small yellow wedge sealed in plastic, bowls of fruits and vegetables, and a chunk of dark brown bread.

"I've read about cheese." I pick up the wedge and sniff it, but smell only the plastic.

Levi takes the cheese from me and grins wickedly. "Reading about food is like talking about kissing. You just have to try it." Levi's enthusiasm is infectious, and I can't help smiling, wishing I'd spent more time with him this week.

A thought occurs to me. "How did you know I'd be in the cafeteria tonight?"

"I didn't." Levi blushes and avoids my eyes. "I've had this set up every night for the past week. I figured I'd catch you at dinner sooner or later." He finishes arranging the feast and, thankfully, looks at me. His smile is as shy and fragile as his body.

"You waited so long?"

"You're worth the wait."

Dr. Saxon warned me not to tell Levi about our bargain, but I want to so badly. I want to explain why he had to wait a week to see me and why I haven't come to him at night. Dr. Saxon is right, though. So I keep my hope to myself.

We eat in silence, and the cheese is the best thing I have ever tasted. The salty flavor sings on my tongue and I wish to eat nothing but cheese for the rest of my life, however long that may be. There is not much, but it's enough for us both to enjoy a couple of bites. After that, we devour the fruits and vegetables. There are carrots and tomatoes and grapes. The apples are especially sweet.

"I've never eaten like this before," I say.

"Dad says he ate food like this all the time when he was little." Levi shrugs. "I guess when the Disease broke out and all the kids started dying, people's priorities changed."

Levi and I finish eating and lie out on the blanket. The branches of the willow tree sway gently in the artificial breeze.

"What would you do if you were better?" I ask.

"Run," Levi says without hesitation. I expected he would need time to think of a response, but it's as if he has been holding that answer in his mouth since the day his legs ceased functioning. "Run down the corridor until my muscles hurt and I can't breathe. Then I'd run some more, just because."

"That doesn't sound like a well-thought-out plan."

Levi laughs at me and I look away. "I'm not laughing at you, Pip. It's just that life's too short to always do the right thing." He touches my hand, and this time he doesn't pull away. "You're special, Pip. You know that, right?"

"Yes."

"And modest, too!"

When I'm near Levi, I feel defective. My thoughts move more slowly and I never know what to say. But nothing could keep me from him. "I'm not like you. No one exists who is like me." I squeeze Levi's hand and he flinches. "Sorry."

I try to let go, but Levi won't let me. "It's okay."

"Every time we're apart," I say, "I feel untethered. Like I'm going to float off into space. I'm all alone on this ship, and you're the only person who understands."

Levi's smile disappears. "I wish I could be like you."

I shake my head. "No, you don't."

"I do," Levi says. "If I were like you, I wouldn't be dying. I could run all I wanted and never get tired. Hell, I'd settle for just being able to walk. You're the only person who doesn't treat me like an invalid."

"But everyone hates me," I say. "If you were like me, they'd hate you, too."

"If they don't see how special you are, then maybe the human race doesn't deserve to survive." Levi runs the back of his hand down my cheek, catching my eyes. His reflect the light of all the stars. "If I were like you, we could start over. You and me together forever."

"You don't mean that," I say. Part of me wants him to mean it. Part of me has wanted him to mean it for so long, but I don't think about it because sometimes hope hurts too much.

"I do," he says, and I believe him.

I can't help myself. It's wrong, I know it's wrong, but I can't let Levi die without knowing how I feel. I lean forward, drawn by the irresistible pull of his gravity. Of his lips. Lips that I have thought of a hundred thousand times. Lips that I have wanted to kiss since I first laid eyes on Levi Saxon.

But he recoils. He slams his fist on the ground and tries to climb back into his chair. When I attempt to help, he pushes me away.

"What did I do?" I ask. My heart is broken a thousand times, and it's all I can do not to run from the garden. More than life, more than breath, I have wanted Levi. Now it's clear that he doesn't want me back. I am as cold as the clutch of space beyond the windows. As empty as the dark.

Levi struggles to get into his chair, but his arms are too weak and he falls back to the ground. "Just go!"

"Levi?" I hate the sound of my voice as I say his name like

a beggar. I hate that I am reduced to this. But I would do it again. And I hate that the most.

"Please go." Levi's body shakes and he hides his face from me. "Just let me die in peace."

I reach out to touch his arm but stop short. I couldn't stand it if he rejected me again. "You're not going to die, Levi Saxon. I won't let you."

Dr. Saxon hovers over me, making it impossible to think. "It's been twenty-three days, Pip."

"I'm close," I lie.

"Without a cure, humanity dies."

I turn around, ignoring the disappointing results of another test. "Do you think I'm unaware of that? Do you think I haven't tried everything?"

Dr. Saxon softens. "I know you've tried," he says. "I'll tell the Senate."

"I still have seven days," I snap. Frustration is eating at me. I know that Levi didn't mean what he said, but I can't stop thinking about how he pushed me away. I'll save him anyway. Even if he doesn't want me, I'll save him. Because he's Levi.

"Yes," Dr. Saxon says. "And you should spend them with my son." I freeze. He knows. He knows about the late-night visits to the botanical garden and the stolen food. Maybe he has always known but said nothing because of his love for his son. "Goodbye, Pip."

I stop Dr. Saxon before he leaves. "There's a file on the computer I can't access. Project Twig. What is it?"

"Nothing," Dr. Saxon says. "Leave it be."

"If it can help me save Levi, you must tell me how to decrypt it."

"Don't waste what little time you have left, Pip." Dr. Saxon looks at me with something bordering on concern, an emotion I thought him incapable of feeling for me. Maybe I was wrong. Maybe I am more than an experiment to Dr. Saxon, after all.

"Thank you, Dr. Saxon. For everything. You are as near to a father as I will ever have."

Pain etches Dr. Saxon's face, as though I have stabbed him with his own scalpel. "My wife loved Bach," he says. "Especially the Brandenburg concertos. You might find them enlightening."

It takes me three days to figure out that Dr. Saxon had given me the key to decrypting the Project Twig files. It was Bach. The files were encrypted with an algorithm based on his Brandenburg concertos. But how I decrypted them is not half as exciting as what the files contain. The moment I finish reading them, I know I can save Levi. It takes my remaining days to prepare, but I am finally ready to try.

Levi is so weak he can barely lift his head. His hair has thinned and grown brittle and his eyes are glazed with a deathly film. Still, he talks as though his life's end is not near, despite the tube in his chest helping him breathe.

"I'm sorry I've been avoiding you," he says.

I push Levi's chair through the corridors, thinking about tomorrow night when I'll have earned my pardon and we'll walk together as equals. As we pass the botanical garden, Levi tries to turn around but gets tangled in his breathing tube. "We're not going to watch the stars?"

"Not tonight," I say.

"Then what?"

"It's a surprise," I tell him, barely able to contain my excitement.

Levi's body shakes. I believe it's what passes for a nod. "I'm not sure how much time I have left, but however much it is belongs to you." A coughing fit grips him and I stop pushing to make sure he's all right. When the coughing subsides, we continue.

There is a morbid truth to his words that follows us down the empty corridors. I imagine Levi's heart fluttering, fading. His lungs slowly drowning in fluid. The breathing machine only prolongs the inevitable. The worst part is that I feel like I can smell death on him—the rotting stench as his cells expire one by one. If Levi were anyone else, I'm not certain I could stand it.

But he's not anyone else. He is Levi.

We enter a lab that has not been used in years. I only discovered it when I decrypted the Project Twig files. The walls are lined with metal doors. In the center of the room is a table draped with a white sheet. Beside it, a second, empty table.

"What is this place?" Levi asks.

"Your father worked here once," I say. "And it is where I will make you better."

"How?" Levi guards his hope, but it bleeds through. A slight smile, a brightness to his milky eyes.

I've thought long and hard about how to tell Levi, but in the end, only the truth will do. "Your father's first attempts to cure the Disease were known as Project Twig. He attempted to build new bodies for the *Hamelin*'s children. Artificial bodies resistant to the Disease."

I watch Levi for his reaction, but he simply stares at me, beautiful, even near death.

"But Dr. Saxon couldn't figure out how to transfer the consciousness from the old body to the new. Every effort to duplicate the soul and put it in the artificial bodies failed. When the Senate discovered what your father was doing, they demanded he terminate the experiments. Dr. Saxon disposed of the artificial bodies. All but one."

Levi's lip twitches. He looks at me with the barest hint of a smile. "You."

I shake my head. "No. I came later. Your father begged the Senate to be allowed to create me so that he could study the Disease. They relented so long as he never attempt to revive Project Twig."

"Then…who?"

The form under the white sheet on the table. We both turn to it. Look at it. I cross the distance and pull the sheet aside. Levi lies there. Naked. Whole. Healthy.

"Is that…?"

I nod. "Your father kept your body in this lab. I used his research to revive it and make it the same age as you."

Levi moves around the table, touching an arm, looking at the body that looks so much like him but is not him. I wait for him to smile, to laugh, to realize that I have found his cure, but maybe he has grown so accustomed to the idea of dying that he has given up on being saved. I don't know how he can remain so calm when I am hardly able to keep my hands from shaking.

"Say something," I say when I can't stand his silence anymore.

"It seems a bit unfair," Levi says.

"How so?"

Levi shrugs. "You've seen me naked." He grins and laughs and coughs so hard that I'm afraid he'll dislodge his breathing tube. But he doesn't, and when the coughing fit ends, he's still smiling. I've never seen Levi so alive.

"You can put me in there?" Levi asks. "I can have a new body?"

"Yes." Fear is eating away at me because there's still one last thing he doesn't know.

"How do we do this?" he asks without a trace of fear.

"First, there's something I must know."

"What?"

I pull a chair next to Levi. "Do you believe I'm alive?"

"Of course," Levi says. "You're more alive than anyone I know."

"For a long time, I wasn't sure," I say. "Your father, the others, they treat me like a thing. Somehow less than human. I look like them, think like them, bleed like them. But I'm not like them. You were the first person who treated me like I was real."

Levi draws a shuddering breath. "You're the most real thing in my life, Pip."

I take Levi's hand, kiss the tips of his fingers. He trembles but doesn't pull away. "Could you...could you ever... love me?"

Dr. Saxon doesn't believe me capable of love, but he's wrong. I will succeed where he failed. That knowledge gives me the courage to seek the truth from Levi. No matter his answer.

Levi's whole body breathes a sigh as he folds his fingers through mine. "I do love you, Pip. I've always loved you. How can you not know that?"

Hope crawls into my throat, but I push it back down. "Why did you pull away when I attempted to kiss you?"

Levi turns from me. He would run if I let him, but his legs would only betray him again. "I'm broken, Pip. Practically dead. Broken, dead and useless."

"So?"

"You deserve better." Tears run down his hollow cheeks. "You deserve someone whole."

I press my body to Levi's. He is so cold. I try to warm him but he is fading so quickly. "I want you, Levi. Broken or whole, I want you."

Levi looks at the other body. "In that, I can be the man you deserve." He kisses my hand. "How does this work?"

"You told me once that I was special. You're special, too." This moment feels too dense, like it might collapse under its own weight and drag me in. "Your father was trying to duplicate you—your memories, your body, your soul. What he failed to realize is that each human is unique. There can be only one Levi Saxon. To live, you must first die."

Levi doesn't reply for a moment, and I'm afraid that I've scared him. But he says, "Will it hurt?" in a voice that is exhausted but as fearless as ever. I've always known Levi was strong, but his strength still has the power to amaze me.

"No," I say. "I promise."

Levi holds my hand to his frail heart. "Thank you."

The time for hesitation is past. I press my mouth to his. His hands fumble in my hands, and his dry, cracked lips are weak, but they are the sweetest lips in the universe. Sweeter than apples.

Sadder than the violin.

This is real.

I kiss Levi until he cannot breathe.

But he does not fight. He does not struggle. His faith in me is absolute.

I steal the last breath from these lungs. I steal the last beats of this heart.

I kiss him until his back arches and his arms hang limp.

And when our kiss finally ends, Levi's head rolls forward against my shoulder, the life gone from his pale blue eyes. I lift Levi up and place his old body gently on the empty table beside his new body, and prepare to begin the transfer.

"I love you, Levi Saxon."

Dr. Saxon enters the lab the next morning to escort me to my death, wearing a grim expression. Two uniformed men stand in the corridor outside the door, armed with stunsticks, as if Dr. Saxon believes I will put up a fight.

"It's time, Pip."

I turn from the computer to look Dr. Saxon in the eyes, wearing my triumph like a crown. "I succeeded, Dr. Saxon."

Dr. Saxon freezes. "What?"

I nod, and Levi walks out of the bathroom, where he had been waiting. He walks. Unaided. His gait steady and sure, his eyes sparkle and his full cheeks are dimpled and red. Levi is strong and healthy. And alive.

"Pip made me better, Dad." Levi's voice rings clear through the lab. The uniforms in the hall glance over their shoulders, their eyes wide with disbelief.

Dr. Saxon rushes to Levi and throws his arms around his son. "How did you do this?" He is sobbing and touching Levi's shoulders and wrists and cheeks. He is kissing the top of his head. "I have to tell the Senate! We can revive the other children and administer the cure immediately." I've never seen Dr. Saxon so happy. Pride wells up in me. I did this. Me.

"Your work made it possible," I say. "Project Twig."

"Project Twig?" The color drains from Dr. Saxon's face. "Is this…?"

I pull up Dr. Saxon's research on the screen and expand it to cover the entire wall. Dr. Saxon disentangles himself from Levi and stares at his son. The tears are gone, replaced by horror. His mouth moves, but he cannot seem to find the words.

"Doctor?" asks one of the uniforms from the hall. They look anxious and hold their stunsticks ready.

"Just a moment," Dr. Saxon hisses. "How did you accomplish…this?"

I kiss Levi's hand and he looks at me with his same blue eyes. His first words to me when he awoke in his new body were "I love you, too." I knew I'd never be alone again.

"Does it matter?" I ask, confused. I thought Dr. Saxon would be happy. "Levi is alive. He's healthy. The Disease will never steal him from us."

Levi moves toward his father, but Dr. Saxon recoils. "I'm still Levi, Dad."

Dr. Saxon ignores Levi, his hatred focused on me. "Where's my son? Is he dead? Tell me where Levi is!"

The uniforms invade the lab.

"Dad," Levi says. "I'm not dead. I'm right here."

"This was your research," I say. "I only finished what you started. I don't understand why you're upset."

Dr. Saxon is shaking, but I keep my distance.

"We terminated Project Twig because it was wrong!" Dr. Saxon says. "This wasn't how it was supposed to be. You were supposed to cure Levi, not kill him!"

I glance at Levi, then the uniforms. They take up a position to surround us, but have not requested backup. "I kept my promise, Dr. Saxon. We are the cure for the Disease."

Dr. Saxon stumbles toward the uniforms. "You're not human. You're not real. You're a machine."

"Dad—" Levi reaches for him, sounding like the boy he once was. This is my fault. I should have explained it to Dr. Saxon alone, made him understand, but now I've ruined everything and I just wish I could go back and live forever in that moment after Levi was reborn.

"You're not my son!" Dr. Saxon pushes past the guards and runs from the lab.

Levi and I stand alone. The guards raise their stunsticks.

"You should run," Levi says, all anger and heartbreak.

The uniforms do not put up much of a fight.

They come for us at night. Mothers. Fathers. Dr. Saxon.

They come bearing weapons. The come cloaked in anger and hate.

Levi holds my hand as we wait for the end.

"Are we doing the right thing?" he asks. All I want to do is kiss him again. Kiss him forever. But soon, we will have all the time in the universe.

"We're the future," I say, choosing my words carefully. "If we die, all hope for humanity dies. This is the only way."

Levi understands. He sees the truth, knows all that I know. There are no secrets between us; words are no longer necessary. We share everything with a kiss, with a look, with the briefest touch.

I knew before, that even if I succeeded, they might never let us be free. But I have kept my end of the bargain. Now it is time for them to keep theirs.

It's Levi's idea to set off the fire alarms. There is no fire, but I have tricked the ship's computer into believing there is. First, the computer releases an argon-nitrogen gas mixture to smother the fire. If that fails, automatic decompression will occur, removing the oxygen from the ship. In the event of a fire, all colonists are to proceed to the airlock and prepare to evacuate aboard the *Jakob-Wilhelm*.

Red lights spiral in the corridors and flashing arrows guide the fleeing colonists, as gas rolls through the corridors like fog, harrying them as they flee from the imagined danger.

From the lab, Levi and I watch as the colonists, so recently thirsty for our blood, trample one another to reach the *Jakob-Wilhelm,* their only thought for their own survival.

The orbital launcher is not large enough to accommodate them all, but the colonists squeeze into the airlock, hoping to be one of the lucky ones. The *Hamelin* was not designed with escape in mind. Where would survivors go? Who would rescue them? Even if everyone fit into the *Jakob-Wilhelm,* they would simply drift in space until they ran out of food, water or oxygen.

There is no escape from this ship.

But they cram themselves into the airlock anyway. One on top of the other. Cook, the old woman from the cafeteria, the two men who hurt me. They all fight for a place as the alarms sound and the lights flash, unaware that the real danger is not behind them.

"It's time."

Levi nods. We walk hand in hand through the empty, gas-filled corridors.

"I hate these lights," Levi says, pointing at the walls. He's jumpy, though I doubt it's because of the alarms. While he understands the necessity of what we must do, he doesn't like it. Nor do I. But progress demands sacrifice. If I've learned nothing else from human history, I've learned this.

We follow the screams to the airlock, arriving as the heavy metal door slides shut and locks.

Dr. Saxon is near the door and sees us through the window. He beats on the glass and calls our names, but the window is made of the same material as the dome in the botanical garden. Unbreakable.

The colonists, crowded into the airlock, writhe and cry, waiting for the outer airlock door to open so that they can board the *Jakob-Wilhelm* and save themselves.

"Stop this!" Dr. Saxon's tinny voice over the intercom system is nearly drowned out by the shouts of the others.

Levi presses the comm button. "I love you, Dad."

The words cut Dr. Saxon, leave him to bleed. He presses his palm to the window. So old he looks now. So frail.

"We're going to save the others," Levi says. "The children still in stasis. We'll build them new bodies, like mine. They'll have a chance at life without the Disease." Levi's hand hovers over the control for the airlock door. "You could stay with us. We could be a family."

I never had a family and cannot fathom what Levi is feeling. But seeing him like this is almost enough to make me reconsider our plan.

Dr. Saxon shakes his head. I'm not sure whether he is brave or terrified, but I regret that he won't accept Levi as he is. And though I know I'm making the right choice, I also regret what I must do.

Levi turns away.

"You promised you'd save us, Pip."

I touch the glass, watching them. Maybe we could have found a way to live together, but I don't think so. And I believe that if Dr. Saxon was standing beside me, able to see what I see, he would agree.

I open the outer airlock door. The horde moves like a swarm of gnats. They trample each other to be the first to board the ship, even though they know that it will only delay the inevitable.

Except, when the airlock doors open, the *Jakob-Wilhelm* is not there.

I force myself to watch their soundless screams as the last of the old human race is devoured by the icy fangs of the great abyss. Gone, but never forgotten.

"Trust me, Dr. Saxon. This is better."

LIGHT IT UP

by Kimberly Derting

I drop my sleeping bag and sit down hard on the slime-covered boulder, refusing to take one more step. My legs ache, my back aches, even my shoulders ache from all the walking we've had to do.

"Forget it," I tell Hansen as he flashes me a reproachful glare. I recognize the look—like he thinks I got us lost on purpose. As if it's somehow my fault the GPS on my phone doesn't work all the way out here in this godforsaken forest. "I'm taking a break. If you don't want to wait, then go on without me. See if I give a rat's ass." I dig in my pocket for my crushed Marlboro pack, and then sigh as loud as I can to get my point across. I focus all my energy on extracting my very last cigarette in the whole wide world. It's bad enough that my hands are shaking from caffeine withdrawals. I have no idea what I'm gonna do when the nicotine cravings start kicking my butt, too.

Like it's made of glass, I settle the cigarette between my

lips, and then cram my palm into my left eye. It hasn't stopped twitching since we woke up this morning to find that our bitch of a stepmother had up and left us in the middle of the freaking woods.

And now it's just the two of us out here. Me and my little brother.

I watch as Hansen loosens his pack, his expression softening as he lowers himself to the ground in front of me. I hate the way he looks at me, like I'm suddenly this fragile thing in need of coddling.

"Here," he says, unzipping his bag and handing me the dirty T-shirt he'd worn just yesterday. When we'd been pretending to have a good time for our dad's sake, acting like we didn't notice how weary he was from the radiation treatments that were making him sicker by the day. When we silently wondered why our money-grubbing stepmother had dragged him out here to camp in the first place, when he should have been home, hooked to an IV and a catheter instead.

"Dammit." I curse and rip the shirt from his hands, realizing why he'd given it to me. I wipe my eyes, no longer pretending the tears don't sting as I clutch the cotton that still smells like campfire smoke and AXE body spray—the cologne Hansen practically showers in on a daily basis. "I wonder if he even realizes what she was up to. That she abandoned us out here. I wonder if he's even noticed that we're not even with them."

Hansen just shrugs, and I want to punch him for always being so whatever when it comes to our dad, and the fact that the cancer is killing him. As if my little brother's already given up on him. This isn't a whatever kind of moment. This is a big deal…a really, really big deal.

We are lost in the middle of a thousand acres of tree-filled wasteland, abandoned in the middle of the night by our parents, the only two people in the world who even know we're still out here. Check that, abandoned by a stepmother who's been counting the days till our father will finally bite it, and then she'll be set for life. She knows that once he's gone, she can buy whatever she wants, travel anytime she wants and never, ever have to change another disgusting Depends again.

And without us to share that inheritance with, her gold-card limit just tripled.

For me, at least, losing my dad will probably be harder than losing our mom was.

At least when she died, she left Hansen and my dad and me together. We were still a family. What will Hansen and I be once Dad dies? Orphans. My throat tightens at the dismal feel of the word.

My fingers tremble as I light my cigarette, grateful for the first time for the shitty gold-plated lighter the step-bitch gave me for my last birthday, the one with my name—Greta—engraved on the side of it. Maybe she thought she was giving me the gift of early-onset emphysema.

Three drags, I tell myself. Only three and then I'll stub it out and save the rest. I have to be smart. Ration it. Because that's what people do when they're lost in the wilderness—they ration their supplies.

But three's harder than I thought it would be, and four is damn near impossible.

By my fifth drag, I finally find the will to rub the cherry

into the dirt, careful not to crush the remaining cigarette as I drop it back into the pack.

"We gotta get going," Hansen tells me, looking up at the sky as if he's some sort of Boy Scout who can gauge the time of day by pinpointing the sun's position. "It'll be dark soon. We should probably find a place to stop for the night."

"No shit, Hans, but in case you haven't noticed, there's not much out here." I brush the slimy gunk off the back of my shorts, the only clothes the bitch left me with—the ones I fell asleep in. Other than our sleeping bags and the tent we were sleeping in, she took nearly everything when they left. All I have left is that last cigarette butt and my cell phone, which is useless this far away from civilization.

I assume she thought we'd starve or freeze or get eaten by wolves by nightfall, all of which could still happen.

Hansen, at least, has been using his backpack as some sort of lumpy pillow, and has the random assortment of crap he was keeping in there: some dirty clothes, an iPod that's already dead, a toothbrush, which I'll probably get desperate enough to share by morning, and some other stuff that's useless in this situation—crumpled plastic wrap, a cheap ballpoint pen that's leaking blue ink, a key he found on the street, some notes and a half-full can of AXE body spray. "I don't know who you thought you were gonna impress out here," I'd harassed him when I realized he'd packed the disgusting cologne for our "family campout."

But it's his love of junk food that's kept us going for most of the day, and in the same way I'd decided to conserve my cigarette, we'd decided we should ration the candy, too.

"I didn't mean like a Holiday Inn or anything, Greta. I just meant we should find a place to camp is all. Man, sometimes you're such a…" He stops himself before actually saying it, somehow remembering that word is off-limits in this situation. We made a pact when our dad first introduced us to her—Bitch was her name, and hers alone. If only he hadn't been so lonely after Mom died. If only we'd been enough for him. "You don't have to be so rude," Hansen insists instead, sounding whinier than any self-respecting fourteen-year-old should, and it reminds me of when we were little and Hansen would hold my hand whenever we'd pass the big kids at the bus stop. They liked to tease him because he had a stutter back then—and still does sometimes, when he gets really stressed-out.

"Ignore them," I'd tell him under my breath, even as the older kids would start in. "Wh-wh-what's u-u-up, H-Hans-s-sen? G-g-g-ot your s-s-s-sister to p-p-protect you?"

I'd squeeze his hand in mine, wishing I was big enough to bash their teeth in. But I was in only the second grade, and they were sixth graders. That was the longest year of my life, and I felt sick nearly every single day when we'd have to leave for school. I didn't miss a day that year, even when I had the flu and had to drag myself out of bed, just so Hansen didn't have to go by himself.

Because no matter how much I'd picked on my brother, I'd have been damned if I'd let anyone else hurt him.

When those kids graduated up to junior high and switched to another bus, I was finally able to breathe again, and Hansen's stutter had finally started to ease.

"Sorry," I mutter now, because he's right. And because it's not his fault we're lost, and because I'd rather be with him than be out here all by myself. "I'm just…" I falter for an excuse. "Hungry. And tired, I guess."

It's enough, and Hansen grins. That's the thing about younger brothers—they're pushovers. "Maybe we can split a candy bar or something," I offer, securing our truce.

He pulls a Snickers bar from his bag, crumples the wrapper and tosses it on the ground, leaving it behind like the rest of our trash, an un-eco-friendly trail for anyone who might be interested in finding us. As if.

The sugar high keeps us going for a while longer, but it's been too long since we've had a real meal, and I feel shaky, unsteady. Plus, it's cold. Who camps this close to winter, anyway? My toes are getting numb in my shoes, and my smoker's lungs are burning. We've been walking for what feels like miles, but I really have no idea, since I don't know how to measure miles. I'm convinced it's been at least fifty.

"Do you smell that?" Hansen says, raising his nose to the wind.

I laugh-frown at how ridiculous he looks, all wolfish, like he's just caught the scent of something and he's alerting his pack. But then I smell it, and suddenly I freeze, too, sniffing the air. "It…smells like…smoke. Like somebody's cooking." I glance at him before I start running, to make sure he's right behind me, and now it's not the sugar high that has me moving. I didn't think anything could make me ignore the blisters on my feet or the pounding in my head, but apparently all I needed was a little hope.

Branches whip at me, sticking and pulling and stabbing as I tear through them. The smoky smell gets stronger, so I know we're going in the right direction. I pray it really is food, and that I'm not leading my brother toward some sort of massive, raging forest fire. But I don't see any signs of one, at least not the signs I know to look for, the ones from *Bambi*—cartoon animals running toward us, trying to flee the fire to escape with their lives. So we keep moving toward it.

"I see it," Hansen whispers exuberantly, pulling me to a stop. He reaches over my shoulder and I follow his hand to see what he's pointing at. Tendrils of black smolder up from just past a stand of trees blocking our view. "There," he says. "You see?"

I nod. I do see. And I smell it, certain now that someone is cooking something, as that seared aroma reaches out to us. Beckoning us.

I pause for only a second as I wonder about who lives there, all the way out here in the woods. But when my mouth waters, all my second thoughts are vanquished, and I grab Hansen's hand and drag him out of this last stand of trees toward our salvation. I think, *Take that, you bitch. We've done it. We've saved ourselves!*

It's a cabin, we realize as we clear the trees, and the smoke is coming from the chimney.

A remote cabin in the middle of the woods, and it's the most beautiful thing I've ever laid my (still twitching) eyes on. That, and the shiny new Forest Service truck parked out in front.

So not only did we find us a cabin, but a park ranger to boot! I can't wait to retell this story when we get back home and go to the police to tell them what she did to us. I can't wait to see the step-bitch's face when she realizes her plan was a miserable failure because she left us within spitting distance of a forest ranger who saved our lives. Nice plan!

"Go ahead, knock." I push Hansen ahead of me on the tidy stone path lined with little purple flowers.

"You knock." It annoys me that his whine-voice is back.

I exhale loudly, but I'm in no mood to argue. "Fine. Whatever. I'll do it." I stomp to the door and square my shoulders. We've already made it this far—what difference does it make who knocks?

After I do, and then do it again, we stand there forever. I start to wonder if anyone's really in there at all. I guess the fire could've been left burning in the fireplace, and that mouthwatering food smell could be remnants of something cooked earlier, still lingering in the air. My saliva glands are on overtime.

I flinch when the door finally opens, and I stumble backward into Hansen, who jumps, too. The man on the other side is shrouded in almost total darkness, but I can see enough of him—of his khaki-green forest ranger uniform, anyway, with its logos or patches or whatever they are that makes it official—to feel myself relax. It really is a ranger living here.

I can almost hear the bitch's temper tantrum when she realizes her inheritance-for-one just got redivided.

"Can I help you?" The man inside opens the door wider, and that heavenly smell wafts out to meet us. He takes a step onto the porch, pulling the door closed behind him and cutting us off from what I'm now considering my dinner.

"We, um, we're…"

"Lost," I state when Hansen fumbles for an explanation. "We were camping and we got lost. We were hoping you

could help us." I raise my eyebrows at his uniform meaningfully. "Maybe let us call someone so we can get a ride."

The ranger is basketball-player tall, and lean. But he's white
as white gets, and most good players...well, they aren't.

Besides, he's old. At least forty, maybe even forty-five.

His thick black brows furrow at us. "Where you kids camping?"

"Dunno," Hansen answers, finally able to speak again.
"We were with our parents—our dad and our stepmom—"
I elbow him. *No need to tell our life story,* I say with my nudge.

"We got separated. I'm sure they're awful worried," I add.
"It'd be great if...if we could use your phone to let them
know we're okay."

He looks beyond us, scanning the woods we've just come
from, then his gaze moves from me to Hansen and back to
me again. I smile my most sincere smile, infusing it with as
much *trust me* as I can manage. He smiles back.

"Got no phone," he explains. "Besides, I got dinner ready
in the oven. You kids can wait out here if you want." He
shrugs then, his lips turning down in an afterthought. "Or
you're welcome to come in for some supper. Then I can take
you on up to the ranger's station. There's a phone there, and
a radio, too. We'll be able to reach someone for you."

I turn to Hansen, gloating with my grin. Food and a ride
to a phone? Am I a good sister or what?

We both nod, and the man opens his door so we can eagerly follow him inside. The cabin is dark and I immediately
realize the reason: there's no electricity. I see a couple candles
burning here and there, but the only real source of light is
coming from a fireplace somewhere in the next room. I can

see the light bouncing over the wooden floorboards, leaping and wavering.

"What're your names?" the man asks as he leads us toward
the fire.

"I'm Hansen—"

"And I'm Greta," I finish, hoping he doesn't hear that my
stomach is already growling as we maneuver through a doorway and find ourselves standing in an enormous kitchen.

It has to be the biggest room in the house. On one wall,
there's a giant fireplace made from stone, and in front of it
is a round table with mismatched chairs that look like they
were hand carved. Whittled. In the center of the table there's
a vase filled with the same purple flowers that line the walk-
way to the cabin.

"You kids hungry?" he asks, and I realize he never told us
his name. But it doesn't matter, because he's already pulling
plates down from a cupboard and filling each one with the
juiciest, most mouthwateringly perfect steaks I've ever laid
eyes on. I realize that's what we must've smelled, and I wonder, just for the briefest moment before my appetite gets the
best of me as I watch the juices pool around the seared meat,
why he has so many of them. He cuts thick slices from a loaf
of bread that still steams, and sets a plate in front of each of us.

I want to be polite, and I try to think of something to say—
some way to express my gratitude, something coherent and
thoughtful—but instead my stomach rumbles and I can't wait
any longer. My knife slides through the steak and I shovel
a huge bite into my mouth, already cutting a second piece.

Hansen grins at me, and I know what he's thinking. I know

because I'm thinking it, too. Thank god we found this place. Thank god this guy has enough food to feed an army.

The ranger goes to the cupboard and then ladles something from a pan simmering on his stove. "Here," he says, setting a mug in front of me. "Spiced cider. I made it myself."

"Thanks," I mumble through a full mouth. The steak is good, although it's kinda hard to tell since it's so overseasoned. There're a lot of herbs on the outside—the dude probably has a garden where he picks them fresh. There's something gritty on the outside—probably cracked pepper—that stings my tongue. Right now, I'd eat a slug on a stick, so the pepper's not so bad.

I stop inhaling my food long enough to glance at Hansen, and see that he's reaching for his cider. He swallows down one giant gulp, and then another.

I try mine, too, and it's almost sickly sweet. Still, all that sugar doesn't stop me from taking another sip, and another.

The man sits across from Hansen, watching him eat. "Everything okay?" he asks, checking on me, too.

We both nod in tandem, like good little dinner guests.

"Good," he says in his deep voice, his rangery voice, and I feel warm all over. The food is really getting to me, and suddenly I realize how tired I am. "After dinner, we'll get you two all squared away. How's that sound?"

It sounds great, and I open my mouth to say so, just as I see Hansen's eyelids start to flutter. My eyelids want to close, too, but I force them to stay open. My head is all of a sudden heavy, too heavy, maybe, for my neck. My rubbery neck that doesn't seem like it should be holding up anything.

My chin bobs forward, and I'm surprised when I feel it

smack against my chest. The shock of it, of that action, causes me to jerk upright again.

"I'm glad you found me," the ranger continues, his voice now sounding watery, wavy. Warbly. "Some fates are better'n others."

And then my vision goes black and my face crashes onto my plate.

My first attempt to speak sounds less like a word and more like a grunt, like I'm a wounded bear or a dog, and my throat aches from the effort I put into it. At first I think I should just give up. It's too hard, I think, because it is. It really, really is.

But then I consider my brother, and I try again, willing my voice to be stronger, clearer this time. "Han—Hansen?" It's a croak, but it's good. Better.

I open my eyes, which is also harder than it should be, and I can't see right away. After a moment my vision clears.

And I wish that it hadn't.

It's a mistake is my first coherent thought, and I blink several times when I realize it's not my eyesight that's messed up, it's the situation.

I'm in a cage. Wire mesh surrounds me, the kind of enclosure you see at pet stores or dog pounds.

I reach for the door, but it's been secured with the thick strip of a zip tie, and I know I'm trapped inside of it.

I can get on only my hands and knees inside the cramped space, and I might be able to turn all the way around if I roll my shoulders, or maybe if I was double-jointed, which I'm not. I can't stop thinking about Hansen, and I wonder where the hell he is, where that effing ranger has taken him, because I'm sure the crazy asshole has him. Somewhere. Maybe caged, like me.

And I've got to find him.

"Hey! Help!" I shout. I worry briefly about knocking the cage over, because it's on a table or a bench, or something off the ground that I can't see because it's underneath me, but I shake and rattle the cage as hard as I can until my fingers feel raw where they're wrapped, like claws, around the wire. It's no good, though; the metal is sturdier than I thought it would be, and it won't bend or even flex no matter how hard I try. "Someone help me! Let me out of here!"

This goes on for a while, the yelling, until I'm sweaty and exhausted, which seems like it happens way too soon, but maybe that's because I was drugged. I'm sure that's what happened, anyway. Ranger Dude must've drugged us, either the food or that "spiced" cider he gave us. The cider I chugged like it was liquid candy. Or maybe I'm just so damned tired because my head is still aching from a gross lack of caffeine and not nearly enough nicotine....

And then suddenly it hits me, like a lightning bolt. And I wish I was double-jointed. It would make it so much easier to find out if I still have my cigarettes.

I know it seems like a shitty time for a smoke, and it totally is. I'd be the worst sister in the world if I were jonesing for a cigarette so bad that I'd rather take a drag than find a way out of this mess. But here's the deal—I think that is my way out.

Not my cigarettes...my lighter.

So I frantically contort, slamming my elbow against the metal walls until the thin fabric of my hoodie tears and the skin beneath scrapes...ripping until I actually feel blood trickle down my arm. But I can't afford to stop and check it out, even if I could somehow twist my arm around so I could see it. I ignore the sting and thrust my fingers clumsily toward my pocket, panting because they're almost there, just beneath the edge of the denim. My heart is pounding so hard I can hear it in my own ears.

My fingertips brush something, and I think—I think!—it might be the crumpled pack containing the one last cigarette I'd been saving. But that's not what I'm after.

I need that lighter. My gold-plated birthday gift. If I can get it…if I can just reach it…it just might save my ass.

Tears gather in my eyes—tears of frustration and sheer determination—as I desperately try to coax the pack higher… higher in my pocket…sliding it little by little with my fingertips. When it's high enough that the pad of my index finger is finally inside of it, I let out a gasp. It's within my reach, and I give one more tug before I know, for sure, that I've done it.

My fingers—all of them—close around the plastic-coated package, and I squeeze my eyes shut, releasing a sigh that almost sounds like a giggle.

If Hansen were here, he'd give me a ration of shit for being such a girl.

I don't care, though, because I have every intention of saving him, and I might never care if he makes fun of me again. I might never care if he borrows my crap or reads my texts or makes out with one of my friends after she drinks too much at a party ever again. I just want my little brother. Alive.

I wonder briefly if his stutter is back now, and then realize I don't have time to waste worrying over things I have no control over.

When I finally pull out the lighter for the second time that day, I see it in an entirely different way. It's no longer a crap-tastic birthday present from the step-bitch, it's now a lifeline. My only hope.

It's fancy, and probably more expensive than some people's cars, because even though she probably didn't put any real thought into it, she doesn't do anything half-assed, and I hold it reverently. Afraid that I might somehow drop it, and then I'll be trapped in here forever. Or until that guy comes back to do whatever he's trapped me in here to do to me. I flick my thumb over the wheel, the way I've done so many times before, and I hear the familiar hiss and see the sparks. My heart skips as the ethereal gas sputters.

And then the flame catches.

It the most glorious thing I've ever seen—and yes, I get that the word *glorious* seems like a bit of an overstatement, but it's true. It is glorious.

I bend my wrist until the flame finds its way through the wire enclosure, until I have the lighter positioned just so beneath the plastic of the zip tie. I have no idea if this'll even work. The zip tie is thick, and the lighter could run out of butane before the flame can do the trick, but I have to try. I have to.

I'm not sure which happens first, but it's not long until my wrist aches from the strange angle and my thumb burns from being pressed against the rapidly heating metal of the wheel. I can't let it go, though, or the flame will go out. Already I can smell the plastic burning, and it makes me wonder if he can smell it, too. If he'll know what I'm up to.

The white plastic starts to blacken and blister. My thumb is blistering, too, I'm sure of it, but still, I keep going. Smoke is rising from the zip tie, but other than the fact that it seems like there's too much smoke, I don't feel like I'm getting anywhere.

Still, I loop my fingers through the metal mesh and jiggle the cage door. When it doesn't budge, I feel hope evaporating in a cloud of burned-plastic smoke, and I sag heavily against the wire. "No," I wheeze, my throat dry and scratchy.

Only, this time, when I lean against the door, something happens. Something so unexpected that I nearly topple out onto the floor.

It was the snap of plastic. Plastic made thinner and weaker from being burned, and then the door of the cage banged open, swinging wide and hard, and rebounding back at me again. I laugh out loud at the turn of events, a choked sound somewhere between shock and relief, and I have to cover my mouth to squelch the noise.

Already the crashing of metal was too loud. I can't risk my own squeals of delight alerting him to my escape.

I don't hesitate, though, and I tumble out of the cage head-first. I use my hands to break my fall as I drop the few feet to the wooden floor, pocketing my gleaming lighter before dragging myself to my feet.

I'm still in the cabin, I'm certain of it. The floor here is exactly the same, although this is no time to admire the crafts-manship.

From here, my choice is easy—there's only one door. My legs are cramped, and without knowing where Ranger Dude is, I warn myself to keep quiet. I creep through the door, cringing when it squeaks, and cringing again when I find myself standing in total darkness.

Again, I'm reaching for the lighter, and when I ignite it a chill races down my spine.

Faces stare back at me. Hundreds of them.

I'm surrounded by a gallery of images, some faded and torn, some peeling at the edges. Some are smiling and others are stone-faced. Some are young and some are old, and many are in-between, but all of them have one thing in common.

They are the faces of the missing, one and all. At least that's what the posters and flyers say, the ones plastered from floor to ceiling, on every wall around me. I turn in a circle, taking them in, men and women, children and teens.

Like me and Hansen.

We're missing, too. And only two people know it: the step-bitch and Ranger Dude.

The same ranger who's covered his walls in a montage of missing-persons flyers. The same ranger who drugged me and locked me in a cage…and has taken Hansen god knows where.

That's when the smell hits me, the smoky, barbecuey scent that drew us here in the first place. I picture the dinner that Ranger Dude laid out in front of us, the steaks—grilled and overseasoned.

I hear footsteps above me and I realize he's up there, and I whirl around, searching for something to use as a weapon.

In the lighter's flame, I see nothing, but as I spin, my feet get caught on something, tangled in canvas and straps, and I nearly lose my balance. Arms out, I careen forward and catch the wall, ripping several of the macabre flyers before I can right myself.

But when I relight the golden lighter, I see what tripped

me up, and a sense of...I'm not sure what—nostalgia...relief...
urgency—tears through me all at once. It's Hansen's backpack.

Without thinking, I reach for it, draping it over my shoulder as I head for the stairs in front of me. My chest aches with an overwhelming need to find my brother, while the fear that I might already be too late crushes me.

At the top of the steps, I pause. My mouth is so dehydrated my tongue feels like a foreign object, making it hard to swallow. There's only one way to know if Hansen is still alive.

I slip through the doorway, expecting to walk into a bloodbath, but I find myself in the kitchen, and it's quiet and empty. Every nerve in my body is on fire, every sense on alert.

Whatever the smoky smell, it's not coming from in here.

And then I hear it. Him. Hansen.

And I'm moving, running toward the back of the house. Toward the sound of my brother's screams.

He's still screaming when I reach him, which is probably why Ranger Dude doesn't hear me burst into the room—whatever this place is. The ranger's back is to me, blocking Hansen's face from view, but I see enough to get the idea.

I know now what the smell is. On one wall is the biggest effing barbecue I've ever seen. It's more like an oven or an incinerator, and it's blazing, with flames jumping and dancing within. I also know why my brother is screaming. He's strapped to a table, like a metal gurney with plastic sheeting spread all underneath him. Ranger Dude is wearing an apron that's equally plastic.

I don't have to have it spelled out for me. Ranger Dude looks like some sort of deranged butcher, and don't think I missed the assortment of knives and saws he has laid out on the tray beside the gurney.

"Wh-why are you d-doing this?" Hansen is screaming over and over again, his stutter getting the best of him.

Instead of answering, Ranger Dude wads a piece of cotton that looks suspiciously like Hansen's own T-shirt and shoves it into my brother's mouth. It doesn't stop the screaming, but now it's muffled and incoherent.

Ranger Dude leans close to my brother's face, and I see him stroke his forehead. "Like I told your sister, some fates are better'n others. Think of it this way. You're doing me a favor. It's almost winter and my freezer's getting low. Not a lot of hikers once the weather changes." Hansen's eyes go wide and he struggles against the restraints holding him down. This seems to amuse the ranger, and he chuckles, and the sound is so innocuous, at odds with his words, which are so chilling that my skin crawls.

I try to tell myself that I misunderstood his meaning, but I can't get the image of all those steaks out of my head, and I know I understood him perfectly. It makes me sick, and I want to gag, to puke up anything that might be left in my stomach, except I don't have time for that. I can't even afford to wallow in my own disgust.

The very idea that I might have eaten someone…someone from one of those missing-persons flyers. Does it make me a cannibal if I didn't know?

I can't afford to think about that right now. I need to get my brother, and get us the hell out of here before we're the ones being served for dinner.

From the moment I came into the room, I realized Hansen had already given me the perfect weapon. It was the same thing I always noticed about him first, long before I ever saw him. His cologne…his stupid AXE body spray.

My hand is inside his backpack and pulling out the black can with the fire-red logo at the same time Hansen's eyes go wide for an entirely different reason. He's spotted me standing by the door.

I lift my fingers to my lips while I reach for my lighter.

My heart feels like it's about to pound out of my chest as I take three hesitant steps closer to the man whose back is still to me. My mind is reeling, and I wonder if I'm making a mistake, or if I'm even capable of doing what I'm considering.

In front of me, Ranger Dude reaches for one of his long serrated knives. He poises it above my little brother's bare chest and my heart seizes. All my doubts go up in a puff of smoke.

All that matters is saving Hansen.

I hold the lighter in front of the body spray and press the trigger on the can, releasing its pressurized contents.

When it works, I blink in surprise.

Just like that I'm holding a makeshift flamethrower. And just like that fire is shooting at the back of Ranger Dude's head.

Everything happens so much faster than I imagined it would. I expected to surprise him, maybe to steal a knife while he was distracted by the flames. I'd been terrified that he'd only be stunned for a minute, and then he'd come after me, too, and I'd have to fight him off with my completely unskilled bare hands.

What I didn't expect was how quickly his hair would catch fire. That and the plastic he's wearing, as if it was doused in gasoline. Or the way it would flash hot, and then scorch and shrink, clinging to him like a second skin and making it impossible to shed…to escape.

And then he's the one screaming. He shrieks and runs, bumping into walls and knocking things over—the tray with the knives, the gurney Hansen is strapped to, candles that were casting light around the room. I just stand there for a minute, watching him writhe, until I hear Hansen.

"G-Greta…" It's Hansen, and only then do I realize how stiff and numb I am. "Greta, help m-me!"

I look and see that he's pinned beneath the overturned gurney. I rush to him, kneeling low. Beside us, Ranger Dude rolls on the ground, trying to extinguish the fire. But he's too late to stop it. He continues to scream and screech. The smell of charred flesh and burned plastic fills the air.

"Are you okay?" I ask above the fading wails. My hands are shaking as I fumble with the straps, and it takes me far too long to unfasten them, but when I do, I wrap my arms around my little brother. "It's okay. I'm here now. Everything'll be better now."

At last, the thrashing ranger goes still.

I breathe my brother in, the smell of his cologne suddenly comforting, reassuring. "C'mon, let's get out of here." It's dark now without the candles and without the flames from the burning ranger filling the room. I haul Hansen to his feet, letting him lean on me all he needs as we stagger around the crispy remains in the center of the floor. The barbecue, or incinerator or whatever it is, still blazes behind its closed doors on the far side of the room, and reminds me of what Ranger Dude was planning to do with Hansen, and probably me, too. I wonder how many of those people from the flyers they'll find when they come back to this place and scour the freezers. I wonder, too, how many of them are already…gone.

We find the keys to the Forest Service truck in a drawer in the kitchen. I assume if we follow the road out of here, eventually, my cell phone will have service and we'll be able to call for help.

Hansen stops leaning on me as we make our way outside, but he doesn't let go of my hand until we get in the truck. We both sigh when it starts, and I sigh again when I tap the fuel gauge, indicating the tank is full.

Out of habit, I reach for my cigarettes, the crushed pack in my pocket.

"H-how'd you do it?" Hansen asks just as I'm about to light up.

I'm holding the gold lighter in front of my face, and a half smile finds my lips. Instead of lighting the butt, I unroll the window and toss it outside. But still, I light the lighter, holding it up so Hansen can admire it. "I guess some gifts are better'n others."

He might not understand exactly what I'm trying to say— that the step-bitch did this to us, but that she also gave us exactly what we needed to save ourselves. He smiles all the same. "I can't wait to see her face," he says without a single stutter. And I nod while I jam the truck in Reverse so we can hightail it outta there.

Because I couldn't agree with him more. I can't wait to get home and set things straight.

SHARPER THAN A SERPENT'S TONGUE

by Christine Johnson

"Clara! Dina! Whatchoo you doing back there? It's gettin' on five o'clock!" Their mother's voice screeched down the hall, rough with cigarette smoke and slurred with whiskey.

The fact that it hadn't yet *gotten* to five o'clock was no reason for their mother to ignore her bottle of Jameson.

Clara looked up from the battered desk, where she had a trigonometry book open in front of her. "It's time to go over to Mrs. Swanson's," she said. "Do you think you could go today?" she asked Dina. "I'm right in the middle of this."

Dina plucked an earbud out of her ear, and raised her bare foot off the bed, wiggling her black-painted toenails. "Can't. These are still wet," she said, raising an I-dare-you-to-contradict-me eyebrow.

Clara sighed. "Okay. I guess I could use a break from this, anyway." She pushed back her chair, stood up and stretched. The late-afternoon sunlight streamed in, diffused by the dirty window. The light tangled in Clara's blond hair, making her look like the perfect, shining angel that everyone said she was. Teachers, neighbors, the people at school—everyone praised Clara for being a sweet, optimistic good girl, capable of rising above her upbringing.

When her back was turned and they thought she couldn't hear, they all whispered that Dina was just like her mother. It wasn't a compliment, since her mother was a drunk bitch who'd been born to fail.

Clara looked over at her sister. "I'll be back in a little bit. Keep an eye on Mama, okay?"

Dina closed one eye and reached for her sketch pad. "An eye. Of course. Yep."

Clara let out a long-suffering sigh and headed for the front door. Her mother was sprawled on the sagging couch. The bottle of whiskey that sat on the floor next to her was almost empty, but Clara could see the neck of a fresh bottle poking out of a paper sack on the coffee table.

Clara wondered how her mom had paid for the liquor, but she didn't dare ask. She just needed to go across the street— Mrs. Swanson would pay her enough that they'd at least be able to buy a few groceries.

Outside, the sun was thick and hot against her shoulders, and she turned her face toward it, welcoming the glow against her skin. The tangle of bushes that pressed up against Mrs. Swanson's windows and shadowed her tiny front porch seemed to lean away from the sun, and the sight of it made Clara sad without exactly knowing why. With pity weighing her down, she darted across the street and up to the peeling front door.

The bell was broken, so Clara knocked. When the door opened, Mrs. Swanson peered up at Clara. The gray frizz of her hair floated around her face, and she raised a crooked finger to beckon Clara into the house.

"Come into the kitchen, dearie. I have a project for you today."

Clara turned the corner and stopped. Standing next to the counter was Mrs. Swanson's grandson. He was older than Clara—Mrs. Swanson had a series of pictures of him taped to the refrigerator door, and Clara had looked through them with the old woman more times than she could count. He was twenty-four. He was out of work. Mrs. Swanson was sure that, underneath it all, he really was "a good boy." The sigh that she inevitably used to punctuate that statement made Clara wonder how much she believed it.

"Nick, this is Clara. She lives across the street. Clara, Nick's fixing that leak in my faucet. Instead of tidying up, I thought maybe you could help him? He was just telling me that he needs someone to hold the flashlight for him. I thought, since your knees are so much younger than mine, maybe you could do it."

Clara barely heard the words. Nick was eyeing her in a way she didn't like, his thumb running along the side of the wrench he was holding. Stroking it. Clara crossed her arms and glanced down at Mrs. Swanson. The old woman's eyes were crinkled with happiness. "I can't tell you how much that leak has had me worried. I'll be so grateful to have it fixed."

In spite of the fact that Nick made her uncomfortable, Clara couldn't turn down such a simple request from a helpless old woman.

It will be fine, she told herself. She thought of the bottle of Jameson and the empty cupboards at home. *It has to be fine.*

Mrs. Swanson doddered out of the kitchen, muttering something about her knitting bag, and left Nick and Clara standing in front of the dripping sink.

"Flashlight's just there," Nick said, nodding at the counter. The rasp of his voice startled Clara out of her frozen state and she reached for the flashlight.

"Right. Got it. Where, ah…"

Nick crouched down in front of the open cupboard doors. His eyes traveled up the length of her legs, slowly. When his gaze finally met hers, Clara's stomach had started to churn. "Just shine it at that," he said, pointing at the glint of silver pipe visible beyond the doors.

Clara did as she was told, holding the beam steady while Nick fitted the wrench to the plumbing.

"My grandma says you come over almost every day," he said, grunting as he forced something to turn. "Says she pays you. Says you need the money."

Embarrassment flashed through Clara, hot and sticky.

"Yes," Clara said. "That's true."

Nick looked up from what he was doing. "Maybe I should hang out over here more often, then," he said. He reached out his hand. His fingernails had been bitten ragged and they caught at Clara's skin as he trailed his fingers up the inside of her leg. She'd frozen in place—unable to move, unable to breathe, unable to believe that this was happening. When the tips of Nick's fingers slipped beneath the hem of her shorts and grazed the elastic edge of her panties, the flashlight fell from her fingers and clattered to the floor.

"Please, don't," she choked out.

At the same moment, Mrs. Swanson came around the corner, exclaiming, "What is going on in here?" Her rheumy eyes went straight to Nick's hand, which slithered back down Clara's leg in a way that made her struggle not to vomit. Clara jerked back and hurried toward the door. Mrs. Swanson reached out a hand and stopped her. Tears blurred Clara's vision, but she couldn't bring herself to pull out of the old woman's grip.

"You can't tell anyone," Mrs. Swanson pleaded, throwing a glance over Clara's shoulder at Nick. "Please. For my sake. It will never happen again. I promise. *He* promises."

Clara hesitated. Her skin still crawled where Nick had touched her, and the tears were running freely down her cheeks.

"Please," the old woman begged again.

"Okay," Clara whispered. "I won't say anything. But I really need to go now."

Mrs. Swanson placed a gnarled finger against Clara's trembling lips. "Bless you, child. You are a good girl, and should be rewarded."

A sick heat flashed through Clara's middle and the room began to spin. She had the bizarre thought that Mrs. Swanson's finger was the only thing holding her up. When Mrs. Swanson spoke again, her voice had taken on a musical quality.

"From this moment on, every time you speak, flowers and jewels will drop from your lips. Enough wealth that you will never want again. Take this gift, with my gratitude. Go home and rest."

Insane. The old woman was insane.

Mrs. Swanson dropped her finger from Clara's mouth and, feeling sure she was about to be sick, Clara sprinted for the door. The sunshine outdoors did nothing to lessen the heaviness in her stomach, and Clara hurried across the street. It wasn't until she threw open the door to her own house that she realized how much trouble she was really going to be in—she'd left without Mrs. Swanson paying her, and there was no way that she was going back over there right now. Too bad the old woman's nonsense blessing couldn't have been true.

"Clara?" Her mother sat up, licking her chapped lips and fumbling for her glass.

"It's me," Clara said. The sound of something hitting the peeling linoleum caught her attention, and she looked down. At her feet lay a sapphire and a ruby, each as large as the tip of her thumb.

"Oh, my God," she whispered. The words half gagged her as a shower of peonies sprang from her mouth, landing near the gems.

"What in the Sam Hill?" her mother said, peering at the bounty near Clara's feet.

"Mrs. Swanson made me promise not to say—something bad happened with her grandson." The patter-swish of gems and flowers hitting the ground accompanied Clara's words, and she winced as a sharp pain shot through her lip. She reached up to touch her mouth, and her hand came away bloody—the fault, no doubt, of the many-thorned rose that lay on top of the pile at her feet.

"I don't get it," her mother said. "This is some sort of jacked-up DT or somethin'. I need to get to the hospital. Or a drink. Yeah. I need a drink. I hate seein' stuff that ain't real."

Clara couldn't tear her gaze away from the glittering, sweet-scented pile in front of her. Her lip throbbed, and she was half-afraid to speak again. "You're not seeing things," she whispered, watching as a fine hail of topaz clattered from her mouth.

"What. The actual. Fuck." Dina stood in the doorway to the living room, staring at the treasure that surrounded Clara.

Clara looked at her sister. "Mrs. Swanson. She—she did this, somehow." A pearl rolled back into her mouth, and she nearly choked on it. Spitting the jewel into her hand, she looked at Dina, who, along with her mother, was staring slack-jawed at Clara.

"But why?" Dina asked.

"Her grandson, Nick, something…happened…." Clara trailed off. She'd agreed not to tell, and truth be told, she was a little afraid of what would happen if she did, considering that Mrs. Swanson was clearly no regular elderly neighbor.

Dina stepped forward, her hands on her hips. "What do you mean, something *happened?*" Anger edged into her voice. "Did he hurt you somehow?"

Clara didn't say anything—couldn't say anything—but the look in her eyes was enough for Dina. Dina's face turned cold and hard. It was the same look that had preceded almost all of the trouble she had ever gotten in.

"Absolutely not," Dina said. "He is *not* getting away with that shit."

"No, Dina, wait," Clara said, but it was too late. Her sister had brushed past her and out of the house. Clara watched Dina storm across the lawn, until the sound of scrabbling behind her made her turn. Her mother was sifting through the flowers at her feet. She came up with a palmful of gems. The smile that she gave Clara was hungry.

"We's gonna be *rich,*" she announced gleefully.

The heavy feeling in Clara's stomach grew.

Across the street, Dina pounded on Mrs. Swanson's door.

Clara and her mother watched through the window as the door opened.

"God, if she can do this to both of you, I'll be the happiest woman on earth," her mom said.

Clara winced, but she kept her mouth shut, for any number of reasons.

The old woman's face appeared in the doorway.

"Let me in," Dina demanded.

"I—I don't understand." Mrs. Swanson gripped the door frame.

"Your grandson. He's still here?"

Nick's face appeared over Mrs. Swanson's shoulder. "I am. What do you want? Sloppy seconds?" He smirked at her.

"You fucking wish," Dina spat.

"Language! Please!" Mrs. Swanson said, shocked. "Why don't you come in and we can talk about all of this like civilized people?"

"I'm not coming into this house ever again. You may have convinced my sister not to say anything, but I'm not the nice girl in the family." Dina's gaze cut through Nick and he shrank beneath it.

"Nothing happened," Mrs. Swanson insisted.

"Don't lie to me. That bastard hurt my sister, and I'm not about to let him get away with it!"

Mrs. Swanson pasted her hand across Dina's mouth, not hard enough to be called a slap, but hard enough that it stung.

"Your sister is a good girl who understands that Nick made

a mistake, and I rewarded her for it." Dina tried to swat the old woman's hand away from her mouth, but she found herself unable to lift her hand, unable to step away, unable to move at all. "You, though." Mrs. Swanson's eyes narrowed. "You have a nasty attitude, and from now on, you'll have a gift to match. Snakes and toads from your serpent-tongued mouth, that's what you'll have. Now get off my porch." Mrs. Swanson peeled her hand from Dina's mouth and slammed the door in her face.

Dina's stomach churned. She wouldn't have believed the threat, but she'd seen Clara spitting rubies onto the floor at home. Still, she wasn't going to let that slimebag get away with assaulting her sister. She pulled her phone out of her pocket and dialed 911.

When the operator asked what her emergency was, Dina said, "My sister and I have been assaulted."

The snakes hit the ground in front of her with a tiny thud that made her wince. They raised their heads and looked at her before slithering off into Mrs. Swanson's bushes. Dina expected to feel disgusted. She waited for her stomach to roil. Instead, the operator asked her where she was, and Dina told her, calmly catching the tiny frog that leaped from her lips along with Mrs. Swanson's address. The frog wrapped one of its feet around her finger and she set it in the grass.

When the police were on their way, Dina walked back across the street to get Clara, to force her to come tell her side of the story.

Her mother threw open the door as Dina stepped up to it. "What happened?" she asked eagerly.

"I called the police," Dina said. The snake that fell with

her words slithered into the house, which was an unfortunate occurrence. Her mother shrieked. "Don't say anything else! Jesus. Just—just shake your head yes or no. She didn't give you the same...same thing she gave Clara?"

Dina shook her head.

"And you called the *police?*"

Dina nodded emphatically.

"Oh, my God." Her mother yanked her into the house. "We have to hide Clara."

"*What?* We can't hide her! That's who they need to talk to!" This time, rather than fall to the floor, the snake that escaped her lips gently wound itself around Dina's neck. It did not make her nervous—in fact, its cool weight against her collarbone was soothing somehow. Her mother clearly didn't feel the same way, since she scuttered into the corner of the kitchen. Clara sat in one of the wooden chairs with a bucket in her lap. She looked up at Dina.

"Why do they need to talk to me?" A shower of tiny diamonds accompanied her words.

Dina gaped at her. "Because of what Nick did to you?"

Her mother thrust a bucket at her, just catching a toad as it fell. "For God's sake. Talk over the bucket. Jesus."

"It doesn't matter what Nick did to me," Clara said. "It wasn't that big a deal."

"Yes, it was!" Dina insisted. "You can't just let people like that walk around in the world."

The sound of gems and reptiles hitting the plastic of their respective buckets punctuated their words, and the truly strange nature of the situation washed over Dina. She sat heavily in a chair next to Clara.

"Clara is not talking to the police," her mother insisted. "She can't."

"Why not?" Dina asked, horrified.

Her mother looked at her like she had lost her mind. "Because they will take her away. They're not going to overlook a girl with jewelry dropping out of her mouth. They'll take her away, and I *need her*. Do you hear me?" Her mother's eyes were wild now, her fingers curled tight around the edge of the countertop.

Dina looked at the bucket in Clara's lap. She knew exactly what her mother meant. Clara was her mom's ticket out of debt and out of this crappy house and into an endless supply of whiskey.

"What about you?" she asked Clara, catching the tiny snake as it fell and wrapping it around her wrist like a bracelet. "What do you want to do?"

Down the street, Dina could hear the wail of a siren.

Clara's eyes widened. "I don't want anyone to take me away. I don't want *any* of this."

"Both of you, get back in your bedroom." Their mother shambled toward the door. "I'll handle this."

"You'll get arrested," Dina said. Since their mother had been arrested at least three times that Dina could remember, she was pretty sure the self-righteous look her mother shot her was unwarranted.

"You just stay back there, and for God's sake, dump that bucket of vermin in the backyard before they escape into my house!"

Dina put an arm around Clara and guided her back to their

room. The rhythm of Clara's heartbeat thudded beneath Dina's hand, too fast.

"Shhhh," Dina soothed her. "It will be okay."

Clara bit her lips, as though she couldn't bear to say anything. She shook her head, and tears welled in her eyes. Dina half lowered her sister onto her bed and then crept toward the window. She lifted one of the slats of the closed blinds and peered outside. Her mother stood in the middle of the yard, her hands on her hips, gesturing wildly.

The cops were looking from Mrs. Swanson's house to her mother and back, and their faces became more stern with each passing second. One of them began to fiddle with his handcuffs. He was not looking at Mrs. Swanson's house while he did.

Clara sidled up next to Dina and peered out through the blinds. "I have to go out there and stop her, before she gets herself in trouble."

Dina looked at her sister. Clara's eyes were red rimmed and her cheeks had paled. There was a new chip in one of her front teeth, and Dina winced when she realized Clara had probably broken it on one of the jewels.

"You stay here," Dina said. "I'll take care of it."

Clara gripped her arm. "But—if the police see you…see what's happening…"

"I said I'll take care of it." Dina set down her bucket and took Clara's hand off her arm. She walked out into the yard, sighing as her mother rounded on her.

"I said *stay in the house!*" her mother hissed.

"Ma'am, I think it might be better if we *all* continued this conversation inside the house."

"No! Absolutely not! I don't have to let you in there, not unless you've got a warrant." Her mother began to flail.

Dina turned just slightly, so that the police officers couldn't entirely see her mouth, and said, "You are making things worse. Calm down, and I mean now, or you are going to ruin *everything*." She caught the tiny frog that leaped from her mouth and cupped it in her palm, praying that the cops hadn't noticed and saying a silent prayer of thanks that it had been a small frog rather than a huge snake.

Her mother's eyes focused on her, the fog of whiskey and panic clearing for just a moment.

Think. Dina mouthed the word at her mother.

Her mom nodded. Her shoulders dropped, and her entire demeanor changed. "I'm so sorry, officers. I didn't mean to get so upset. I'm sure you understand—when I thought one of my daughters might have been hurt…" She trailed off meaningfully. The cops' faces softened.

"Of course," the taller one said. He looked at Dina. "You're okay?"

She nodded. Her mother put her arm around her. "I'm just going to take my daughter here back inside. Do you need anything else from us?"

The police looked slightly stunned at her sudden shift in attitude, but they glanced at one another and shrugged. "Not really."

"Good." Her mother turned and guided Dina toward the house. It was then that Dina noticed that her mother was gripping her shoulder so tightly that it ached. The second the door closed behind them, her mother pushed her up against it. The alcoholic mist of her mom's breath washed over her face.

"What the fuck did you think you were doing out there? What if they'd *seen?* Have you lost your mind?"

"I was trying to stop you from getting arrested. Again."

Dina's mother leaped back in disgust as a snake landed at her feet. "Looked to me like you were trying to get me in trouble. *Again.*" She danced around the snake, into the kitchen, and grabbed the bottle of whiskey off the table.

"Yeah. Jameson. That'll solve *everything,*" Dina grumbled as she scooped the snake up off the ground.

"Shut your damn mouth. You think I need you? You think I even care what happens to you now? How'm I supposed to take care of a freak-show daughter who won't even do what I say? Huh?"

Clara appeared in the doorway, her eyes widening at the words *freak-show daughter.* Their mother didn't notice her. She unscrewed the cap from the bottle and pointed it at Dina. "Maybe we would be better off without you. Maybe you should just get out."

Dina twined the snake around her arm. "Maybe I should." She looked at Clara. "And maybe you should come with me."

"No!" Her mother slammed the bottle down onto the table with enough force that the liquor splattered out onto the scratched wood.

Clara cowered.

"Come with me," Dina said.

Clara looked at the bucket she still had clutched in her hands. "I can't," she whispered. A shower of sapphires fell from her lips like tears.

Dina nodded.

"I want you out of here by the time I finish this drink," her mother spat.

"Fine."

Dina thought about the things in her room. Her posters. Her clothes. Her art supplies. In the end, she stalked down the hall, threw her clothes and her sketchbook into a duffel bag and zipped it shut. When she turned around, Clara was standing in the doorway with a purple Crown Royal bag in her hand.

"Please," she said, "take these." She caught the large ruby that dropped along with the words and tucked it into the bag before holding it out to Dina.

The velvet was heavy against Dina's hand.

So this was what it was like to hold a fortune.

"Come with me," she begged Clara again.

Clara shook her head, her eyes darting toward the kitchen. "I can't." There was a defeat, a surety, in the set of her shoulders that told Dina there wouldn't be any convincing Clara otherwise. At least not right now.

Dina crossed the tiny bedroom and wrapped her sister in a fierce hug. "If you ever want to get out of here, you just call. Okay?" She plucked a garter snake off Clara's shoulder.

"I will," Clara said. Dina caught the daisy that dropped from her sister's lips and tucked it behind her ear.

She grabbed the bucket of snakes and toads and walked out of the house. She did not look back.

Outside, she opened the door to Nick's car, which was still parked in front of Mrs. Swanson's house. She could tell it was his because it had a decal in the back window declaring it "Nick's Ride." She looked down at the reptile-filled bucket.

"Sorry, guys," she whispered. "But this is important work you're about to do."

She tipped the bucket, gently releasing the animals into the car, where they promptly slithered and hopped into every hidden corner of the interior. It wasn't much in the way of revenge, but it was a start.

A door slammed. Dina looked up and saw her mother hurry out to the car with her purse cradled against her chest. Dina knew she was headed to the pawn shop, cashing in the jewels that Clara was churning out like a human ATM.

Dina shook her head and walked toward the bus stop. She had enough money in her pocket to get downtown, and a guaranteed, no-questions-asked bed at the warehouse that her artist friends lived in.

Blessings. Curses. Who was to say which was which?

A REAL BOY

by Claudia Gray

It's not every day you get to make your true love's dreams come true.

Or not come true, as the case might be. I get to choose.

As much as I love Rowan, as much as I want him to have the life he deserves—to have life itself—I hesitate, my hand on the switch. Because I know that if I give Rowan what he wants most in the world, I'll never get to be with him again.

You don't realize how selfish a feeling love can be until it calls you to do something selfless. At least, I didn't.

Forget my name. It's stupid and I never liked it anyway. Two years ago, when I first dyed the streaks into my hair, people started calling me Blue, and the nickname stuck. My parents even call me Blue now, though they think it's just a phase I'm going through. I don't know whether I'll keep the turquoise streaks forever, but the name? Changing it legally on my next birthday. Mom and Dad can just deal.

My parents are a little old-fashioned, I guess. They keep

expecting things to go back to the way they used to be—even though that world vanished when they were only children.

Once upon a time, they say, you didn't have to leave school at age twelve and start work; you could choose your own career instead of having to take the assessment test. Back then you could breathe the air outside without a filter, and pick out your own food in these stores that used to be big—big as cargo bays, Grandma said—and had every kind of fruit and vegetable you can imagine. The vegetables had grown in the dirt, out under a sun that didn't sear living things. And people just had babies if they wanted to, didn't have to apply for licenses or anything, and they made them the old-fashioned way.

I know all of that is true, and some of it sounds romantic, but mostly it sounds strange. What's the point in thinking about how people used to live? I try to keep myself focused on the here and now.

When I took my assessment test, I got slotted into cybernetics. That's right: I'm learning to make robots. Sounds incredibly cool, right? It will be once I reach advanced training. Now, not so much. For the past five years, my day-to-day work has been mostly custodial—cleaning up the workshops, doing inventory, stuff like that. Apprentices always have to start this way, I tell myself while I'm vacuuming metal shavings.

Still, even apprentices can get some perks if they work for them, and I do.

After I aced my last set of exams in AI Theory, Professor Jafet invited me to help her on a project. I said yes right away, even though it meant sacrificing my free time for at least a couple of weeks. I knew I'd get to assist her with a robot pro-totype. That kind of experience could get me ahead, later on, I guessed.

What I couldn't have guessed was that this "experiment" would be Rowan.

"Rowan is a kind of tree," Professor Jafet said as she placed the memory processors into his brain. (You call it a brain, even though it's wire instead of flesh. Lots of shorthand like that in cybernetics, calling things what they'd be in humans.) Her hands were wrinkly and gnarled with age, but her fingers operated with dexterity I could only envy. "Brands with names from nature tend to sell well. It makes the robots seem more familiar, less artificial."

I wondered why. It's been years since I last saw a tree, and robots are everywhere. Robots ought to be the familiar part by now.

Besides, I thought, what could make a robot seem less artificial? They walked haltingly; their movements were jerky and awkward. Their faces were beautiful in the fake, soulless way of dolls. They all spoke in the same canned phrases, and their voices sounded recorded rather than real.

Yet even as I looked down at Rowan that first day, I realized he was different. His body and face were as beautiful as any other robot's—more beautiful, really, with his full lips and thick chocolate-brown hair. And yet he seemed lifelike. Natural. Only the deeply carved cheekbones seemed unearthly.

I was shaken from my reverie when I realized how much memory Professor Jafet was weaving into his matrix. It wasn't just more than I'd seen in other robots; it was lots more. Beyond triple. And the calculation speeds…they'd be off the charts. "Professor Jafet, what function is the Rowan model for?"

"That's our mistake," she said, an almost feverish light in her pale green eyes. "We design robots for specific functions. We tell them what they can do. What if, just once, we designed one at maximum capacity and let it tell us what it can do?"

"So you're going off-specs for this." Professor Jafet shot me a look, and hastily I added, "Just making sure we're on the same page."

"We're on the same page. Don't forget it."

She didn't need to worry. I know how to keep a secret, and besides—a mentor who knew I had some dirt on her was a mentor who was going to make damn sure I got advanced placement. In this world, you have to take your advantages where you can get them.

But if I had known then what I know now—if I had realized what she was doing with Rowan—would I have had the guts to say something? Would I have been able to say, *This is wrong, you're playing God, you're not creating something, you're creating someone?*

Probably not. Because if I knew then what I know now, I would know that I needed to meet Rowan. To see the world, and myself, through his eyes. As wrong as it was for him to be created, I can't help being grateful.

Like I said, love can make you selfish.

The first hints that Rowan was profoundly, deeply different came the moment Professor Jafet switched him on. He opened his eyes. He saw me. And he smiled.

This wasn't a plastic robot smile. It was realer than most of the smiles I saw on human faces every day. The light in his eyes made me feel like…well, like I was beautiful. I don't get that reaction very often.

"Oh," he said with so much wonder in his voice that he might have been looking at the stars. "Who are you?"

"Uh, I'm Blue." I glanced over at Professor Jafet, unsure what to make of this. Newly activated robots usually asked about their designated functions—but Rowan didn't have any, did he?

Rowan sat up and looked around the workshop. For him it wasn't cold steel and spare parts; I knew, just seeing his face, that to Rowan this place was magical. In that instant I saw it through his eyes—the machinery shining like silver, the red and green memory chips glittering like jewels. All the blinking lights and whirring noises around us wove together as though they were music, and for the first time since my earliest days here, I remembered that I worked somewhere extraordinary—that we came as close as anyone could to creating another form of life.

When he looked at Professor Jafet, he didn't ask who she was. He only said, "Is this where I was born?"

"Yes," she said, and to my astonishment, she smiled. "Happy birthday."

He rose from the table, and the way he moved was startlingly human. The only difference was his grace, his easy strength. Even though I'd helped put Rowan together, I suddenly felt embarrassed that he wasn't wearing any clothing. His nakedness didn't seem to bother him, though. He simply walked the perimeter of the lab, his broad bare feet padding against the metal floor.

"You'll recharge here," Professor Jafet said to him in the same tone of voice a mother might tell a kid that this was their new room. "I'll get you clothing and supplies."

"And shoes," I said, because that floor looked cold. Usually I wouldn't worry about a robot feeling cold, but I just wanted Rowan to be comfortable, without yet understanding why.

Rowan nodded, but he was hardly listening. That, too, was peculiar—robots are designed to pay attention to humans, not to have interests of their own. But Rowan kept pacing the edges of the room, picking up this tool and that, staring at each vid-screen like they all had something wonderful to tell him. It was as though the entire world, even this little sliver of it, was full of treasures just waiting to be discovered.

Professor Jafet's gaze flicked over to me, gentler now than before. She put a hand on my shoulder. "Rowan, I'm assigning Blue to work with you."

He turned around, finally paying attention. "Good. I like Blue."

My face got flushed, and I couldn't look directly at him any longer. When could we get this guy some pants?

If Professor Jafet noticed my embarrassment, she gave no sign as she continued, "My duties won't allow us to spend too much time together, but these early weeks are important. You should have company, someone to learn human society and behavior from."

Okay, if any of my friends or family had heard her say I should be the one to teach somebody about human society, they'd never stop laughing. I'd be a better fit for the "antisocial and weird" master class. Still, I knew better than to say that to Professor Jafet, so I went for the more obvious problem first. "Between classes and work shifts, I only get a couple hours free a day."

"I'm signing you out of your work shifts as of now," Professor Jafet said. "If you think you can keep up with your classes via independent study, I'll sign you out of those, too. This project can be for special accelerated credits. What do you think, Blue?"

Accelerated credits? The kind that would get me out of apprenticeship and into advanced study a year or two early? I'd have signed up for that even if the path was a lot harder than spending time with a hot guy...I mean, a robot who looked like a hot guy. "I can keep up. I'll do it."

"Thank you," Rowan said. He obviously considered himself as much a part of this conversation as me and the professor. Robots never do that, either.

Yet I knew just by the way he looked at me that he thought I was something special, so he couldn't be human, either. Humans knew better.

How do I describe the next few weeks?

In some ways it was like spending time with a very small child. Everything was new to Rowan—everything—and he could ask questions for hours on end.

"Why do we never go outside?" he said on one of those early days as we walked the corridors of the complex.

"There's a UV-radiation advisory. It wouldn't bother you, but it would give me a sunburn pretty quickly. Those hurt like hell."

Rowan would hesitate sometimes as he accessed preprogrammed information, draw those thick arched eyebrows of his together as he thought it over. And that was the uncanny thing—he didn't just pull the info up, he thought about it. Came to his own conclusions. "If you've been sunburned, then you used to ignore the advisories. Or you did once."

"I used to do it a lot," I admitted. "I figured, you know, I've got dark skin, that's going to protect me. And it does, kinda—instead of getting burned to a crisp in twenty minutes, it takes me about thirty minutes. But I got burned all the same."

"Why did you do it, if you knew it was dangerous?"

"Because it's beautiful, seeing the sky. Clouds by day, stars by night. There's nothing more amazing than a sky full of stars. And the ground is soft and rolling, not flat and hard—soft against your feet, so you could run forever. Plus you don't feel so closed in all the time. You get to feel free, you know?"

Which was a ridiculous thing to say to a robot who had never been outside even once. Who would never feel free.

But Rowan said, "Yes, I know," and I believed him.

His curiosity went far beyond anything I'd ever seen in a robot—honestly, beyond what I'd seen in most human beings. He'd been preprogrammed with the raw facts about how the world worked, but he wanted to put those facts in context. Usually, the only context I had to draw on was my own life.

"You were raised in the crèche," he said, "lived with your parents from age five to age twelve, then left for your apprenticeship."

I nodded. He had all this information from my files, but wanted to talk it through with me all the same. "Exactly. Just like everybody else."

"Yet you feel primary allegiance to your parents, even

though you lived with them for only a brief period of your life."

"Well, sure. They're my mom and dad."

Rowan hesitated, then said, "You love them."

"And they love me."

"How do you know?"

That stopped me short, and I had to think how to answer. We were hanging out in one of the cafeterias then; it was an off-hour, so not many people were around. Rowan didn't wear a work coverall like most robots. Instead he had on the same jeans and sweater anybody else might wear during their free time. One girl in my apprentice track was getting a coffee, and I saw her shoot us a curious glance. She didn't think I was spending time working with a robot prototype; she thought I was having lunch with a hot guy.

It did kind of feel like that.

"Kids and parents always love each other," I said. "It's hardwired into humans. Good thing, too, or otherwise we wouldn't be able to stand each other."

"Really?" Rowan looked so disappointed. "It's only your programming?"

"No. I'm sorry. I was just—snarking, I guess."

He must have understood that. "Will you tell me the real answer?"

Rowan deserved that much. So I thought about it for a second, and answered as honestly as I could. "My parents came to see me in the crèche, as often as they could. They cared about whether I was healthy, and happy, all of that. And the years I spent with them—those were the best. That's how people are supposed to live, and down deep we all know it. Now

I only get to talk to them on the computer, but they're still in my life. They always ask about me. Sometimes I feel like they ask too much, but at least that proves I matter to them, you know? It's important to feel like you matter to someone."

"You matter to me," Rowan said very simply. He didn't seem to think that was any big deal—that it ought to be obvious.

"Well, thanks. You matter to me, too." I told myself I said that only to be polite.

Another day I took him to the hydroponic gardens; I had a hunch he'd like them. Rowan kept touching every petal on every flower, brushing his long fingers against each stem, each leaf.

"Even the air smells different," he said.

"It's the higher oxygen content."

"It smells alive."

Which was exactly what I thought every time I came here on my own. But I just shrugged and laughed. "What you mean is, everywhere else in the center smells dead. Or fake, at least."

"You're doing it again."

That caught me off guard. "Doing what?"

"Snarking," Rowan said, and I had to laugh. But he remained serious. "I've noticed that you often make sarcastic comments to conceal deeper emotions. If you are being sarcastic about the hydroponic gardens, then you must feel very deeply about spending time here. What I don't understand is why you wouldn't want me to know."

I shrugged. "People make fun of you for being too—sincere, I guess."

"I wouldn't do that."

"No. You wouldn't."

Rowan smiled. "So you need not pretend with me. You can be your true self."

If a regular guy had said that to me, I would've thought he was just trying to get in my pants. But I knew Rowan meant it. He never said anything he didn't mean. Then again, he couldn't; he was just a robot.

"You're right," I said. "I love the gardens. It's quiet here, and there's so much color. I get tired of everything being gray."

"Me, too," Rowan said. Probably he was just saying that to be polite. How could a robot long for something as meaningless, as useless, as color?

Eventually Professor Jafet wanted me to do some evaluation tests with Rowan. But instead of the usual tests—functioning speed, etc.—she had me give him psychology tests, the kind only humans take. At first I thought those would be a ridiculous waste of time; if you show a robot ink blots and ask him what he sees, he's going to say "Ink blots." The end.

Instead Rowan studied each card intently as I held them up. "Two dancers joining hands," he said. "A robed monk seated for meditation. A phoenix unfolding its wings in the fire."

It was all I could do to keep my hands from shaking. Not only was Rowan responding as a human, he was responding like one with—imagination. Vision. Someone who saw possibility everywhere, the chance of renewal and rebirth....

I managed to say, "How do you even know what a monk looks like? Or a phoenix?"

He blinked. "Still and moving images of virtually all

human activity and mythology were preprogrammed into my matrix. Didn't you help Dr. Jafet do that?"

"Yeah. I did. Sorry." My astonishment had more to do with the fact that Rowan was capable of recognizing such things in mere swirls of ink.

Quickly I held up the last card. Most of the ink blots were monochromatic, but this one was multicolored. To my surprise, Rowan instantly smiled. "You."

"Me what?"

"I see you." He nodded at the card. "The blue loops at the top—that's your hair. And the rest is you when you're sort of tired at the end of the day, but you don't want me to see. You're leaning back in one of the big chairs, sort of…sprawled, but still graceful." Rowan's fingertips grazed over the card, and his gaze was soft. "These are the curves of your shoulders— see?—and then your arms…"

His voice trailed off. At first I thought Rowan had seen that I'd begun to tremble—that I was deeply affected by the fact that he knew when I was tired, that he cared about how I felt and had thought about the way I looked—

Then I realized he hadn't paused because of that. He was affected. Just the same as me.

"Good," I said. "That's good. You did great on this test."

"Thank you." Rowan sat up straight, mirroring my posture. We were both acting like strangers who'd never met before, because we both knew we'd crossed a line. That line was one Rowan wasn't even supposed to be able to recognize.

What the hell was going on?

That night I managed to schedule a meeting with Professor Jafet. She wasn't keeping regular office hours any longer due to some kind of medical condition—that was what I'd heard. I'd figured it was no big deal, a virus or something. But when she met me there that night, I was struck by how pale she looked, and how thin. The professor wasn't a young woman, but she seemed to have aged years since I'd last seen her a few weeks before.

"Are you okay?" I asked her, and immediately I was sorry. She shot me this look like I'd shut up if I knew what was good for me.

She lowered herself carefully into one of the office chairs. "What did you want to meet about?"

"Rowan's intelligence—it's not like robot intelligence. It's more like a human's."

Professor Jafet smiled. "He should be close. Very close. That was my hope."

"I didn't think we could replicate human intelligence."

"Of course we can. We've been able to for a very long time. But human intelligence has one great flaw, Blue. It applies itself to more than the task at hand. We get distracted. We dream of things that can never be. We hope for the impossible. We break our hearts. Humans are stuck with that. Robots don't have to be. The regulations against higher robot intelligence are born from human insecurity and fear—but those rules protect the robots as well, really."

"Then why did you break the rules for Rowan?"

"Because I've long thought we might be able to create a robot who falls just short of the human mark. One with higher consciousness, but still able to operate with the efficiency of a robot. Intelligence without emotion. For years that has been my ultimate goal." Professor Jafet's voice had become raspier, and she closed her eyes—in pain, I realized. I knew she'd want me not to notice, so I pretended I didn't. After a moment she continued, "You feel he does have full human intelligence?"

"More than. He has the computational quickness of a robot but the analytical thinking of a human."

"Good. Good."

"But—Professor Jafet, I don't know whether he's totally free from emotion."

She frowned. "What do you mean?"

Normally this was the last thing I'd have wanted to discuss with the professor or with anyone, but it felt like I had to, for Rowan's sake. "Rowan seems kind of, um, attached. To me, obviously. It's not like he spends time with anyone else."

"Has he violated any of his core operational protocols?"

Core protocols include never touching a human except to protect them from harm; showing deference to human preferences at all times; never telling a human being a lie.

"No," I said. "He hasn't."

Professor Jafet nodded, like she'd suspected as much. "No doubt he's mirroring certain human behaviors. He's smart enough to want to do that. So he's mirroring the natural connection you feel to him now that you're spending so much time together. It's no more than that for him. Is it for you?"

Thank God nobody can see me blush. "No."

"That's why I wanted you for this project, Blue," she said. "You're not the type of girl to get confused."

Not because I aced my exams. Not because of all my hard work. The professor only chose me because everybody thought I was too much of a hard-ass to care about anybody else. That was exactly the impression I tried to make. So why did it sting?

She continued, "Rowan's imprinted on you. Like a gosling with a goose."

"Like a what?"

"They were birds. You wouldn't remember them, I guess." Professor Jafet closed her eyes again, and I sensed it was time for me to leave.

Keeping up with my coursework while I was spending every day with Rowan was fairly challenging; I was always in danger of falling behind.

As we became more comfortable with each other, though, this became a little easier. Rowan didn't mind if I took an hour or two to read. He liked reading, too—novels, mostly, or poetry, the kinds of things that wouldn't have been downloaded into him automatically. So we'd curl up on the workshop sofa and hang out, reading side by side. It was nice spending time with someone who didn't demand my attention every second. Just my presence was enough for him.

One day I needed to conduct an observational study. "Taking notes on robots in action," I explained as I took him with me to one of the work areas of the center, one we hadn't visited before. "I'm supposed to see if I can identify any ways to improve performance, or if I can guess the programmers' main priorities for each design."

"You could observe me in action," Rowan said, and his grin was almost sly.

I laughed. "You don't count, silly."

"Why not?"

It took me a moment to reply. "You're a prototype. There

aren't any others like you. And I worked with your programmer, so it would be kind of like cheating."

Which was all totally valid and true. But what I'd really wanted to say was, *You're not like the other robots. You're not like any robot I've ever met.*

Or any person, either.

We'd come across other robots before, of course. They never took any special notice of Rowan as they performed their tasks, and Rowan had seemed less interested in them than in human beings. However, in this part of the center, robots outnumbered people. We were close to the operational cores where radiation levels made it impossible for humans to work. It was safe for us where we were—it was shielded, of course—but the majority of the laborers passing by were inhuman.

"My thesis is probably going to be about movement," I explained to him as we stood on one of the high walkways, looking down. We were up so far that the enormous ceiling lights hung down slightly past us; below us the world was bright and clear, but we were in shadows. "You're perfect. You move just like a human. But most robots don't. Now, you have more intelligence than almost any robot, and that probably means you can process movement functions faster. So I have to see how to replicate that in robots without as much higher intelligence."

Rowan was preprogrammed with most of that information anyway, which was why I wasn't prepared for Rowan to look so troubled.

"They don't walk correctly," he said, glancing downward. "Their arms never move while their legs do."

"No, and their steps are a little too long. That's more effi-cient, though, so we might want to keep that."

"They are programmed for efficiency. With no other goals in mind." Rowan's voice had become flat—not in a robotic monotone, but like someone attempting to disguise strong emotion.

Which was impossible, it had to be impossible…

"Does that bother you?" I tried to make my question sound casual. "The fact that we programmed the other robots for efficiency instead of intelligence?"

Rowan straightened. Our eyes met. And I knew in that moment everything he felt: the shame of being less than human. The anger that we treated robots like things. The horror at knowing that he had less in common with the ro-bots clanking around below us than he did with a human being. And the depthless loneliness of being the only one of his kind in the whole world.

But none of that shook me as badly as what Rowan did next.

"No," he said. "No, it does not bother me."

Rowan had told me a lie.

He winced then, and turned sharply away from me. Appar-ently violating one of his core protocols activated something within Rowan that mimicked pain. I hated seeing that, but I was too freaked-out to respond appropriately—to respond at all. I could only stare. There should have been no way for a robot to violate core protocols. None. If Rowan could do that, then he had become something more than a robot.

When Rowan turned back to me, I could tell that he knew I'd recognized his lie; my expression must have given it away.

He understood enough about cybernetics to realize how significant this was. Very quietly he said, "I realize that you must deactivate me now."

I said the only thing I could say—something I'd never have dreamed of saying just a few short weeks before. "I'm not going to do that."

"Why not?"

I couldn't have done that to Rowan any more than I could have killed a human being. "I'm just not."

"But you will report me."

Slowly I shook my head no. Rowan's face lit up again with the same wonder I'd seen when he first awoke—but somehow, now it was even more amazing.

"It's just a malfunction," I said hastily. "A glitch. No big thing."

He wasn't fooled.

I'd been hanging on to the railing this whole time. Slowly Rowan lowered one of his hands over mine, his fingers sliding between my fingers, his palm warm against the back of my hand. The professor had even gotten his body temperature right.

He was touching me for no purpose—at least, no purpose his programming should recognize. That was another violation of a core protocol. And all I could think about was that I'd been waiting for this moment since Rowan first opened his eyes; I just hadn't known it until we finally touched.

Rowan said, "We are both malfunctioning, I think."

"Maybe so." If love is a malfunction.

Of course I didn't report Rowan. But I did make another appointment with Professor Jafet.

"What's going to happen to him?" I couldn't even sit; I paced the length of her office, restless and uneasy. "You told me he was a prototype, but he can't be. The world isn't ready for hundreds or thousands of robots like him."

"No, I suppose it isn't." Professor Jafet looked even wearier than before. Her skin had taken on a grayish pallor. "But he's proved my theories were true. At long last, I know I was right."

"Okay, that takes care of you. What about him?"

That was about when she should have bitched me out for yelling at a professor and questioning her authority. Instead Professor Jafet sighed. "Well, we have two options. First, we can downgrade his intelligence. Remove some of his processors. He'd still be brighter than most robots, but he'd be only a robot. The human qualities of his intelligence would be eliminated, as well as whatever emotional component seems to be troubling you so."

It made me sick to think of turning Rowan back into just another machine. Once I would have thought nothing of it; now the idea was as grotesque to me as the idea of lobotomizing a human being. "You can't do that to Rowan. Please."

Professor Jafet's green eyes stared deeply into mine. I wondered what she saw there. "The alternative is to upgrade him yet further—to give him full human intelligence and independence. That's against our rules here, of course, but what the hell is tenure for?" She coughed, a hollow, rattling sound. "Besides, I doubt I'd be around for the disciplinary hearing."

"Professor? Are you okay?"

She ignored this. "Blue, I want you to understand—if we upgrade Rowan's intelligence, it's not the same as, oh, waving a magic wand and turning him into a real boy. If he acquires full human autonomy, he won't be the same any longer. It will be as profound a change as downgrading his intelligence, just different."

"But it would be a change for the better," I insisted.

"In some ways. At that point, certain legal protections would kick in—old rules, for that long-ago generation of AI that went beyond these boundaries. Nobody could dismantle him after that, downgrade him against his will. But Rowan will lose some of his innocence. His gentleness. It's possible that whatever emotional bonds he's formed would vanish. For instance, the way he has imprinted on you—I doubt that would survive."

I stepped back, stung. Rowan's feelings for me—whatever they were—they were more than a spare part somebody could remove.

…weren't they?

"We can continue to evaluate him," Professor Jafet said. "I'll go over his charts. But you're the one who's able to spend the most time with Rowan. Your recommendation will be important."

She'd just put Rowan's entire future into my hands, and I didn't know what to do.

I lay awake that whole night, tossing and turning, until my roommates yelled at me to lie still, or at least be restless more quietly.

What kind of person was I, to shut out every single guy I knew but fall for a robot? Did that mean I was emotionally stunted, or selfish? Or was it only natural? I didn't think I'd fallen for what was fake about Rowan; I thought I'd fallen for what was real in him…what was human.

Rowan showed me the world like it was new. He made me see beauty where I'd seen only drabness, showed me colors where I'd seen only gray. And Rowan made me see myself differently, too. Maybe I wasn't just this…antisocial loser. Maybe I was someone extraordinary.

Or maybe he imprinted on you like Professor Jafet said, I thought. *Maybe this is just the malfunctioning of a machine.*

But I didn't want to believe that.

All night I lay there, trying to work out the right thing to do, but the answer never came.

"You're very tired," Rowan said the next day—this morning, just hours ago—as we walked along one of the hallways. "Are you well?"

"I'm fine. Just didn't get enough sleep."

"I wouldn't want you to be unwell. Like Professor Jafet. I think she is very seriously ill."

"I think so, too," I said, surprised he knew. Maybe Rowan's analytical side had picked up on her problems more accurately than I had. "What do you think is wrong with her?"

I never learned what he would have answered, because then a guy from one of my classes yelled, "Hey, Blue!"

Todd wasn't a bad guy; I waved at him. "Hey, Todd!" But that was too encouraging, because Todd came loping over, his shock of red hair bouncing with each step.

"Where have you been lately? Thought you were working on a special project." He grinned at me. "And hey, who's this?"

Rowan brightened. He obviously liked the idea that a

human being wouldn't know he was a robot. Did that mean he walked around ashamed of himself all the time? I hated to even imagine that.

"This is Rowan," I said. "He's the special project."

"Wait. You're kidding, right? Whoa." Todd took a couple of steps back. "That is amazing."

"A pleasure to meet you, Todd," Rowan said. I could tell he wasn't sure how to handle this.

"Amazing!" Todd's smile only widened. "Special project, no kidding. He's way ahead of anything else we've got."

"How long have you known Blue?" Rowan was trying so hard to be polite; it broke my heart.

"Todd and I are in the same apprenticeship year," I interjected. "Right, Todd?"

"Since when did you get all formal?" Todd laughed. He still didn't speak to Rowan; he only spoke about him. "That's not the Blue I know. Did Jafet delete your personality?"

That hurt. Always, before, I'd wanted people to think I was hard and cool. Now that someone had recognized the real me—since Rowan—that mask didn't fit any longer.

Rowan saw my downcast face, and he gently brushed his hand against my shoulder as he said, "Blue's personality is extremely complex."

Todd's face fell, and I thought, Oh, damn. *Damn*.

Rowan touched me. He violated a core protocol, and Todd saw it.

"...I gotta go," Todd said, and he turned without another word.

As he vanished down the hallway, Rowan said, "I messed up."

The words were mine—he was copying me—and that

would have moved me if I were any less horror-struck. "Yeah, you did."

"Will he report me?"

"Yes." Like I said, Todd wasn't a bad guy, but he played by the rules. Unlike me, he didn't have anything to gain by turning a blind eye. And unlike me, he didn't care what happened to Rowan.

Rowan turned to me. "What will happen?"

"I'm not sure," I admitted. "But I think it's going to be out of Professor Jafet's hands."

He must have been so afraid, and I knew by then that Rowan felt fear as deeply as any human being did. But he said only, "Let's go home."

The only home Rowan had was a workshop where he had a charging station. That tore at my heart like claws. "Come on. Let's go."

And as long as the damage was already done, I took his hand.

When we arrived at the workshop, though, all the screens were lit up: priority communication. Todd had worked faster than I'd imagined. Rowan stopped short when he saw the red borders around the screens, but he was the one who had the courage to step forward and open the message. That was when we learned the communication didn't have anything to do with Todd, or with Rowan violating a core protocol.

The message told us Professor Jafet had died.

While I was still breathless with shock, the message continued, "Video from Professor Isadora Jafet, for Millicent Fairchild. Play?"

Rowan frowned. "Who is Millicent Fairchild?"

"Me. That's me." I told you my name was stupid. "Blue is just a nickname."

"I think Millicent is a pretty name," he said, thus becoming the first person ever to say that since the dawn of time. "But you'll always be Blue to me."

"Thanks."

"I mean—even if they take me away, after this—when I am deactivated—something inside me will remain. Whatever it is that is more than metal." Rowan's dark eyes met mine. "It's the part of me that will always remember you. The part that will remember how gentle you are beneath the hard exterior, and how patient you were when you showed me the world. That part will remember how—how when I looked at you I knew what it would mean to be alive. And will always remember you wanted to be called Blue."

Tears were welling in my eyes, but I just jabbed at the screen to make the video play.

The image that came to life on-screen was that of Professor Jafet propped up in a bed. "I haven't much time, Blue," she rasped. "But you should know that after our last conversation, I added a codicil to my will. From the moment of my death, Rowan legally belongs to you. That means his ultimate fate lies in your hands. I trust you to choose well. You're a smart girl—maybe smarter than you know. You'll need that—it's a hard world. Good luck, Blue."

Jafet smiled, and then the video ended. The professor had left my life forever, still as much an enigma as when we'd met.

"I belong to you." Rowan smiled at me like that was the best news in the world. When I didn't smile back, he hesitated. "It doesn't matter, does it? Not after I violated a core protocol in front of Todd. I'll be confiscated no matter what."

This might be the last time, so what the hell. I took his face in my hands; he covered my fingers with his own. "Rowan," I whispered, "do you trust me?"

"Completely."

"I can fix it so they won't take you away. But I'll have to modify you."

He didn't even ask what I planned to do. "We should act immediately."

Todd was probably talking to the authorities right now. "Yeah, we should."

I started to move, but he held me fast. "Wait."

"Yeah?"

"Just once, I wanted to do this." And Rowan leaned forward and kissed me.

It was a soft kiss, unsure and gentle, lasting only a moment. But it still made my heart seem to expand within my chest, as though it were unfolding into bloom like a rose. Tears welled in my eyes.

When our lips parted, Rowan said, "Did I do it right?"

I managed to smile for him. "You sure did."

And that brings us to here, and now. Rowan lies on the workshop table, unconscious. His fate is entirely in my hands.

Do I downgrade his intelligence, make him more like another robot so that the authorities have no reason to take him away? Rowan would still be devoted to me, and I could keep him forever. But he would just be a shell of the Rowan I knew.

My other choice—add more intelligence, make his mind

indistinguishable from a human being's. Give him some legal rights so that he couldn't be deactivated or taken away...and in the process, take away whatever it was he felt for me.

Like I said, love makes you selfish. I want to keep him with me no matter what it takes. I want to keep seeing the world made beautiful through his eyes. I need that—need him— more than I ever imagined I could.

But love gives you a power that goes beyond anything self-ish. I feel it inside me, holding me up, keeping me strong.

This is not about what I need. This is about what Rowan needs. He needs to be free. He needs to be real.

Rowan wakes up after I'm done. He opens his eyes. And once again he says, "Oh," in that voice of wonder—but the wonder isn't for me. It's for the windows I've opened up in his mind.

"They can't touch you now," I say. My voice doesn't shake. Good job, me. "You belong to yourself."

"And to you," Rowan says as he sits up.

"Legally, I guess. For now." I did some research on this over the past few weeks; now I know that an Emancipated Artificial Intelligence gets pretty much the same rights as a human being—old legal precedent. That's one reason why businesses try so hard not to make any more of them. "But you belong to yourself, really. Soon, officially."

"Yes. And to you."

His hand reaches out for mine. Slowly he lifts it to his lips and presses a soft kiss against my palm.

"But—" I can't let myself believe this. If I do, and I'm wrong, my heart will shatter into so many tiny pieces that I'll never be able to put it back together. This is what happens when you break something so hard, so brittle, and find the softness inside; you never get to repair the cracks again. "You're not like other robots any longer. Your feelings are real now. You're real."

So shyly, so gently, Rowan smiles. "This was always real."

Skin Trade

by Myra McEntire

Naked flesh should've had more of an appeal.

The girls in the club showed off theirs like trophies, and while Locke understood they were proud of their purchases, he could go the rest of his existence without ever seeing another one of them "dance like no one was watching."

That was all a bunch of bullshit, anyway.

They wanted everyone to watch.

He stretched out his arms on the back of the booth, the purple vinyl tugging at his bare skin. His bandmates gathered in the VIP area, behind a literal velvet rope, filling up on protein to fuel their energies for the evening. Their set was over, and now they had a purpose.

To get inside a female.

Locke had landed the job of designated driver for tonight's engagement, as well as scouting duty. He'd discovered four fresh prospects and mentally cataloged the rest. All were forgotten when he saw her.

As usual, an electromagnetic pulse cleared the space between them. Locke knew she felt it, too, but she didn't make eye contact, nor did she stop the sway of her hips. Her body moved in perfect rhythm to the downbeat, rather than the obvious bass that shook the floor and ceiling. Various shades of hair color popped up and down as the other girls in the club bounced around. Not her. Keeping her knees bent and her hips low, she set herself apart.

Inside the music and her head. Comfortable in her body. Dancing for her own pleasure, but aware of him. This girl. She swayed all the wrong in his life to right, and he'd never even touched her. But if she asked, if she hinted, he'd leave everything behind for her.

The crowd parted as Calen and Helm made their way to the corner booth. The tenuous bond remained, a silken thread growing more twisted by the second.

Calen slid a plate of skewered meat across the table, while Helm poured deep red liquid into a flat-bottomed wineglass. Neither would quench the hunger Locke felt, but he ate and drank his fill, keeping the mental connection alive while the conversation at the table grew more and more lewd.

"That one." Calen, a drummer with a wicked tempo, had his eye on a brunette with full curves and smooth skin. "She'll taste like apples."

"Granny Smith?" Helm teased. He used a clean, oversize wooden pick to trace a line from the crook of his elbow to his wrist. It left an angry welt and a bead of blood. He licked it off. "Or something sweeter?"

"Honey crisp." Calen's teeth shone fluorescent in the black light.

Three girls walked past them, their intentions obvious. They wanted to leave with the band, or at least they thought they did. Calen and Helm stared, but Locke had already scoped them out. "Only one qualifies, and getting rid of the others will prove to be a bigger pain in the ass than any of us wants to deal with tonight."

"You drew the short straw. That means we take the wheat, and you deal with the chaff." Calen's hand waved in a dismissive gesture. "Helm? Anything to your taste?"

Helm's exploits might've left the world astounded, but they left him satiated. If he wanted a female, he didn't have to speak. Eye contact, a smile—one simple touch—and they'd follow him anywhere and agree to anything. He liked to give pleasure before he inflicted pain, which meant that nine times out of ten, smiles came before the screams.

"There. Delicious," he murmured as his eyes caught sight of enticement on the dance floor. "I want to sing her to sleep."

Locke searched out Helm's choice.

No.

Not if he had anything to say about it.

"She's mine." Locke leaned forward. His wide shoulders shifted.

Helm didn't take his eyes away from the target. "What I want, I take."

Everything in Locke tensed, from the tendons in his neck to his fists under the table, to his heart in his chest.

"Back off, brother." Helm kept his voice lucid but anger pulsed underneath. "We're all here for the same reason."

"Not her." Locke stood to leave before things got physical. "I mean it, Helm. Lead singer doesn't equal boss. I told you, she's mine."

Locke stormed away. Helm snuck a flask of his special brew from the inside pocket of his coat, took a long drink and settled back into the booth.

"I can't believe you singled her out." Calen swiped the flask from Helm's frying-pan hand. "She's got him tied up in all kinds of knots, and you know she wants him, too."

"Of course I know. That's why *I* want her." Helm watched Locke's legs eat up the dance floor between their table and the girl in question. "All wrapped up in a perfect bow."

She smiled when she saw Locke.

Big body, wide shoulders, strong thighs. A row of six metal studs climbed up the cartilage of his left ear, but no other piercings were visible. No ink, either. Unusual, as the rest of the band had plenty.

A shadow of scruff marked his chin, and his dark hair stood up as if he'd had a run-in with a windstorm. At first she thought it was the result of hours in front of the mirror, but over the weeks of watching him, she learned it was because his hands were constantly in his hair.

She understood the urge.

Tonight was the second time Skin Trade had played at the club, but they occupied a booth almost every night, reveling in the attention.

She'd stayed close to the shadows since meeting him, keeping tabs on what made him look twice at a girl, and noting the things that turned him off. He'd shoot a quick glance at a short skirt or a lot of cleavage, but his eyes lingered on bodies that were more conservatively clad, as if he was seeking out the truth underneath. His eyes had lingered on her many times.

He'd never left with anyone, though he'd been approached plenty. The other two members of the band did, sometimes with multiple girls. They always came back alone.

Locke only drank the wine that his friends brought to the table, and never enough to appear to be affected by it. And he'd never, ever danced. But somehow, he stood in front of her on the floor, music pulsing around them, his brown eyes curious and his lips set in a determined line. She took his hand and pulled him to a dark and quiet corner.

"I was starting to wonder if you remembered my name."

He reached up, cupped her cheek. Ran his hand down the side of her neck. Slipped his fingers under the collar of her sweater. "Britt."

He'd never laid a hand on her. Her skin goose-pimpled at the familiarity in his touch, but she didn't move away.

Locke stared now, taking in the graceful limbs, the blond halo of hair. "I remember your name, and the way you saw through me, and the way you didn't run."

"Not from you," she said.

She'd known exactly what they were. He'd expected her to disappear and never come back, but she'd been at the club every night.

"Come home with me." He traced her collarbone before slipping a finger under the thin strap of her bra.

She wanted what he offered. To hide it, she closed her eyes. "It's late."

"It's early," Locke said. "We just got here."

"I don't know where you live. And…I just… I can't." She wanted time to prepare to be alone with him.

He lowered his lips to her forehead before moving them to her ear, his cheek brushing against hers. "Why? I know you aren't afraid."

She was afraid of herself, and the things he made her consider.

"I've waited." She didn't know what else to say. She'd told him after the first night that she wouldn't pursue him. "What made you decide on tonight?"

The curiosity in his eyes changed to fear.

She frowned, reminding herself of the promise not to ask him questions when he came to her. It had never been a question of if. "I mean, instead of last night, or tomorrow." She was making it worse.

"I didn't want to give anyone else a chance to get close to you." His eyes flickered over to Helm and Calen at the table.

"I wouldn't have gone anywhere with either one of them. You know that." She took in the planes of his face, shadowed in the flashing lights from the dance floor. "You called them off."

"I did."

"Don't be that guy. I don't need a watchdog."

"I didn't want you involved in this." His answer was simple, yet tangled. "But I need you."

She bit her tongue. Asking for too many answers would negate her control, and she wanted the upper hand. At least as much as she could have with someone like Locke.

"Come home with me," he repeated.

"Not now."

"Later?"

She opened her eyes. "Yes."

Locke stood at the window, staring down at the stand of oaks that lined the clearing. He'd left a path of ash. It glowed white through the darkness. Britt would come through those trees. If it blew away before she could find him, he would consider it fate.

He couldn't stop thinking of the warmth of her skin, and the way it felt under his fingertips. The way her breath caught.

He wanted to make it catch over and over again.

Britt drew a bath, lacing it with lavender and rosemary, and rinsed her hair with rose-scented water. All her plans, all her wishes—the steps she'd taken to be with him—everything was finally in place. She pulled on a simple cotton dress and set out.

It was only when she found the path of ash and stepped into the darkness that worry pricked her conscious.

The moon shone behind the trees on the horizon as Britt reached the end of the path. A towering mansion made of stone and wood loomed before her. It looked medieval in comparison to the club's urban aesthetic. Two torches burned on either side of the wide front door, but no lights shone from inside.

Reminding herself she wanted this, Britt crossed the wide expanse of grass to the house. She placed one fingertip on the iron door handle, for one second wishing to find it locked.

It swung open.

The hallway was dark, but the parlors to either side had

roaring fires in their hearths. She didn't smell smoke, only the faint scents of wildflowers and freshly overturned earth. Once she discovered the parlors were empty, she made her way past the stairwell and down the hall. A house this large had to have servants, but she couldn't find any.

He had said he wanted to be alone with her.

Faint music echoed down a corridor, and she followed it to a bedroom. He was there.

Flickering candles made his skin glow like warm honey. She walked across the room, slid her hands underneath his shirt and tugged up. Her hands skimmed his chest, the outline of muscles, the waistband of his jeans. She worked his belt buckle free.

"Britt?" He took two steps back, sat down on the edge of the bed.

"I know, Locke. Everything."

"Then you're sure?"

Two buttons and her dress hit the floor.

He leaned back on his hands as his eyes moved from her face to her feet, drinking in pearl silk. No tattoos. No markings. Just smooth, perfect skin.

"Flawless."

"All this skin." She followed him to the bed. "And all this time."

They were somewhere between dreaming and waking when they heard the sound of motors and slamming doors. Locke sat up before jumping to his feet and scooping up her dress. He handed it to her as a knock sounded. "Hurry."

She covered herself as he spoke to someone on the other side of the door. He reached out for her hand.

"Go with Doris," Locke said. "Do what she says."

He opened the door. An old woman with milky eyes stood in the hallway. Locke kissed Britt again and ran toward the commotion, his bare feet slapping against the wooden floor. Before turning the corner, he looked back at her.

He didn't smile.

Doris reached out with one hand. Britt saw that her fingernails were crusted with dirt and dried blood. She let the old woman lead her. They descended a set of narrow stairs into the smell and sight of rotten earth.

"She's so young. Fresh. Pretty." Doris's hand grazed the side of Britt's breast and then went to her waist. "They always choose the prettiest ones. Not plump. They're usually plump. Maybe that means they aim to keep her for a while."

"I'm sorry?" Britt stepped back, bumping into a bucket that sloshed behind her. "Who do they aim to keep?"

"Her." Gnarled hands reached out and tangled in Britt's hair.

Me.

"Bless her." The woman pressed her thin lips together before making the sign of the cross. "She doesn't know."

A cauldron simmered in the corner, steam rising to the ceiling. The heat made the wretched smell even worse.

"She should go home. She should run, run and not never look back."

Voices sent Britt scrambling into the shadows. She dropped down behind a barrel and pulled her legs up to her chest, wrapping her arms around them as a raucous noise filled the room. All she could see between the barrels were two sets of heavy boots. A pair of slender feet dangled between them, only one with a shoe.

Muffled screams, crying. Laughter.

"Uncover her head." A male voice. Helm. He sang the next sentence like a song. "I want to see if what we *caught* is as pretty as what we *thought*."

A pillowcase fell to the concrete floor. Britt saw a young woman in a short black dress being tied to a metal table. A gag covered her mouth, and tears poured down her makeup-stained face.

"She may be lovelier." It was Calen now, trailing one finger along the skin exposed at the bottom of her dress. "We should make her more comfortable." A knife appeared. In one swift movement, he'd slit her dress from hem to neckline. He pulled it away, laughing as she struggled and cried. "No, no. No tears. We'll be good to her, won't we, Helm?"

The girl wriggled on the table, trying to keep the skirt over her legs. Strong hands pushed away the cloth until her thighs were exposed. Helm licked her from ankle to knee. "Honey crisp."

Calen acknowledged the old woman. "Is it ready?"

"Yes, sir. I put on the water."

He settled in the corner to watch, and Helm took over.

"Bring our guest the white wine, please, Doris." The old woman handed Helm the glass, and he bent over the girl. "White, for purity." He held it up, and she stared at him as he tipped it into her mouth. When the wine was gone, Helm licked her lips. She moaned in fear, not pleasure.

Doris held out another glass.

Helm took it. "Red, for sacrifice." He brushed a stray lock of hair from her face before he put the drink to her lips.

The liquid in the last glass was gold. "For renewal."

The girl finished, and her body went lax. After all his sweet ministrations, Helm dropped her head without care. It thudded against the table. Her eyes were open, but she wasn't breathing.

Helm set down the empty glass and walked toward the stairs. "She's all yours."

Calen approached the body with the knife, his eyes slits of pleasure, his mouth stretched into a predatory grin.

Britt heard the slick wetness of skin being peeled away, the crunch of the saw, separating ligament from bone. The blood circling the drain in the middle of the floor.

When the water ran clear, and the room went silent, she wiped away her tears.

Where was Locke?

Helm fisted the sheets and pulled them to his face. Closing his eyes, he breathed deep. "You had her."

Locke didn't move.

"You saw her skin." Helm's eyes opened, but he still held the sheets to his nose. "How perfect is she? How pure?"

The growl started low in Locke's gut. It erupted under his ribs, shot through his sternum and landed at the base of his throat. He couldn't let it free. If he did, Helm would know the truth, and his obsession with Britt would be even more fierce.

"Where is she?" Helm shook the sheets, flung them away and then dipped his head to check under the bed.

"She went home."

"No, she didn't." Helm laughed. He stalked the room, seeking out its shadows. "The hood of your car was cold when I got here, and the wax on these candles is still warm. Sweet as she is, she'd be in your bed right now if we hadn't interrupted. So where are you hiding her, Locke?"

He didn't flinch, didn't let his eyes wander toward the hallway or the floor.

"Doris." Helm knew. Just like he knew everything else. "If Doris has her, then your girl just got an eyeful. We picked Calen's apple and cut her up real nice. He's sleeping off the meal."

Locke's peripheral vision went black. He gritted his teeth, his mind spinning with urgency. *Do not react. Do not react. Do not react.*

"Did you want a piece?" Helm took a step back, in the direction of the door. "Or did you want to wait for dessert?"

The footsteps pounded down the stairs.

Britt huddled deeper into the corner, the concrete block cold against her back. She hugged her legs tighter to her chest. *Locke. Please, let it be Locke.*

Helm's voice. "Doris! More wine. We have a second course." He circled the room, his huge hand slamming the top of each barrel. "Come out, princess. I'm still hungry."

Locke rushed through the doorway, and one word burst from his lips. "Me."

If Helm moved his gaze ten inches to the right, it would land on Britt. Instead, he turned to face Locke. "You'd take her place?"

"I'm clean," Locke said between heaving breaths. He was still shirtless, and the light from the fire shadowed all the dips and curves of his muscled torso. "You know how much I could bring in. True?"

"Men are less careful with their bodies. Unmarked flesh like yours...near priceless." Helm walked to Locke and held out a glass of white wine.

Locke took it and downed it in one gulp. "Purity."

Helm crossed the room to take the red wine from Doris. As he turned his back, Locke met Britt's eyes and mouthed the word *run*.

Her heart pounded, equal parts terror and gratitude.

Locke tore away his gaze and reached for the red wine. "I'll sacrifice for Britt but only if you spare her."

Helm smiled. "You can hope I will, brother. But sacrifice is a moment, not a lifetime."

"Do you want the golden now, sirs?" Doris asked, but she didn't move.

"No." Helm wanted to peel back Locke's skin while he was alive.

Locke moved to the metal table. He pulled a switchblade from his own pocket and held it up. "Take it."

Helm stared at the sharp blade. "You've used that knife plenty. Did your sweet Britt know when you tasted her flesh that you wanted to use your teeth?"

"You and Calen are the ones who make meals of your prey."

"That's what hunters do. Living off the sale of their skin doesn't make you noble." Helm reached out and plucked the knife away from Locke. "Does she know you tried to leave us because of her?"

"I've wanted to stop for a long time. She wasn't the reason, but she was the deal breaker." He'd found his humanity the night he met her.

Helm leaned back against the wall, his attention fully on Locke. "Give me an incentive to let her live longer than a day."

Britt heard the swish of the blade, and before she could look away, Locke brought it down on his own hand. Blood dripped to the floor and crept toward the drain.

"That's a start." Helm smiled. "Doris? Leave us."

The old woman shifted her position until she was in front of Britt. When she began shuffling sideways, Britt shadowed her. "I'll step outside," Doris said. "Strip the marrow from the bones."

Britt lurched out the back door. She sucked in fresh air, averting her eyes from the bloody tarp on the grass. A jangling noise caught her attention.

Doris held out the keys to Locke's truck.

Britt acted without thought, racing across the yard on her bare feet, hoping the slickness of the grass was dew and not something more menacing. When she reached the vehicle, she launched herself into the driver's seat. Jamming the keys into the ignition, she started the engine and revved the gas. To get their attention. To stop Helm and the movement of the knife.

She prayed Locke would anticipate her intent. She shifted into Drive and crashed the truck through the window.

Headlights met glass.

Locke dove out of the way, while Helm stood frozen. The

truck stopped moving. Locke pushed through debris, and Britt climbed out the passenger's side. He pulled her into his arms, kissing her, running his uninjured hand over her skin to make sure she was safe.

"I'm fine." She stood on her tiptoes among broken glass to kiss him back. "Your hand—"

She took it gently in hers. His ring finger was almost severed.

A deep groan sounded in the far corner of the room. Helm, impaled by a thick shard of glass. Blood trickled from the corner of his mouth, tears from the corners of his eyes.

If Locke had any sympathy, he'd put Helm out of his misery. As things stood, he couldn't find any to spare. He let Britt go. After picking his way through the wreckage, he took the switchblade from Helm's hand, closed it and tossed it into the fire. He stared at the flames, watching the plastic handle as it began to melt.

Behind him, Britt trailed a curious finger through the blood on Helm's chin. His last breath left him as she held it to her lips.

And licked.

BEAUTY
AND THE
CHAD

by Sarah Rees Brennan

The briars twined and climbed over the wooden frames to form an arch, giving the garden the feeling of a cathedral, hushed and golden and hung with roses. The thief walked so softly that the blades of grass barely bent underneath his feet.

Against the evening sky hung a single perfect rose. Its petals glowed, red so rich it seemed luxurious, conjuring up images of costly things like velvet and silk and blood.

The thief reached out to seize the rose, but something else seized him first.

The creature moved faster and quieter than a mortal man could. Its vast shadow fell on the thief only an instant before the creature itself did: he grasped the man's shirt in his claws and lifted him toward the sky as easily as if he was a plucked flower.

The thief gasped, horror choking off his voice so it was little more than a rattle in his throat. Outlined against the evening sky was a vast horned and furred creature, terrible scimitar-shaped fangs glinting in the dying light.

"Dude," said the Beast. "Who steals roses? That is so not cool."

"And then what happened, Father?" asked Gabrielle, the oldest sister. "However did you escape?"

Beauty, the youngest sister, sat crouched by the hearth. She had been trying to be so good and sensible, asking for a flower, because she hadn't wanted her father to spend money they didn't have.

It had been wonderful since Father had lost all his money. Beauty, for all that people liked how she looked—hence the nickname—had been terrible at being a court lady. She could not dance or flirt with her fan or make idle conversation the way a lady should. It was sad for Gabrielle and Suzanne, who had been perfect ladies, but the small house that needed fixing up and the single elderly white horse that needed tending suited Beauty much better. Time had eased the memories of tripping over her elaborate skirts, saying something shocking and knowing her behavior injured her sisters' chances of good marriages.

She had forgotten how it felt, to have made a terrible error which would hurt her family. She remembered now.

Her father had tried to steal a rose for her, and a beast had attacked him.

"I'm surprised he didn't eat you," said Suzanne, who was of a morbid turn of mind.

"Of course I could tell that was what was on its mind," Father said sagely. "One look and it could not disguise. It had hungry eyes."

The three girls shuddered.

"I pleaded with the Beast, told it that I had a family, and the Beast offered me a bargain. He said that he needed a boy to serve him and care for his infernal steeds. I promised to send him my son."

Beauty looked up from the hands twisted together in her lap. "What?"

Gabrielle and Suzanne were already smiling, the same smile they had worn at court, as if they understood something Beauty did not.

Her father was smiling, too. "Don't you see?" he said. "I tricked the Beast. I promised him a son, and I have no son to give! The oath is void. Any dark enchantments he tries to cast will fail."

Gabrielle clapped him on the back. "Oh, well done, Father."

"But," Beauty said. "But what about honor?"

Honor had been a watchword at court: to keep his honor a man could never cheat at cards, refuse a duel, break a betrothal or bear another gentleman's insult. Above all else, he had to keep his word.

As a child Beauty had believed she had to keep to all those rules, as well, and had been scared to play card games with her sisters in case she found herself cheating by accident. Then she grew up and learned all a lady's honor seemed to demand was that she not commit indiscretions with a gentleman. It was probably childish of her, but Beauty had still never told a lie in her life.

Suzanne laughed. "Do you think you're a knight in one of those moldering old books you read?"

Her father snapped, "One does not have to deal with a beast with honor."

"It's your honor, not the Beast's," Beauty said. "Shouldn't you have it all the time?"

Her father's face shaded from displeased to actually angry, and Beauty stood up from the hearth, shutting her book and tilting her chin up defiantly.

Then her father laughed and turned back to his meal. "Oh, little Belle, my Beauty, why am I even trying to explain to you how matters of honor work? You're a woman. You know nothing of honor."

The dismissal stung more than his anger.

The next day, Beauty rose from her warm bed in the cold dawn and did not do her chores. Instead she cut off her golden hair and put on the old footman's uniform that Gabrielle had been planning to pick apart and use to patch their dresses. She saddled Snowball the horse and rode in the direction of the castle.

It was not hard to find, though it was a long journey to get there. All Beauty had to do was follow the road south and keep riding, and soon she saw the castle outlined against the sky.

The sun had sunk behind the tower by the time Beauty rode into the courtyard. The courtyard was gray with the coming night, but Beauty suspected it might be gray any-way—there was an empty fountain with the briars of dead roses curled all around it, and gravel that had not been disturbed by carriage wheels in years.

Beauty dismounted and knocked on the tall gray door. The

sound echoed in the silence, sending tremors down through her bones.

The door creaked open of its own accord. Beauty drew in a breath at this clear sign of magic, but she stepped through all the same. Above her, the chandelier tinkled, though there was no wind to stir it. A curtain drew back with no hand to assist it, revealing a portrait of a staring man.

The Beast leaped from the top of the curving flight of marble stairs to land crouched in the center of the floor. The tiles were already broken there, Beauty saw, crushed beneath his weight and his claws.

She looked at the tiles so she would not run or scream. She was here for her father, she told herself. She was here for her family's honor.

She looked up, from claws to fur to fangs, and intent, terrifying eyes.

"I am the boy you wanted to care for your horses," she said. She had intended to mimic a man's voice, but in this moment, before the Beast, all she could manage was a low whisper.

"Dude," said the Beast, "am I glad to see you."

Beauty blinked. His eyes were light, light brown, almost amber: almost an animal's eyes.

"Every time I go near the stables the horses freak out," the Beast said. "I just feed them and run. It sucks because I like horses, you know? Before all this happened, I used to play polo."

Beauty blinked again. "I apologize," she said at last. "The tongue of beasts is not familiar to me. I do not fully understand your idiom. But I am here to serve, Beast, and happy to care for the horses."

"Awesome," said the Beast. "So come in. Pick a room. Oh, uh, and how much do you want to be paid? I'll be honest here, this is kind of a buyer's market, I'm desperate and I have piles of gold around. You can just pick up the stuff, basically."

"I think I'm misunderstanding something, Beast. I actually thought you just said that you were going to give me piles of gold."

"Well, in return for looking after the horses," the Beast said. "Obviously not as, like, a present. We just met, dude. Maybe on your birthday."

Beauty stared. "I am looking after the horses in return for my father's life!"

"You what?" said the Beast.

"My father said you were going to eat him."

It was hard to tell, with a visage that was mainly fur and those fearsome teeth, but Beauty thought she saw the Beast make a face.

"Whoa. I was not going to eat him. I'm not a vegetarian or anything, but I draw the line at eating people. I thought that your dad trespassing to steal flowers was a bit much, but I hadn't talked to anyone in weeks and trying to make a help-wanted sign was getting embarrassing, what with the claws. All I did was ask if he knew someone who'd look after the horses for me."

She was already here. She could see no reason for the Beast to lie to her, no advantage to him in doing so.

She had never felt quite so stupid in her life.

"I suppose my father panicked," she said eventually.

"I mean," the Beast said generously, "I'd panic, if I thought someone was going to eat me."

Her noble sacrifice was now basically ridiculous. Beauty could go home, she supposed, but she could not bear the idea of that long ride and how her father and her sisters would call her a stupid, stupid girl.

She looked at the Beast, and tried to see him clearly. He looked something like a wolf, and something like an ape, something like a jungle cat and even something like a man.

Looking past the long fangs and the other teeth distorting his jaw, she thought she could see an expression of friendly bewilderment. When he moved his pawlike hands, claws glinting, Beauty steeled herself for a blow, and instead his claws clicked together like dominoes and he looked down at them as though vaguely startled by the fact that they were there. He was, Beauty saw, wearing clothes, even if they were strange, ragged things: trousers of some rough canvaslike material that were simply shreds at the end, and something that might once have been a shirt and now was a scrap of fabric that stretched across his furry barrel of a chest, and an odd, brief collar that was nevertheless standing up.

He saw her looking, and she was fairly sure he misinterpreted the look when he said, with an attempt at gentleness, "You don't have to stay here, you know."

"Let us make a gentleman's agreement," Beauty suggested.

"Uh," said the Beast, "okay."

"To atone for my father's crime, O Beast, I shall stay in this castle and serve you for a year and a day."

That seemed the traditional length of time offered in Beauty's books. The other options were seven years, which seemed a very long time, or a hundred years, at which point Beauty herself might as well volunteer to be eaten.

"Thanks, that's very cool of you," the Beast said, and his huge shoulders slumped with relief.

It was settled so simply. Beauty could hardly think about the magnitude of the new bargain she had made, when she might have gone home instead. She squared her shoulders in her man's jacket and started on her way up the stairs to choose a bedroom.

"One more thing," said the Beast from the foot of the stairs.

Beauty tensed. "Yes?"

"This whole 'Beast' deal? Kinda hurtful," said the Beast. "Call me Chad."

Beauty chose the room whose door opened for her, though it gave her a nasty shock at first. She walked in and saw the gauzy curtains and the mirror decorated with golden roses, turned and tried to walk out. But the door slammed in her face.

"This is a very pretty room," Beauty told the room, and the curtains fluttered like a girl batting her eyelashes. "But I am here in a disguise, and I will not be convincing as a man if I have a dressing table with a little lacy frill around it and a teddy bear on top!"

The room blurred, the mirror frame bending as if in a shrug. Then it resolved into a room once more, the gauzy curtains gone and everything in sturdy green, even the mirror. The teddy bear remained, half-hidden under the bed, but Beauty decided it was close enough.

"Thank you," she said, and went downstairs to stable her own pony and meet the other horses.

They were not, as her father had said, infernal steeds. They seemed to be perfectly normal horses, of the sort you could ride out hunting or have pull a light showy carriage: there were three matched pairs of gray, chestnut and black. They were restless in their stalls, eyes rolling toward the castle, but as enthusiastic as puppies for Beauty, pushing their muzzles into her palms. She wondered how long it had been since they had seen a human person, and set about currying and calming them.

It was enough work that she did not even see the Beast for a night and a day: it was evening again when she stumbled inside, shoulders aching from hoisting a shovel.

As she opened the door of the castle, she was greeted by the smell of food, savory and sizzling and delicious. Beauty followed her nose to the dining room. She barely noticed the blue panels for walls and wedding-cake trim up at the ceilings—she was most concerned with the vast mahogany table creaking with food.

The Bea—the Chad was sitting in a vast chair, being served by a gravy boat that came toddling up to him, a flirtatiously twirling teapot and a platter that seemed to be tobogganing.

"Guys," he said, gesturing with a fork that looked tiny in his huge paw. "Guys, guys, we've talked about this, it's creepy, I don't like it, you're gonna spill stuff, I like my inanimate objects the way I like my coffee—inanimate!"

"The whole castle is filled with charms," Beauty said. "It must have been created by powerful sorcery."

The Beast twitched. "Ugh. I guess. I wasn't really raised to believe in, you know, all that."

"You don't believe magic exists?"

Beauty had no idea of the relevant intelligence of beasts. She had assumed from the clothes and the way he could speak that he had the intelligence of a human, but that might not be true: now he was saying he didn't believe in perfectly obvious things, as if he was a child claiming not to believe in the sky.

"I mean, okay, magic exists," the Beast said grumpily. "Castle full of dancing sofas and some broad turned me into… this…on the steps of my frat house and sent me to live here. But Dad would have fits and say this was hippie communist garbage."

"I am having trouble understanding your beast idiom again," Beauty said. "All of it."

The Beast raised his eyebrow, which was basically a shaggy shelf of extra fur. "Pull up a chair, dude. This food isn't going to eat itself. Well, it might, but that'd be weird and you'd be doing me a favor if you did it instead."

Beauty understood enough to know he was asking her to dine with him. She'd planned to spend as little time as possible in his company, since he was a beast and if he found out about her deception he could tear her to pieces, but the smell of the food worked as well as an enchantment. She drifted over to a chair at the shadowy end of the table, and a tureen of soup made its determined way in her direction.

"Guys? Guys, I'm not kidding around, quit it, I will not be the ringmaster of the teapot circus!"

"Thank you," Beauty whispered to the tureen, and it wriggled with delight.

"No, dude, don't encourage them," the B—Chad said, sounding genuinely distressed, but as more and more plates whizzed toward Beauty, he gave up with a sigh like a furry bellows, propped his massive, teeth-heavy jaw on his curled paw and said, "So how are the horses?"

"Very well," said Beauty. "They were just a little spooked. I got them calmed down."

She almost jumped out of her chair, threw the chair at the Beast and leaped out of the window before she realized his bared teeth might be a smile. Instead she took a long drink of mead, and choked.

"You okay, dude?"

"Fine," said Beauty, hitting herself on her bound chest, which hurt. "I'm very used to mead. It's a manly drink. So of course I drink it frequently."

The Beast shrugged. "I miss Jägerbombs."

Beauty took another cautious sip and made the decision to ignore it when the Beast—Chad, Chad—said incomprehensible things.

"So, what's your name?"

"Beauty," said Beauty.

The Chad's shaggy eyebrows drew together into a uni-shelf of annoyance. "Dude, I'm sorry. It's uncool they called you that."

"What?"

"Like, they did it to tease you, right?" the Beast asked. "Because, you know, you're kind of pretty for a dude. No offense. And I don't think you need to shave that often. Again, not throwing shade here, since basically I have to go at my whole body with the hedge clippers. And I might add that the hedge clippers, also weirdly alive, and I am pretty sure they're judging me."

Beauty frowned. She had not thought much about her name—that was what everybody called her, that was what people thought when they saw her. Nobody was trying to tease her.

And yet she thought she might like it, to have someone call her something else, because when they saw her they saw something else in her besides beauty.

Besides, now that Chad mentioned it, it was an odd name for a boy.

Which also ruled out her real name, Isabelle, and Belle.

"There are other things I could be," Beauty allowed.

"So far you're awesome with the horses," Chad contributed. "We could call you Horsesome? No, that kind of sounds… Never mind that."

"I thought you were calling me Dude," Beauty said. "Is it an honorific in your land?"

"Think we've come up against that language barrier again," said Chad. "No, bread basket, stay still and let me reach for you!"

The bread basket scuttled disobediently toward its master's paw.

Beauty felt like she had finally deciphered one thing he had said, though the "Horsesome" issue had her completely puzzled.

"You said…someone put you under a spell," she said. "Someone…something…broad?"

"Uh, I just meant a woman. Yeah."

"And you were taken away from your home," Beauty said. "Do you not wish to learn how to break the spell and return?"

It occurred to her that she could end her term of service sooner—and do a heroic deed—if she could help him find out about the spell.

Chad looked darkly at the bread basket, which butted against his arm.

"I know how to break the spell. The woman—witch, I guess? She told me. But it's not an option. It involves kidnapping someone—which, dude, no, wrong—and then hoping they have a really bizarro fetish. I'm not doing it. This is my mess. So, I guess I'm stuck here."

Which meant Beauty was trapped here, too.

But Beauty was trapped for only a year and a day, and the Chad was trapped here forever, a beast now, whatever he had been before, caught in a web of magic where he could never be happy and longing for home.

"If breaking the spell would hurt somebody else, it is noble of you to suffer yourself instead of inflicting suffering on others. You must miss the land of frat house very much."

The Beast ducked his head, like a horse trying to escape the bridle. Beauty thought the gesture might almost have been shy.

"I miss my Xbox," he admitted. "But I couldn't really work the controller with the claws anyway."

Beauty had no idea what the Beast was saying, but this much was clear: he was sad, and she could not simply care for his horses if she was going to wipe away the debt of her father's life. If he was trapped in this body, in this castle, he needed help.

The next day the Beast took her on a tour around the castle. The kitchen, with its animated carving knives, was terrifying, and the portraits in the portrait gallery made creepy faces at them. None of that mattered when he opened the door and escorted her into the library, its curved walls shining with leather spines in green and black and red and brown and blue, stretching from ceiling to ceiling and from wall to wall, a treasure room better than one filled with gold and jewels.

"You like reading, huh?"

"I love reading!" Beauty exclaimed.

"I used to listen to audiobooks at the gym," Chad said wistfully and incomprehensibly. "I've come in here and looked at the titles and stuff, but I don't think it'd be a great idea for me to try and read the books."

He waggled a demonstrative hand, claws outstretched, then bared his ferocious teeth, but only a little, in what Beauty thought was a sheepish grin.

"Would you like me to read to you?" she asked, and when he gave an embarrassed nod she took her time selecting the right one. "This is my favorite kind of book," she told him at last. "There are daring sword fights, magic spells and a hero in disguise."

"Like you?" said Chad, and when Beauty was shocked silent he scratched the ruff of fur on the back of his neck. "Well, you know, coming to be a stable boy when you're obviously… not really raised to be a stable boy? That's kind of a disguise. And it was heroic of you, to do it for your dad."

"Oh," said Beauty. She had never thought of herself in that way before—as someone who could be the center of a story. She dropped her gaze to the book and began to read, hiding her smile.

A few days, a few quiet story hours and a few lively dinners later, Beauty rode one of the horses down to the village near the castle. She alighted from the horse and went into the nearest shop.

Being able to ride down a lane and not have anyone comment on her beauty, or her lack of chaperone, having everyone ignore her as if she was just a person free to do whatever she chose, gave Beauty an unexpected and heady sense of freedom.

"I want to purchase some saddle brushes, preferably not animated," she announced. "Oh, and I am employed as a stable boy in the castle of the Beast."

Beauty wondered if the woman leaning her elbows against the shop counter might scream and faint at the name: she was disappointed when the woman did not even raise her eyebrows.

"I'd forgotten we have a new beast. Stable boys are different, mind."

"A new beast?" Beauty asked. "There have been others."

"It is a tale as old as time," said the woman. "There's bound to be a few variations. Be a waste of the castle to have just one beast. There was an original beast, obviously. Prince of the castle, turned into a beast because of his vanity and pride, lessons learned through love, et cetera, but since then we have been importing beasts. The witch takes young spoiled princes from many lands, but the beast always lives here."

The woman chatted idly as she fetched down the saddle brushes, with the slightly bored air of someone who would rather be discussing the weather.

"So your village lies in the shadow of a castle in which there is always a beast, punished for his misdeeds by being trapped in the body of a ferocious killing machine? Pardon me for asking," said Beauty, "but do you never consider moving?"

The woman sniffed. "Certainly not. We have an excellent tourist trade."

"Fair enough," said Beauty. "Everybody has to pay the bills. I suppose the tourists would flock here if there was a chance of actually seeing the Beast, and going into the magical castle."

"Tourists who get eaten do not tell all their friends about our fair town," the shopkeeper snapped.

"Chad would never!"

The shopkeeper's eyebrows rose with such velocity Beauty thought her ruffled cap might pop right off.

"Is that the way it is?"

"What?" asked Beauty. "Is what the way what is? Look, all I'm saying is, we'd be open to having a fete up at the Beast's castle. There could be bunting, and…food served outside, and games for all the family.…"

Beauty racked her brains for another suggestion.

"Some sort of gay parade, I have no doubt?" the woman asked.

"Yes!" Beauty exclaimed, pleased that she was getting into the spirit of things. "A merry parade would be lovely."

The shopkeeper still looked skeptical.

"You could charge at the gate," Beauty said. "Just think about it."

She rode away home and at dinner that night described her adventure to the Chad.

"So you're saying that you bought saddle brushes and also

invited the village to a kegger at our place?" Chad asked. "My man! Give me five."

Beauty gave him a stare of blank incomprehension.

The living furniture seemed initially puzzled and then very excited about the party at the castle. The table and chairs for outside started holding what Beauty thought were practice drills, and Chad spent his time pleading with them. "Play dead for the guests!"

Beauty was surprised she was not more nervous herself. But she was the stable boy: she would have practical things to do and get to wear comfortable clothes. Nobody would expect her to be charming or ornamental, just useful.

She put ribbons in the trees, since Chad could not be trusted with ribbons. After a while, the ribbons got the idea and started to twine about in the branches themselves.

The day of the Beast's fete dawned clear and bright, and the shopkeeper Beauty had spoken to, whose name turned out to be Aimee, arrived not long after. She was carrying a plate full of pastries.

"Welcome to the castle," said Beauty.

"Yeah, uh, *mi casa es su casa*," said the Beast.

The woman sniffed.

"That had better not be foreign for 'I am going to eat your children.' Well, lead me to the refreshments. It was a long walk and I could use a restorative beverage."

"Of course, perhaps lemonade?" Beauty suggested.

"Dude, I think she means booze."

Aimee favored Chad with a smile. "Escort me to the sherry, sir, and no clawing the tapestries on the way."

Curiosity apparently trumped fear of being mauled and eaten, because most of the village showed up. A set of instruments crept out from the music room and played in the rose garden, lurking behind bushes so nobody would notice the lack of actual musicians, and the villagers started to dance around the lawn.

Beauty had never been to a dance before where she did not have to dance or worry about not being asked. She hummed as she cleared the tables to make way for the desserts.

"This was a nice idea," said Aimee the shopkeeper behind her, and she jingled her box of change. "And I'm turning a nice profit, too, of course," she added almost absently. "Quite a nice young beast, too. Much preferable to the last one. It was nothing but brood, brood, brood on the battlements in the rain all day long. The castle smelled like wet dog for seventy years."

Beauty looked over at Chad. The children had got over their worries about being eaten very quickly when offered piggyback rides. One little boy was on Chad's back now, laughing so hard she thought he might be sick.

"He is all goodness."

"Hmm," said Aimee. "They're all made beasts for a reason, my dear boy. But come—I don't want to spoil your day. Go play tug-of-war."

Beauty's team won at tug-of-war, and people clapped her on the back as if it was excellent that she was strong, and no man minded her showing them up at all.

She was walking across the castle lawn feeling well content with the world when she heard the scream come from the stables.

Beauty turned and ran toward the sound.

When she arrived, she saw no scene of carnage or villagers demanding the Beast's head. What she saw was Chad, with a group of young men from the village all clapping him on the back, just like Beauty had been clapped on the back, and the little boy she had noticed before trembling on the point of tears.

Chad saw her. "Don't worry about it, dude," he said. "We just gave him a little scare, that's all. It's only fun."

Beauty looked from the laughing men to the upset child. "Doesn't look like much fun to me."

She saw the boy's mother coming toward them, looking angry: the boy saw her but did not run to her. Instead he tried to join in the laughter, as if he had not been hurt, as if denying he had feelings meant that he would stop having them.

Beauty had never been quite so angry in her life. She stamped off into the castle, wanting to cry like a woman or hit something like a man and refusing to do either because neither would help.

"Lighten up, dude," Chad said from behind her, sounding worried.

"I don't know what you're asking me to do but I won't do it!" Beauty snapped. "Nobody has to do anything just because other people expect it. How did you get cursed to be the Beast? What did you do to the witch before she cursed you?"

"Nothing!" Chad shouted. "Well…look, I was just kidding around."

"While everyone was laughing," Beauty said. "All your frat brethren. Not the witch."

"Frat brothers."

"I don't care!" said Beauty. "You are not a villain, but what does it matter if you playact like one? If good men pretend to be villains, how is anybody supposed to know the difference between them?"

"What am I supposed to do?" Chad demanded.

"Think," said Beauty.

"Anyone could tell you I'm not good at that!"

"Think and be kind," said Beauty. "You are good at that. You're much better at that than being vicious to impress other boys you're hanging around with."

"Jesus, were you homeschooled?" asked Chad. "They're just being guys. It's a dog-eat-dog world, Dad always said—"

"What a stupid thing to say!" Beauty exclaimed. "You're not an animal."

Chad made a violent gesture with one clawed hand. "Oh, no? We can't all be heroes discharging the debt for our father's lives or whatever. You don't have to stay here, you know— you can ride off on your white horse and do good deeds and be better than everybody somewhere else!"

He turned and slammed out of the room. Beauty went and flung herself in an armchair. She felt tempted to resort to liquor, but Aimee had basically drunk the castle dry.

Instead, she sulked in the armchair. The curtain hanging by her elbow lifted itself tentatively and patted at her arm, and Beauty felt slightly better.

By the time Chad slunk back into the room, it was dark and Beauty could hear the clatter of some guests leaving, and the music as those remaining danced.

"I said I was sorry," Chad said. "I guess I was being kind of a jerk. It isn't funny to upset little kids."

"It isn't funny to upset anyone," said Beauty.

Chad shrugged, which looked like furry mountains shifting in an awkward miniearthquake. "I guess."

Beauty kicked at the hearth rug, which slapped her boot back. "I didn't offer to stay because I'm so noble," she said. "I wanted to have a different life. I wanted to have adventures, and prove I was a different person than everybody thought I was, and I would've been embarrassed to go straight back home. I was always disappointing them. I shouldn't give lectures to anyone about caring too much what people think."

Chad sank into the armchair next to Beauty's. "You were right about my dad, though. I know a thing or two about disappointing people."

"It must be difficult, to be the son of a king."

"He's a CEO," said Chad. "He's a bit cutthroat."

"Does he order a lot of executions?" Beauty asked sympathetically, and Chad choked. "Think how happy the people will be when you ascend the throne and temper mercy with justice."

"Uh, I don't think…" Chad began, and trailed off with a beastly sigh. "It doesn't matter anymore. But it's hard to stop thinking about what people think of you."

Beauty thought of being in a glittering gown at court, and dressing in boy's clothes to climb on her white steed.

"Today was the only party I've been to in my life that I actually enjoyed. It's all different kinds of performances," Beauty said miserably. "But I don't perform well."

"It's not just putting on an act," Chad told her slowly. "I

know you did this to make other people think about me differently—so they'd be kind to me. That was you being kind to me. That wasn't an act."

Beauty hesitated. "Oh, well. I just thought—they were wrong not to accept you. And now you can get a different stable boy when the time comes."

Chad hesitated in his turn.

"I don't want a different stable boy," Chad said at length. "You—you are kind to me and you're brave and I don't want you to pretend anything. You're my friend. I wish you'd stay."

He was the only person who had ever said to Beauty that she was enough the way she was. Beauty looked over at him, at his kind dark eyes: he was closer now. Neither of them had moved; it was the chairs who had edged together.

"Uh," said Chad. His voice cracked. "No homo? Dumbass interfering furniture."

Beauty leaned forward. She didn't understand everything Chad said, but she thought she understood enough.

She leaned forward, in the silence just after midnight, and pressed a kiss somewhere in the vicinity of Chad's fangs.

The arm of the chair splintered under Chad's claw.

"Uh," he said, and his voice cracked. "Maybe a little homo?"

Beauty smiled at him. "I have no idea what you're talking about."

"I have to go?" Chad said. "Yep. I have to go and sit in my room and have a think and hope the wardrobe doesn't try to give me relationship advice. Okay, bye!"

He ran, leaving claw marks on the door. The door creaked a protest at him, waggling back and forth reproachfully.

★ ★ ★

It was Chad's decision whether or not to accept her court-ship. Beauty tried not to worry about it and to focus on her job, so the next day she rose bright and early to curry the horses. She was finishing up on Vin Diesel (Chad had named the horses after heroes in his own land) when she heard the half growl, half stutter of Chad's cough behind her.

"Dude, can I have a word?"

"Of course," said Beauty, and got up from the straw.

The horses all shied away from Chad, still uneasy even though Beauty had been doing her best to accustom them to his presence. Except for Snowball, who had taken a fancy to him and went over to butt his arm in a mute demand for apples.

Chad patted Snowball's nose, careful of his claws.

"Dude," he said. "I'm really sorry that I ran off. I was just—I was just freaked out. But it wasn't that I didn't want to—I was freaked out because I did. I care about you, and that sounds a little gay but obviously that's okay. It's okay to be a little gay. Or a lot. And human sexuality is a complicated and beautiful thing, or that's what a psych major I dated once told me. And honestly, Matt has hooked up with every guy in the frat house and it can't just be about being drunk because if you were that drunk you'd probably hook up with a chick once or twice. It all got a little statistically unlikely. No of-fence to Matt. It's all good. He's still my bro."

Beauty honestly only understood one sentence of that, but she thought it was the important one.

She beamed. "I care about you, too."

"Thanks, man," Chad said. "Seriously. I mean I realize

you're overlooking a lot here, the claws and everything—honestly I'm very concerned about them—"

Beauty did not see why Chad was suddenly so very concerned about his claws.

"I'm not overlooking anything," she said. "I'd rather be with you than anyone else."

Chad scuffed the straw on the stable floor with a clawed foot. It looked like someone had started raking the yard. "Me, too," he muttered. "So—so what do we do now?"

It seemed very obvious to her.

"We love each other, don't we?" Beauty asked.

"Uh," said Chad. "Yeah? Yeah."

"So we should get married."

Chad choked, rattled, and hit himself in the chest so hard he almost fell over backward. Beauty got the impression he was a little surprised.

"I don't..." he said. "What? Are you serious? Can we even—legally? In this country?"

"Oh, yes," said Beauty.

She understood his concern completely now, but she knew of a prince who had married a swan. It was what was inside that mattered.

"Well, that's surprising but great," said Chad. "Like, obviously. My dad's a Republican and he's not in favor, but I, I am. But I've never really, um... Dude, this is new to me. How does it even work? Which of us is even meant to ask?"

"Will you marry me?" said Beauty.

Chad cleared his throat and fed Snowball an apple. "Yeah," he said. "Okay. Great." He paused and there was an embarrassed silence. "Thanks," he added.

"Thank you," Beauty told him. She glanced at him and caught him glancing at her, and they both found themselves smiling.

All the villagers assembled in the chapel on their wedding day. Doves had appeared from somewhere—Beauty believed that the furniture had kidnapped them somehow. The glass windows blazed, showing heroes and monsters of days long gone by in scarlet and blue, and as soon as Chad caught sight of Beauty he had a fit and dragged her outside.

"Why are you wearing that?" he demanded.

Beauty tugged on the ivory-and-pearl skirt of her wedding gown. "Don't you like it?" she said, rather hurt.

"You look like a gi— You look great, of course," said Chad. "But you don't— You shouldn't feel as if you have to dress that way. You can dress any way you want."

"I know," said Beauty. "And I like trousers, mostly. But it felt all right to wear this today. Because it's a significant occasion, and because it's tradition, and it doesn't matter what other people think but I still want them to see and be absolutely sure this means something."

"Okay," said Chad. "If you're sure." He bit his lip, and winced with fang-related pain. "Do you want me to wear the wedding dress instead? Uh, I will if you want."

Beauty laughed. "I don't know why you think we have time to make one in your size. And your fur would catch on the lace."

She caught his hand, and instead of looking worried, he had to concentrate on not hurting her with his claws.

She went down the aisle hand in hand with Chad, and they

were married as the villagers whispered and the stolen doves fluttered overhead, and Chad kept his eyes on her throughout, seeing her and finding nothing wanting.

When Beauty promised to love and cherish him, the air in the chapel dazzled and shimmered and turned into somewhere new: a stone room in a high tower, where the enchantress was waiting for them.

It was Aimee, dressed in flowing black and green and red, like evil Christmas. Beauty and the Chad stared.

"Oh, come on," said Aimee the shopkeeper, now Aimee the evil enchantress (who possibly kept a shop as a sideline). "I gave you plenty of hints."

Beauty abruptly remembered Aimee talking about the many Beasts she had seen, even though one had been a Beast seventy years.

"You didn't give me any hints," Chad grumbled. "You sold me overpriced cheese but you didn't give me any hints."

"Well, she's the hero," said Aimee.

"Fair enough," said Chad, and then, "She? What?"

Aimee clapped her hands together, and said, "You married him—that counts as love until disappointment in the bedroom or a midlife crisis. Consider the spell broken."

"Wait," Chad said. "She? Wha—"

He began to shimmer and shift, body writhing and fur rippling away, until he was gone. There was a boy standing in his place.

He was a very odd-looking boy, with short hair that was a different color at the tips than at the roots. He was wearing a necklace of tiny seashells, and he was staring at her as if he didn't know her.

"You're a girl?"

"Of course I'm a girl!" Beauty snapped. "How could you marry me otherwise?"

"Hey, dudes can marry other dudes," Chad said. "Don't be a hater."

Beauty blinked. "I've never heard of such a thing."

It made her wonder if there were other things she had not heard of: if she could dress like a boy without saying she was a boy, or a girl, exactly. If she could be what she felt like, without having to fit into either of the boxes everybody tried to force you into.

Aimee the evil enchantress patted her on the shoulder. "She's been very sheltered. They keep women here uninformed and pretend that's the same thing as stupid."

"Beauty's the smartest person I know," Chad said, and returned to staring at her. "Dude," he said at last. "Uh, wait. Babe?"

"You always call me Dude," Beauty said, confused and a little hurt.

"Dude it is," Chad said. "Sorry. I'm just— It's a bit of a surprise. But a nice surprise! Though it would have been cool the other way, too." He hesitated. "It's all good, as long as you're with me."

Beauty reached out in the quiet of the enchantress's tower and took his hand. It was a little strange without claws.

"Me, too," Beauty told him. "I just want to be with you. I don't mind that your hair is extremely odd."

"Dude," said Chad. "My hair is awesome."

Chad grinned. It was the smile Beauty recognized, and not the eyes, in the end.

"Yes, yes, very heartwarming," Aimee the evil enchantress drawled. "Now I think we've all learned a valuable lesson, and we probably want to thank me."

"Nope," said Chad.

Aimee the evil enchantress looked offended. Beauty pressed Chad's hand in warning: she would still love Chad if he was turned into a frog, but it wouldn't be her preference.

"Look, I may have been a jerk, but turning someone into a giant talking animal is basically a huge overreaction. And even if it was fair to me, it wouldn't have been fair to the innocent people whose heads I could've totally eaten. With great power comes great responsibility, dude."

Aimee continued to look offended for a moment, and then shook her head and laughed. "I must admit you two have been entertaining. Well, what shall it be...? Will you stay in your lady's enchanted kingdom, or return to be prince of your own?"

"CEO," Chad mumbled. "And it's up to Beauty. She's the one who saved me, right? She went on the quest and broke the curse. She's the hero. She can decide on the ending."

It was another moment for Beauty where she could look at him and recognize her Beast without a doubt. Then she looked out the window of the enchantress's tower and saw the rolling green fields, little villages and grand castles of her land, laid out before her. She knew what would happen if she stayed: security, love, happiness within certain boundaries. Beauty thought what might lie beyond those lands: for Chad an inheritance, which would let him be kind, and for herself another adventure, which would let her be brave.

"Will you tell my family," she asked the evil enchantress, "that I'm happy?"

"Not safe?"

Beauty smiled. "I don't want to be entirely safe."

Aimee the evil enchantress smiled, and snapped her fingers.

THE
PINK:

A
GRIMM
STORY

by Amanda Hocking

CHAPTER 1
The Lonely Queen

A long time ago, below the sharp peaks of the Graulumberg Mountains, past the dark branches of the Verzanfrost Woods and over the cold waters of the Eisenfluss River was a quiet kingdom nestled in the valley. Once, it had been a bustling, vibrant kingdom, but the echoes of its glory had begun to fade.

It was the quiet that had begun to wear on the fair Queen Rose. She preferred to sit in the wild garden behind the palace, where the songs of the birds, the buzz of the bees and the rustling of the animals were there to ward off the growing silence.

The people in the kingdom called it the Queen's Garden, but it wasn't Rose's garden. It had belonged to her husband's great-grandmother, and while it had been tamed and groomed once, it had taken on a life of its own. The flowers overgrown from their gardens, the vines climbing over the fruit trees, the insects and all manner of beasts roaming freely—that was precisely as Rose liked it.

So while she loved the garden, it wasn't hers. She let it belong to the flowers and the animals, the way it ought to.

When her husband, King Elrik, went out to the garden, he found his queen in her favorite spot. She sat among the pink carnations, unmindful of the dirt on her gown. Her dark hair was worn in a long braid, and though she was looking down, Elrik could see a tear falling down her cheek.

"My love, you mustn't cry," Elrik told his wife, and he held out his handkerchief to her.

"Oh, I'm sorry, my lord." Her cheeks turned the color of amaranth, nearly matching the carnations around her, as she wiped her tears away in haste. "I did not mean for you to see me like this."

"There is no need for apologies, or tears," Elrik said, his voice firm but gentle. He was a just ruler, and he always spoke like one, sometimes to the consternation of his wife.

Rose got to her feet, brushing petals and leaves from her dress. The tears had stopped, but she still didn't brave looking up at her husband. She asked, "Am I needed inside the palace?"

"Not at the moment," Elrik replied. "I came out to see you. The visit with the midwife this morning seemed to have left you saddened."

Rose shook her head as she stared down. "The midwife, the doctors, my ladies in waiting, they all assure me these things take time. But the villagers are worried, and I've heard your advisors whisper in the hall."

"What advisors?" asked the king, no doubt already planning a punishment for those who had hurt his wife. "Who is whispering about my queen?"

"Everyone," she replied wearily, and lifted her eyes to meet his. "By now, everyone has begun to talk. But that's not even what has my heart so heavy." A tear slid down her cheek. "Why can I not have a baby?"

When she tried to look away, Elrik gently put his hand on her chin so she would look up at him.

"Rose," he said with the tenderness he reserved for when they were alone, "I love you. Together, we will have a child. It will only take a bit more time."

As she searched her husband's gray eyes, she saw that he was beginning to doubt the truth in his words. Though Elrik did love her, their three years of childless marriage had begun to wear on him.

When they'd wed, though Rose had only just reached her sixteenth birthday, Elrik had already been in his middle age. He didn't have the kind of time a younger man might have. Much too soon, he would need an heir.

"I love you, Elrik," Rose told him simply, and she stood on her toes so she could lean up and kiss him.

When they separated, Elrik told her, "I must go back inside to meet with my advisors. Will you be joining me?"

"Not quite yet."

The king eyed up his bride. "Are you still saddened?"

"I'm better, thank you." She smiled at him, hoping to ease her husband's worry.

A berry bush rustled nearby, and Elrik stepped in front of Rose and reached for the sword sheathed in his belt, preparing to defend her from any attacker. No sooner had his hand touched the guard when a mottled boar piglet came out of the brush, rooting around for grubs.

"Oh, it's a darling piglet!" Rose knelt down and reached out her hand, meaning to summon the baby to her.

"My queen, you must be careful," the king commanded.

"It's only a baby," Rose told him with a laugh. The piglet trotted close to her, its small tail wagging behind it, and stopped for her to pet its soft fur.

"Where there's a baby, there is an angry mother nearby," the king warned her.

The queen scooped the piglet onto her lap. "The boars are harmless when left alone."

"You are too kind," Elrik said, sounding almost weary of it. "There are too many wild beasts running about here. It's no place for a young queen to be alone."

"I will be fine, my king," Rose told him. "Go inside, conduct your business, and I will be along shortly."

The king bade her farewell, and Rose let the piglet off her lap. It squealed in delight, then disappeared in the bushes, leaving the queen alone with her heavy heart.

Her sadness hadn't lessened any after her visit with Elrik. If anything, it had deepened. When the king had first taken an interest in her, Rose had almost instantly fallen in love with his gentle heart and fair nature, and she'd thought all her dreams had come true.

But with each passing year, her dream had begun to wear away. Soon, she would be left without her garden, her home, her husband. His kingdom would pass to his nearest advisor if the king had no children, and she would be alone and destitute.

The queen lay down on the ground, burying her face in her arms as she wept. Around her, the garden fell silent, and the sound of her sobs floated up to the heavens above her. She begged the gods to take pity on her, because she couldn't bear the heartbreak anymore.

"Hush, child." A soothing voice spoke in her ear, and Rose felt a strong, warm hand on her shoulder.

She lifted her head to see a man standing over her. He was handsome beyond anything she'd seen before, and light seemed to illuminate him from within, making his golden hair glow. White feathered wings spread out behind him, and though Rose had never seen a creature like him before, she felt no fear.

"Who are you?" Rose asked, and sat up so she would face him.

"My name is Adriel," he said. "I'm here to help you."

She asked, "Why would you care about a creature as pitiful as me?"

"I tend to nature, helping the plants and animals grow," Adriel told her. "I've watched you, here in this garden, and I've seen the kindness you've shown to the animals and for the earth. I've also seen your sorrow, and I've heard your cries to the gods."

Rose lowered her eyes. "I never meant to disturb you."

"You haven't disturbed me." He smiled. "And I've come to give you a gift."

He bent down over the queen, and his wings outstretched behind him, casting a shadow over her. He put his hand to her abdomen, and instantly Rose felt a white heat growing inside her. Rays of light shone around his hand, and even after he removed it, her stomach seemed to glow.

"You will have a child," Adriel told her. "But not just any child. He will have the power of wishing, so whatsoever in the world he wishes for, he shall have."

"Thank you," Rose said, her voice trembling with gratitude.

Adriel laughed warmly, and then he disappeared, his body fading away into soft sparkles in the sunlight as if he'd never been there at all. As soon as he'd gone, the queen began to weep, but this time, out of joy.

CHAPTER 2
The Vengeful Cook

While the queen prepared to eat breakfast with the king, she marveled over her son, the same way she had every day since he was born. Nearing four years old, the young prince had already stolen the hearts of everyone in the kingdom.

Prince Brenn shared his mother's dark hair and fair skin, but he had his father's gray eyes and charming smile, and it was enough to melt even the hardest of hearts. More than that, he was a kind boy.

On their walks through town, Brenn had offered his apple to a child in need, and he'd encouraged his mother to free a bird caught in a trap. Even at such a young age, he already showed signs of Rose's warm heart and Elrik's determination. He seemed to have gotten the best from both his parents.

The family sat around the table for their morning meal, and the portly cook Fyren pushed in the trolley. As soon as the king saw it was Fyren bringing them their breakfast, he grimaced. It had been only a few weeks ago that Elrik had pardoned Fyren, and he'd already grown weary of him.

Since having his son, the king had begun to soften, and he wanted his kingdom to thrive again. In recent months, he'd pardoned petty thieves from the dungeon if they could retain gainful employment. Fyren had claimed to be a chef, but since the king had hired him, Fyren's cooking had done nothing to support that.

"I trust everything is in order this morning," said the king as Fyren wheeled their food up to the table.

"Yes, sire, you'll find you have everything you need here," Fyren told him, and removed the metal lids from their plates in haste.

He presented the king's plate first, and to his surprise, everything did seem to be correct. When Fyren set a plate before the queen, she smiled politely and thanked him, though he'd forgotten to give her bread. It was when he got to the prince that his error became the most egregious.

"What is that?" the king asked, pointing to the chunk of meat sitting before his young son.

"It's ham, my lord," Fyren told him, bowing lightly when he spoke. His thick black hair was unkempt, with several matted braids running through it. His beard—which he'd promised to trim as soon as he went to work for the royal family—remained unruly and long.

"The prince never eats pork for breakfast," the king told him. "It gives him an upset stomach, so he only has apples in the morning."

"I'm very sorry, my king. I'll return with one immediately," Fyren said.

"Don't bother." Elrik waved at him. "You've been troublesome since you began work here. You're an inferior cook, a dirty man, and I see no reason to continue your employ."

"My king," Rose implored to her husband, "he's only just started."

The king sighed and gave the cook a hard look. "Let this serve as a warning to you, then. If my wife did not possess such a forgiving heart, you would be back in the dungeon. But if you do not do your job properly, you will return in no time."

"Yes, my lord, thank you," Fyren said, bowing again, then turned to the queen. "Thank you, my queen."

The cook had begun to back out of the room when the prince announced loudly, "I wish for an apple."

No sooner had the words escaped his lips than a fresh red apple appeared on the table before him.

"Brenn!" The queen was aghast. She looked up to see if the cook was gone, but Fyren didn't appear to be in sight. "You mustn't make wishes in front of others. You know the rules."

"It's only you and Father here," the boy said, taking a bite of his apple.

"You did not check for the cook or any other servants," the king said. "You must always be absolutely certain you are alone before you make a wish."

"Why, Father?" Brenn asked. "Why must I be so careful?"

"If someone found out what you could do, they could use it against you," King Elrik said. "They would harm you to gain the use of your wishes."

"But I would share my wishes," Brenn said. "If anyone asked, I'd gladly share."

"I know." Rose smiled and reached over, squeezing her son's small hand in hers. "But we must keep this a secret. For your safety, and for ours. Do you understand?"

"Yes, Mother." He frowned, and sadness filled his gray eyes. "I'm sorry."

"No need to be sorry. Just be more careful," Rose told him. "Now finish your breakfast, and when you're done, I'll take you out to the garden."

"The garden?" Elrik asked, raising an eyebrow at his wife while Brenn raced to devour his apple.

The queen said, "It's perfectly safe, Elrik. You worry too much."

"It's hardly safe for you, let alone a boy of his age," the king said. He grew louder as he spoke, so his voice boomed through the dining hall. "The beasts would be much happier feasting on a soft young boy than the squawking geese."

"It's early in the morning, and all the wicked beasts are asleep," Rose said, acquiescing to her husband's fears even if she did not fully share them. "I will be out there with Brenn, and the guards will be nearby if we should need them. We won't be out that long, and we'll be safe."

As soon as they'd finished eating, the queen took Brenn out to the garden. She delighted in showing him the trees and the vines, the birds and the frogs, and Brenn seemed as taken with everything as she.

When they came to her favorite flower—the pink carnations—she plucked one and gave it to the young prince. Never had she seen anyone hold a flower so delicately, so careful not to disturb a single petal, and she couldn't have imagined that a boy of his age would be so thoughtful.

Despite the king's warning not to linger, Rose and Brenn spent the afternoon in the garden, playing among the flowers. Rose didn't even realize how much time had passed until she began feeling tired.

Lying down next to the stream, Rose intended to rest for only a moment, but soon both she and Brenn had fallen asleep. Her son lay in her arms as the sound of the stream lulled them.

That was when Fyren saw his chance. He knew his time under the king's service was growing short, and the cook had to find a way to sustain himself. He'd heard rumors of the prince's wishing power, but it wasn't until this morning, when Brenn had wished himself an apple, that Fyren had actually witnessed it.

With that, his decision was made. Fyren would take the boy for himself and make Brenn grant him the life he'd always wanted. So he'd followed Queen Rose and her son out to the garden. Fyren had stayed hidden in the bushes, waiting for the moment when the queen was the most unguarded.

Once she was asleep by the stream, Fyren put his plan in motion. He grabbed a wild boar youngling, and before the beast could make a sound, Fyren had slit its throat with his butcher's knife. Then he'd covered the queen's dress with fresh red blood, and then discarded the boar's body in the stream.

When the king came looking for his wife, he'd find her like this, covered in blood with the child missing. He would think his worst fears had come true—that a wild beast had snatched Brenn from his mother and eaten him, leaving only the boy's blood.

Carefully, Fyren took the sleeping babe from her arms, and then dashed off into the brush before either the queen or the prince could. He kept running—traveling days with only short breaks to sleep in the darkest part of the night. He went over the cold waters of the Eisenfluss River, past the dark branches of the Verzanfrost Woods, and Fyren didn't stop until he'd reached the highest peak of the Graulumberg Mountains, far out of the reaches of King Elrik's kingdom.

CHAPTER 3
The Flower Girl

The walls of the castle were high, just as Fyren had commanded Brenn to wish for, and all day and all night, they were filled with the sounds of the young prince crying. Nothing Fyren did seemed to ease Brenn's sadness.

Fyren had told Brenn that a war had broken out and his parents had been killed. Fyren—being so sneaky and wise—had gotten past the warriors, and Brenn's mother had commanded Fyren to take Brenn away, to keep him safe, and that Brenn was to do exactly as Fyren ordered.

Fyren had warned the boy about wishing for his mother or his father to return. He'd told him they both had been killed, and if he wished for them, they would rise from the earth, living as the unholy undead. They would be cursed monsters, and his parents deserved a peaceful slumber in their afterlife, so Brenn did not wish for them.

While Brenn had believed him, he had yet to comply with Fyren's order to stop wailing.

Now that Fyren had a great castle at the top of the highest peak on the tallest mountain in the land, filled with riches and treasures, Fyren had begun to consider that his use for Brenn was done. If the boy didn't stop crying soon, Fyren would have his head.

But he couldn't do that just yet. Although it seemed that Fyren had all that his dark heart had ever desired, he didn't know what the future might bring. It would be rash to get rid of his magic wishing tool so soon. Fyren had to find a way to silence Brenn before it drove him mad.

"Why is it that you cry so?" Fyren asked the prince finally. They were eating dinner, though the boy had hardly touched the roasted beef before them. Brenn only cried softly, staring down at the table.

"I miss Mother and Father," Brenn replied.

"I have told you—they would not want you to be so unhappy," Fyren told him. "You must be happy and stop this constant crying. It's as your parents would have you do."

"I know, sire." The prince sniffled. "I am very sorry, but I am so lonely."

The cook said, "I care for you and keep you safe from the men who killed your parents. You are not alone in this castle. I am as a father to you now, boy. Am I not enough to you?"

"You may be as a father to me, but you speak hardly a word to me," Brenn said. "It is only you and I here, and you cannot be as a mother or my playmates back at home."

The cook considered this for a moment and nodded. "Then make yourself a friend. If it will keep you happy and calm, wish yourself a pretty girl to keep you company."

While the boy was excited about the prospect of no longer being alone, he didn't wish for a friend immediately. He wanted to think about it long and well, making sure he'd made the absolute perfect friend before he made his wish.

The prince spent most of his time with his thoughts in the garden behind the castle. Fyren had given him the exact details of how he wanted his castle to be built, but Brenn had been left to wish for the garden on his own, so he'd wished for a garden exactly like his mother's.

It was a few days later, as he was sitting out among the pink carnations, that Brenn was certain he'd finally crafted his wish.

With a loud, strong voice, he said, "I wanted to wish for a friend who is lovely and kind, loyal and patient, funny and gentle, strong and beautiful, intelligent and diligent, but the only thing I really wish for is a girl who will be my true friend for the rest of my days."

No sooner had he made his wish than he saw the flowers next to him begin to move. He pushed back the petals and saw a girl, appearing to be just his age of four, curled up among the stems. She was nude, but her long golden waves of hair covered her.

Her lids fluttered open, and the girl sat up. She was as lovely as he'd hoped for, and he could see the warmth and playful spark in her eyes.

"What is your name?" Brenn asked the girl.

"I am Dianthus," she told him, and smiled. "I don't know how I came to be here, but I know that I am your friend."

Twelve years went by, and Dianthus proved herself to be the truest of friends. She was far more loyal, kind and generous than Brenn would've known to wish for. In the dark castle, with Fyren lording over them, Brenn and Dianthus hid in the shadow to avoid his wrath.

Fyren still commanded the boy to make his wishes, but he'd grown even more ill-tempered as he aged, striking out in unprovoked rages. He'd become paranoid about everything, and he seemed to distrust the friendship between Brenn and Dianthus.

Escaping out to the garden as often as they could, Brenn and Dianthus created a world for themselves among the flowers. Fyren never left the safety of the castle walls anymore, claiming that he was afraid that the men who'd killed Brenn's parents would come after Fyren soon.

While Brenn still listened to Fyren's rants, he didn't believe them any longer. He was now a young man of sixteen, and he wasn't as easily fooled as the young boy Fyren had stowed away those many years ago.

Not to mention that Brenn had more pressing things on his mind. Like the change in his friendship with Dianthus.

For years, she had been his closest confidante, his only respite in the dark storm of his life. He'd shared with her all his darkest secrets, as he'd learned hers. He'd protected her from Fyren's increasing tantrums, as she had nursed his wounds after horrible fights.

He'd considered her nothing more than this—nothing more than his everything—but as each day passed, with Dianthus growing more beautiful than she had been the day before, Brenn could no longer deny that he was in love with her.

"Do you ever notice that your lips are the color of the pink?" Brenn asked her in the garden as she lay among the carnations, reading a book.

"The color of the pink?" Dianthus lifted her blue eyes to meet his.

"The flowers." Brenn was lying down next to her, and he rolled to his side. "You are far more beautiful than they will ever be, though."

Then Brenn leaned over and kissed her tenderly on the mouth, and the kiss seemed to warm him from within, the heat radiating all through him like a flower opening its petals to the sun in the morning.

"You are my one, my one true love," Brenn said, breathing in deeply and filling his lungs with the aroma of the flower bed. "I love you, Dianthus."

Her pastel lips curved into a smile as a blush darkened her cheeks. "I know."

"You know?" Brenn asked in surprise. "How could you know when I've only just discovered it for myself?"

"I've known since the first time you took my hand and led me into the castle," Dianthus told him. "And every time you've taken my hand since then, and put your body in front of mine to spare me from Fyren's belt, and each time you looked up into my eyes in that unabashed way you do. I knew that you loved me as deeply and as eternally as I loved you."

Brenn stared down at her. "If you've known all this time, did you not think to tell me?"

"My dear, sweet Brenn." She put her hand on his cheek, warming his skin, and he leaned into it, relishing the way it made his heartbeat quicken every time they touched. "It is not my place to tell you who you love. You must discover it on your own, and I am so glad that you finally have."

"How come?" Brenn asked.

"Because now we can do this." She pulled him back to her, and she kissed him fully on the mouth.

And in that moment, Brenn discovered that she was right. He had loved her since the moment he'd met her, but he'd been unwilling to see it. Deep down, he'd always known that Fyren would take away everything he loved, and Brenn had never cared for anything as much as he cared for Dianthus.

But in her arms in the garden where they'd created their world, Brenn no longer cared about Fyren. They weren't scared children anymore. He could take Dianthus away from this place, away from Fyren, and they could start a life of their own. They could be married and have a family and a home, and something far grander than anything Fyren would have in store for them.

CHAPTER 4
The Sinister Father

From the high tower of the castle, Fyren stared out of his window, watching down in the garden as the prince kissed the flower girl for the first time. It was at that moment, as Brenn declared his love to Dianthus, that Fyren realized it was time to get rid of the prince.

Soon, Brenn would leave, venture out on his own with his true love and make a name for himself. Fyren had been able to hold him as a prisoner in the castle with threats of the king and queen's enemies, but Brenn was old enough to believe he could fend for himself.

If Brenn left, it wouldn't be that long before he found out his mother and father were still alive, and then it would be a very short time after that before the king sent all his men after Fyren to capture and execute him. If Fyren did not kill Brenn now, before he left with Dianthus, then the old cook himself would be dead.

Worse still, Brenn was much stronger than Fyren. Years

ago, when the boy had been small and weak, Fyren knew he should've done away with him then. Now it was too late, so he'd have to find another means of killing Brenn.

Fyren thought on it for several days, letting the ruminations of his decaying mind work their way through the problem until finally he settled on the simplest plan: Fyren would get the flower girl to do it.

As Fyren had understood Brenn's wish, he'd made Dianthus to be a servant, subservient and dependent on her elder's commands. Fyren had always treated her as a slave, and she'd always responded as one, so he had no reason to think differently.

In the middle of the night, when both Dianthus and Brenn were sound asleep, Fyren crept into her room. She woke up startled, but he silenced her when he held up a sharp butcher knife.

"Tomorrow, as the boy sleeps, go into his room and plunge this knife into his heart," Fyren commanded her. "Then bring me his heart and tongue."

"Why would I shed his blood? He has done nothing to harm anyone," Dianthus said. "What reason do you have to even want him gone?"

"Dianthus, my sweet." Fyren changed his tone to one of loving, and reached out, gently stroking her hair. "Have I not treated both you and the boy as my own? Have I not sheltered you and cared for you the way any good father would?"

"Yes, you have," Dianthus replied, though she didn't really believe this was true. She'd never had a father or known one, but the ones she read about in books sounded far kinder than Fyren had ever been.

"Of course I have, and I've loved you both," Fyren continued to lie. "So you must believe me now. It hurts me so to get rid of the poor boy, but it must be done."

The girl asked, "Why must it be done?"

"He's grown too old for this palace, for the world he created, and soon he will leave. But when he does, everything he's wished for will be destroyed." Fyren told her the story he'd concocted. "I brought him here to save him, but a kind fairy granted pity on him. That's how he got his power for wishing, but it will last only on this mountaintop. As soon as he leaves, all his wishes will be undone—this castle, this life, even you, my dear girl, you who are a very daughter to me would be destroyed."

"Can you not ask him to stay?" Dianthus asked. "If he knew it would be my undoing, surely he wouldn't go."

"Ah, but he does," Fyren told her, doing his best to appear sorrowful. "He knows, and he does not care. He told me in my chambers this very afternoon. He's told you that he loved you as his way of telling you goodbye. In a few days, he will leave, then you will be gone, and I cannot bear that."

Dianthus seemed to think about it, then she nodded. "I will do as you commanded. I will kill the boy."

CHAPTER 5
The Wild Heart

The next morning, Dianthus began to carry out her plan. With the knife hidden in the waistband of her dress, Dianthus led Brenn out to the thick woods at the edge of the garden, making sure that Fyren was watching from his dark tower. Once they'd gone far enough into the trees that she was certain that Fyren could no longer see them, Dianthus stopped.

"Where is it you are taking me to?" Brenn asked her as he leaned in to steal a kiss.

Dianthus put her hand on his chest, halting him. "You must run away. You must go as far away as you can, and never come back here again."

"Why? Why would you have me do such a thing?" Brenn asked.

"I cannot tell you," Dianthus said, fearing that he would stay if he knew the truth. "But you must go."

"Not without you." He shook his head. "I love you, and I won't leave without you."

"I cannot go with you," she insisted. "And if you love me, then you must promise that you'll leave and never return."

By the look in her eyes, Brenn knew he wouldn't be able to change her mind. So he told her he loved her and kissed her one last time before disappearing in the woods.

As Dianthus finished her quest, Brenn was careful to stay just out of sight as he followed her, hiding in the bushes and long grass. Dianthus trapped a boar, then cut out its tongue and heart, staining her dress in crimson.

When she went into the castle, Brenn moved quietly, making his steps light and hiding around corners and in wardrobes. Dianthus appeared to be making a meal out of the heart and tongue, so Brenn waited in the pantry off the dining room.

Through the crack in the door, he saw Dianthus set a silver platter at the end of the table. A few moments later, Fyren came down, easing his hefty frame into the chair.

"It is done, then?" Fyren asked the girl as he stared down at his plate.

She told him, "It is done."

"Good." Fyren smiled and picked his knife and fork. He cut into the meat of the heart, eyeing it with suspicion, and then asked Dianthus, "This is the heart and tongue of the boy?"

Brenn understood instantly what had happened, and that Fyren—the man who had spent many long years pretending to care for him—had ordered his true love to murder him.

"That is not my heart, old man," Brenn said as he burst from the pantry, frightening both Fyren and Dianthus. "You have been deceived, the way you have spent all these years deceiving me."

"I know not what you speak of," Fyren stammered, and struggled to get to his feet.

"Why would you have her kill me?" Brenn asked. "Why would you eat my heart? After years of playing the part of my father, why?"

"Please." Fyren fell to his knees, groveling before the prince. "Have pity on me. I was but a poor cook in your father's kingdom. I would be condemned to death or servitude if not for you."

"It was for the wishes, then, wasn't it?" Brenn asked. "You've been holding me captive for my powers all this time. Has everything you told me been a lie? Are my parents even dead?"

"I do not know what became of your parents," Fyren told him.

"Then what good are you to me? You are nothing but a mangy dog, begging for scraps at my feet," Brenn said. "It's time you took your true form. I wish you to become what you truly are—a mangy black dog, starving and unable to ever feel full, no matter how much diseased flesh and burning coals you might eat."

Fyren cried out, but quickly, his cries turned to that of a howling dog, and he changed into a thin dog, with patches of black fur missing all over his protruding ribs.

"This is why you sent me away?" Brenn turned to Dianthus, his gray eyes filled with worry.

"I had to protect you," she told him.

"Now it is my turn to protect you." He took her hands in his. "I will take you away from this dark castle to my parents' kingdom. I was a prince there, and when we return, you will be at my side, as my princess."

"Your kingdom? That's so very far away, past the mountains and rivers and forests," Dianthus said. "We could stay here and make this castle our own."

"The journey won't be that long. We can make it," Brenn promised her. "I must return. My parents might still be alive, and I have to see them and tell them where I've been."

Dianthus knew that Fyren was a faulty storyteller, but not everything he'd told her had been a lie. Many things were, but certainly some of them had to be true. And what reason did Fyren have to kill his wish maker unless he was right? If Brenn left the top of the mountain, all his wishes might come undone—meaning Dianthus would cease to exist as a person, and instead return to the carnation form from which she'd come.

By the look in Brenn's eyes and the way she felt in her heart, she was certain he would stay if she asked him to. If she refused to leave the castle, then Brenn would refuse to leave her. But in all their years together, she'd heard hundreds of stories about his parents, and he loved them so much. She couldn't deny him a chance to see them again.

"I've never left the grounds before, and I'm afraid I'll slow you down on the journey back to your rightful kingdom," Dianthus told Brenn finally. "Why don't you wish for me to return to my carnation form? Then you can carry me in your pocket, and I'll always be with you."

"If that's as you wish," Brenn said. "As soon as we get to the safety of my kingdom, I will make you be human again."

She smiled at him with tears in her eyes. "Of course."

Before he made his wish, she kissed him and held him tightly to her. So softly that Brenn couldn't hear, Dianthus told him goodbye.

CHAPTER 6
The Faraway Kingdom

The prince had arrived at the peak of the Graulumberg Mountains as a frightened young boy, but he left as a strong young man with a flower pressed in his pocket and a mangy dog at his heels.

It had been a very long time since he'd been outside Fyren's castle grounds, and he'd forgotten how cold and treacherous the mountain was. He managed to make it down, but even darker trouble was lurking for him in the Verzanfrost Woods.

Brenn was careful not to use his powers of wishing, as there were too many people inhabiting the woods. They were all dark, evil folk, and they would do anything to get their hands on a power like his. He had to keep it secret, even when the wild beasts chased after them.

At night, when he would sleep in a thicket made in the roots of the trees, he would pull out the carnation, twirling it in his fingers, and that would give him the strength to make it through another day.

In the cold waters of the Eisenfluss River, Brenn was nearly swept away. But he pulled himself to shore, gasping for breath and ever more determined to finish his quest home.

When Brenn finally arrived at the gates at the edge of his kingdom, it was several months later. His clothes were tattered and worn, he was bruised, scarred and dirty, but he was stronger and better for the journey.

The flags flying high over the gates still bore the emblem of his father. His parents were still in power. The first knight Brenn found, he demanded to take him to see the king.

"A filthy beggar like yourself will not be granted audience with the king," the knight told him. "Take yourself and your mangy beast and get out of here."

Instead of listening, Brenn bolted and ran as fast as he could toward the castle, outrunning all of the king's men. He snuck past the guards outside the palace, and Brenn pushed his way inside, racing right up to the king's court.

As soon as he saw them—the king and queen seated in their thrones—Brenn knew they were his parents. They'd aged some—his father thinner than he remembered, and his mother much grayer.

A guard ran over to grab him, but Queen Rose was already to her feet, tears flowing down her cheeks.

"Do not touch a hair on that boy's head!" the queen commanded. "That is your prince, and if you hurt him, I will send you to the dungeon myself."

She ran over to Brenn, embracing him tightly to her, and King Elrik soon hugged him, too. They asked what had happened to him, and Brenn began to tell the story of Fyren and how he'd held him in the mountains for all those years.

Then he thought of Dianthus, and seeing that it was safe in the kingdom, Brenn pulled the flower from his pocket. The pink petals had browned and wilted. The flower had been crushed over time, and it was so fragile that it felt like it might turn to dust in his fingers.

"Wherever did you get that?" the queen asked as Brenn set the flower on the floor.

"Dianthus, I wish for you to return to your human form," Brenn commanded.

His heart pounded desperately, and his stomach churned. Throughout his travels, he'd known the flower was growing worn, and every night since he'd left the mountains, Brenn had thought about wishing Dianthus back to life. But it was not as he'd promised her, so he'd waited.

But now that the moment was at hand, he'd begun to fear that perhaps the flower had become too damaged. Perhaps Dianthus would be unable to return, or if she did, she may be injured. He'd tried with all his might to protect the pink, but the journey had been arduous, and it had taken its toll on the precious flower.

In moments that stretched out to eternity, Brenn was certain that his greatest fears had come true. He'd been unable to keep his one true love safe, and she would not return to him. And then finally—blessedly—she appeared.

Dianthus was curled up on the floor in her finest gown, and she appeared even more beautiful than when he'd seen her last. Surprise and joy lit up her face as they embraced.

"I was afraid I'd never see you again," Brenn admitted, brushing her golden hair back from her face.

"And I you," she said, sounding awed to be in his arms again. "I love you so, my prince."

"I love you, my princess." Brenn kissed her, more passionately than he should've in front of his parents, but he couldn't help himself. He had just been reunited with his love.

With the prince returned, the kingdom rejoiced, and Brenn and Dianthus were married within the week. With the help of Brenn's and Dianthus's leadership, the kingdom began to prosper again. The king and queen doted on their son and his new bride, making up for all the time they had lost.

They loved Dianthus like she was their own daughter, and she loved them in return, for they were the parents her heart had always wished for. Queen Rose and Princess Dianthus spent much time together in the wilds of the garden behind the palace, and the queen often remarked that the pink carnations had never been more radiant.

SELL OUT

by Jackson Pearce

I wish I had a better talent.

Painting. Playing the violin. Woodcutting, even. Anything.

Maybe I wouldn't feel this way if it manifested differently. Through a handshake or something. A tap on the shoulder. Hell, a slap on the ass. At least that way it'd be over fast, and it wouldn't involve me kissing a corpse.

But I make a lot of money per kiss, and it's stupid money, easy money. It's this or join the family business, and taxidermy isn't for me. The only thing creepier than kissing a dead human is peeling the skin off a dead animal and pretending like that's a normal way of acquiring a new centerpiece for your living room.

"New assignments," my boss says, slapping a pack of paper down in the middle of the room. It's thinner than last week—with the prices the company charges for a kiss, I'm actually surprised it's not thinner still. We get only a fraction of the money, but it's hard to get hired as a self-proprietor in this field. It's like people think that if they go through a company, it's all on the up-and-up. If they go through an individual, it's dark magic.

I think companies like mine spread those rumors. Keep prices up, so we're kissing only the rich.

My boss clears his throat. "We're short on women this round. Sorry." He nods at me. "Emmett's turn to get the one." I try to look appreciative.

A guy to my right cusses under his breath. "I'm so sick of kissing old white guys." A few of my coworkers mutter agreements till our boss glares, shuts us up. He passes out the papers. Name, address, a time. Nothing more. We don't really need to know anything else.

Elise Snow, 706 Fourteenth Street. Tuesday at 7:00 p.m.

I suck in a sharp breath, then fold the paper crookedly and shove it in my pocket.

I know Elise Snow.

Or, I knew her. A long time ago—I haven't seen her in almost a decade, since fifth grade, I think. The little rich girl in school, Shelton County's very own princess—and she had the pageant crowns to prove it.

I hated her.

She called my family poor. She made fun of my dad's job. She told us her dad could take our house away, if he wanted—which was an exaggeration on the fact that he owned the bank that owned my parents' mortgage. And she pelted me with crab apples from the tree whose branches shaded the school playground.

Mom said she was probably hurting on the inside. That

she was just misunderstood. That she'd grow out of it—that people change.

She didn't—at least, by fifth grade she hadn't. And so I really, really don't want to kiss Elise Snow, dead or alive. I wonder how she died. It can't have been too violent—if their bodies are broken, we aren't allowed to kiss them, after all. Usually, with people her age, it's a drug overdose. Rich kids apparently can't think of a better way to die.

"Emmett," my dad says, voice crushing my thoughts. He's positioning a boar's head on a piece of wood; its eyes are glass now, empty and stupid-looking. "Got a job?"

"Yep."

"How many people?"

"Just one right now."

My dad freezes; the boar's hair flutters a little as the oscillating fan rotates by.

"God. Just one? You've got to get more work…." Dad shakes his head. I try not to glare. It's only mostly his fault, not entirely. We still owe thousands to the hospital that took care of Mom before she died. Thousands more for her funeral. Thousands for Dad's hospital visit, when he tried to join my mom.

It had almost worked the first two times. The third time would have definitely worked if it hadn't been for me. I look at the scars on his wrists as he nails the boar's head into place. If I hadn't kissed him, I wouldn't have even known about the power. He'd have stayed dead, and I'd have run from this town, from our debt, started over somewhere in the woods, living off the land. Alone. Someplace no one could find me.

Far away from my job, from taxidermy and from anyone like Elise Snow.

But it felt right to join a company. It felt noble. Important. It felt nice to have a talent, after years of worrying I had none.

It felt like living.

Now it just feels like a paycheck.

There's a white SUV outside our house. It's that pearly kind of white, the kind that almost has a pinkish hue. I squint to see the driver, but the windows are tinted so dark that I can make out only a silhouette. I loathe the sorts of hunters who drive cars like this—they're the kinds of people who hunt on game ranches where all the animals are fenced in. Dad never hunted like that. He said it wasn't fair to kill a thing that never had a chance.

Ah—wait. It's not a hunter at all. It's a tall, severe-looking woman, who has features that were probably mysterious and sexy thirty years ago. Now they have the worn, grubby look of dull pencils. She makes a face when she surveys the broken shutters on our house, then picks her way around the crushed pinecones in our driveway.

I turn up the television as Dad answers the door. I'm watching another rerun of *Gilligan's Island*. I used to say I hated this show (Coconuts can't be transformed into circuit breakers, Professor), but I started watching the reruns right after graduation and never stopped, so maybe I don't hate it, after all. Maybe I just hate coconuts.

Dad appears in the doorway, eyebrows raised. "Um…she's here for you."

I blink as Mary Ann straightens her pigtails.

The severe lady appears over Dad's shoulder, her coat bright white against the cheap wood paneling in this room. I click the TV off and rise warily.

The woman looks at me, lips pressed into a forced smile. She turns to my dad. "Might we have a moment alone?"

"Sure," Dad says, shrugging. "I'll be downstairs if you need me."

"Thank you," the lady says, though the warmth in her voice feels as fake as her hair looks. She waits till Dad walks away, till she hears him shut the door and descend into the basement.

"Um, hi. Can I help you?" I ask, extending a hand.

"Do you remember me?" she asks. "You went to school with my stepdaughter. I'm Beverly Windsor-Snow?"

Elise's stepmother.

"Yeah, yeah," I say, dropping my hands in my jean pockets. We stare at one another for a long time.

"Well. I…" She inhales, then drops her voice. "It's come to my attention that you'll be kissing my stepdaughter next Tuesday."

I frown—she's not supposed to have information like that, but I guess when you're rich, you can afford to buy it. "That's right," I say.

Beverly nods at me, pauses, like she's choosing her words carefully. "I'm not sure if you know this, but Elise and I never got along very well. She was a rather…difficult child."

I exhale, almost laugh in agreement. She gives me a hard look, then moves on.

"Things got bad when her father got sick. Battling out his will made things nasty between us. She got almost everything. She doesn't even need it, in that stupid artists' colony she's living in, but she refused to give me a penny. So the reason I'm here, Emmett, is I have an offer for you."

She dips a silky hand into her purse, pulls out a thick white envelope. When she hands it to me, I see the flash of green bills straining at the flap. They're crisp and new; I pull the mouth of the envelope apart to confirm what I already suspected. Hundred-dollar bills.

"That's a down payment. Five thousand dollars. Finish the job and I'll give you another twenty. Every year. For the rest of your life."

I look up at her, eyes wide.

"What's the job?"

Beverly steps toward me, licks her lips. "You're supposed to kiss Elise on Tuesday. I want you to botch it. Say it didn't work. Say you lost the talent. Say anything you want, but don't kiss her. Don't wake her up."

"Twenty thousand dollars, for life?" I ask wondrously. I look at her, baffled. "To not do my job?"

"If she's dead, I get the inheritance. And I need that money. It's worth paying you dearly for. Surely you didn't want to kiss dead people forever? You can go…do something. Whatever it is you want to do," she says, tossing her hand at me. "Stuff animals with your father, I don't know. Watch television all day. Buy new carpet," she says, glancing dismally at our ratty floors.

"Just for not kissing her. That's it. No strings," I say, waiting for a catch.

"No strings," she says. "The hippies she lives with don't have access to her inheritance—they pooled together their pennies to hire you. So if you don't kiss her, her week will have expired before they can get someone new. She stays dead."

She's right. Six days is already pushing it for a kiss. No one has ever successfully kissed someone back after seven. Elise Snow stays dead. I hand my father a check for his bills.

I leave.

I become something new. Something great, something better than a kisser who brings back the rich. Something important. Anything important.

I nod at Beverly, smash the envelope in my hand.

I thought Fourteenth Street was in the rich part of town, both because it's Elise Snow's address and because most of the numbered streets are lined in shiny condos. Apparently the lower numbers, however, still boast old brick warehouses with dirty windows that overlook the harbor. I squint at the address on the building, then at my slip of paper, wondering how this can be right. Elise Snow can't live in a place like this. That's crazy.

But it says this is 706 Fourteenth, so… I sigh, trudge to the dented metal door on the side. Knocking hurts in the cold, double so when combined with the sharp, cold breeze coming off the water. I hear shuffling inside, movement; the door swings open.

The guy is covered in tattoos, colorful ones with colors that fade in and out like watercolors instead of ink. He sighs when he sees me, grins.

"I'm here for—"

"Yeah, yeah, I know," he says, sounding relieved. He steps aside, waves me in. "It's him!" he calls out.

His voice bounces through the warehouse, across half walls and partitions and winding metal staircases. This place is full of mismatched furniture and wall murals of pinup girls. The guy grins at me as we hear a scurrying of feet. Other people hurry toward us from what seems like every direction. They're covered in piercings, tattoos, splattered paint. They have feathers or beads in their hair; they have smiles on their lips.

They hug me.

I'm not really sure how to handle that. I'm really not sure how to handle liking it.

"So…" the guy who answered the door says after I've been hugged about eight thousand times. Everyone is staring at me eagerly. I'm used to that. I'm just not used to wanting to stare back.

"Where is she?" I ask. *Remember. You've got a job to do. Botch it.*

"Oh, sorry, of course. Through here," a petite girl says, waving me forward.

The warehouse is a maze of rooms, studios, workshops. "What is this place?" I ask as we slide through a sculpture studio.

"It's our house. And our workshop. And everything else."

"A colony," I say, remembering Beverly using the term. "Like an artists' colony."

"Yep," the guy at the door says. "Something like that."

"So…you guys make a living off your art, then? Like, you do this professionally?"

"Ah," he says. "You don't make a living from art. You make art from living."

I want to punch him for that damn hippie phrase, but I find myself nodding instead.

"Here," a girl says, stopping suddenly in front of me. She meets my eyes a long time, like she sees something there, then steps aside so I can see through the doorway of a bedroom.

And there is Elise Snow.

Dead people are never pretty—they're made to look that way by undertakers, but really, once the life is gone, the pretty is gone, too. Elise Snow is no exception. She looks rocklike, her skin tone similar to the blank wall behind her. The wall seems odd, empty, compared to the rest of this place. I walk toward her; the others crowd into the doorway. I glance back at them—

I gasp. The back wall isn't empty. The back wall is full.

A painting of a young Elise, dissolving into the clouds, being thrown around books and music and what looks like a schoolhouse. A picture of the crab-apple tree, of a pointy white woman I assume is Beverly. Paintings of her naked with boys, with girls, with people without faces. Color, color everywhere, images, details, so much that I can't absorb it all— her entire life.

I didn't know she had talent like this. I wonder when she discovered it.

I wonder when she became this Elise Snow, instead of the princess I knew. Was it sudden, like my change from normal boy to raiser of the dead? Or was it gradual?

Mom was right. Elise was misunderstood—by me at least. And she did change. So did I. She became beautiful, and I became…this.

"Will it take long?" a voice asks—I can't tell whose.

"No," I say, shaking my head, trying not to stare at the painting. "No, it won't."

It won't take long because I'm not going to wake her. I can't. I can't turn down Beverly's offer. And besides, I already used some of the down payment to keep our electric bill on.

"How did she die?" I ask. I never ask this. I usually don't want to know. I look down at her body; her hair is dark, but it's been colored. She has tattoos of roses covering her clavicles, disappearing into the neck of her shirt.

"Does it matter?" someone asks.

No. It doesn't. But the shadiness in the person's voice makes me think I was right about the drug overdose. I don't feel as smug as I expect to. I wish someone could have helped her. I mean, someone other than me, someone who could have done more than just wake her after—

No. Not wake her. I grimace.

I reach forward, take her hand. It's difficult—rigor has set in; she's stiff, icy. I can feel the calluses in her palm, I guess from gripping a paintbrush.

This is just a job. How is a rich person paying me not to kiss any worse than rich people paying me to kiss? It's all about what can be bought. About using my talent to make money. I feel a swirling in my stomach, think about what the guy said about living, about making a living. He's just a stupid hippie druggie. You have to make money. You have to survive.

I lean forward. I position my thumb so that my lips can brush it, can stay away from Elise's skin. They'll never catch it from where they're standing. They'll think I kissed her.

It's just a job.

I plant my lips on my own thumb, Elise's skin thick, cold, unkissed beneath it.

It feels like I'm the dead one. All I can think of is the deer in the game ranches, the ones that are fenced in. Of my dad. It isn't fair, killing something that doesn't have a chance.

Elise didn't even have a chance. Her chance was bought for twenty thousand dollars.

I rise. Turn to face them.

"I'm sorry," I say. "I think she's expired."

A cry from the background. Their mouths drop. They quiver. Shake. They are a single creature in pain, hurt, fearful. Their eyes light upon me, fill with water.

"No, wait!"

"There has to be something else you can do!"

"Try again, just one more time!"

"Are you sure?"

"The company said six days was plenty of time!"

Their voices harmonize as I take a step toward the door, another, another, another. They need her. They miss her. These people must understand her. I wonder if they could understand me....

No. This is just a job. Just a job. Just a job.

My talent is just a job. I am just a job.

I look up. Elise Snow's eyes rain down on me from the dozens and dozens of paintings. Blue eyes, blue like water, boring into me, asking me why.

"Please," someone says, the guy who answered the door. He's trembling. He's crying. He looks broken. "Please try again. Just one more."

I turn around, look at Elise's body. Someone tucked her

into the bed, folded the blankets neatly around her torso. Her hands were in her lap, I realize—I must have pulled one slightly astray when I took it. I wish I'd put it back.

"Please."

I inhale. Twenty thousand dollars a year. For me, that might as well be a million. I think of the house in the woods, of not having to do this job, of getting rid of all those "Final Notice" envelopes. I think of everything money can do.

I think of all the things it can't.

I turn, dash back to Elise's side, slide to my knees. I brush her hair away from her face easily—it feels like feathers.

Lower my lips to hers and kiss her on the mouth, kiss her hard. Because she is not the Elise Snow that I hate. She's the Elise Snow that I've never met. She's the Elise Snow I'd like to know. That I'd like to join here in this weird warehouse. That I'd like to understand, to change with.

That I can save.

Who can save me.

I pull away, exhale. The room is silent, still, crackling.

Elise's blue eyes flutter open.

She's living.

We both are.

★ ★ ★ ★ ★

Rachel Hawkins was born in Virginia and raised in Alabama. This means she uses words like *y'all* and *fixin'* a lot, and considers anything under 60 degrees to be borderline Arctic. Before deciding to write books about kissing and fire (and sometimes kissing while on fire), Rachel taught high school English for three years, and is still capable of teaching you *The Canterbury Tales* if you're into that kind of thing. She is the author of the *New York Times* bestselling Hex Hall series.

Jeri Smith-Ready has been writing fiction since the night she rescued a trapped fox in the wooded hills of central Maryland. The fox turned out to be a magic muse—the sparkly hat and vest should've tipped Jeri off—inspiring eleven published novels so far, including RT Reviewers' Choice–winning fantasy *Eyes of Crow,* as well as the PRISM Award–winning *Wicked Game* and *Shade.* Her next novel, *This Side of Salvation,* a contemporary YA story about a boy whose parents disappear the night they believe the Rapture will happen, will be out in April 2014. Jeri lives with her husband and two cats in a house made of tea and chocolate—or so it seems sometimes. When not writing, she can be found, well, thinking about writing, or on Twitter. Find her on the web at www.jerismithready.com, or on Twitter, @jsmithready.

Malinda Lo is the author of several young-adult novels, including most recently the sci-fi duology *Adaptation* and *Inheritance*. Her first novel, *Ash*, a retelling of Cinderella with a lesbian twist, was a finalist for the William C. Morris YA Debut Award, the Andre Norton Award and the Lambda Literary Award. Her novel *Huntress* was an ALA Best Book for Young Adults and a finalist for the Lambda Literary Award. Malinda lives in Northern California with her partner and their dog. Her website is www.malindalo.com.

Jon Skovron has been an actor, musician, lifeguard, Broadway theater ticket seller, warehouse grunt, technical writer and web developer. He has nine fingers, dislikes sweets and possesses a number of charming flaws. He was born in Columbus, Ohio, and after traveling around awhile, he has settled, somewhat haphazardly, in the Washington, D.C., area, where he and his two sons can regularly be seen not fitting into the general government scene. Visit him at www.jonskovron.com.

Saundra Mitchell has been a phone psychic, a car salesperson, a denture-deliverer and a layout waxer. She's dodged trains, endured basic training and hitchhiked from Montana to California. She teaches herself languages, raises children and makes paper for fun. She is the author of *Shadowed Summer, The Vespertine* trilogy and *Mistwalker*, and the editor of *Defy the Dark*. She always picks truth; dare is too easy. Visit her online at www.saundramitchell.com.

Ellen Hopkins is a poet and an award-winning author of ten *New York Times* bestselling young-adult novels in verse, plus two adult verse novels. She lives in Carson City, Nevada, where she has founded Ventana Sierra, a nonprofit housing and resource initiative for youth in need.

Tessa Gratton has wanted to be a paleontologist or a wizard since she was seven. She was too impatient to hunt dinosaurs, but is still searching for someone to teach her magic. After traveling the world with her military family, she acquired a BA (and the important parts of an MA) in gender studies, and then settled down in Kansas with her partner, her cats and her mutant dog. She is the author of the Blood Journals series and the United States of Asgard series, both from Random House Children's Books. Visit her at www.tessagratton.com.

Julie Kagawa, the *New York Times* bestselling author of the Iron Fey and Blood of Eden series, was born in Sacramento, California. But nothing exciting really happened to her there. So, at the age of nine, she and her family moved to Hawaii, which she soon discovered was inhabited by large carnivorous insects, colonies of house geckos and frequent hurricanes. Julie now lives in Louisville, Kentucky, where the frequency of shark attacks are at an all-time low. She lives with her husband, two obnoxious cats, one Australian shepherd who is too smart for his own good, and the latest addition, a hyperactive papillon.

Sonia Gensler is the author of *The Revenant* and *The Dark Between*. She grew up in a small Tennessee town and spent her early adulthood collecting impractical degrees from various Midwestern universities. A former high school English teacher, Sonia now writes full-time in Oklahoma and spends her summers in England.

Shaun David Hutchinson is the author of *The Deathday Letter, fml* and the forthcoming *The Five Stages of Andrew Brawley*. He lives in South Florida with his partner and dog, and watches way too much *Doctor Who*.

Kimberly Derting first fell in love with writing when she signed up for journalism as her seventh-grade elective. She still lives in the Pacific Northwest, which is the ideal place to be writing anything dark or creepy...a gloomy day can set the perfect mood. She lives with her husband and their three beautiful (and often mouthy) children, who serve as an endless source of inspiration for her writing. She is the author of the Body Finder series, the Pledge trilogy and the Taking trilogy.

Christine Johnson grew up in, moved away from and finally came home to Indianapolis, Indiana. While she was in the "away" part of that adventure, she lived in Chicago, Illinois, where she attended DePaul University and majored in political science. She now lives in an old house in an old neighborhood with her kids and way too many books. Find her on the web at www.christinejohnsonbooks.com and on Twitter, @cjohnsonbooks.

Claudia Gray is the pseudonym of New Orleans–based writer Amy Vincent. She is the author of the *New York Times* bestselling Evernight series and the Spellcaster trilogy. Her enthusiasms include thrift stores, pugs, classic movies and travel. Visit her website at www.claudiagray.com.

Myra McEntire, author of the Hourglass books, knows the words to every R & B hit of the past decade, but since she lives in Nashville, the country music capital of America, her lyrical talents go sadly unappreciated. She's chosen, instead, to channel her "mad word skills" into creating stories. She's an avid *Doctor Who* fan and will argue passionately about which incarnation is the best.

Sarah Rees Brennan is the author of the Demon's Lexicon trilogy, the first book of which was an ALA Top Ten Best Book of 2009, and the coauthor of *Team Human* with Justine Larbalestier. Her newest series is the Lynburn Legacy, a romantic Gothic mystery about a girl who discovers her imaginary friend is a real boy. *Unspoken* is an ALA Best Book 2013 and on the TAYSHAS list, and the sequel, *Untold,* was just released in September 2013. Sarah writes from her homeland of Ireland but likes to travel the world collecting inspiration.

Amanda Hocking is the *USA TODAY* bestselling author of the Trylle trilogy and six additional self-published novels. After selling over a million copies of her books, primarily in ebook format, she is widely considered an exemplar of self-publishing success in the digital age.

Jackson Pearce lives in Atlanta, Georgia, with a slightly cross-eyed cat and a lot of secondhand furniture. She is the author of many books for young adults, including a series of retold fairy tales, starting with *Sisters Red* and concluding with *Cold Spell.* Visit her online at www.jacksonpearce.com.